Beach Cottage Haven

Donna Munro

Beach

Cottage

Haven

Donna Munro

Warm Witty
PUBLISHING

Warm Witty Publishing
Sunshine Coast ☺ Queensland ☺ Australia

Donna Munro

First Published – 2022
This edition published by Warm Witty Publishing
Sunshine Coast, Qld Australia
www.donnamunroauthor.com

The National Library of Australia Cataloguing-in-Publication

Creator: Munro, Donna, author.

Title: Beach Cottage Haven / Donna Munro.

ISBN: 978-0-6452629-6-4 (paperback)

Subjects: Romance fiction.
Australian fiction.
Contemporary women's fiction.
Adventure romance
RomanticsSuspense
Beach fiction

Typeset in Times New Roman 12pt by Warm Witty Publishing.
Cover artwork by Donna Munro.
Printed and bound in Australia by Ingram Spark.

Chapter One

2019

Pepper Cassidy's nostalgia hit her like a nail gun to the heart. Cutting the car engine, she stared at the blue beach cottage. *Home, maybe?*

To her right, on the idyllic Queensland beach, waves surged over rocks, booming and rhythmic like a heartbeat. Seagulls screeched above, gliding in a baby-blue sky. They swooped into the ocean, pinching fish from a school of mullet close to the shore. Lemony eucalyptus and frangipani blended with salty air in a fragrance so familiar it hurt deep in Pepper's chest. Yesteryears' memories swirled, making her dizzy. She steadied her wobbly legs, placing a hand on the hot car bonnet, glancing at Livia to check she missed the stumble. *Why, after all this time, have I chosen to come back here?*

'We're finally home.' Liv glanced around and yawned, stretching one slender arm over her blonde head.

'It's a bit cliché returning to my hometown. I honestly never thought we'd settle back here,' said Pepper, giving Liv at least some of her thoughts. Leaving the car, they strolled to the cottage. She brushed the dusty weatherboard surface, and dry, faded aqua-blue paint came off on her fingers. *One thing noted on the list of things to do.* Rubbing her hands down the side of her jeans, she bit her bottom lip before saying, 'Oh, well, new year, new life, I guess.'

The stand-alone garage on the left-hand side came into her vision, even though she told her eyes not to stray there. Goosebumps popped along her arms. She quickly averted her gaze, avoiding Liv's questioning look by walking towards the veranda, gulping back her fear. Lantana trailed over the rail and into the gutter.

'Your hometown, Mum. My sea change,' said Livia, pulling an

1

earphone from her left ear. 'The beach is amazing. I'd forgotten it's this close. What was I, about four last time we came here? It seemed miles away when I was little. It's like right there. Wow!'

'Nearly five.' *The same age as me when Dad went to war.* 'You can hear the surf. It's beautiful at night. I remember it lulling you to the most peaceful sleep.' Considering how much Pepper dreaded moving back to Blueshell Beach, finding one pleasant memory was reassuring. A two-hour drive north from Brisbane with crawling traffic for the first hour hadn't helped her apprehension. *Too much time to think.* She inhaled a deep breath of salt air, stretched stiff shoulders, and stepped on the timber stairs. The second one sunk and creaked. *Another thing noted on the list of things to do.*

Livia strolled to stand beside Pepper, taking in the ocean with wide eyes like the first beach she had ever seen. Her young face was hopeful. 'Oi, check him out.' Liv pointed, grabbing Pepper's shoulder to make her face the north. 'Bit old, but what a six-pack and those arms,' Liv said, elbowing Pepper's ribs.

Pepper gazed at the fine specimen of a man jogging shirtless along the goat-track path winding around the beach in front of their home. A large dog with pointy black ears and tan fur ran in front of him close to his feet. It wore no collar or lead but didn't stray far. The man glanced at her, holding her gaze for a second before facing the track. A small smile tugged his lips. The barking dog loped towards them, seeming excited by the prospect of new people. The man whistled, and the big dog stopped, tilting its head towards his master, triangle ears raised at the command.

'Awww, he's so cute. Hello, boy.' Liv grinned at the pet.

The dog hunched low, returning to its owner with his tail between his legs. They jogged, but in the dog's exuberant state, it circled back to happy-bark at them, causing the man to trip over the mutt. He righted himself in one fluid movement, said something to the dog, patted its head and glanced over his shoulder with irritated eyes.

Pepper stifled a giggle and placed her hands over her mouth.

Liv enthusiastically flapped a hand towards him. 'Hi.'

He shook his head but didn't wave; instead sprinted the rest of the track with the dog following closely.

'Not very friendly.' Liv laughed. 'That was pretty funny, though. Mum, mum?' She waved a hand in front of Pepper's face. 'Earth to Mum.'

Her mind was still holding a vision of the guy in her head. Her dropped jaw was having trouble returning to her face. To cover her weird reaction to the guy, she asked, 'Since when have you noticed six-packs?' She ruffled Liv's hair, ignoring the weird something stirring deep inside.

'Who doesn't?'

A tiny niggle of worry about Livia's comment stayed with her. *Don't grow up, Livy.*

At fourteen, Livia had already developed a womanly shape, much to Pepper's concern. Unlike Pepper, Livia took after her father's side — tall, with long angled limbs and her mother-in-law's enviable model body. At least Liv didn't have their snobby, mean disposition. *She takes after you, always wearing a bright smile.* The thing mother and daughter shared most was the unique colour of their violet eyes. People always commented on their eyes—eyes the same as her father.

Pepper opened a screen door and inserted a key in the intricately carved timber door. It would have looked more at home in a place like Bali or Zanzibar. Her mother had imported it from Morocco, and her dad lovingly installed it. A recollection so happy, Pepper smiled. In 1970, the year Pepper was born, he'd devotedly built the house. *In a time before he changed.*

'Come on, Mum, open the door already!' Livia said, startling Pepper from her thoughts. Liv glanced at the mobile phone in her hand. She smiled before tucking it into the back pocket of her jeans.

'I'm trying. The key's a little stubborn. It hasn't been used in months since Nana went to the nursing home.' Pepper jiggled the key, and the lock clicked. She pushed the door wide open. The hinges didn't even creak. At the same time, a gush of memories surfaced like ghosts circling over her head.

The mudroom flowed to the sunroom facing the veranda, where faded cane lounges took in the picturesque view. Beyond, the main lounge room housed the old purple velour sofa and a huge Persian rug that never seemed to match the décor, but the carpet held favour with her mother.

Daylight streamed on the kitchen benches from a circular

skylight. The cabinetry, dated lime melamine with curved metal edges, was art deco at its best or worst. Pepper wasn't sure which, but she knew she had shitloads of work to do renovating it back to a proud little beach house. At least the modifications would keep her busy enough to forget things. A folded note sat like a teepee on the bench.

She unfolded it. *Welcome home, Pepper. I'm so sorry for your loss. Meg was a dear friend. It's terribly sad. I've been feeding Chloe until you arrived as I said I would. Poor thing seems to be pining but must be eating all her food because she's looking on the chubby side. She's an adorable cat. I just loved looking after her. Any questions, just give me a call. Mrs Charlotte Walters.* A phone number at the bottom was written in a different pen ink as if an afterthought.

'It's all so old,' said Livia, running a hand over the velour lounge. 'Jeez, who'd put purple with that rug?'

'Your grandmother,' Pepper said with a catch to her throat. The rug seemed to lift and roll. She steadies her feet. No ocean breeze to do that, and the rug was heavy. *Odd.*

Liv didn't seem to notice. 'Oh, sorry, Mum. Are you okay? You look a little rattled?'

'I'm fine. It's just strange being here after all this time.'

'You didn't come back much because of Granddad, right?'

Pepper glanced away, trying to ebb the flow of tears pooling in her eyes. Changing the subject, she opened a door. 'This will be your room. It was mine growing up, at least when I wasn't at boarding school. The bay window has views of the beach.' She strolled over to where a bench seat tucked under the windowsill. The view wasn't as clear now that the native bush had grown. 'I read here, escaping into books when Dad was —,' she trailed off, taking a deep sigh. 'Anyway, what do you think?'

'It's so huge compared to my room in Brisbane. I can put my bed here.' She spun around, pointing to a blank wall. 'My Five-SOS poster could go up here.'

'Sure, but after I paint. What colour do you want your walls? I'm doing shades of white everywhere else, but you can choose in here.'

Livia shrugged her shoulders, but the smile remained. 'I'll think about it.'

Liv's room led to an adjoining patio taking in the backyard. A double cat bowl for food and water sat near the door; a small pet bed wafted of cat piss and mould. A couple of deck boards were rotted black like stumps burnt in a bushfire. *Add it to the list of things to do.*

'Chloe, here pussy,' Pepper called, but there was no sign of her mother's cat. Probably under the house in the shade, where their old dog Mahli used to sleep.

She strolled to the second bedroom, the one her two brothers shared. She could see the overgrown backyard from the grimy window where they would chuck a football or wrestle each other and her on the freshly mowed lawn. Having boisterous brothers made her robust even though she was small. Fighting with them taught her how to beat boys and later men at their own game. She never backed down when she knew she was right while working in construction, which helped her business thrive, and the primarily male tradesmen respected her.

The room would be a spare room or an office for her company, Pepper C Construction, at least at the start. Anyhow, Rob wouldn't be coming back to the house any time soon. Tim definitely wouldn't.

Pausing at the door to the main bedroom, Pepper sighed. She opened it slowly, hearing the familiar creak of the hinges. Her mother's scent wafted. Pepper lifted a pillow and held it to her face, sniffing deeply. *Lavender mixed with the spicy vanilla and sandalwood Coco perfume.* The tears came. She muffled them with the pillow, but they dampened her face until she felt Livia's thin arms wrap around her shaking shoulders.

'I miss her too, Mum.'

Pepper dropped the pillow to hug her sweet daughter. 'I know, darling. It will get easier one day. This house brings back all the memories.' The sooner she packed up her mother's things, the easier living in the house would be—*another thing for the list.*

'I could take this room instead.'

'No, it's okay. Once we renovate, it will be fine. We'll have to camp out in the lounge or outside while we get at least one room habitable. We'll do yours first.'

'Why don't we stay in the garage instead. It looks like there's a loft?'

'No.' Pepper said it too abruptly. 'It's um, dirty, and it's locked.' She glanced at the floor, scuffing her feet over a worn section of laminate flooring. *Add it to the list.*

'We could break the lock and clean things,' Liv said. 'It looks like a Miami condo, well, if you renovated it.'

'I said, no, Liv. Just drop it. The garage is out of bounds.' Livia was clueless about what happened in the garage, and Pepper planned to keep it that way. She couldn't face it yet, either. What happened in there could never be erased from her mind but moving forward meant it had to be. *One day at a time.*

Chapter Two

Back in 1980

If only Darius never went to war.

Darius leaned on a crutch, watching from the damp sand. He squinted towards splashes five metres past the shore. Pepper dove under a wave, popping up like a champagne cork to swim further past the breakers. *Only a kid, and she could outswim her old man.*

Resisting the urge to scratch his arms where shrapnel wounds puckered the skin, he kept his eyes to the surf and his daughter. Only thirty, but he felt older; war expunged the youthfulness from him. Watching Pep's strokes, an indulgent smile played on his thin lips. It exaggerated the lines around his nicotine-stained mouth, at the same time revealing a rarely seen dimple. The smile lingered. A deeply hidden pleasure, caressing his broken heart like a secret gift.

Poor little Pep didn't know he smiled at her or because of her. She swam further out, rounded the rocky outcrop where rips lurked and swam back towards the shore. Though her arms were skinny as wattle tree branches, she ploughed through the basil-green water like an Olympic prodigy. It was her dogged determination to please him. Why she kept trying, he'd never know because he couldn't give her anything in return. *Not a skerrick. Not a crumb.*

A seagull squawked nearby. He ducked, pulse rate accelerating and swung his crutch at the bird, almost losing his balance. A swear word burst from his lips. *Just a seagull. Not an IED. Not the enemy lurking in the shrub of Nui Dat. No chopper booming like thunder above the bush.* His skittering glance took in the beach around him. Pulling himself up before the anxiety took control, he struggled to find calm. *Breathe, mate, breathe.*

Darius sighed, leaning heavily on the crutch, counting slowing heartbeats. Glancing down at the plaster cast wrapped from ankle to knee where pain throbbed across his shattered shin, he shook his head—*bloody idiot.*

Swaying off-balance, he stabbed the crutch in the sand, righting himself. Once again, he'd let everyone down. A drunken stupor—a trip on the stairs—a staggering fall—smack-bang on the gravel driveway, where his tearful wife found him and called an ambulance. The haunting déjà vu of the siren made him fold into himself while nightmares swamped his mind. Enough Bundy Rum to kill a crocodile didn't push the horrors out.

From the water, the child shot an angelic smile his way. As she neared shore, he knuckled a tear under his eye. *Poor kid.* No hugs, kisses or endearments from him. How could he do that to her, Meg asked? Darius didn't have an answer. At least not one he could readily pull from his muddled brain. It's not like he'd tell his wife anyway. Some things remained better left unsaid.

In the garage, he'd written words in his curling scrawl, sniffing the strong ink of the fountain pen, the same stuff he used to write letters home when he toured Vietnam. The journal helped clear his thoughts, sometimes. Other things were too hard to put on paper. He scribbled the reasons he couldn't show the poor mite the love he knew she craved. One day she would understand the things haunting him most.

'Ya can do better. Come on. Ya swam further last week,' he yelled, trying to keep the awful accusations from his voice. But they remained. *Uncontrollable.*

Saltwater dripped from Pep's skin, the damp red swimsuit riding over skinny hips. Brown hair plastered her pretty face, masking one eye. In the other vivid-blue one, tears bubbled—because of him. She blinked them away, biting her bottom lip, saluting and turning. With the longest strides she could manage on such pin legs, she ran back through the shore to dive into the ocean like a dolphin. Pep's strokes became sloppy, her anger at him evident in a rush to swim far because he wasn't satisfied with her first effort.

Wincing, he shot another disgruntled look at his broken leg and the soldier crab crawling on his toes. 'Bugger off,' he yelled at the tiny crustacean before glancing back to the surf. The swell peaked and grew angry since she'd first swum out. Whitecaps surged and crashed over the rocks. A fast sweep sucked the shore with the reversing surge, pulling with it clumps of pungent red seaweed. No tiny brown-haired child bobbed in the ocean.

Darius's eyes widened. His heart faltered, like the hand of God clamped his aorta. It twisted his veins further, making him gag. He scanned everywhere. Out past the sets and jagged rocks, to the horizon, along the shore, but the sweep told another story. A rip must have carried her around the headland near the blowhole. *God, fuckin sake. I've killed ma daughter.*

Tears, salty and raw, slid down his rugged face. Without bothering to wipe them, he lurched to the shore, his movements sluggish because of his busted leg. He waded into the warm sea, not caring if the bloody cast crumbled, scouring the ocean for a sign of Pep. Tripping, he fell into the water face first. Pushing with hands planted in the sand, he turned over, spitting salty water. Hunched in the calf-deep foam, he thumped down with his hands, splashing his face to mingle seawater with salty tears. *Fuckin' useless piece of shit! Get up. Look for her.*

Pulling himself up, dragging the wet cast, he staggered from the shore and spun to face the rip sweeping the rocks. His panicked brain scrambled for a solution. *Where are you, Pep?* Her tiny head popped clear for an instant before it disappeared, where the blowhole sucked anything in its path. His eyes grew wide. Fear pooled in his gut, twisting his insides. The blowhole whooshed water into the air, spraying like a massive whale. *Jesus!*

His shoulders slumped, and his throat filled with bile. *Pep in the underwater cave. Pep smashed on the rocks. Drowning. Dying.* He squeezed his eyes, fighting to shut down the images of rocks and surf pummelling her perfect little body. *There's no use!* No way to save her. Why did he push her so hard?

'You useless, fuckin' piece of shit bastard,' he yelled to the high heavens. Pathetic as when the sniper shot Joey. *In the thick of the jungles of Vietnam. Members of the platoon spread along a ridge concealed by thick wet plants and mud to their knees, not knowing friend from foe or tree root from snake in the sludge. Him and his best mate Joey, rifles cocked over their shoulders, wearing even* cockier grins, stood side-by-side when the whip of a sniper shot sliced the air.

They were so close, Joey's blood and grey matter coated Darius's cheek, dampened his hair and filled his right ear. Too in shock to clean it off, too stupefied to move, minutes passed before he could look to his right where Joey lay dying.

He should have died instead. *I can't do this again? Can't lose anyone else.*

Staggering back to the sand, he flung himself down, punching until he created deep holes in the sand, and his strength ebbed. He kneeled, reaching for the crutch lying on the sand, lifting it to stand with a sodden cast. With power born of wrath, he snapped the crutch across his cast, shattering the timber in two. By the time he'd hobbled home, dragging his leg like a useless appendage, the sun was sinking behind the back of the blue house, casting a burning red glow like hell.

Poor Meg. Through the kitchen window, she hummed to herself, oblivious to what he would do. She'd never forgive him. The delicious aroma of a baked lamb dinner wafted. His favourite, though the thought turned his stomach. He'd miss it — even her and her worrisome, though beautiful, looks. She'd be better off without him.

Wiping his nose with his arm lost some of the snot and tears, but he could barely see through blurry stinging eyes. Lifting the heavy garage door, it slid towards the ceiling with scarcely a sound. He'd oiled the hinges only days before, like other things, in case they were needed.

***

Pep let the rip take her, trying not to panic in the darkening water. *It's only those who panic in a rip that drown,* Daddy always said. Thoughts of being dragged out to sea lingered, but she pushed them aside along with the dread in her gut. A shadow loomed under her feet—goosebumps skittled down her back. Fear lodged in her throat, but she tried to swallow it down without drowning. She tucked her feet under her bum; petrified sharks lurked below. Though she swam through the water keeping her head high to avoid swallowing any, the surge forced her under more times than she could count. She sputtered for breath, eyeing the looming rocks and bracing her hands.

10

The rip sucked her around the rocky headland, her arms scraping rocks, bleeding, and sore knees and muscles cramping. She fought control against the undertow, pushing the growing panic from her brain. Verging too close, her head smacked the north side near the blowhole. Stunned by the hit, she blinked and shook her head. With trembling fingers, she pushed hard away from the rocks.

The blowhole rumbled as she passed. A tall waterspout showered her like rain. Her skin spiked with bumps—a close call. Almost sucked into the blowhole. She shivered and ploughed on, feeling a tug of water pull her feet. The undercurrent continued to take her around the rocks to Moon Beach. Coughing, she spat saltwater from her mouth, trying to keep steady breaths.

The water slowed to rolling waves. It happened so quickly Pep barely realised she was out of the rip's grasp. Scratches and bruises hurt her arms. Her knees stung, and her head ached, but she found enough energy to wade to shore on wobbly legs.

'I made it!' she yelled, spitting seaweed from her parched mouth. Of course, no one heard her boast. She coughed, spitting more salty sludge. Her fingers shook when she pulled seaweed from her hair. With the last of her strength, she punched the air in triumph. Able to negotiate a rip at only ten years old. Tugging tangled hair away from her eyes, she glanced up the goat-track path. *Wait until I tell Dad.*

After regaining her breath, she ran through sand and bush, her bare feet stinging from bindies and stones. Her heart thumped louder than the chorus of cicadas humming in the bush. Would this be the moment he would finally be proud? Might he take her in his big arms and hug her tight? Would he call her Princess Pepper, like he did before the war?

Wrapping her hands around wet shoulders to still the shivers, she stepped off the sandy track to catch her breath. The beach was deserted. Dad's looming figure wasn't staggering on the beach or the track. Why wasn't he looking for her?

She turned towards home, hoping he was waiting with a warm towel. Mouthwatering roast dinner beckoned from the kitchen window. She blinked and raised her eyebrows — the garage door was up. *Dad only goes there when—*

Boom! A blast echoed around the beach cove, loud and sharp. Light flashed from within the garage. Gunpowder mingled with salt, roasting lamb and frangipani. Her breath hitched in her throat. She could have outrun an attacking dingo to get to the garage. *Daddy, no!*

He lay slumped over his desk, a bottle of rum spilled onto the concrete floor mixing with red-almost black blood. His face stared at her with lifeless violet eyes: *blood, so much blood.*

Screams filled the dusk air like hungry fruit bats overhead. Heartbeats later, she realised the cries were her's. The sound muffled to sobs when her mother's warm hand gently covered her lips and eyes. Safe, soft arms wrapped around her like a blanket.

It's my fault.

Chapter Three

2019

'There's a light on next door. I wonder who lives there,' Livia lifted a fork to her mouth. 'Oh, yum. These baked beans are like a-laaaa-cart!' She teased.

'I'll go to the local store for groceries tomorrow. There wasn't any point until the fridge arrived.' Pepper glanced at the enormous fridge, dwarfing the small kitchen.

'I don't get why you have a shipping container when we have the biggest garage. Couldn't it have been put in there?' Livia asked, glancing outside past the shipping container to the neighbouring house. 'See.' She pointed with her fork. 'One light like a reading lamp. Must be some sort of scrooge, not using electricity.'

'Don't be so nosy.' Pepper ignored the garage comment. 'I wouldn't mind curling on the lounge with a book myself. I'm so glad Mum upgraded the electrical wiring a few years back. I always wondered why she never updated anything else.'

'Like the retro-as kitchen? And the godawful rug?'

'She loved the kitchen and the rug; it was a souvenir she bought in Morocco, so a treasure. She must have vacuumed it a million times. Never had a crumb on it.'

'She went overseas?' Liv's eyes were wide.

'When she was in her late teens with your great grandparents. Never again after she married Dad.'

'Why? She lived all those years alone. Travel would have been good for her.'

'I guess she could never leave Dad or his memories. It's why she didn't quit this house.' Pepper shook her head, blinking back the tears pooling under her eyelids.

The faded lime dining room curtain lifted and curled as if a sea breeze had snuck in. It was odd because the night was still. The only sounds were the boom crash of waves and humming cicadas.

Liv placed her hand over Pepper's. 'Mum, let's not dwell. As you always say, there's a sunny side to every situation; you only have to step out of the shadows. Don't you think Nana and Grandad are casting pretty gloomy shadows over you?'

Pepper smiled. It was nice to know Liv listened to some words of advice. 'You're right, sweetheart. Let's make some fun plans for tomorrow.'

'A swim at the beach, then veggie garden?' Liv grinned, standing to scrape the remnants of her dinner in the bin. 'I'll wash up if I get to go to the nursery and meet with my friend who works there.' She winked.

'Friend? What friend?'

'Goes to Blueshell Beach High, so we'll be at the same school when term starts.' Livia busied herself at the sink, a sure sign she was evading further scrutiny.

Pepper cast her eyes towards the neighbouring house. 'You can have your garden, but I'm starting on the house renos.' The person in the adjacent house shifted in the chair, and the lamp illuminated a man's profile. 'It's most definitely a guy over there.' Pepper squinted for a better look. The man stood, faced the window, clearly lit by the lamplight. He looked her way with a frown on his handsome face, shutting his curtains. 'Oh, shit.' Pepper ducked.

'What? Did you get a look at who it is?'

Pepper laughed. 'God, he got a look at me, staring like a peeping tom. He shut his curtains.'

'And you called me nosy. So, was it the hot guy?'

Pepper held her hands to her face feeling the flush of her cheeks. 'Yep.'

'Well, that's awks. The way to pick up a guy is to look like a creeper — not!'

'I won't be picking up any guy, let alone one living 10 metres away.'

'But he's saucy. You said so yourself.'

'Hotness is not a criterion for the ideal man. Besides, I am not looking, and he's too young. After what your father —.' Pepper baulked, gulping back the almost slip of her tongue. She could have ranted, but it wasn't fair to Liv. 'Sorry.'

'Don't be, Mum. I know he's an A Grade asshole.'

'Liv, the language?'

'Mum, he is, and anyhow you swear like Gordon Ramsey.'

'You know that's because I work on building sites. It's part of my job.'

Liv rolled her eyes.

***

Keegan's dog lifted his fuzzy head, letting out a rumble deep in his throat, followed by a fart. His long nose twitched for a scent, ears pricked for sound. There was a warning of something different in the air, but Gus was a lazy, content dog who settled back at Keegan's feet.

Keegan turned his head towards the window, trying to push Gus's awful lingering fart away with one hand. Someone from the house next door must be watching him. He'd always had a sixth sense for that kind of thing. Probably the years of being in dangerous, frontline situations. *Well, except for that one time.*

Holding the book open to mark the spot, he placed it on the lamp table. He stood to face the window. Gus let out a sigh, settling his head further onto his paws.

Keegan spied the pretty woman leaning over her dining table, chin on her hands, watching him from the metres separating their homes. His lounge window ran parallel to the kitchen of the funky blue cottage.

She must have realised he saw her because she ducked out of sight for a moment.

He pulled the curtain across and hid behind the block-out fabric, peeking to see what she would do.

The daughter moved, placing a hand on the woman's shoulder, glancing towards him with a grin. Was she teasing her mother? They had to be mother and daughter, surely. Other than their heights, they were too similar not to be. The woman's head rested in her hands. He willed her to look up. *Doesn't hurt to see your beautiful face again.*

He missed his old neighbour, Meg, and her soft, gentle ways of

15

being neighbourly without being nosy. He wouldn't approach the younger women, but having them nearby, so lovely and happy, made him crave something he didn't know he wanted. *A connection.*

Moving away from the window, he cursed himself. He wasn't in Blueshell Beach to make friends and, stunning woman or not; he didn't need the complication. *But damn, she was easy on the eyes.*

He picked up the book, a biography, Turia Pitt's *Everything to Live For*, a relevant memoir to help him pull himself together, but all it did was make him feel weak and useless. If brave Turia could go through almost burning to death, survive and remain upbeat, who was he to complain about PTSD? *If I even have it.* But the psychiatrist said he'd probably fight the disorder forever. He didn't have the classic signs anymore, wasn't angry, didn't drink. He was calm and fine—*most days.*

He slammed the hardcover book shut. It would be impossible to read with the woman on his mind. He hadn't reacted to a female in so long there'd be cobwebs growing on his cock.

When he first saw her standing in front of the cottage with the teenager, he felt self-conscious with their gazes upon him, especially when he almost tripped over Gus. Jogging by the two houses fronting Blueshell Beach, his and old lady Meg's, was his ritual. Always alone, well, except for Gus. He wasn't expecting anyone as he rounded the goat track. When her pretty eyes flashed something, it intrigued and chuffed him. Did they hold a note of desire? *Wishful thinking.* She quickly covered it, not before he noticed — her electric glance holding for an instant. He could be mistaken, but he doubted it. *More wishful thinking.*

In town, women flashed looks his way, some brazen and shameless, but they didn't do anything to break the iceberg he'd built around himself. Whereas she seemed like the Titanic crashing into the ice instead of the other way around. Pieces fell away at a rate of a global-warmed glacier. He didn't know if he were happy or terrified. One thing he did know, his sleeping cock was suddenly awake. He glanced at his lap, totally baffled by how he was feeling. Love, even lust, didn't take one look at someone. He didn't believe in first-sight-romance mumbo jumbo.

Gus raised big hazel, intelligent eyes. 'Mate, I must be going a

16

little stir-crazy isolating myself, eh?'

Gus tilted his head sideways.

'You've never endured woman problems. Sorry, mate, no pun intended, but you have no balls.' Keegan chuckled. He hadn't heard the sound of his laughter even longer than he'd experienced a woman-induced hardon. 'I can do without a distraction like that. Plus, we have work to do, right?' He glanced at the textbook he'd been avoiding for Turia Pitt. Getting back to work should be his priority.

Gus's tail thumped on the timber floor.

'The ladies don't bother you, Gus. Maybe that's the best way for a guy to be. No balls, no complications. So, I plan to admire her from a distance, you know, like a nice painting, but not get too close, or the beauty will be spoilt. Right?'

More tail thumping.

'Great. That's my plan, then. I just hope they aren't the nosy type.'

Gus let out a yap as if he agreed.

'Yep, Gus, we only need each other.' He rubbed the fur on Gus's narrow neck. Gus preened. 'Don't you dare go being friendly with them.' He wagged his finger at the ex-Air Force recruit.

The dog, a Malinois, was supposedly the most trainable breed, but Gus possessed obedience difficulties. He liked people. There was no way in Haiti he would take down a baddie or stay calm enough to find an IED before it exploded. Anyhow, the Air Force's loss was Keegan's gain. The dog was loyal as a barnacle on a whale. Keegan didn't know what he would have done without the companionship of Gus. Especially after what happened two years ago. A time he'd rather forget.

Chapter Four

Pepper parked the car in front of the neighbour's driveway. 'I'll go in and see if he needs anything in town,' she said to Livia, who pulled earphones from her ears and raised her eyebrows. 'Never mind. I'll be back in a moment.'

'Any excuse to meet him, Mum,' Livia said, chuckling. 'No swearing, panting or doing that eye flutter thing you do.' She wound down her window, ever the stickybeak.

'He's our neighbour. We need to meet him. And I do not eye flutter.' Pepper tilted her head and flickered her eyelashes with over-the-top exaggeration.

'You do swear, though.'

'I'll keep it in check. I'm not on a building site, just meeting our neighbour.'

Livia jammed the earplugs back in her ears, singing to her favourite band. 'Push me away, push me away. Then beg me to stay, beg me to stay, yeah.'

The front screen door of the house creaked opened and shut with a clap. A dog loped in front of the man, eager and excited, twirling a full circle in front of Pepper's legs.

'What do you want?' the man said in a deep voice. His hands shoved in the pockets of his shorts made his pecs look rather appealing under the stretch of a tight t-shirt. He was muscular in a trim way, not beefcake, more a bar of delicious chocolate. *Mouthwatering.*

His skin was dark, perhaps he was European, and his almost black hair peppered with grey waved around his face, thick, lush and on the longish side like Brendan Fraser in George of the Jungle. His eyes were charcoal with lashes so thick they shadowed his cheeks. Pepper took a deep breath. *Holy fuck, even better up close!*

***

Keegan's dog, Gus, circled the woman's legs giving her the where-you-been-who've-you-seen sniff. She dropped a small hand to the dog's nose, revealing calloused hands and dirty, chipped nails, not in keeping with her neatly brushed pulled-in-a-pony-tail hair and pretty face. 'Hey, buddy,' she said, 'What's your name?' She glanced at Keegan with a smile. 'The dog won't answer me. Could you?' She tilted her head.

Gus whoofed. *Don't you turncoat on me, dog.*

'It's Gus,' Keegan said. She ruffled his dog's neck in the place Gus liked most. He lifted his hand to his neck, fingers trailing the scar from ear to mid clavicle, a habit he'd been trying to stop.

'Hey, Gus, aren't you a beautiful animal.' She bent beside the dog, giving her full attention.

Gus lapped it up, licking her face, and she didn't even flinch. *Friggin traitor, dog.*

'So, hi. I thought we'd introduce ourselves and see if you'd like anything in town.' She grinned a broad, welcoming, pretty-as smile, her small hand outstretched.

His fingers twitched, but he did not reach out. Deep laughter lines accentuated the vivid colour of her Elizbeth-Taylor eyes. *Ignore those eyes too.*

'I'm not up for chit-chat.' Keegan released air through pursed lips. His fingers scratched his neck where the long-gone ache once lingered, but mental scars remained.

'You could say, thanks for asking—no need to be rude. I'm your neighbour. We're trying to be friendly,' she said, shaking her head, so her short ponytail bounced, making her look young and full of spunk.

'Well, sorry, luv. I'm not the neighbourly kind.' Keegan frowned. Why didn't women just leave things be? He was quite happy with his solitude. *But, damn, she was charming.*

'So, you can't answer me as to whether you would like anything in town since I'm going there?' She raised neat eyebrows and turned her palms to face the baby-blue, cloudless sky.

19

'Nope.' He shook his head, glancing past her to the idling ute with an empty flatback tray. It had seen better days, with dints along the sides and peeling signwriting, the first word missing from— C Constructions. Probably the husband's work ute. The teenager in the passenger seat smiled a broad hello, with an earphone in one ear.

'Come on, Mum. Obviously, Mr Grouch wants to be left to himself,' the teenager called from the idling car.

'Gus, here,' Keegan called. The dog was slow to respond, making Keegan's temper loom. 'Now!'

Gus's ears pricked. He cocked his head, trying to understand Keegan's odd reaction to the woman. He figured it wasn't the dog's fault for liking her. She was friendly, cheerful, clearly adored dogs and sexy as a Cherry Ripe advert. *What's not to like?* But Keegan couldn't go there. He didn't need a complication messing up his plan to win Joe's love back and return to work.

'Okay, if you're sure,' she said, turning back to the car.

'Yep.' *Nope.*

Looking over her shoulder with a cute grin and a wink, she said, 'My name's Pepper, and this is my daughter Livia. We live too close not to be acquaintances, if not friends. We'll be back. Might need sugar or something at some point, huh?'

Keegan shook his head, rolling his eyes, trying to keep the smile he held inside from transferring to his eyes. His jaw twitched, keeping unspoken words at bay.

'What's your name?' yelled the teenager Livia.

'Keegan.'

'See ya, Keegan and Gus.' Livia waved.

Pepper hit the accelerator, turning the car from his drive, spitting sand and dust in the tyres' wake.

Keegan watched them until the car was out of sight, wondering why he'd been abrupt, rude and unfriendly. Saying hello wouldn't have hurt, but no, he'd reverted to the old habit of not letting anyone get close. *Better that way.* So, why did he feel an ache in his gut the size of a pineapple?

Could have asked what happened to dear old Meg? At least show some concern. The lady kept to herself, but she was a lovely old duck, though a little odd due to senility. They hadn't talked much, but he'd

20

kept an eye on her when her friends weren't around. When she fell down her steps, he called the ambulance, administered first aid, and kept her calm. *How long ago was that?* He scratched his head. Probably a few months or so. He hoped she was okay.

***

Pepper pretended to be engrossed in the label of a fertiliser bag. Livia and the boy moved closer, looking too familiar and friendly for someone Liv had recently met. Lumbering the heavy load, she walked to the counter of the Garden Nursery. To the attendant, a lady about her age with a mass of red curls and a pretty porcelain white face, she asked, 'Is this good for — um?'

'Fertilising plants. Yes. But I can see your attention is more on Ross and his new friend.' She tilted her red head towards Liv and the boy.

'The new friend is my daughter, Livia.' She dropped the bag on the counter. 'I guess vegetables need fertiliser, huh?'

'Sure do. And you'd better watch out. That boy has fertilised more paddocks than a prize bull.'

'Really? He's so young.' Pepper's heart stopped. Livia was clearly flirting with the boy, hips jutted forward and flipping her long blonde hair. 'What's his surname?'

'Ronson,' she said in a sing-song British accent.

A name from a long time ago. 'Not related to you? I guess you're from England.'

'Hell no. And yes, Cork. I try my best to sound un-British, but after 30 years here, it sneaks back occasionally. I only work here and wouldn't employ that little piece of shit. Oh, sorry, you look like a bit of a lady. I shouldn't be swearing.'

Pepper laughed. 'Fuck no; you shouldn't.'

The woman slapped the counter. 'You are one funny bugger. My name's Maisy, stupid old name handed down for generations, but that's me, Maisy Stewart. I live the north side of Moon Beach, the pink house if you ever want to call in for a cuppa. I heard you're doing up Meg's blue house. You're the daughter, right?'

'Yes. I am. Pepper Cassidy.' What a lovely friendly woman. Maybe returning to Blueshell Beach wouldn't be so bad after all.

'Sorry to hear about her. I guess she's finally with Darius, though.'

21

'You know about Dad?' Pepper's fingers shook. She curled them on the counter to still them.

'Whole town does, sweetheart.' Maisy laid her hand over Pepper's. 'Most who went to school with you are still here. I know a few. It's how I know your story. Myself, I got here in '96. I guess you were off in the big city by then, luvy.'

'Yes. I was married that year. Unfortunately, I'm divorcing soon. It's strange to be back after all this time, but sometimes you don't plan your future.' *Understatement!*

'I find it better that way. Never planned to stay here.' She laughed. 'I was travelling my way around Oz, but I fell in love with the place, plus a bugger of a man. So, I'm still here.'

'Still with the bugger of a man?'

'Sure am.' Maisy winked.

'Guess he's not such a bugger then, huh?' She giggled but glanced at Livia, and the laughter died.

'Seems a bit keen on him. Best you nip that in the bud. Sorry, I don't mean to be nosy.' Maisy scanned the barcodes of the herbs and vegetable plants Livia had stacked in a metal trolley.

'It's okay.' Pepper's heart twisted, watching her blossoming daughter flirt with the young man, a boy with a reputation and a surname that stirred unwanted memories. 'I'm aware of the Ronsons, unfortunately. A friend married Bobby. Is that their son?'

Maisy stacked the plants in cardboard boxes. 'Sure is. Bob's in jail for assault, and poor Judith can't keep that boy out of trouble, nor herself.'

'Such a shame. Judith was so kind.'

'Sucked in by a good-looking man with a devil's heart.'

'Mmm, and probably why Livia thinks the son is hot stuff. He is a nice-looking boy.' Pepper angled her head.

'Too much like his old-man, though. Keep your eye on him, Pepper,' said Maisy. 'He works hard enough, though. I've got to give him that.'

Pepper tapped her credit card on the EFTPOS to pay for the supplies, biting her bottom lip. 'Livia, are you ready to go?' she called, receiving a narrow glare from the young man. He winked at Liv before smirking towards the counter. *Don't mess with a mumma bear, mate.*

'Have you met your sexy neighbour yet?' Maisy asked, making Pepper's heart skitter. She dropped the credit card.

'Keegan, yes.' Pepper laughed, hoping a blush hadn't hit her cheeks. She bent to pick up the card and slipped it back in her purse. 'He's not very friendly.'

Maisy chuckled, deep and throaty. 'Good luck getting him to say more than three words. Plenty of single women have tried to woo him, but he's not taken the bait once. Pretty much keeps to himself. Hangs out fishing with my man, Trev, sometimes and surfs a lot.'

'Makes you wonder what his story is, doesn't it.' She pushed the trolley to the side, waiting for Livia, who was waving to Ross over her shoulder as she strolled to the counter.

'Maybe you'll be the one to pry it out of him,' Maisy said.

'Doubt it. He seems about as approachable as a pond full of crocodiles.' She laughed but felt sick at the thought of Livia liking Ross Ronson.

Maisy chuckled. 'Don't forget my invitation to call in any time. I think we'd get on like a house on fire.' Maisy turned her attention to another customer.

'Come on, Liv. Let's get this stuff home. I have a hardware order arriving at the house soon. We've spent longer here than expected.'

Livia strolled beside the trolley, turning back several times to shoot smiles at Ross. 'What does that mean, Mum? I told you I had a friend who worked here.'

'You forgot to mention that person was a boy.' She raised her eyebrows.

'So, a girl can have boys who are friends? He's really nice.'

'Just be careful, sweetie. Some people aren't always as they seem.' Why did Livia turning boy crazy coincide with all the other obstacles in her life? *Mum's death. Husbands' betrayal. Restructured business. Moving town. Renovating. Divorce.* She doubted she had the energy to cope with anything else.

Livia huffed, pulled her phone from her pocket, shoved earphones in her ears and ignored her during the drive home. She helped silent Liv set up a raised garden bed, filled it with soil and left Livia to plant the herbs and vegetables.

She returned hours later to check on Livia's progress. As she rounded the house and walked the wire fence line towards the vegetable garden, she stopped short with her mouth agape. The sight in front of her was so mouthwatering she was a waterfall.

Keegan was in a yoga headstand pose, his arms each side of his head, stretched with sinewy muscles. Shoulders and back bunched, well-defined rivets of muscle and deep olive skin, tapering to a narrow waist and smooth backside. His legs angled directly above, toes pointed. There was no shake as he held the posture, so still she could barely see him breathing.

'How long's he been doing that?' she whispered to Livia.

Liv glanced over, lifting dirty hands from the soil. 'Ages, maybe twenty minutes.'

'Wow!'

'I think you're *wowing* about more than his yoga posture,' Liv said, 'kinda makes you a hypocrite, Mum.' She shoved a bunch of coriander into the soil, pressing it down before placing a name tag in the earth beside it.

Pepper gulped. 'No. It's just such a goood headstand.'

Liv snorted.

Keegan must have heard them because he angled his knees and tuck-jumped to the grass. He waved and said, 'Good luck with your garden, Livia.' Grabbing a towel lying on the lawn, he wiped his face and strode towards the house. 'Hey, can you keep the noise down tomorrow?'

Pepper nodded but had no idea why, because she wasn't going to stop renovating the house. 'You've been talking to him?' she asked, dragging her eyes away from the magnificent man before glancing at Liv.

'Yeah, so. Hey, how good does this look? All the bigger veggies to the back and herbs to the front. We'll be self-sustainable in no time.'

'Great job, sweetheart.' *But what did Keegan say?* 'Better clean up. The sun's going down.

'Thanks.' Livia brushed the soil from her hands. There was some on her face too, making her violet eyes stand out. 'It was fun. I have gaps, though. I could fill them with chives. Can we go back to the plant nursery through the week?'

24

'Weren't chives on your list?' Pepper pursed her lips—*an excuse to see Ross again.*

'Must have missed them,' Liv said, not meeting her eyes. 'I need a shower. I'm filthy.'

Pepper followed Liv, glancing over at Keegan's house, hoping to get another glimpse of him. *Stupid.* Was she a crazy middle-aged, sex-starved woman or what? Slapping her hand to her forehead, she ignored Keegan's side of the fence.

Get with the real world. It had been a lovely interlude watching Keegan's yoga pose, but it was time to make serious decisions. *File renovation plans with the local council. Divorce Ian. And find out what Ross Ronson was up to with Livia.* Even without Maisy's well-intentioned warning, there was something about the young man's look that didn't sit right. Or, was it only his surname that bothered her?

Chapter Five

Keegan ran with his heart surging with adrenaline. He glanced back. The man's shadow followed. He upped his pace, rounding a bend, skidding to a stop in front of the ambulance. With balled fists, he banged on the closed back doors, screaming for help. His paramedic partner, Renee, was nowhere in sight. *Move. Hide.* But his body froze. The ground spun. Pain ripped his neck. His head lolled. *Blood. Fear. Anguish.* Joe, in his peripheral vision. The shadow loomed arm raised, knife glinting.

'Noooo. Not Joe. Not—' Keegan sat with a jolt, his focus clearing. *Bedroom.* It was a while before his heart seemed to join his chest as if he were still in a dream-state above his body. He ran a finger along the straight scar on his neck, then over his forehead where sweat pooled. *Calm. Deep breath.* A nightmare.

Gus pawed the bedspread, whimpering, before leaping on the mattress to lick Keegan's cheek. Every time a nightmare hit with intensity, Gus was drawn to him like he was a dog treat.

Keegan took a deep breath, feeling Gus's fur curl over his hand. His fingers caressed the dog's neck, giving comfort to both dog and man. Heart rate gradually slowed to a semblance of normal. Six months ago, he would have drowned the nightmares in a bottle of bourbon, but with Gus by his side, he no longer coped through the booze. He was stronger. *Closer to Joe.*

Stretching his arms above his head, he pushed his palms together in a salutation to the sun. Since he was an atheist, he could hardly call it prayer, but in his way, it was a thank you for being alive and getting through another day. And, it was another step closer to bringing his son, Joe, back into his life.

He didn't blame Sherry. She did her best to deal with his all-consuming role as a rescue paramedic and the resulting PTSD. And, if he were honest with himself, he hadn't been kind enough to her with the burdens she carried as his wife. He didn't let her in to help deal with it. Shutting her out was the stupidest thing he'd done. Not so much because he lost her, but because he failed Joe. Missing Joe's tiny, eager face did more than any knife to the throat. It tore his insides to pieces. Problem was no one could see it or understand how he felt. Least of all, Sherry.

'Thanks, Gus. I'm good now.' He ruffled the dog's ear. 'A surf will clear the head. You can run on the beach and go sniff out some soldier crabs.'

Gus, whoofed as if he understood, bolting for the front door. Keegan stood naked, gazing out the window towards the surf. Not a big swell, but it didn't matter. He needed saltwater on his skin more than the thrill of catching big waves. Slipping boardshorts over his hips, he followed Gus outside where his board hung on a rack near the back door.

By the time he'd reached the shore, the nightmare had receded to another part of his brain. Digging his toes in the sand, feeling the cool grit, sent calm through his nerves. Peace reigned again. He took a deep breath of salty, seaweed air and smiled.

Gus frolicked past chasing seagulls, splashing water over his calves. Keegan waded in, duck dived a small wave, popped up behind it and paddled out. The pressure of fibreglass below him, coconut wax and the temperate water were a tonic. His arms propelled him forwards, and the ache in his shoulder muscles was familiar and reassuring. Surfing was not only fun, but it also pushed his body against the force of nature; ocean and swell. There was nothing like it for seeing your insignificance in the scheme of things—no better place to recharge mental energy and appreciate life.

Turning the board to face shore, he sat on the deck, head over his shoulder to check the swell. It was small and would take a while to build enough for him to catch a wave. He turned his attention to the blue house visible on the rise. Another truck idled in the driveway, unloading supplies. He frowned. More timber meant further hammering, sawing and whatever the hell else went on in the house.

27

It was probably time he told his new neighbour she was ruining his serenity.

It's why the nightmares returned. Noises did that. The reason Keegan chose the house he did. *Noiseless.* Only rolling surf, aquatic birds and the occasional torrential downpour.

Damn that infuriating woman. A smile took his lips hostage. There was something about Pepper that intrigued him. It was a long time since he'd been interested in a woman the way he was with her. Maybe talking to Livia over the fence about her vegetable garden was a way to find out more about her beautiful mother without asking outright.

Feeling water surge below him, he turned to see the mounting swell. He paddled into the curve, pushed up with his hand, jumped to his feet, planting them goofy-foot forward and rode the wave, letting out a whoop of delight. Gus barked from the shore, hearing him with perfect dog precision, before being distracted by sea-tumbleweed rolling over the sand.

***

'Thanks, Tom. I appreciate you dropping it off on a Sunday,' Pepper said, signing the invoice and handing the delivery driver a copy.

'Are these the new doors, Mum,' Livia asked, trailing her fingers along the raw timber, slanted to look like shutters. 'They'll look great but still give privacy.'

'Yeah, I'm using plantation doors and windows to keep with the beach cottage feel. I don't want the cottage to lose its charm.'

'It has no charm.' Liv rolled her eyes. 'But it will now. Are you going to avoid the drop saw today?'

'No. I'll need to cut the skirting to finish your room.'

'Keegan wasn't too happy about the noise when I talked to him over the fence yesterday.'

'I got that, but surely he knows it's only temporary.' Pepper glanced over at his house, but he was nowhere in sight, and neither was his faithful pooch.

'It's something about the serenity. He says he does yoga to keep calm. I guess the noise is messing with that.' Liv shrugged her shoulders.

'Did he say much over the veggie garden?' Pepper fished for more information on the mysterious, quiet, sexy-as-Henry-Cavill-neighbour.

'I talked more than him. But I could tell he was mad at you.'

Pepper placed her hands on her hips. 'Well, he has no friggin' right. I'll damn-well build my house when I like. Seriously, does he think he owns Blueshell Beach?'

Liv tapped her on the shoulder. 'Ah, maybe you should ask him. He's right behind you.'

Pepper wanted the ground to swallow her like quicksand — *the quicker, the better.* Fanning the flame on her cheeks, she turned to face Keegan. He had a curled fist over his lips as if he were about to discreetly cough.

'I'm not stopping the noise,' she said before he could take a breath, let alone speak.

His handsome jawline twitched, and slate eyes glanced around the building site. 'I can see that.'

'So?'

'How long?'

'How long's a piece of string?'

'Do you always talk in riddles?'

'She does,' Livia said with a smirk.

'If I can get all the supplies I need and fit the kitchen, as long as council approve the walls I'll take out and the extra level, probably April.'

'Easter? Are you serious?' He ran a hand through his thick black hair with greying sideburns.' His cheek twitched again, and Pepper guessed it was to keep his temper in check.

'I'm sorry, but I have to do it right to honour Mum.' *And Dad.*

It was like the air left Keegan's lungs. His broad shoulders slumped slightly. 'Oh, Meg, your mum. Sorry. I only heard about her yesterday.'

'From me, Mum,' said Livia. 'Noone told him she died at the nursing home. Did you know he was the person who strapped her hip and waited for the ambos when Nan had her last fall?'

Keegan nodded. 'I'm sorry for your loss.' His glance hit the ground, not meeting Pepper's eyes.

She should be ashamed for assuming it was one of her mother's friends who had been at the house. 'Thank you,' she managed to say, over her tripping tongue. 'It was quick once the Alzheimers took hold.' Pepper blinked at the tears pooling behind her eyelids.

'I'll leave you to it.' Keegan lifted hooded eyes slightly before turning away.

'You're not going to read the noise act to me?'

'Nope.' He shoved his hands to nonexistent boardshorts pockets. The loose singlet over his back barely concealed a single riveting muscle. *Damn, it was unfair how good he looked.* Pepper glanced at her workwear, stained with sawdust and dirt. *Must look about as appealing as a pile of shit.*

'So, no words about the noise?' she asked.

'Are you trying to push my buttons?' Keegan turned back, striding towards Pepper.

Livia laughed. 'Well, she pushes mine all the time. It must be your turn.'

He stood over Pepper, glaring down at her. He wasn't tall, perhaps five-ten, but towered over her petite size. He didn't intimidate her, she'd put bigger men in their place, mostly as their boss, but she was always fair. 'No, of course not. It's just that I was going to agree to sawing and hammering at better hours to suit you. If you'll tell me what they are?'

He harrumphed. 'None.' Pepper could feel his warm, fresh breath on her face and the scent of surf wax and male musk.

'I can't do—*none* or my house will never get completed.'

He raked a hand through his long fringe. 'Where are all your workers?' He glanced around, tapping one foot, clearly irritated.

'I'll only need some for bigger things. I'm doing most of it myself.'

'Serious? You'll never get it done, and you'll keep me in hell.' His jaw did the twitchy thing again, and he rubbed his neck over a long scar.

'Well, if I had neighbours helping it would get done faster.' Pepper placed her hands on her hips and raised her chin to him. She wondered how he got such a scar. It was his only flaw but somehow seemed a perfect imperfection.

His eyes bulged. 'After 9 am and finish by 4.' He shot it over his shoulder, long legs already striding away back to his barking dog.

'Tell Gus between nine and four too,' she yelled, receiving an arrowed dark-eyed glance in return.

'Mum, what's with you,' Livia asked, shaking her shoulder. 'Why do you weird out around him?'

'I do not weird out.'

'Really. Why are you placing newly cut skirting boards in the skip bin?'

Pepper glanced down at her hands, holding perfectly cut timber. *Damn, Keegan!*. What was with the guy anyway? He had to have a reason for being such a damn pain. *What was his bloody story?*

31

Chapter Six

'Hi, Liv. How are you doing with the garden?' Keegan asked, leaning the surfboard against his house. Approaching her, he passed the clothesline, grabbing a towel, rubbing it against his wet skin.

'Not bad for a novice. I Googled everything, but I must admit I copied how you've staked your tomatoes.' She brushed dirty hands down her thighs. The garden was thriving two weeks since her first planting. 'Been for a surf?'

He shook the water from his hair like a shaggy dog. A saw buzzed next door, making him wince and forcing a headache to his temple. 'Yep, it usually relaxes me, but with the racket you're mother's making, that won't last long.'

'You should try yoga,' Liv said with a grin. 'Mum likes when you do yoga.'

'What?'

She giggled. 'Never mind. Hey, you've been 'round these parts for a while. Do you go to town much?'

'Nope.'

'Do you know the Ronsons?'

'Kinda.'

'Like, Ross. Have you met him? I have, and he's just about the sauciest guy I've ever known. He works at the garden nursery, you know.'

'Yeah, I've met the kid.'

'You never offer much.' Liv frowned. 'I want to know all about him.'

'Why?'

'Well, don't tell Mum, but I like him, like heaps.' She twisted her fingers to her lips, making sure he knew to button his. 'Is his family nice? He doesn't say anything about them, but I'm curious.'

'Look, Liv. I don't butt into other people's business, but I have heard his dad's in jail. Maybe you should set your sights on another young man.' By the dreamy look on her pretty, young face, it was unlikely.

'No way. He's like so snatched.'

'Huh?'

'You'd probably say good looking, like lit!'

Seriously teenagers talk like aliens. 'Right. You like him.'

'So much.' She stared into space, her face taking on a dreamy quality.

Uh oh! What to say to a teenage girl he barely knew and was probably going to the wrong side of the tracks? It wouldn't end well. He scratched his head, trying to come up with something more helpful. 'Just be careful, eh.' What more could he say? She was a vulnerable young girl, and he didn't want her in harm's way. He was flummoxed.

Of course, he had Joe, but little boys were another kettle of fish compared to teen girls.

'What's that sound?' Livia asked, glancing past Keegan towards his house.

'I can only hear your mother hammering her heart out on some poor piece of timber.' Keegan shrugged his shoulders, but between the racket next door, he heard high pitched meowing. 'Kittens?'

'Sounds like it. Can I come over and look?'

'Sure.' *Where was Gus?* It sounded like the meowing was coming from under his house, and his dog was nowhere in sight.

Liv climbed the low metal fence and ran to the stumped house. 'Look, there they are in that corner. Your dog's with them. I hope he's not hurting them. Here, boy.'

Keegan bent down, squinting. Gus ambled towards them before licking Liv's face. Seven tiny fluff balls followed the dog, rolling and tumbling over each other until they reached the dog. Gus lay down, letting them snuggle against his belly, with puckering mouths and sweet meows.

'OMG, look at that. The kittens think Gus is their mummy,' Livia cooed, rubbing her hands together.

'Where's the mother cat?' Keegan scratched his head.

'Who knows. Looks like they are abandoned. Gus is now a mummy. Sweet!'

Keegan sighed. 'What the hell do I do with that?'

'Well, they'll need milk, obviously.' Liv glanced up, rolling her eyes.

Not so obvious to a bloke, even though he'd been a paramedic. 'Would they need special formula?'

'Google is sure to tell us.' Livia stood away from under the house, whipping a mobile phone from the back pocket of her denim shorts. 'Righto, it says, goats milk, kayo syrup and non-fat yoghurt, plus a little gelatin.' She glanced at him. 'You do have stuff, right?'

'Who drinks goats milk? What's kayo? The yoghurt and gelatin I can do.'

'How old do you reckon these cuties are?' Liv asked, picking up a bundle of fur with her free hand. It cried louder but curled into her palm, watching with huge green eyes. 'You hungry, bubba?'

'Their eyes are open. If they are like puppies, at least two weeks.' Keegan picked up a runt-looking kitten with orange stripes. The rest of the babies were grey and white, with fluffy fur, whereas it had a shorter coat. 'Well, look at this guy. The oddball.'

'Let's call him that,' Liv said. 'What about the others?'

'Hey, let's not get attached. These are not my cats, and surely someone owns them.' Keegan frowned.

'You don't like cats?'

'I'm a dog person, but they are cute.' He admitted with a grin, bringing the kitten to his face and rubbing the fur against his cheek. Weird how babies of any kind did that to most people, not all. He knew that well enough. 'Jesus, Gus, you look way too comfortable with a litter of kittens. You are the weirdest Air Force recruit ever.' He chuckled.

'You were in the Air Force?' Liv asked.

'I—um. Hey, do you think you could watch these little fellas while I run to the store and see if I can get some goats milk and kayo, whatever that is? I thought it was a betting app.'

'Maybe the pet store has something better. You should try there first. Do you have a blanket or something to make them more comfortable? Actually, a big box so they don't get lost?'

'Yep. Grab three. I'll take four and get them up to my deck.'

Liv scooped kittens into her arm, grinning wide. 'This is awesome.'

'Mmm.' Keegan shrugged. What was he going to do with a damn litter of kittens? He could look after himself and Gus—but kittens?

'Where will they go?'

'Doghouse.' It was timber with a large opening but unused because Gus quickly asserted himself as an inside-beside-Keegan kinda dog. He placed the kittens in the pet bed and went in search of a blanket. He returned to find Gus inside the doghouse with the kittens.

'Look, he's blocking the entrance so they can't get out,' said Liv. 'Smart dog.'

'Stupid dog, never even knew it was a doghouse until now.'

'Kitten house,' Liv said with a giggle. The kittens meowed louder. 'Better get that milk. And kitty litter too. You don't want them doing their business all over your deck.'

'I'll see what I can do.' Keegan ran inside, shrugged a shirt on, grabbed his keys and ran to the car. Could the kittens die of starvation if he wasn't quick enough? There was no way of knowing how long it had been since they fed off their mother.

He pressed the electronic key towards his car, but a large delivery truck parked over both driveways blocked his exit. He got in and honked his horn, only to receive a one-finger salute from the driver. Pepper strolled down her drive.

'Hey, Keegan,' she called in her ever-cheerful voice. 'He'll just be a minute.'

'I don't have a minute. Can the bloke edge that way? I need to get out.'

'It won't take—'

'Now!'

Pepper shook her pretty head. With her hands on her hips, over an enormous toolbelt that made her look like she had a tyre straddling her hips, she still looked cute.

She pleasantly asked the driver to edge further over her side of the road. She turned to wave him off, shooting him a tilted look of concern.

'Kittens, and Liv's with them,' he yelled out his open window before driving towards town.

When he returned home, he found the street quiet. Only the sound of booming surf and aquatic birds filled the air. It almost made him whistle until he noted Pepper had joined Liv on his deck. With a frown, he retrieved the bags of kitten stuff from his back seat and locked the car. How could he avoid her if she kept dropping in?

'Did you get what we need?' Liv said it like she'd moved into his bloody house to nurture kittens he didn't even own.

'Kitten formula in a can, milk formula, bottles, teats, toys, blankets, training pads, a bag of kitty litter and some tray contraption the girl at the pet shop recommended,' Keegan said. He glanced at his hands carrying full bags, feeling stupid he'd bought so much for pets he wasn't planning to keep.

'Well, hot damn. I reckon that's about the most words I've ever heard come from your mouth,' said Pepper, looking fresh and pretty in a loose yellow blouse and faded denim shorts revealing lovely tanned legs. *A serious distraction.* She playfully elbowed his ribs, and he hid his smile.

'Here,' he passed the bag to Liv, not knowing what to do next, especially with Pepper so close he got a whiff of perfume like roses. *Intoxicating.* 'How come you're here?'

'Liv called and said you had kittens. Your last words out your car window were rather cryptic. I'd finished work, and who can resist cute little kitties.' She smiled, and her whole face lit up. Unlike him, she didn't avoid a smile. She thoroughly enjoyed it, sweet pink lips taut and white teeth showing, along with an adorable dimple on each softly lined cheek. He couldn't tell how old she was, about his age. She must have been young when she had Liv.

'You can have the kittens. I have no idea what to do with them.'

'Don't be silly. Gus is doing a great job. We'd better get some formula into them. The funny one—'

'Oddball, Mum.' Liv cuddled Oddball to her chest.

'Yes, Oddball's meowing his little heart out, telling us he's starving.'

'Right. I'll do whatever,' he said, strolling inside. He turned to find Pepper close behind him.

'I'll help. Give me the bottles, and I'll fill them per instructions.'

'You don't think I can read them?' He passed her the formula and bottles.

'No man can.' She pulled reading glasses from her pocket and eyed the label, then looked over the top of them at him. 'Yes, I need reading glasses.'

'No. It's not that. I'm noticing the woman, not the glasses.' *Idiot! Why say that?* No use in telling her he thought she was hot. *What was the friggin point?* 'I'll head back to the kittens with these extra blankets.' He took off outside before she could see his embarrassment.

One to be standoffish and relaxed with the ladies, he wasn't used to being so awkward. It frustrated the hell out of him. Pepper made him say dumbass shit as if his cock was speaking for his brain. The pressure in his boardshorts proved it. He passed Liv the blankets and toys. 'Here.'

Pepper's soft footfalls had him edgy. 'Grab a bub each and let's get these kitties fed,' she said cheerfully, passing each a bottle. Liv, cross-legged on the floor near Gus and four kittens, Pepper sat beside him on his outdoor couch, which was way too close but the only seating. Their thighs touched, and she shifted slightly away, trying to get the teat into the kitten's mouth, or was she avoiding him. 'So hold the bottle at this angle and keep forcing it gently into their mouths until they suck. Oh, there you go, Keegan, you've done it already.'

His kitten slurped and sucked hard on the bottle, and he felt a little surge of joy or pride or something undefined. But it hadn't been that many years ago he'd fed formula to Joe. Pepper stared at him with her incredible eyes with a broad, encouraging smile. He couldn't help but smile back. Not a full smile, but it was close.

***

Pepper watched Keegan, feeling a tug deep in her belly. A beautiful, compassionate man caring for tiny, helpless animals with such patience, how couldn't it tug at her heart? She tried to keep attention to her kitten, but her eyes kept dragging back to his gentle hands, the half-smile on his bristled mouth, his thick hair falling over his mesmerising dark eyes.

'Mum? Earth to Mum,' Livia said. 'My baby's full. I need another bottle.'

'Okay.' Reluctantly, she stood from the couch, instantly feeling devoid of Keegan's warmth. Placing her kitten inside the kennel beside the dozing dog, she went inside to fill more bottles. She glanced around Keegan's home. It was minimal but had books stacked on the shelves and was tidy for a man living alone.

A picture of Keegan with a young boy of about five sat on top of a low bookshelf. They were smiling into each other's eyes and looked too alike not to be father and son. He still wore a wedding ring. She'd noticed, of course, but where was the picture of his wife? There was one featuring a family gathering, big, Greek or Italian, with smiling, laughing faces and the evidence of much love. The home didn't look like it had a woman's touch, and Maisy hadn't given any indication the wife lived in Blueshell Beach as well.

'You took a while,' said Livia. 'My kittens are furious.' She giggled. Pepper passed her a new bottle sitting back next to Keegan, feeding a kitten with the remnants of his first bottle. She handed him a full bottle, and their fingers brushed. *Electricity!*

'Thanks. How often do these little fellas need feeding?' Keegan asked.

'Every three hours.'

'Shite!' He raised his dark eyebrows.

'Shit is right because they'll probably do plenty of that and peeing as well.' Pepper laughed. It was cute how he didn't swear in front of them. She'd have to be more cautious with her gutter-worksite language.

'I can help,' Liv said, snuggling a kitten to her ever-growing breasts.

'I'll have to set the alarm. It's fine. I wake up most nights anyhow.' But she noticed his frown and knew waking up to seven hungry kittens would give him little sleep.

'Maybe, Liv and I could take over every couple of nights to give you a break. See how you go.'

'Mmm. We'll see.'

'Hey, Liv, have you seen Mum's cat yet?' Pepper asked, moving her bottle at a better angle. The kitten in her hands wasn't as good a sucker as the others. 'Come on, kitty.'

'Chloe,' said Keegan.

'Yes, that's right. Mum's cat hasn't been around. I wonder if these are hers. Probably not, though. She always got her cats desexed and kept them inside away from the native animals.'

'There's been ferals from time to time.' Keegan stood to place his last kitten inside the kennel.

Pepper did the same. 'Would you look at that! So cute.'

'Food comas,' Keegan said, 'speaking of—sorry, Gus.' He lifted a storage box lid and pulled a dog food bag and a bowl to feed the dog. Gus turned from his surrogate duties to fill his belly before returning to his adopted brood with a fart and contented grumble.

Pepper shot Liv the we've-overstayed-our-welcome look, and Liv reluctantly got to her feet. 'Anytime you need help, Keegan, just yell over the fence,' she said, giving each kitten one last pat.

'You've helped plenty. Just need to find the cat owner.'

'I'll put a notice on Facie,' Liv said, reaching for her phone.

'Facie?' Keegan asked with raised eyebrows. He looked beat.

'Facebook,' Pepper said, 'teen-speak.'

'Mmm.' Keegan nodded.

'Okay, we'll leave then. We're only over the fence if you need us.'

'Gus and I will be fine, thanks.' He strode inside, ending all conversation with the slap of his flyscreen door. Through the door, he called, 'Thanks for your help.'

Though it had been rather adorable watching him with the kittens, being in his house had brought more questions than answers. *An absent son and wife. What happened to his family?*

Chapter Seven

Sand rubbed Pepper's bare feet in a soothing massage. She strolled along Moon Beach, enjoying the sun and salty air blessing her skin. Aromas familiar and delightful pushed distant memories to the surface. *Good ones.*

Her and her brothers' skimboarding along the shore, giggling and gleeful. Their mum, trailing unhurriedly, collecting seaweed and shells—constantly glancing up to check they were safe. She called them to put more zinc on their ever-peeling noses—carefree days when her father was away for work and the household no longer walked on eggshells.

Shielding her eyes from the sun, she glanced towards the pink house on the rise to the northern headland. She'd been looking forward to visiting her new friend, Maisy, especially since their last conversation at the plant nursery where Maisy dropped a hint. 'I'm home all day tomorrow. I'd love a visitor. Call over.'

In light of Keegan probably having little sleep due to the kittens, Pepper decided it was a good day to give him a break from the noise. She was enjoying a day off to explore a place that changed her life but somehow was timelessly similar—rocks, sand, dunes, vegetation all similar. The changes were the new homes, bigger and flashier, lining Moon Beach. Only Maisy's cottage remained a reminder of that time.

She remembered the house well. Her friend Judith's family, once lived there. For years Judith was her best friend until Bobby came between them. Judith had been head over heels for the bad boy Bobby. Unfortunately, Bobby made it clear he preferred Pepper even though she wasn't interested. She'd never do that to Judith. It was a shame Judith believed all the bullshit Bobby spewed instead of hearing her best friend out. It was a friendship Pepper missed, especially when she moved to the city.

A seagull hovered close, flicking her out of her reverie. She couldn't change the past, but it was time to make her future and Liv's as happy as possible. Climbing the winding track to Maisy's house, her thoughts turned to Keegan. A man of so many contradictions and secrets, making her head spin, churning with what-ifs. What if he was a serial killer? *No way.* They didn't nurture kittens. What if he was madly in love with his wife and she was just away on holiday? But there were no photos of her. Where was the son? Why didn't he work? And, mostly, how was he so damn sexy with no friggin clue of the things he was doing to her.

Tapping softly on Maisy's screen door, she took in the picturesque cottage as she waited. It was the same colour as when Judith's family lived there but intricately repainted the same pink with new white trims. The colours blended with the Hamptons white cane furniture on the deck facing the ocean.

'Hey, luvvy. I was hoping you'd turn up. Such a lovely day for a walk, huh!' Maisy said, opening the door and ushering her in. 'Come meet my bugga of a man.' She laughed, tossing red curls over her shoulder. 'Trev, where are you?'

'Coming, love,' a tall man said, walking towards them with a wide grin. 'Struth! You must be Meg's girl, Pep. I think you were a couple of grades older than me, but I remember your face.'

'I am. You went to Blueshell High?' She shook his long-fingered outstretched hand. 'Only Mum and Dad called me Pep. I haven't heard it for years.'

'Yes. Oh, sorry. Always putting my boot in my mouth.' He frowned, but his eyes were still twinkling.

'Don't be. It's kind of nice, actually—gives me a feeling of deja vu. What a charming home,' she said, glancing around. *Pretty. Tidy. Homey.* 'My friend grew up here. You've kept the character beachy and inviting. I'm trying to do the same with Mum's house.'

'I'm sure you will. I hear you're a hot-shot builder. It should be a cinch. Nice to meet you again, Pep. I'm heading outside to tackle some never-ending weeds. Let you girls have a natter.' He chuckled before kissing Maisy on the cheek and winking.

Maisy preened. 'Okay, sweety. So, Pepper, coffee or tea?'

'Tea would be lovely.' She watched Trevor stroll outside. 'Did he hang with the Williams boys? The youngest was his best mate, right?'

'Sure did.'

'No wonder he looks familiar. He was a cute kid who loved his footy. He seems like a top bloke, Maisy.

'I'm lucky. You'll hear around town there's been some domestic violence going on. There's a shelter in at Whalebone to house some of the poor luvs. So sad, huh? But never here. My man wouldn't hurt a bumblebee, let alone me. He's a good one. Milk, sugar?'

Pepper shook her head. 'I'm glad you're happy.' She took the offered tea. 'Thank you.'

'Let's head out to the deck and watch the surf. I saw Keegan paddle out about half an hour ago. Probably still out there.' Maisy winked over her cuppa, taking one of the single cane plush chairs.

'Huh, why would that matter to me?' She hoped a blush wasn't colouring her cheeks. Of course, she could blame the hot tea, but it wasn't the truth.

'You ask questions about him any chance you get, plus you get this look.' Maisy puckered her lips and tilted her head, patting her chest. 'Love is in the air.'

Pepper choked on the tea, and her eyes watered. 'What? No. I'm not even divorced yet. I'm not interested in Mr Grouch.'

'Oh, really! Body language and your voice taking a higher pitch would argue otherwise.' Maisy laughed. 'Sorry, luvvy. I enjoy watching love stories unfold. Let me have my fun. I can help matchmake if you like?'

'No. Maisy, stop.' Pepper put her cup of tea on a coffee table between them, wiping her eyes. 'Nothing is going on between Mr Grouch and me.'

'So those glances out to the surf are checking sharks haven't got past the headland? Or is there a hot, near-naked man getting your attention? Oh, speak of—. He's catching a wave now. Can't half tell with those bright yellow boardies.'

Pepper's eyes followed Maisy's pointing finger. Yup, there he was in all his glory, riding a wave like a pro. Chris Hemsworth didn't come close to how hot Keegan looked surfing. Pepper withheld the need to fan her face.

Maisy flicked her fingers in front of Pepper's eyes. 'Mmm, you should plead guilty as charged.'

Pepper sighed. 'So, I find Keegan attractive. I can look. It doesn't mean I want to touch.'

'Oh, you don't want to touch that stud muffin? Sure.' Maisy rolled her eyes.

'You're not to tell a single soul if I admit how I really feel.'

'Shoot.'

'Yes, I'm into him—a lot, but he's not giving any signals, and he's married with a kid, so I can fantasise all I want, but it ain't going anywhere.' She shrugged her shoulders.

'Wife? No way.' Maisy sat upright.

'He wears a wedding ring.'

'Really? Not a single woman in town has mentioned that.'

'No morals, perhaps.' She raised her eyebrows and gave Maisy a lopsided grin.

'Hey, Trev,' she called to Trevor, who moved to a spot near the verandah where the clover was taking over the cooch grass, like soldier crabs over sand.

He sprayed the clump of green weed and glanced up. 'What, Maisy?'

'You've spoken to Keegan. Is he married?'

'Yup.'

'What? You never told me that,' said Maisy, glaring at her husband.

'Don't matter. It's over, he said, just hasn't had time to formalise it or something. He's got bigger stuff going on in his life.'

'Like what?' Pepper asked, trying to hide her excitement at the fact Keegan might be available. Maisy shot her a glance with a smirk.

'Dunno. Didn't say. Bloke doesn't divulge much.'

Pepper's shoulder's slumped. *Give me a crumb.*

'Thanks, Trev. Back to it,' said Maisy with a joking laugh. 'Why don't we have a dinner and invite Keegan?'

'No. That would be embarrassing. Plus, he has kittens to look after.'

'Why?'

'They stowed under his house, motherless, and now his dog is surrogating them, and he's getting up every three hours to feed them. Poor bugger.'

'No mother cat in sight?' Maisy rubbed her arms.

'Did you just get chills?'

'Yes, because if those kittens are motherless, I'll bet the mother's dead.'

'Wildlife?'

'Possibly, but, old Glenda, in that new townhouse over yonder, was beside herself when she found poor Tootsie dead. She suspects foul play?'

'Why would she think that?' Pepper shook her head, sipping tea.

'Tootsie has always come back to her. As they say, cats have nine lives. She always expected he wouldn't pass away on the side of the road all twisted up. Maybe a car, but she reckons someone did it.' Maisy shrugged her shoulders. 'She's got her theories.'

'Poor Glenda. It must have been traumatic.'

'Yeah, enough for her to insist the police investigate.'

Pepper put the tea down with a tiny shake of her fingers. 'Mum's cat Chloe is missing too.' Something that seemed harmless, like an older woman's cat dying, took on new meaning. Goosebumps trailed her arms, and she rubbed them as Maisy did the same.

'Two cats, maybe. Do you think there are more?'

'Could be, but don't worry, luvvy. It's probably only a coincidence. Glenda is a bit of a worrywart.'

'I hope you're right. I still wonder where Mum's cat got to. Her friend only fed it the day before we arrived in town. We've searched the two blocks around the house. And another cat is missing since Keegan has a brood of kittens without a mother cat. Weird coincidences.'

'Maybe you should fill him in. And, while you're there, maybe tell him how you feel.' Maisy angled her head, her eyes boring into Pepper.

'No way. He's too young. I've got more than enough complications in my own life already without a man muddling it further. I'll just gawk at him in private. I'm seriously doing nothing about it, so stop.' She raised her hand. 'Thanks for the tea. I'd better head back.'

'Oh, yes. Go now, and you'll accidentally on purpose,' she raised her fingers in exclamation marks, 'bump into Keegan when he alights like Aquaman from the surf.' Maisy laughed, patting Pepper's back as they both stood.

'You don't stop, do you?' Pepper said with a laugh. 'Goodbye.' She hugged her new friend.

Turning to wave before striding down the goat track to the beach, she held a smile. It was good to have made new friends in her old hometown. Yes, she could have used the road on the other side of Maisy's house, but what was the fun in it on a beautiful day where the beach beckoned? *Be honest—and a certain man.* Maisy was right on so many counts. Was she so transparent? Perhaps Maisy was more astute than most. Keegan certainly hadn't got the hint.

As if on queue, he ran from the surf as her bare feet reached the shore. The water was warm over her legs. At the sight of him dripping wet, between her thighs was hot and wet as well. She watched him near, trying to think of something funny, witty or wise to say. She held her sandals in one hand, swaying them at her thigh.

Water slicked Keegan's tanned, undulating muscular body. He shook his long hair, spraying water around him like he was a hot smouldering model in some men's cologne commercial. *Oh, my fuck.* And that was seriously something she wanted to do.

'Hey,' he said, so familiarly, like they always met at the beach. He flicked the legrope over his board, tucking the board under one well-defined arm. No tattoos, only smooth skin, the colour of caramel chocolate.

'Hi. Nice surf?' She managed to say despite the saliva pooling in her mouth.

'Could be bigger swell, but can't complain.' He smiled the almost-smile that set her heart fluttering around her chest, seeking escape like a swarm of butterflies.

'Yeah, I guess.'

***

Keegan gulped at her beauty. She was wearing a strappy pale blue sundress that curved over her hips and flicked over her thighs, accentuating slender legs and perfectly curved body, small pert breasts and creamy golden tan. Loose, tawny-brown hair touched her

45

slender shoulders, bouncing as she walked. He'd seen her coming down the hill and timed his paddle inshore to perfection.

'You heading home?'

'Yep.'

'I'll walk with you. I've got to tell you something—'

'I want to help you,' Keegan said, surprising himself.

'Pardon? With what?'

'Your house. Help you get it done quicker. I could bring the kittens and Gus, but I think he'll cope with them for a bit. You're doing too much yourself.'

'Oh, right. Wow, I'm surprised, but, yeah, tomorrow I could do with a hand.'

How did that pop out of your mouth, mate? What use would he be to her anyway? She seemed more than capable, and he was about as handy as a spoon cutting a steak.

'Other than having kittens, I have the time,' he said truthfully.

'Great. And about the cats.' She shot him a puppy-dog eyes look, the brilliant violet colour more startling in direct sunlight.

'Cats?' She stepped in beside him, and he tried to curb his longer gait. She was tiny but perfect in every way, making it near impossible for him to concentrate on walking, thinking, talking, let alone—*cats.*

'Someone else's cat was missing and found dead. Maybe the kittens' mother is dead too, but I'd like to search more for Chloe. Maybe they've been spooked or something. I did hear a dingo a few nights ago.' She held a hand over her forehead, shielding the sun as she glanced up at him. Almost close enough to kiss if he bent down to her.

He'd usually carry his board in his right arm, but it was strategically in his left, so their bodies could occasionally brush. *Electric every time.* He wasn't obvious. There was a risk to that. *Rejection.* Compartmentalising his feelings clearly wasn't working. She pulled him to her like a loyal dog on a lead, and he was damn-well wagging his tail, tongue hanging out dripping saliva.

'What?' It finally sunk into his brain. She was serious about searching for the missing cats. 'Where have you looked? I could try the cliffsides. Hopefully, Chloe, or the mother of the kittens, haven't had a fall or met with a dingo. I'll check it out for you.'

'Good. I'll keep putting the flyers Liv made about her missing around the streets. She raised her shoulders, looking glum. 'I hope a person isn't hurting the cats.'

'Why think that?'

'Maisy's friend got the police to check about her cat's death. Sort of sounds serious.'

'Are you talking about the Glenda woman?' He rolled his eyes.

'Yeah, why?' Long eyelashes blinked up at him.

'I heard the ladies gossiping in town. I think she likes the attention. She's called my mate, Dane, a cop, about someone knocking over her garbage bin. She calls them all the time.' He shook his head.

'Oh, that kind of trouble maker.'

'Pretty sure her cat died of old age. It was about fourteen or something.'

'Oh, Maisy hadn't mentioned that.' She giggled. 'My stupid imagination has gone from lost cats to dingos stalking pets to some weird shit like someone deliberately attacking poor defenceless cats. How silly am I?' She shrugged her shoulders.

His brain jumped to a memory that made his mind jolt—a man stabbing his wife. Him trying to save her with gauze, pressure, speed. The cuts to her severed major arteries. *She never stood a chance.* Her last words haunted him. *He killed our puppy. I should have known what he was capable of.* He never saw the man come up behind them.

Keegan reached for the scar on his neck; the movement made his skin brush Peppers. *Warmth, comfort. If only.*

'Keegan, hey, are you okay?' Pepper asked, snapping him out of the vision.

'Yeah, of course.' Her hand was on his arm, soft and reassuring.

She watched his eyes, not paying attention to where she was walking and tripped over a piece of driftwood. On her hands and knees, she said, 'Oops!'

He reached for her gritty sand hand and pulled her up, trying not to laugh.

Blush coloured her cheeks while she patted the sand from her hands and knees. 'You did look kind of stunned a minute ago.' She went straight back to her question. 'Are you sure you're okay?'

He changed the topic. 'Any word on if kittens were missing too?'

He asked, thinking of Livia sitting with the litter.

'No. Seems to be only grown cats. At least so far.' Pepper rubbed her bare arms. 'Should we be worried? I thought I was overreacting.'

'The kittens will be fine. There'll be a reasonable explanation for the rest. Hopefully, your Mum's cat will turn up soon. What about old Charlotte? She loved your mum's cat like her own.'

'We asked her already. She hasn't seen it. I feel like I've let Mum down by not finding her beloved cat. I thought Chloe would come back for a feed. I've been leaving food and water out. It goes untouched.' She frowned. Her eyes shone with unshed tears. 'I'm changing Mum's house, which some days is harder than others and I guess adding the cat to it, and it's—'

'Overwhelming.'

'Yeah. I miss Mum so much. It hurts.'

He didn't know if he should reach for her and give her comfort. *Too late.* She stepped further away.

'You're still grieving. Give it time.'

'I know.'

'I'll see what I can do to find both missing cats. Maybe someone took them home but hasn't seen one of your flyers yet. Liv did include the abandoned kittens too, didn't she?'

'Ah, no.' She smiled. 'Liv thinks they're too little to leave the litter yet.'

'No wonder she's always offering to watch them.' *Cute kid.*

'Livia's with the kittens now?'

'She said it was better than watching the veggie garden since nothings growing quick enough for her.'

They neared between their houses. 'I'll come to get Liv. Thanks for being so kind to her, Keegan.'

'She's a great kid. Anyhow, I don't know what I'd do if she weren't helping with the furballs.' *Plus, it's an excuse to see you.*

Livia waved from the deck with a kitten on either side of her lap, leaning a bottle to each.

Keegan dropped his board, stepping close to Pepper, who smiled up at him. *Open your arms. Take a chance.*

Pepper, still on the brink of tears after talking about her mum, stepped closer. He hugged her, feeling the warmth and salty tears on his chest. Was it wrong to want so much more than to hold her? She looked up, and her sweet lips were so close he could almost taste them. Before he could contemplate that further, she stepped away.

'Sorry, I've overreacted. I—um. It's, you know, missing Mum and all that.' She turned from him, striding to the deck.

'Thanks for looking after them, Liv,' said Keegan, as Pepper leant down to pet a kitten.

When they left after lots of last pats of the adorable kittens, Keegan stood on the deck wondering if his life were about to implode again. *Knives. Blood. Cats. People*—swirled through his brain like a whirlpool. The slightest thing brought back the day he almost died. He crushed his hands to his skull, ignoring the depression medication sitting in his medicine cabinet.

Would he leave this town, too, if the demons came back full force? Or was it finally time to crush the devil and find the happy life he deserved?

Chapter Eight

Pepper hammered another nail with a satisfying last bang. Keegan probably wouldn't come, and she'd be disappointed once again. Why would she even put herself out there? It wasn't only because he was good-looking. Something else stirred her in a way she'd never felt. But of course, as Liv and Trev said, he had a wife, kid and even more hangups. 'Bloody men!' She swallowed, aligning the skirting board through cloudy vision and hammering another nail into the timber.

Heavy footfalls neared, followed by a deep cough. Her heart skipped more beats than a pile driver. With head held low, she turned to find Keegan shrugging his broad shoulders. She gulped, not able to avert her gaze.

His hands jammed deep in his jean's pockets. Firm biceps bulged under the taunt green t-shirt splattered in colourful paint stains, like some Ken Done design. Her mouth watered, and it was nowhere near lunchtime.

'Oh, hi. You came.' Her gaze strayed to his face. Perfect, with just the right amount of Don Johnson stubble. She gulped. It was hot in the house, but the temp had skyrocketed since he entered the room. 'And, you look ready to work, which is great.' She stood, snapping her thoughts to construction mode. *For fuck sake, the man was sex on legs and had no friggin' idea.*

'Uh, huh. What men were you mad at?' An almost smile turned his thick lips, and he raised a dark eyebrow.

'Oh! That.' She turned, tripping over a pile of skirting boards.

She steadied herself against the cool wall, earthing her zip-roaring nerves. Keegan leaned closer as if to stop her falling. *Damn, one reach out to touch wouldn't hurt.* Her fingers twitched — *one touch.*

No. She clenched her fingers on her trousers.

She feigned an I'm-fine smile. *What did Keegan ask again?* Bloody men? *Yeah.* She waved the hammer. 'I was talking about the timber yard. They stuffed up a few things, timber size, quantity, quality.' *Nice save.* She twiddled with the protective goggles slipping over her head. An oversize reflective shirt tucked into navy cargos, hitched with a toolbelt bulging with paraphernalia. Before, it felt practical, but now it was daggy under his gaze.

'Great look.' He raised a brow, smirking.

When you want a broken floor to swallow you up, it never happens. Her cheeks heated. 'It's important to dress for the occasion. You know personal protective equipment and all that.' She took a deep breath stilling her heart. *Sure, tell the hot guy why you look so damn unhot.* 'I have spare goggles if you need.' She tossed a pair, almost slapping him in the face with them.

I look as attractive as a bag of mushrooms. Why hadn't she worn jeans and a t-shirt instead of construction gear? *Habit.* Things needed to change, especially when Keegan was around. Trying to impress a guy looking like a stop-n-go roadworker was stupid. Running fingers under her hair wouldn't fix the problem, but she did it anyway. Sweat pooled on her neck, sticky and damp. *Definitely need to up my game.*

'What do you do for a job anyway?' she asked, tucking her shirt deeper and tightening the tool belt, feeling like a damn potato sack.

'Stuff.' He shrugged his broad shoulders, eyes smouldering. Maybe she didn't look so bad after all.

'What kinda, stuff? Like, do you build things, push things, pull things?' She winked.

'Nope, don't own a Hilux.' A small smile tugged his perfectly kissable lips.

So, he did have a sense of humour, after all. 'Do you work in town?'

'Nope.'

Seriously? The conversation was worse than laying a brick wall. She took a deep breath. *Oh boy, he may be shit-hot, but his conversational skills are exasperating as hell.* She kept the daggers she wanted to shoot him in check. Okay, he wants to work without talking. She was hearing him loud and clear. 'Can you use a saw?'

Pointing to a stack of skirting boards near the drop saw, she waved the hammer.

'Nope. Not handy with a saw.' He scratched his head. His mouth moved slightly as if he were tumbling words over his tongue. 'I'm handy with a gun.'

'What?' Only yesterday, Livia joked about him mentioning hairy situations. Probably a war hero. A veteran. Just what she needed. *Like friggin' hell. He'll end up like Dad, bitter at the world. Didn't war always do that?*

Much as her libidinous neighbour attracted her, she couldn't go through with the torture all over again. *No way.*

***

'Anyone you want me to shoot?' Keegan tried to contain a smile, 'Perhaps those bloody men?' If she wanted to picture him as a gun-toting hero instead of a failed paramedic, who was he to argue with that?

Pepper furrowed her brow, holding the hammer in mid-air, a perplexed look flashing across her incredible eyes. She had no idea how cute she looked in the get-up, especially when she got clumsy and talkative.

'Plenty, but, ah, no thanks.' Watching her response, he ran a hand through his hair. If Livia hadn't been so nosy, he never would have led her to think he was ex-defence force. He didn't correct her assumption, especially when she said her mother knew about PTSD. At least it sounded worthier to suffer anxiety as a soldier rather than a civilian. It wasn't as if he were ashamed; he'd been proud of his emergency work before it got too challenging. Though it didn't hurt to let Pepper think he was braver than he was. What did it matter if he kept the truth to himself for a while? At least until he had Joe back in his life and got a new job.

He curved his lips into a semblance of a smile to let her know it was a joke. But the joke was on him. He'd no more shoot a charging feral pig, let alone another human.

A cute blush coloured her cheeks the same as when she'd tripped. Damn, he'd wanted to touch her. Feel her perfect skin. Find that human connection he hadn't allowed himself to believe he was missing—*until now.* She'd pulled back, going all worksite busy, giving him the brush. Perhaps she thought he was too young. *Too messed up. Too broken.*

She wasn't wrong.

He dug his hand further in his pockets, shifting from foot to foot. She'd be able to talk underwater. Now for some reason, she was speechless.

'What about painting?' she asked with a hopeful slight angle to her head. It made the goggles slip, and silky hair covered one vivid eye. Young Elizabeth Taylor eyes. The same as her daughter's.

'Yep.' He pointed to his shirt. 'I did my place.'

'What? For a preschool?' She laughed. 'Did you paint every colour of the rainbow?'

'Yep.' His lips twitched. It wasn't the first time she'd tried to make him smile. In this instance, she nearly succeeded. A gorgeous, funny, talkative woman like her needed someone more together than him.

'Great. Well, you'll nail this since it's certainly no rainbow. One wall, one colour.' Placing the hammer in her tool belt, she lifted a tray and roller, almost dropping it when her fingers sizzled on his, sending a shock of sensations twisting through every nerve. It took all his resolve not to step closer. Paint slashed across her flushed cheeks, accentuating amazing eyes. For a professional builder, she was clumsy as a baby elephant and just as cute. 'That wall's been sanded and cleaned. There's a cutting-in brush on the paint tin over there. You do know how to cut—'

'Cut in? Yes. My speciality, in fact.' He wouldn't be able to help her on the building side of things, but the finishing stuff was a breeze. There was nothing like slow painting to soothe the nerves and help you forget the shit in the world.

'Okay, great. Thanks. We're doing this open lounge area, then the kitchen, which is behind that tarp, once the new cabinets arrive.' She turned back to the drop saw, wielding it like most women brandished a nail file. *Hot, capable, and efficient.* His kinda woman. It seemed she was badass, and he was broken. She might be his kinda woman, but sadly he doubted he was her kinda man.

***

Pepper slid the timber through the saw with ease and precision, pretty much on autopilot. The loud buzz filtered her hammering heart because Keegan whipped her into his whirlwind. Her senses spun, and her insides twisted deliciously, all that without a working womb. Maybe the menopause was fuelling the hot flushes. Her heart twisted. *Growing older sucked.*

She glanced at Keegan through her safety glasses. *Nope.* Definitely the hot man, not a flush in sight. It was nothing to do with procreation either; lust slicked her inner thighs like coconut oil. If only he were older, her cellulite and wrinkles wouldn't matter so much.

Keegan worked slowly and meticulously, his large hands dwarfing the brush, his wedding ring catching a glint of light. A reminder of his marital status. He painted with care, more like creating a masterpiece than painting her old cottage walls. Hands so gentle, they couldn't possibly be the hands of a killer.

The man seemed a contradiction. If he were suffering PTSD, she couldn't see it, except for him being a man of few words. He didn't remind her of her father. Perhaps he was further in his recovery and wasn't the cranky, haunted man she remembered. Keegan showed glimpses of humour, though a little dark, lurking under the surface.

Pepper tried to make him laugh. She hadn't seen a full-blown smile yet. Barely saw if his teeth were perfect or not. It made her wonder what the sound of his laughter would be like, deep and hearty or a small chuckle. Pepper was the kind to belly laugh so full she could wet her pants or stop breathing. *Would he find humour in that?*

He turned, shooting her a look over his shoulder. 'Are you checking my work?'

'No, not at all.' *Your hot arse, maybe.* 'You're painting a damn sight better than me.' Her cheeks flushed. 'Anyhow, I'll cut more skirting board to add to the next wall.' She busied herself at the drop saw. 'I do appreciate you helping.' *And being easy on the eyes.*

'Got nothing else to do.'

'You don't work?' she asked.

He shrugged his shoulders, dropped the roller in the tray and turned to face her. 'You ask a lot of questions.'

'What's wrong with giving answers?' She smiled.

'Sometimes people don't want to talk, you know.' He stretched his arms over his head. The movement made his t-shirt rise to show muscle crevises and a trail of dark hair. *Oh, my Lord!*

Pepper gulped, dropped the saw to cut the skirting boards, the screaming noise ending further discussion. Instead of laying each board down with care, the way she usually would, she banged each piece on the bench, trying not to shoot Keegan angry glances. Getting him to talk was like trying to park a bus in a single garage.

Keegan continued painting, seemingly oblivious to her frustration.

'Why the fuck don't you ever say anything?' she asked, dropping the skirting board to clatter on the floor beside him and placing her hands on her hips.

'You swear lots for a petite woman,' he said, furrowing his brow where he had white paint like a Harry Potter lightning scar.

'So what if I do?'

'Just a little shocked is all.'

Livia walked around the tarp dividing off the kitchen with a plate of sandwiches in her hands. 'See, Mum. Told you he'd be too straight to endure your swearing.'

'Liv,' Pepper warned, shaking her head.

'Mum is glad you'd come to help,' Livia said to Keegan, winking.

'I'm—,' she shot Livia a daggered look, 'Yes, of course. We'd never get it finished by Easter otherwise.'

'I checked on the kittens again,' said Liv. 'They've put on weight already. My friend Ross reckons they need solid foods now. Should I try them on it, Keegan?'

'Sure,' said Keegan. He stood back to admire his painting, stretching his arms over his head. Pepper ogled his back muscles and bum in tight jeans. Livia raised her eyebrows, grinning, pushed the sandwiches towards her.

Pepper reached for a sandwich, shaking her head at Liv. 'Keegan. Have a break,' Pepper said.

***

'I'll head home for lunch. You eat your sandwiches,' said Keegan, wiping his brow and trying not to let the smell of fresh ham, cheese, chicken and eggs tempt his tastebuds.

'No, you can't. I made plenty,' said Livia. 'You and Mum eat. I'm going back to the garden after seeing the kittens anyway. See ya.' She shot Pepper a wink.

Keegan half-smiled, reaching for an egg sandwich and sitting on a camp chair. 'Thanks, Livia.' He bit into the bread. 'They are delicious,' he mumbled.

'No probs.' Livia skipped out to the front porch, fishing her ever-present mobile phone from her shorts.

'She's a great kid,' said Keegan with half a mouthful of sandwich, so his cheek's chipmunked.

'Yep.' Pepper's eyes followed her daughter as she strolled to the vegetable garden with the phone to her ear. 'Is she saying much when she talks to you?' Her pretty eyes held his, pleading for honesty. She took a seat beside him, the plate of sandwiches between them on a small table.

'Some.' What could he say? Tell Pepper her daughter was seeing the local town tool and break Livia's trust?

'She's closed up to me. It's not like her. We always talk.'

'I bet.' He grinned. 'It'd be who comes up for air first.' It felt good to smile again. But he was dodging her question. Also, she was sitting so close on an old camp chair he could smell her shampoo. *Could run my hand through that silky hair, bring her face to mine, kiss —*

'Keegan! I asked you what she's saying. I need to know if she's okay.'

'She's fine.' At least Liv will be when I get my hands around Ross Ronson's neck. 'She said she doesn't miss her dad. I think she does.'

'Of course, but it's difficult.'

'Why? What happened?' *Diversion.* Always a good tactic with a patient, even better with a woman with questions. He bit into another sandwich, watching her face baulk, cheek bite, then bottom lip tug.

'It's as complicated as any marriage break up. But ours was tenfold. We owned a business together. He was running it to the ground with his gambling issues and women. The business was worth fighting for more than our marriage.'

'You or him?'

'What?' She scrunched her eyebrows together, dropping an uneaten sandwich back on the plate.

'Who fought for the business more than the marriage?'

Her open mouth could have caught twenty flies. 'Me. He didn't fight for anything, not even Liv.'

'Do you still love him?' Keegan asked, brushing crumbs from his jeans and not meeting her eyes. All he could hope was that she would say no. He took a breath, waiting.

'No. I'm not sure if I ever did. What about your wife? Why are you separated?'

'Complications.' He shoved another sandwich in his mouth and stood. 'Well, back to the painting.' He mumbled. Inside he was doing a happy dance that she no longer loved her soon-to-be ex-husband. He faced the wall, painting, hiding his smile.

Relief. A chance. But at what cost?

Chapter Nine

The full moon cast a light silver glow over the cool sand and illuminated the booming surf below. Livia's thonged feet flicked sand at her calves, cool but not cold due to a hot northerly keeping the temperature warm and humid. Storm clouds rumbled in the distance, ready to break the humidity during the night.

She found Ross tucked into a dune waiting for her. Her heart skipped a billion beats when his eyes lit upon seeing her.

'I was thinking you weren't going to come,' he said, patting the sand beside him. 'I thought I'd scared you off.' When she sat next to him, he put his arm around her shoulders.

She snuggled into his chest, feeling warm and protected. 'I don't scare easily.'

'Why didn't you want to meet in your garage?'

'Mum's acting all weird about anyone going in there. Thought it best to meet here with a full moon and all.' She touched his handsome face feeling brave. Lifting her lips to his, she kissed him, tasting minty breath and a hint of alcohol.

'Sorry, my friends were doing dumb things. They're just barneys. Don't let them put you off hangin' out with me.' He pressed his lips harder with his hand behind her head as if he couldn't get enough of her taste. 'I've never met a girl like you.'

She pulled away slightly. Her hands rested on his tanned shoulders. 'I've never encountered anyone like you. I don't care about your mates. They're only dudes. It's better than hangin' with city guys.'

'Why so?' His hand trailed down her hip, resting on her thigh. A finger edged lower.

She squirmed, feeling something tingle between her thighs, making her excited and terrified. 'They're boring. The surf culture is way more rad.' She smiled, kissing him again. His finger slid under the edged of her shorts, teasing towards a place no guy's hand had been before. Though her insides were screaming for the attention to continue, she pushed his hand away. 'I'm not ready, Ross.'

'We can do other stuff,' he said, kissing and sucking on her neck until it stung.

'Like what?'

He took her hand and placed it on his crotch. She gasped, feeling the outline of his penis through his boardshorts. 'Just rub it, please.' His lovely eyes pleaded. She complied. Not knowing how to do it but sort of holding what she thought was the shaft and dragging her hand back and forth, she assumed she was doing it right. He'd shut his eyes and groaned. 'That's—ah, keep going, babe. Gonna blow.' He ripped open his fly, exposing his erection. His fingers closed around hers to hold it.

'What? Ross, no, I can't.' It felt smooth and warm, seeming to pulsate under her curled palm.

'Please, babe. I'm so close.' He pushed her hand along the shaft. 'Harder.' He threw his head back. His penis seemed to grow bigger, so hard, and suddenly it jolted. Liquid sprayed from it, some leaking on her hand, warm and sticky.

'Oh, my.' She edged away from him on her haunches, wiping her hands on seagrass.

He ejaculated some more, shook it and stuffed it back in his boardies before laying back in the sand, sighing and smiling at the sky. 'I'm so sorry, Liv. It's what you do to me. Wow!' He glanced at her. 'What's wrong? I can do the same for you.'

She moved closer, unable to resist him, even though she felt out of her depth. 'I just want to kiss and cuddle. I don't need that.'

'Okay. Sure, but that was so rad. Seriously, you blow my mind. Just looking at you makes me want to toss.' He sat up, placing his arm over her shoulders again, squeezing her to him. 'I can wait till you're ready, really I can. Just needed a release, ya know?'

'I kinda get it. I feel things when I'm with you too.' She kissed him, letting his tongue in this time when before she denied him that.

His hands left her shoulders, trailing to her boobs. She caught them. 'Enough of that for today. I want to talk. Plus, I have to get back soon before Mum notices I'm gone. She always does this annoying thing checking up on me before she goes to sleep.'

'You're lucky she cares enough,' he said, frowning. 'My mum's too busy working because Dad's away. She barely knows where I am.'

'I'm sure she loves you,' she said, kissing his cheek. Soft hairs brushed her lips.

'Yeah, probably. Hey, anyway, I wanted to check you were okay after the other night. I promise I had nothing to do with it.'

'I don't get it. Why take drugs? They're too young, let alone how stupid it is. How do they even get them?'

'I dunno. We all did a séance with an ouija board at the start of the summer. Seriously freaked me out, but Hunter and some of the others wanted to explore further. I can do without ghosts. Anyhow, Hunter reckons he gets the same thrill with the drugs.' He shook his shoulders.

'Yeah, Mum reckons there's a ghost in the garage. Did you feel anything different when you walked past?'

'Nope. Only these.' He brushed her breast with gentle fingers.

'The gang's been reading about supernatural stuff like Ouija boards, too. The girls think it's empowering. The guys like the weirdness. Me, I'd rather talk surf.'

She raised her eyebrows. 'Some actually read?'

'Ha, ha,' he elbowed her. 'It's harmless fun. Just join in next time, and they'll let you into the fold. They think you're a stuck up city girl.'

'That's not fair. I've been nice to all of them. Doesn't mean I have to agree with weird shit going on.'

'It's only harmless games. Chill, babe.' He kissed her deeply. 'I'll always protect you. You know that, don't you?'

She wanted to believe it with all her heart, but she was cautious. If her dad could abandon her, couldn't the boy she was in love with do so just as easily?

They kissed some more, and she relaxed in his robust arms, feeling loved but still with a niggle of worry. Something moved in the corner of her eye. *Shadow. Movement. An animal? Was someone watching them?* Goosebumps prickled her arms.

Large raindrops hit the sand, thunder boomed, and a slash of lightning followed, lighting the beach. Livia stood with her hands over her head. 'I have to go.'

Ross stood, taking her hands, pulling her to him and taking one last kiss. 'See you tomorrow, babe.' He ran towards the road. Livia took the goat track back to the house. Though she ran, rain already soaked her. Sneaking sopping wet into the house would be a problem. Her heart thumped with the fear of her mother catching her and took up a different beat from kissing Ross.

***

Lightning flashed, thunder boomed, and as with any sounds in the night, Keegan couldn't sleep. He strolled out to the deck, checking the rain wasn't getting into the kennel wetting the kittens and Gus. The rain soaked the deck edge, but the kennel was under the awning enough to be dry and protected. All slept soundly.

Gus opened one eye, thumping his tail on seeing Keegan. 'Go back to sleep, mate. Just another storm.' He patted the dog's head and took a seat on the couch, watching the flashing sky. A person ran up the road, a shadow in the night. Keegan eyed the guy with curiosity, wondering who would be out on such a night. Lightning flashed, revealing a face. *Ross Ronson.* When the lightning stopped, Ross disappeared.

He'd seen another person earlier and wondered why someone would go to the beach when a storm was building in the sky?

Keegan narrowed his eyes, watching Pepper's house. As he suspected, a mobile phone's soft light showed the shadow of Liv climbing in her bedroom window. No good would come of two horny teenagers meeting after dark.

It should have been none of his business, but he felt a need to protect Liv and, more importantly, Pepper. Whatever was going on with Ross and Liv, he would be finding out. *I'm watching you, Ross Ronson.*

Chapter Ten

The plant nursery was quiet. It was a day so clear, hot and humid most of the town's people were either at the beach, swimming in pools or socializing at barbecues. School returned Monday, and families were making the most of their last weekend of summer holidays.

Keegan passed a stack of fertilizer bags, shooing a fly from his nose. He found Ross sitting on a pile of turf smoking a cigarette.

'You need grass?' Ross asked, smirking at his joke but rising languidly and butting out the cigarette under a booted foot.

'Nope.' Keegan held closed fists at his sides.

Ross baulked. 'Dude, why look so hostile. You a non-smoker or somthin'?'

'I saw you.'

'Dude, saw me where?' Ross scratched his head, dragging one foot in front of the other.

Keegan leaned close. 'The beach last night.'

Ross's eyes bugged. 'So!'

'Take this as your first warning. Harm Liv and you'll have me to deal with.' His hand itched to grab the kid's shirt and give him a fair shake.

'Shit, Dude. The last thing I'd do is hurt Liv. She's my girl.'

'A fourteen-year-old girl.'

'I know. Dude, she's safe with me.'

'She'd better be.' He pointed two fingers at his eyes and then Ross. 'I'm watching you, mate. Best you keep a low profile for a while.'

'Who are you to tell me what to do? You aren't my old man.' Ross stood taller, glaring at Keegan with hostile green eyes in a tanned face.

'Nope. I'm not, but with your dad behind bars, he can't give you advice, can he?'

'Don't talk about my old man. You know nuthin.'' Ross stalked towards a stack of pavers, bunching his sleeves, revealing tattoos. The kid was only fifteen and already wearing illegal tattoos. 'I work hard. I'm not endin' up like him. Don't judge me on his shit. I'm good to Liv. Just ask her.'

Keegan sighed. Perhaps he was too hard on the kid. People judged him on his family and past. He shouldn't do the same to a teenage boy who seemed to be trying to change his path. 'Okay, maybe. Look,' he scratched his head, 'I know she's a pretty girl, and I can understand.' He shooed another fly. 'Her family have been through a rough time. Don't make it any tougher on them. Right?'

'Dude, I won't.' He lifted three pavers and placed them on a trolley. 'I don't go looking for trouble like my old man.'

'Not what I hear.'

'It's my crew, not me. I hang out, don't plan the parties 'n' shit.'

'Whatever.' Keegan turned away, striding towards the exit.

'Who are you to talk?' Ross yelled. 'Word is you killed someone.'

Keegan's heart froze, but he kept walking without looking back. *Ross was right.* He did kill someone, and he'd never forgiven himself.

***

The mouthwatering aroma of barbecued sausages and onions filled the humid air. Cans of beer hissed open among the chatter of neighbours and friends. Keegan eyed them, clutching a bottle of water in one hand a little too tightly. He was in a foul mood after speaking to Ross. *Shouldn't be here.*

Trevor invited him. Since he was one of a handful of friends in the small town, he couldn't say no. Trev was one of the people helping him out of his dark hole. A guy who'd chased his demons and came out the other side. He was a great guy who shared his philosophies only when Keegan wanted to hear them.

'Oi! There you are, Keegs,' said Trevor, slapping his back with his free hand, flipping a sausage with the other. 'Want a snag?'

'No, thanks.' His eyes shot around. Liv was in the yard, throwing

63

a football at a young man. People he'd met a few times, blokes from the pub and the men's shed, a couple of single women, couples, kids and Maisy. She was as kind as her husband. On spotting him, she rose from her foldout chair and walked over.

'Hello, stranger. Haven't seen you in ages.' She grinned, red hair cascading around her face like a halo.

'Keeping to myself.' He nodded, half-smiling.

'I know. Nice to see you out for once. Want a drink?'

He lifted the bottle of water. 'All good.' *Pepper. Sweet smile. Sexy.* She strolled towards him with a plate of nibbles in her hands—cheese, crackers, cabanossi and grapes. Her ironed-straight hair sashayed around her pretty face like silk. As usual, her amethyst eyes twinkled.

'Ah, yes, Pepper is here,' said Maisy, winking exaggeratedly and elbowing him in the ribs.

'Hi, Keegan. Would you like something to eat?' Pepper offered the plate.

'No, thanks.' *Just you.*

'Glad you're here. How'd you fare in the storm last night? Were the kittens okay?'

'Fine.'

'Great. I'd better keep moving with this plate,' she said, smiling sweetly.

His gut twisted. The floral maxi skirt flowed over her hips almost to the ground—an ethereal princess floating on air. She paused in front of a huge Maori man in his fifties Keegan hadn't met. He wasn't a bad looking guy, and by the look on his face, he knew it. The bloke edged closer to Pepper, grinning, laughing, roping her in. Keegan's fist bunched. Jealousy surged, green and hulk-like.

A tap on his shoulder made him turn. 'Hey, Keegan,' said Liv. 'How are our kitties?'

'Fine. Eating, getting fat, shitting and peeing. As you predicted.'

The young guy hovered behind her like a loyal puppy. 'This is Hunter. One of Ross's friends.'

'Hi, mate,' Keegan said, shaking the teenager's sweaty hand. He had a light spray of freckles over a tanned face.

The kids went back to their touch football game, and Keegan

strolled around the party, nodding at people but not holding chatter with any. Pepper was still talking to the baby-boomer dickhead. She giggled like a friggin school girl. Her pretty eyes glanced his way occasionally with intense looks he couldn't quite decipher. He returned to the barbecue.

'Need a hand, Trev?'

'All good. You at a loose end? I know it's hard to put yourself out there after everything, but it's the only way to come back to life, you know.'

'Yep. Trying, Trev.'

'Good mate. It's all you can do, right?'

'Yep. Who's that?' He pointed to the wanker still chatting up Pepper.

'New in town. One of the extra teachers at the high school. Tui or something. Seems okay.'

'Family?'

'Nope.'

Fuck

***

Pepper tried to extract herself from the conversation with Tui, but it was proving difficult. He was a lovely, talkative and yes, even a good-looking man, but he wasn't Keegan. She saw the hurt in Keegan's eyes as he watched. As much as she wanted him to care, it annoyed her he seemed jealous. He had chances to start something.

'You seem distracted. Did you want to empty that plate? We can chinwag again after that,' said Tui in a broad Kiwi accent. 'As a woodwork teacher, I'd like to bleed your builder's brain.'

At least Tui was giving her his undivided attention. His hand brushed hers, but it didn't give her tingles the way Keegan did. 'Sure. I'll be back.' She offered the plate to people sitting at the edge of the garden.

Livia giggled when the boy tackled her to the ground, landing on top of her but rolling over. It was distracting as much as Keegan. Another young man panting and hopeful around her daughter. *What a worry.* At least the boy didn't look like a trouble maker with his boy-next-door looks and politeness. Maybe she should encourage Liv to see more of him instead of Ross.

With the plate almost empty, she strolled over to Keegan.

65

'Hungry yet?'

'Just had a snag, Trev insisted.' He rubbed his flat belly.

It felt like a hand was to her back, pushing her closer to Keegan. She turned to see no one close.

***

Blinking violet eyes at him, thick lashes flutter to her pretty cheeks.'You seem off today.' She tilted her head, almost tripping over her own feet when she crossed her ankles, revealing a split in the front of the dress. It revealed lovely smooth legs he wanted to run his hands over.

'What?' He couldn't wrap his head around what she said when her body was draped in a pretty skirt, making him imagine what was under it.

'I thought we'd built a friendship, but you seem to be ignoring me.'

'Nope.'

'Okay. So what's with you today?'

'Nothin'.' He shot a narrowed gaze towards Tui.

'Oh, I see. Have you met Tui? He's a nice guy. Schoolteacher.'

'So I heard. Go back and talk to him. You seemed to be enjoying the conversation more than talking to me.' He took a swig of water. 'Go, have fun. I'm leaving now anyway.' His cheek twitched as he tried to keep his temper in check.

She grabbed his arm, sending electric shocks to his toes and elsewhere. 'Keegan, talk to me,' she pleaded. Big beautiful eyes bore into his.

'Have fun.' Tossing the empty water bottle in a bin near the barbecue, he turned away from her. *She's better with the school teacher anyway.* What did he have to offer her? *Ross was right.* He was a killer, and he could never get away from it. Yes, it was self-defence, but he was supposed to save people.

Striding down the goat track to the beach, kicking sand with his running shoes, he bunched and unbunched his fists. Taking deep breaths to reign in the anger, he paused to take off his shoes, feeling the soothing sand under bare feet. He strode to the shore, enjoying salty, warm water splash up to his shins. Shutting his eyes to face the sun, he sighed. *Breathe.*

As his mind cleared, he realised the panic attack and anxiety didn't hit as hard as they would have a year ago. He smiled. *Recovery.* Lead lined his gut, wondering if the new bloke would attract Pepper instead of him, but he had to roll with it. The tiniest setback could destroy him and any hope of getting Joe back. He wasn't going to allow that to happen.

Letting the water soothe him, he strode the shoreline towards home, wondering if the ephemeral look Pepper shot him was read correctly. It seemed a look of care by softness to her beautiful eyes. And, she'd noticed he was off. Called him on it. Not many people did. Could it possibly mean they had a chance?

He glanced back at the pink house. Walking away, letting Tui have his chance could be costly. He ran a hand through his hair, then down his neck feeling the scar, knowing he couldn't control the outcome, but feeling frustrated by it nonetheless.

Realistically, Pepper probably deserved a nice, religious, respectable Maori teacher over a failure like him. The only way to fix it was to become the man she needed and be the dad Joe deserved. When he rounded the rise to his home, he looked forward to the distraction of seven defenceless kittens.

Gus barked a welcome. Keegan smiled. Only one thing remained niggling his brains, Ross's mention of his friends causing trouble. He needed to find out what the teen surf gang were planning and keep Livia out of the brewing trouble.

Chapter Eleven

Music blast from the boom-box speakers, doofing too much base, blocking the thundering surf and sending those on drugs into a head-thrashing frenzy. Livia watched them with goose-bumps spiking her skin, despite the humidity and heat.

Hunter grinned lavishly at her. 'Want some?' he asked, offering the pills in his open palm. His illuminated face looked different, older, not a boy-next-door and innocent freckled teenager.

'No, thank you.' Out of her depth, she glanced around for Ross, her lifeboat in the bedlam of a teen party. He talked to a girl about her age, darkly tanned, scraggy blonde hair, a surfer. The girl touched Ross's bicep, squeezing it in a gesture that looked familiar. Livia gulped, feeling jealousy growing but trying to push it back. *Ross loves you.*

His eyes caught hers. He winked, raising the two beer cans he held. He said something to the surfer chick and strolled through the raging dancers to sink beside her on the blanket draped over the sand. 'You want a beer?' He kissed her cheek.

'No, thanks.'

'At least I'm not doing the drugs,' he said, cracking the beer.

'Don't know what you're missing,' said Hunter, his eyes in a weird, narrowed gaze. Hunter's hand touched her thigh. 'Come on, you two, join the party. We've got the music pumpin'.'

Ross grabbed Hunter's hand, twisting it as if threatening to break it. 'Never touch Liv again. And, she said she doesn't want to join in.' His teeth were grit. Beer spilled from the can in his hand, wetting the edge of the blanket.

Hunter raised his fingers in the air, giggling. 'Chill, just getting both your attention. Enjoy your fuckin' boring beer then.' He stood, dancing towards the other kids, throwing his head back to howl at the moon.

'Mad as a cut snake,' said Ross, righting the other beer. He took her hand with his other.

'You'd never know it through the day. He's like a different person tonight.' She shook the chills from her spine. She liked Hunter, and now she wasn't so sure.

'Yep, that's Hunter. Changes tack more than a yacht in the Sydney to Hobart.' He squeezed her fingers. *Reassuring.*

'What are the drugs he's on?' she asked.

'Dunno.' He leant in, kissing her lips. He tasted of beer and boy. She kissed him back with her insides mushy from the sweet sensation but her mind hyperalert to the strangeness of the party. She probably didn't want to know the answer.

The smooch intensified, and he put the beer to the side. He wrapped his arms around her, pulling her hips to lay on the blanket beside him. One leg draped over hers, pinning her. Slowly, he rubbed his body against her until she felt the bulge in his boardshorts. It felt good, but the place was all wrong. She twisted away from him, sitting to wrap her arms around her legs.

'Sorry, babe. You okay?' Ross sat, draping his arm over her shoulders.

'I don't like the party. They're getting out of control.'

'I guess.' He glanced at the dancers. 'Yep, you're right. I'll walk you home. A tink sounded as his foot kicked a bottle on the ground. 'Fuck, Black Label.' He picked up the three-quarter bottle from the sand. 'If Hunter mixes this with those drugs, it won't end well.' He stashed it under his t-shirt with one hand and took her fingers with the other.

They were halfway along the track when a shadow emerged. Liv's heart stalled. She stepped behind Ross, but Keegan's face grew evident in the moonlight. 'What's going on down there?' He asked, with eyes taking them in from head to toe.

'Just a gathering,' said Ross, taking a small step backwards.

'What's under your shirt?' Keegan demanded, shooting her a concerned look.

Ross mutely handed him the bottle of bourbon.

'Seriously. You were drinking this shit?' He judged them, holding the bottle aloft.

Liv shook her head, feeling tears pooling under her eyelids. Keegan was like a father figure, and she wasn't enjoying one bit of his scrutiny.

'I've been drinking beer only, and Liv's drunk nothin'. Ross defended her.

'Better be straight with me.' Keegan edged closer to Ross, who clung to her hand a little tighter.

'He is, Keegan. He's not lying. We weren't into the party like the others. He's walking me home.' Liv hoped Keegan believed them. He sure looked ready to take someone's head off.

'Good, go. When are they winding up down there?'

Ross shook his head. 'Late, probably.'

'Drugs?'

Ross shook his head but glanced sideways at Liv. 'Maybe, don't know.'

'Mmmm.' Keegan's jaw twitched. 'Get her home now.'

Ross cleared his throat. 'I wouldn't try and break it up. There's thirty or so. Let 'em wind down. They'll disperse soon.'

***

'You'd better be right. I'm sick of no sleep.' *Kittens and kids.* Keegan shook his head, trying not to laugh at the irony.

He followed the teenagers walking hand in hand in front of him. They looked cute and carefree. It took him back to a time when he was young and in love on a beach. The girl was sixteen-year-old Christine Bates. He was only fourteen like Liv. He hoped what they got up to in the sand dune wasn't happening between Ross and Liv. He'd always seemed to go for the older girls. Loved they knew what they wanted and how to go after it.

The bottle in his hand reminded him of the alcohol and probably drugs down on the beach. And a point in time, he would have been only too happy to join in. The crew Ross hung with weren't innocent teens watching movies, eating popcorn and having a giggle. They'd advanced to hard-core parties, and their young minds probably weren't ready for the consequence.

70

One job in the ambulance service took him to an out-of-control teen gathering in Logan, south of Brisbane. Immigrant Africans clashed with Maoris in a racially tense situation when rival gangs arrived at the party. A broken bottle slashed one young woman, and two youths were bashed within an inch of their lives. When he attended, they had to treat the victims and deal with a mob, copping shit, spit and the threat of harm, all to save three young lives.

'Are you angry, Keegan,' Liv asked in a small voice, glancing back over her shoulder with sad eyes.

'Nope, Liv.' He scratched his head. *Irritated at Ross for taking you there.*

'Dad would be livid.' Her face turned back, and he barely heard her words drifting in the ocean breeze.

'I'm not you're dad, Liv.'

'Wish you were.' It was a whisper in the air, but he caught it, and it tugged his heart. *If only Joe wished I was.*

'You're just a teenager learning lessons in life.'

'So long as we learn from them, right,' said Ross, over his shoulder.

'Yep. Head home, Liv. Ross is coming with me.'

They turned to stare at him. Liv's mouth was half-open.

'Kiss, whatever.' He waves his free arm in the air. 'Then, Ross, follow me. And, Liv, use some makeup to cover that hickey on your neck, so your mother doesn't see it.' Keegan kept the smile from his lips when they slowly came together for a kiss. He turned, giving them privacy, waiting for Ross to join him. When footfalls fell in behind him, he strode towards his home. Ross kept up.

'Am I in trouble?' Ross scrunched his eyebrows together.

'Maybe, maybe not.' Keegan lifted the bottle of bourbon. 'Was this for later?'

'No.' Ross' voice broke.

'Why do you have it?' Keegan lowered the bottle, waiting for the boy's reply. 'I've seen a lot of alcohol abuse, and this strong shit does not go well with a teenage brain.'

'It's my friend's. He's already off his tree—,' Ross paused. 'He couldn't drink that too.' He pointed to the bottle.

'Okay. I believe you, but if I find out differently, you've been warned.'

Ross scuffed his feet, looking down. 'Can I go?'

'Yep.' He watched him run down the road, not looking back. *Who was the kid, Ross?* The townsfolk thought Ross was the troublemaker. What he'd seen tonight did not justify the tag. But, Keegan knew better than most how people could hide behind a facade of kindness and deep-down be evil. *Which was Ross?*

At the blue house, the lights were on. Pepper's hands were on her hips. Words shot from her mouth like rapid fire. He couldn't see Liv, but she was apparently copping a grilling. Pepper paused, curled a finger to her daughter. Liv walked into Pepper's open arms, and they hugged.

Like a voyeur, his eyes couldn't turn away. When he did, he was blinking back tears. He'd give anything to be able to provide Joe with guidance and hugs. Probably another reason the party bugged him—teenagers with parents who had no idea what they were up to.

Inside his home, he flipped open the textbook on his desk, knowing he could no longer sleep. *Don't give up on me. I'm coming for you, Joe.*

Chapter Twelve

A car engine purred in his driveway. Gus bounded past him, eager and excited, barking his approval of the visitors. The engine cut.

Keegan let the screen door slap behind him, never taking his eyes from the back doors of Sherry's shiny white Range Rover. *How the hell has she suddenly afforded a Rover!*

The door opened agonizingly slowly. He inched closer, holding his breath, waiting for the beautiful sight of his son. Joe clambered out, greeted by Gus, almost knocking the five-year-old off his feet. Joe giggled. *A wonderful tinkling sound.* Joe glance up with cute, big black eyes. His mirror image. 'Daddy,' he squealed, running into open arms. Keegan picked him up, squeezed the tiny body tight, keeping the tears at bay.

Joe kissed his cheek, sweet and soft as a feather. Keegan breathed him in, baby shampoo, fresh, soft skin, *love, connection—son.* Tears pricked his eyes. 'I've missed you, Joe, my boy.' Little hands clasped over his ears, and big eyes stared as if memorizing his face. Tiny lips met his in a sloppy child kiss. 'Can I see the kittens?' Joe asked, in the baby voice gone slightly primary-school deeper in the time they had been apart.

Reluctantly, he set Joe on his feet, pointing to the doghouse on the deck. Joe raced towards it, Gus nipping at his heels.

Sherry strolled from the driver's side, as usual, looking immaculate in a black pencil skirt, matching pen-thin heels and a silky white blouse. She looked like she should have been selling real estate, but she's never worked a day in her life. He had no idea how she paid for the designer clothing, but he admitted she looked beautiful. It irked him. His jaw twitched as she neared.

'Hi, Keegs. You look well.' She observed him over with a grin. 'Really well. A tan suits you.'

'Thanks.' She was saying nice stuff, but he knew she meant none of it. He kept his guard up. 'You look good as always.'

She preened, flicking long, jet black hair over her shoulder. Leaning in, she pecked him on the cheek with cold lips. 'Why keep the wedding ring on? You know it's over.'

'Habit. Plus, it's less complicated.'

'Ah, getting the local women all hot and bothered, are you?' She laughed.

'Nope.' He twisted the ring. It was about time he stopped wearing it, but something always prevented him. *Joe.*

Pepper's ute rumbled past with a tooting horn. Liv waved from the passenger seat. Sherry eyed them with a narrow gaze. 'Your neighbours?'

'Yep.'

'Of course, they're chicks.' She raised perfect eyebrows.

'They can't help that.'

'Are you going to invite me inside? It's a long drive, and I could do with a cuppa.'

'Ah—sure. Are you going to leave with me for Joe for a bit?'

'Not sure.' She possessed all control as usual. He felt powerless and bitter. 'Depends on if you've signed the divorce papers.'

'You make yourself a cup and take your time. I want to be with Joe.' *Steal some dignity and control back.* He hunched down next to Joe, who held two kittens with a priceless wide-eyed look on his adorable face. 'Cute, aren't they?'

'Can I have one?' He rubbed a kitten to his face, kissing the fur and cooing.

'You'd have to ask your mum that.' Again, Keegan wished he was able to make those decisions for Joe.

Sherry raised her eyebrows. 'No, Joe. You know I have no time for pets.'

Even though you don't bloody work. 'Got a job?' he asked.

'Have you?'

Touche! 'Workin' on it.' He scratched his head.

She huffed. 'I have a boyfriend, though,' was her parting shot before her heels clicked over the floorboards. She strode inside to make her cup of tea and probably sticky-beak on his life.

He placed his attention firmly on Joe, touching his baby-chubby shoulder, feeling the warmth. Joe glanced up. 'Don't like him,' said Joe, shaking his head.

'Who?'

'Mum's boyfriend. He doesn't like kids.' He shrugged his little shoulders, swapping out his kittens. Oddball meowed. Joe giggled. 'I want this one.'

'His name is Oddball.' Keegan grinned. He was partial to the weird-looking kitten too.

'Like the dog in the movie who saved all the penguins.' Joe kissed the scruffy kitten, making it meow louder.

'Guess so. Son, don't squeeze them too tight. Be gentle; they're just babies.'

'I'm not a baby. I start school tomorrow.' He said it like he was super proud of himself, making Keegan laugh. It felt so damn good to be near his most precious human being.

He ruffled Joe's dark hair. 'I know, buddy. How good is that?'

'I have all my books, pencils, a ruler too. Mum said you'd pay for them. She has the bill.'

Of course, she does.

Heels hammered the floorboards. Sherry stormed out of the house, leaving the screen door banging against the frame. 'You're on the booze again.' Her face turned furious red. She lifted the bottle of bourbon in the air, swaying it.

'Hang on a minute.' He stood with a hand raised in the air. 'That is not mine. I confiscated it from a teen party last night.'

'Bullshit, Keegan.' She threw the bottle on the driveway. It smashed, spraying bourbon and glass towards her car.

'That's smart.' Keegan turned to Joe, whose eyes were bugging out. 'Stay there until I clean up the glass. 'Gus away,' he called the dog. It lumbered over to sniff the liquid. 'Are you serious, Sherry?'

She pushed past him, pulling the kitten from Joe's hands and roughly pushing it into the kennel where it squealed. Grabbing Joe's hand, she pulled him up, scowling at Keegan, shaking her head. 'You'll never change.'

'I have,' he said, air leaving his lung. Tears dropped down Joe's sweet cheeks. 'Sherry, you're overreacting. I told you it's not mine, and I've turned a corner. I'm doing well. Got my life on track.'

'Bullshit.' She stormed off the deck with Joe looking over his shoulder with sad black eyes. 'Always bullshit and lies.'

'You never listen. Why can't you trust me? Hey, you can't take Joe. You only just got here. Listen to me, Sherry.' His voice took a whining plea. She was killing him.

'Say goodbye when I put his seat belt on. We are leaving.' She brokered no argument.

Joe bawled, rubbing his eyes. 'I want to stay with Daddy. Dadddddy!'

'Shut up,' said Sherry, glaring with narrowed eyes at their son.

'Don't say that to him,' Keegan said.

She stepped aside so he could say goodbye. 'I'll say anything I want. You have no idea how hard it is to single parent.'

'You don't need to single parent. I'm asking you to share.'

'Fat fuckin' chance.'

Keegan ignored her to concentrate on Joe, whose bottom lip trembled with tears rolling over it and down his chin. 'I love you, Daddy.'

'Love you too, Joe. Mummy's got things wrong, buddy. We'll sort it out. I'll see you again soon. I promise.' He crossed his heart, then leaned in to hug Joe to him. It didn't matter Joe's cries dampened his shirt. He wanted to suck in those tears so Joe would never shed any more. 'Promise,' he repeated it to reaffirm it to Joe.

Glancing over her shoulder from the front seat, Sherry shot him daggers. 'Hurry up. We're going.'

'See ya, buddy.' He glanced with a tilted head at Sherry, trying to dissolve her anger. 'It's not what you think. When you calm down, I'll ring you. Okay?' In reality, he wanted to wipe the smugness from her face, say nasty things, get it off his chest, but with Joe's little ears pricked to any fight, he couldn't.

'Don't waste your breath. Drinking again has ruined my trust.'

'I told you.' He took a deep breath steadying his rage.

She raised a palm. 'Talk to it. You'll have to prove more than that for me to let our son visit you alone. His safety is all I'm doing this for. It's not a vendetta because you left. I don't even love you

76

anymore.' She turned quickly, adjusting the rear-view mirror. The reflection told another story when she wiped under her eyes.

And you left me.

With a last squeeze and kiss on Joe's wet cheek, Keegan shut the door and stepped back, forgetting the broken glass was there. The pain hit his barefoot, but he ignored it as they drove away, with his heart hurting so deep he felt mortally wounded.

***

The white Range Rover sped past, hugging too much of the middle of the road, almost clipping Pepper's ute.

'Idiot drivers!' Liv was in the passenger seat, so she pushed the F words aside. The driver, in dark sunglasses, was the one she'd seen at Keegan's. *His wife. Posh. Better than her.*

'Mum, Keegan's hurt,' Livia said, pointing to where Keegan crouched on his driveway with broken glass surrounding his bleeding feet.

Pepper braked, swerved the car into his drive and was out quicker than Usain Bolt. 'Keegan, you're bleeding.'

He glanced up with moist eyes, nodding. 'Doesn't matter.'

'What? You're not making sense. Liv, grab the kitten blankets or a towel, anything.' Liv ran up the stairs, passing Gus, who was whimpering, head resting on his paws.

'Had worse wounds.' Keegan twisted, inspecting his left foot. With pinched fingers, he pulled a large chunk of glass out. Blood spurted from the wound. He didn't wince. Taking the towel Liv passed him. He pushed it to the wound. Pepper's hand reached over to touch his shoulder. He trembled. Whether it was with rage or what, she was unsure, but her heartbeat quickened. There was something more wrong with him than the depth of the wounds.

'Step over here. Let me check you over.' She nodded, gulping, feeling queasy seeing the blood. 'Where's a dustpan and broom?'

'Inside, hall cupboard.' Wiping at moist, dark eyes with his free hand, he sighed. 'Go home, Pepper. I'll look after myself.' His voice was gruff, and his eyes wouldn't meet hers.

Liv returned with another towel and the dustpan. 'I'll get rid of the glass.' Liv swept the glass towards the pan, taking care where she stood, but her sneakered feet protected her from the shards.

'You might need stitches,' Pepper said.

He wobbled to his feet, leaning on her shoulder. Lifting his right foot, he pulled another shard from his heel. 'Superficial. I'll be fine.'

'Why were you just standing on the glass, bleeding?' Pepper asked, taking some of his weight. He limped beside her towards the deck.

'She took him.' He glanced to the road.

'It was your wife and son, right?'

'Yep.' He shook his head. 'First friggin' visit in three months.'

'Why'd they go?'

'She thought I was on the booze.' He shot an odd look at Liv, who turned towards the wheelie bin with the dustpan. There was a shake in her hands.

'Why would she think that? You never drink. Well, I haven't seen you.' The smell of bourbon on the ground wafted. 'Where'd the bottle come from?'

'Not mine.'

'God, Keegan. I'm trying to help you. You're going round in circles as usual. Talk to me.'

'Nothing to say. Go home. I'm fine.'

He let go of her, leaning against the house. Gus sniffed his feet, lowering his whimpers to go quiet. His head angled at Keegan as if the dog were trying to make out what the human thought.

'Are you sure?' Pepper asked, feeling she should stay.

'Yep.'

'Come on, Liv.' Pepper rolled her eyes at him. 'Let's leave Mr Grouch in peace.'

His shoulders slumped. He sat on the couch, lifting the towel to inspect the deep wound.

***

Keegan didn't want Pepper to leave, but he'd been gruff and unkind. *They were only being nice.* How could he ask her to help him stitch his foot now? He'd acted so ungratefully. *Dickhead!*

Taking a deep breath, he bit the bullet, calling to Pepper's retreating back. She opened the car door. Liv was already past their fence running inside, mobile phone plastered to one ear. 'I'm sorry, Pepper. I need help.'

Pepper turned, hand still on the door. 'Well, maybe, I don't want to help you anymore.' She slammed the door, striding towards him.

'I'd deserve it.' He shrugged.

'Damn right, you would.' Her anger deflated as if it wasn't even there at all. 'How can I help?'

'Inside, first-aid above the fridge.' He winced after she stepped inside. The pain was kicking in, and he knew from experience that the cut wouldn't ache at first. It was only later when the nerves caught on to the damage. He couldn't let his mind go to the last time he'd bled. Unconsciously, his free hand trailed the scar on his neck.

'Right, what now?' Pepper returned, placing the kit on the table in front of the couch, sidling in beside him.

'I need a face washer from the bathroom, and we're good to go.'

She stood, shrugging her shoulders. 'Where?'

'Small house. You'll find it.' He fished through the first-aid box for what he needed without looking up.

She returned with the washer, passing it to him with warm, gentle hands. The differences between Sherry and her were staggering. For one, she listened. Two, she was laid back and genuine. Three, she didn't question him with accusations, only with kindness. He thought he couldn't warm to her more, but despite the gash in his foot, and the ache of Joe leaving, he felt content when she sat back beside him.

'I'll have to twist a bit to get to it. Can you hold my leg as still as you can? When I nod, shove the washer in my mouth.'

'What? You're not—' Her eyes grew wide when he snapped open the sterile needle and threaded it with suture nylon. She paled, turning away. He smiled.

***

Warmth seeped through Pepper's hands, holding his calves. Avoiding the wound and the queasiness it induced as he stitched; instead, she lifted her eyes to Keegan's. Beautiful, dark eyes concentrated on the injury, so she could observe him unnoticed. *Nice consolation.*

His eyes occasionally narrowed, long lashes squeezing on handsome cheeks. When the pain intensified, his jaw twitched, but he bit down on the washer, grunting. After what seemed like ages, he pulled the last thread through, snipping the end. The washer dropped to the floor.

'Done.' His dark gaze caught hers. 'Thanks. You can let go now.' A half-smile found its way to his delectable thick lips—*so bloody kissable.*

'Oh, sorry.' She lifted her hand, feeling the loss. Touching him seemed intimate even though all she did was keep him still enough to stitch the gaping slash down the side of his foot. 'You okay?'

'Ah, huh. Just need to do this.' He splashed stinky Betadine over the wound, flinching. Pressing non-stick gauze to it, he tightly wrapped a small bandage. With relaxed movement, he dabbed the antiseptic over the other cuts on his feet, balled up the dirty gauze, tape and other mess, put it aside and shut the first aid kit.

'You're good at that. You should be a doctor.'

Flicking his foot to the floor, he tested it with a bit of pressure. For the first time in ages, he grinned, lighting his face in a way so appealing, she forgot why she was there.

Her lips gravitated towards his. She stopped short. There was more explaining to do on his part before she could give in to the temptation. 'What really happened today?' she asked, wanting to know it but hoping he no longer loved his wife.

He rubbed a hand through thick hair. 'I guess I owe you that.'

'You don't owe me anything. I'm concerned about you, is all. You seemed—lost.'

'Sometimes, I am.'

'Why? Tell me.' She edged closer, feeling warm breath on her cheek. They were too close. Their eyes met. Moments ticked. Heartbeats thundered. Lips met. *Soft. Tentative.* He edged back, black eyes staring into hers as if trying to read her thoughts.

She parted her lips slightly, tongue flitting the bottom one, hungry to taste him further. He seemed to take it as a cue, pushing his lips against hers, nipping, tugging, taking her breath away. Twisting towards her, one arm wrapped around her waist, the other trailed her neck, gently forcing her head closer.

His tongue edged around her lips as if testing her need before dipping inside. Tongues twirled, joining and spinning her like a vortex. It seemed impossible to stop, but her mind flitted to his wife standing on the driveway, kissing Keegan's cheek. *Close. Smiling. Familiar.* Before she drove away, angry and upset.

Pushing her hands to Keegan's firm chest, she felt his rapid heartbeat. 'I can't. We shouldn't—'

His jaw twitched. 'Pepper.' It was a plea from his lips to his eyes. 'You have a wife. *Child.* You have things to sort out before—'

'It's sorted.' He reached for her hand, tugging her back, so she almost landed on his lap.

Though every nerve told her to give in to her lust for him, the rational part of her brain knew not to mess with an angry wife trying to sort out her marriage. She'd been on the other end of that.

Scrambling her mind for what to say to the man she'd fallen for but couldn't have, she blurted, 'I'm dating Tui.' Pushing from his lap to stand, she avoided the hurt in his eyes. It was better. He had to sort his marriage. It didn't mean it didn't hurt deep in her gut.

'The school teacher?' He glanced away, turning his body slightly. 'Seriously? Why kiss me then?' He stood, wincing when his foot hit the floor.

'I—um.'

'Why kiss me?' His jaw twitched.

'You kissed me.' She tilted her head, challenging him to argue.

He raked a hand through his hair, cheek twitching, eyes flashing. 'And, if I recollect, you kissed back—a lot.'

It was tempting to fall into his arms. Ignore the complications. Forget she was still married. Disregard his wife. Overlook the fact she had said yes to a date with Tui, who, compared to Keegan, seemed as insignificant as a fly on the wall.

'I'm confused. I don't know how we got to this.' She blinked back welling tears.

'Well, Pepper, just take your fuckin' confusion and go.' He pointed to her house. 'I can't deal with this today of all days. I thought we were building something, despite all the other shit around.'

'That's the thing. I don't know what the fucking shit is. Are you married? Are you working? How do you feel about me? You don't talk enough for me to know how you feel. Talk to me.' And she wanted him to. If he opened up and told her his marriage ended and they had a chance, she'd step into his arms in an instant.

'It's not just words, Pep. Sometimes there are too many words and not enough,' he sighed, 'passion.' He said the last word so softly, more like a breath than a word.

Pepper couldn't keep the tears at bay, letting them slide down her cheeks unchecked. 'We're friends, right?' She held her breath, not able to lose him completely.

He didn't answer, only stared at his bandaged foot.

'We're better as friends.' She nodded, trying to convince herself.

'Just, go, Pep.' He turned from her, limping inside, slamming the door.

It woke Gus. The dog yelped before barking, cocked its head at Keegan, headbutted the doggy door, and padded inside to console his best friend. A kitten meowed from within the doghouse.

Pepper wiped under her eyes, fished her keys from her pocket to walk to her car. Had she stuffed things up completely? *I'm in the doghouse like those kittens, and I'm not getting out easily.*

Chapter Thirteen

It took Keegan two days to shift the black cloud over his head. Surfing was out because of the stitches in his foot. Yoga helped a little, calmed his breath and mind. Reading textbooks was useless because he couldn't concentrate. At lunchtime, the postie delivered the mail.

The official envelope, stamped QFES or Queensland Fire and Emergency Service, lay open on his knee. A kitten with an engorged belly of food snuggled in his lap. Things were finally going right for him. He lifted the letter, kissing the inky stamp—*my ticket to Joe.*

Raising his eyes towards Pepper's house, he saw her lift a timber stack bigger than her and lumber it inside. The house was coming along. She worked each day doggedly, hammering, sawing, instructing the few labourers she employed. He admired how efficient she was. Wielding saws like most women did hair dryers, lifting heavy things better than some men, hammering nails in no more than two beats, like other women would tap their stilettos on floorboards. In stark contrast to Sherry. *Bloody, selfish, unreasonable, Sherry.*

It wasn't only Pepper's efficiency and craftmanship; she happened to look damn adorable bossing big blokes in her no-nonsense way. Though she swore too much for his liking, it was growing on him. Who was he to judge that? He sensed she did it to fit in a male-dominated job. Many of his paramedic workmates had done the same. He never understood needing to, well, at least until Sherry took the rug out from under him and Joe again.

For some reason, since he'd helped Pepper with painting, she'd toned down the workwear, usually wearing butt-hugging jeans and t-shirts instead of the hi-viz. Either way, she looked adorable. He liked to think the change was for his benefit. It was doubtful, after all, he'd offered to help paint only yesterday. She hadn't taken him up on the offer.

Maybe it was because she turned her attention to Tui, but he questioned that too. Their kiss a couple of nights ago told a different story. There's no way she didn't feel *something* the way she kissed him. Touching a finger to his lips, he relived the memory—again. *Her taste and feel. More.* He wanted so much more.

The kitten stirred. Absently he stroked the soft fur, watching Pepper return for another load of timber. This time one of the tradies took the other end. They looked to be sharing a joke. *Another friggin bloke vying for her attention.*

It was probably his fault she knocked him back. Weakened by his run-in with Sherry, he probably seemed desperate. Every time he got the anxiety under control, Sherry chucked a spanner in his spokes and stood back, laughing at the damage spitting out. *Sherry!*

Since the breakup, he'd remained kind, fair—accommodating. He didn't argue when she called the shots, knowing he had to prove himself because he was the one who stuffed up. But Sherry taking Joe without so much as hearing him out pushed his controlled civility to hostility. It was sad to think his wife's selfish, uncaring attitude forced him to see Sherry differently.

The signed divorce papers remained on his desk in an A4 yellow envelope. He'd planned to give them to Sherry, but after her abrupt departure, he'd had no chance. Always hoping something would save their doomed marriage, he'd kept them for months too long. It was because he love her once, way back in the beginning when he'd asked her to marry him. She'd seemed sexy, kind and sweet, not materialistic and selfish. And the thing that hurt the most was she didn't love him enough to get through the tough days of his illness. Was it too much to ask for your wife's support?

Amicable breakups were possible. His brother's affable split with his first wife was a testament to it. Couldn't Sherry and he have a chance of the same thing? It would be possible if she'd played fair. He wasn't a vindictive man, but there was no way he was putting up with more of that shit.

The hole in his heart could not fill without Joe. It was time to stick up for himself, prove how far he'd come, and demand time with him. If Sherry wanted a fight, she was about to get one. His jaw twitched as he made a plan.

He glanced longingly at Pepper's house before placing the kitten beside its sleeping siblings in the dog house. Gus barely stirred, snoring loudly next to his adopted brood.

'I'm not giving up on you either, Pepper,' he said to thin air. *You're only on the backburner.*

Inside the house, he opened the small laptop on his desk. With quick fingers, he typed his reply to QFES, hearing the satisfying ping as the email shot into cyberspace. On the bookshelf, the photo of Joe smiled at him, forcing a wide grin. Something clicked into place. Optimism surrounded him like an orb. *I'll show you, Sherry.*

***

'Love it, love it, love it,' Livia screamed, twirling around her finished room. Pepper grinned, feeling a deep tug in her heart from the memories of being a little girl in the same room.

Livia chose soft, pale blue paint instead of the white shades throughout the house. The trims were white. A new bed doona with a cover in deep rich navy blue dressed the queen-sized bed. Scatter cushions in all shades of blue plumped against the cane peacock bedhead. Her first adult bed. She bounced her bum on the edge, facing a Five-SOS poster framed on the wall.

'I'm glad you like it.' Pepper strolled over to the bay window, staring at the inky ocean's growing swell. Darkening clouds huddled on the horizon. 'Might be a storm. I'd better move some of the timber and tools.'

'Where will you fit it? One of the shipping containers went yesterday.'

'I'll find somewhere.' Pepper thought of the garage. It had to happen sooner or later. She'd been avoiding it long enough. *But not with Liv here.* 'Hey, you still want to go to your new friend's house?'

'Of course.'

'I'm going to let you go over to Jodi's if her mum is still happy to have you. Then, you can have her over on the weekend to see your new room. I'm only letting you do this if you both do your homework together.' She watched Liv's face light up. Bouncing off the bed, she snatched the mobile phone off the desk near the window reading nook.

'Hey, Jodi. Is it still okay to come over? You're mum's sweet with it? Yay. I'll pack a bag and see you soon.' Hanging up, she said, 'You're the best, Mum.' She hugged her before spinning in full circle with a grin admiring her room. She took photos of the room from all angles.

'Get a move on. If you dawdle, you'll be stuck in the storm.' She was more than happy Liv had made friends with a girl and no longer talked only about Ross.

'What about the stuff outside?'

'I checked on BOM earlier. The storm shouldn't hit for another hour and may not hold much rain. I'll manage.'

Liv stuffed clothes into an overnight bag. 'Can't wait to show Jodi my room.'

As long as Ross Ronson never sees it, Liv.

Liv's eyes darted around. 'I love the bedhead and doona. Thank you.' She hugged her, then shot out the door, waving behind her.

'Love you,' Pepper called into the wind. The garage loomed. She shuddered.

Striding to the roller door, which long replaced the old tilt-a-door, she pulled the thin key from her jeans. She stepped back as a wave of nostalgia wobbled her knees.

Do it, you whimp!

Tapping the phone to feel it was in her back pocket, she pulled it out. Hesitating for a heartbeat, she dialled her brother's number. 'Rob, hey. Sorry, I know you're probably in bed.'

There was a slight time delay in his answer from New York. It was 2 am, but he was a workaholic and always answered his phone. 'Yeah, but still got a laptop on my lap and a wife snoring by my side.' He chuckled. 'What's up? You're in front of the garage, I reckon.'

'Yep.' She bit her lip. A large kookaburra flew overhead and perched on the gable above the door.

'Gonna open it?'

'Would you?'

'Bloody oath and I'd trash anything of his that Mum left inside it.'

'Maybe she got rid of it all.'

'You know she didn't. Come on, Pep. It's just a building; you'd know that better than most. Do you want me to stay on the phone?' She heard his stifled yawn.

'No. Go to sleep. I'll call you tomorrow. Sorry, I—'

'Sis, it's only us now. It's okay. I get it.'

Her lip trembled. She bit it tasting blood. 'Thanks.' The kookaburra tilted its head at her, its beak opening and closing but making no sound.

'You sure you're okay?'

'I guess. I wish you were here, though. Got to do it some time, right?'

'That's the spirit. Get it over with and start your life afresh without his fuckin' bloody ghost sitting on your shoulder. Make the building into something spectacular, like I know you can.' His wife, a beautiful African American, Etti's voice asked in a sleepy Brooklyn accent, who was on the phone. 'I've got to go. I'll call you in the morning. Yours, not mine.'

***

Keegan checked the kittens, fed Gus, and glanced towards Peppers. She paced in front of the garage roller door with a narrow, slumped stance. A phone was to her ear, and she looked sad. When she hung up, tucking the phone in the pocket of snug jeans, she stood for a good five minutes staring at the building.

Why hadn't sh opened it, and what lay beyond the door?

Hands at her sides, her shoulders shook as if she were crying. One hand lifted, dropped again, like she was deciding whether to open the door.

What the hell is scaring you, Pep? He wanted to go to her but held his breath, feeling somehow it was something she needed to do alone.

Goosebumps popped along his arms. He narrowed his gaze. Dark clouds lined the sky, blocking the sun a couple of hours before dusk was due. Wind whipped and howled. A feeling of dread hit the pit of his stomach. Always a bit of an intuit, even from fifty metres away, he sensed she was scared. *Pepper!*

Chapter Fourteen

Pepper stood in front of the garage door, trying to push the image of her father's death to the back of her mind. This time she would open the door. Avoiding a stupid building didn't make sense, though the buzzing in her ears told her otherwise. Structures were her thing, so why should this one haunt her? *Bricks and mortar, right?* To be correct, it was timber, cladding, metal and concrete. *Just a fuckin' building.*

The wide door handle reflected warm sunlight but felt cold at her touch. Her fingers trembled. *Turn it. Lift. Enter.* Simple. *Not so.*

Livia, being streets away at Moon Beach with some new girlfriend, allowed Pepper to step through the godawful threshold without scrutiny. It had taken her the better part of thirty years. Years of inner turmoil and self-loathing, at least in the early days. Biting her bottom lip as her fingers pressed the smooth metal, she twisted the handle. The catch gave way with a grinding click. Taking a deep breath, she slid the door up. It glided along its rollers with a whir and clatter, needing a spray of lubrication after so long remaining closed.

Nausea flipped her stomach. She edged forward on unsteady legs, squeezing her eyes shut, taking deep breaths. Dust, mould, timber, canvas and paint assaulted her nostrils. She twisted her fingers together in prayer, though she didn't have religious faith. *You can do this.*

Blinking open one eye first revealed nothing unusual. She opened the other, scanning the dusty interior. It needed more light to see things clearly, but of course, she was reluctant to notice anything at all. A couple of steps to her left, and she pulled back the heavy curtains, unleashing a cloud of dust. She sneezed, pinching her fingers over the bridge. *Add cleaning the garage to the list of things to do.*

Her heart beat steady. *Not so difficult.* It was just a garage. Nothing to fear. She was too old to believe in ghosts. *Time to bloody move on from the past.* Flicking the switch to her left made the fluorescent bar light high in the ceiling blink three times before brightening part of the area.

She glanced up. The loft spanned the back of the A-framed ceiling, its wide timber beams crisscrossing its length. A place she used to play with her brothers. *Until that fateful day.* Tears formed. She blinked them back, dragging her brimming eyes from her father's desk to the loft ladder. Sweaty, trembling hands gripped the timber ladder. Each shaky step up dredged another memory she'd buried deep inside. She paused, taking a deep breath and pushing the thoughts aside.

The eyes of a builder saw the potential. A mezzanine level, vast space, with picture windows facing the surf. *Wow!* The view of Blueshell Beach showed the whitecaps growing larger in the turbulent ocean. The grey sky grumbled with thunder.

Why didn't the house have another level? Or at the very least a viewing platform. Surely Dad would have seen the potential, or was he too caught up in his own twisted world because of the war? It would have been a long time since Mum climbed the ladder because of her bad hip. Dust mites danced on the benches, bird and rat shits scattered the scuffed timber floorboards.

A scuttle. Tip-taps on the timber floorboard. She jumped backward. *Fuck!* A mother of a rat. Its long, scaley tail disappeared into the shadows. 'Get out of here. Vermin!' she yelled. Placing a shaky hand on her hammering heart, she gave a rattled laugh—*top of the list — pest control.*

Stacks of photo albums filled two plastic tubs. Old timber tea chests with metal edges lined the wall. Near the loft rail, a stack of old toys looked like a frozen moment in *Toy Story*; Mr Potato Head, a Raggedy Anne doll, barbies, action men and board games. Raggedy Anne stared up with round black eyes. Her moppy red hair was tangled and faded.

She reached for the familiar doll, lifting the dress to see the heart

89

on the doll's chest with the words *I Love You, Pepper*. Hugging the doll to her breast forced tears to her eyes. The aging fabric oozed mothballs and memories. An image flashed — Dad yelling. Mum crying. The boys running to their room. Her and Raggedy Anne hiding under her bed. The doll wore her petrified tears. *God, I wish you were still here, Mum.*

She filled her heavy lungs. Braced. Time to face the challenge head-on. Placing the doll gently next to the other toys, she climbed back down the stairs. *Where was Chloe? No way was the cat around if the place was crawling with rats.*

At the bottom, she turned toward her father's desk. She wouldn't lose her nerve again. His dead staring gaze and the blood of the gunshot wound were no longer in the room. They were long gone.

Mum maintained the garage as if keeping a part of him with her. Pepper couldn't understand it, but perhaps it was the only way to cope. Her mother had frozen his desk in time.

The old desk was a salvaged door, sanded down to a smooth finish and attached to garden stumps. He'd done a beautiful job and the varnish still shined. Pepper ran her hand along the surface, remembering her father retreating to the desk. His sanctuary. *I got my building ability from Dad.*

Other than the dust, it was tidy and organised. A stack of leather journals stood neatly held by bookends shaped like a sausage dog head and tail. Her father carved it from a chunk of driftwood he found on the beach. After he'd finished whittling it, he told her he'd make one for the little desk in her room. He never did. *Another promise broken.*

Pens and pencils filled an empty baked bean can, standing like soldiers. Rulers, compass and odds and ends filled a spaghetti tin. A bottle of ink, so deep blue, it looked black, rested in the middle. Dad wasn't a hoarder, but he was practical about waste. Ahead of his time, it seemed.

She strolled around the desk, feeling the cool varnish on her fingertips, admiring the workmanship. *Dad gave me a gift, after all. Talent.* The hand trailing the desk froze. Red stains on the concrete floor. *Blood.*

***

Keegan shoved his phone in his back pocket and ran. His heart lurched. A scenario of what-ifs ran through his brain like pop-up banners. His legs didn't sprint nearly quick enough.

Gus beat him to the garage, galloping through the open roll-a-door.

'Gus, stop.' He followed the disappearing tail, skidding in the gravel as he rounded the bend to run through the door. *Fuck!* His gut clenched. Pepper crouched on the cold concrete curled in a ball of desolation. She was oblivious to Gus licking her face, his tail flapping like a windscreen wiper.

'Gus, off. Here.' Gus cocked his head but obeyed, flopping to his side. 'Lie. Stay.'

Pepper didn't budge. Closed fists knuckled tear-stained cheeks, her cries like a wounded puppy. Brown, dishevelled hair flopped over her pale face. The mobile phone she'd called him with lay on the concrete with a crack through the screen.

'Pep? What is it?' He dragged his hand through his hair. *Shit!* For a woman who was always a blast of sunshine, it seemed the light was out. A chill curled over his shoulders and down his spine, clamping over his heart. He stepped closer. His eyes darted, taking in Pep, the dusty old desk, workbench, an easel with a canvas tarp over it, paints, tools, odds and ends. Blood on the concrete. *What the hell?* He edged closer with fear bubbling through his nerves. Blood was something he was used to—as long as it wasn't hers.

Not hers. Too dry. Thank fuck.

She dropped her hands, bottom lip trembling. Eyes like diamonds met his. Tears slipped over her mouth, down her chin. Crouching, he gently wiped them away. 'Tell me, Pep.' She leaned one cheek into his cupped palm. *Soft. Feminine. Beautiful. So right.*

'How can there be blood after all this time?' She asked, haunted eyes glancing at the stains. 'He did it here.' She pulled her cheek from his palm, shaking her head and shoulders like chills crept over her. He felt the breaking of touch like shattering glass.

'Who did what here? Pep, come on. Let me look at you.' He placed a hand under her elbow, trying to release her from the fetal position. 'Are you hurt?'

'Not me.' *She's in shock.* With no blanket, he did the next best thing, wrapping his arm over her shoulders and bringing her close.

He could hold her forever, but what was the point. He'd missed his chance.

With one finger, he touched the blood on the concrete, dry, still red though. *Recent but not today.* Gus rose to sniff over the stains, letting out a small whimper. He padded outside, no doubt to relieve himself.

Pepper rocked slightly but didn't pull away, instead resting her head on his chest, where his heart hammered faster than she slammed nails. To say the woman made him feel good, even in such odd circumstances, was an understatement. *Soft, velvet warmth. A drug. An addiction.*

As if talking to herself, she mumbled, 'After Vietnam, I let Dad be, especially when he had a mood. Even though I was little, I understood. I gave him space like Mum did.' She took a deep breath. Tears slid from her eyes, pooling on his forearm. 'It didn't matter he still friggin' um, blew his brains out. I — found him —here.' She clamped a hand over her mouth, tears trickling over her fingers onto the old concrete floor, mingling with the dry blood. 'My fault.'

Keegan opened his mouth but shut it again. What could he say? People always tried to tell him how to handle his grief. Who was he to push his opinions on her?

'He did it in here?' *The reason she'd been reluctant to open the garage.*

'Mmm.'

'Didn't you live here until you were eighteen?'

She nodded mutely. He squeezed her closer. The scent wafting from her was as intoxicating as her skin—*vanilla and flowers.*

'You never came in here since?'

'No.' She shook her head until it wobbled. 'I was ten.' She shuddered.

'When it happened?' *You poor little girl having to witness that.* His gut twisted. *How dare her father do that to her?*

'When I nearly drowned. Pepper's eyes flickered to the door towards the beach. A nostalgic look crossed them before she turned her face to his. She was a warm breath away. *So tantalisingly close. An easy kiss.* Pepper needed his ears more than lips. He pulled his arm off her shoulders and stood out of her personal space. Too close was playing with fire.

'Do you understand? she asked. 'His blood is still here. I knew he was haunting me.' She wiped her eyes, blinking at him, standing and stepping so close he could almost taste salty tears.

'It can't be his blood. It's new, not from thirty years ago.' Convincing her would take some doing. Keegan placed both hands on her shoulder, giving her a small shake. 'Pep, do you understand me?'

She squirmed from his hold, striding to the desk. 'He did it here. The blood is there.' Her finger shook as she pointed to the spot. 'He's haunting me.' The paleness left her face to be replaced by flaming cheeks. Slamming her hand along the desk, she slapped the pens and journals. They clattered on the floor along with a thud from one fallen bookend. She glared at a bottle of ink, grabbed it and flung it against the panelled wall. It shattered. A dark blue stain slowly trailed down like ghost tears.

He stood, raising his hands in surrender. 'I know what you think it looks like, but your mum lived here for those thirty years. She painted in this garage. It was tidy as a pin.'

'How do you know?' Her pretty eyes, still moist with tears, zipped around the garage. She wrung her hands together as if giving herself comfort. If only she were willing to take more from him instead of the dickhead school teacher. Could he give it? There was still a risk in it. *Joe.*

'Look, there's her easel, near the window. She wouldn't have left her husband's blood there. There's no way she'd want that memory either. Pep. It's recent.'

'How?'

'Maybe from an animal, a rat or something. I've been here with your mum; she wouldn't do that to you or his memory. I've never seen that stain before.'

Her eyes widened. Huffing, she strode over to the easel, tearing the tarp off the canvas. When it came away, she gasped.

Keegan stepped behind her, gently placing his hands on her shoulders as they stared at the painting. She didn't move from his touch. The picture showed her mum, Meg, two young boys, a little girl and a man smiling from the canvas in bright, cheerful colours. The man grinned the broadest, his head tilted to the little girl, but he was a lighter colour as was one boy. Faded. *Ghosts.*

Pepper placed her fingers over her mouth like a prayer.

'Your family?' He squeezed her slender shoulders, feeling warmth return to her veins.

'Mum.' She didn't take her eyes from the picture. 'My younger twin brothers by two years, Tim and Rob, — and Dad.' She stepped towards it. Keegan let his hands drop to his sides. Even in these bizarre circumstances, her touch was softer than he imagined.

'And you. You were adorable — still are.' He smiled, feeling a pride he didn't deserve to feel.

She glanced over her shoulder, feigned a half-smile. One of his tricks. 'I never knew Mum was so talented.' She brushed her fingertips over her father's face. 'I can't remember him this happy. It must have been before —.' She sighed heavily, her slender shoulders rising and falling.

Keegan stepped backwards, allowing her a moment. He inspected the blood splatter again. On the dried blood, a fine tuft of hair spiked out like a tiny echidna. He lifted it, rubbed the softness between his thumb and forefinger, noting the tabby colour. *Chloe, the cat, was a tabby.* What had happened to Meg's cat?

Best to leave Pepper to her memories before becoming one of them. 'I'll leave you to it if you're okay.'

She sighed before frowning. 'I'm sorry. I overreacted. It's just — opening the door stirred —like an overflowing can of worms or a barrel of monkeys.' Her lips trembled. She was probably trying for humour but fell short. 'Stay, please. I need company.'

Not me, just company.

She tilted her head in a way that skipped his heartbeat every time. He wasn't fooled. She had someone else, and it wasn't him. He didn't have the energy for it right now.

'I can't do this.' He turned from her startled face. Lightning cracking overhead. Plops of large raindrops hit the bitumen driveway, splashing his ankles. With long strides, he retreated towards the sanctuary of his beach shack.

Though, of course, it would be no haven. Her face would haunt him even if he shut his eyes. Her sorrow would seep into his pores if he tried to purge them in the salty ocean when he swam, and her beauty would enter his bedroom and taunt him when he tried to sleep.

No ghost haunted her garage, but she had no idea how much she spooked him.

And, on top of his unrequited lust for her, he had a mystery to solve. *Why was a cat bleeding in Meg's garage, and did it have anything to do with his adopted kittens?*

Chapter Fifteen

Jodi's house was high on Moon Beach Road. There was no way of missing the imposing modern home, with square angles and glass framed balconies. It looked like a concrete warehouse. The view from inside staring out was stunning, overlooking the inky Pacific Ocean.

Livia stood on the patio off Jodi's bedroom. 'Wow, your parents must be sooo rich,' she said, circling her arms wide. 'We couldn't swing a cat on our front deck.'

'Don't talk about cats,' said Jodi, grimacing. 'Mum found Bluey dead in our back shed.'

'I'm sorry. She wasn't pregnant, was she?'

'Not likely, stupid, being he was a male cat. He was like, I dunno sixteen or something. Just old age, I guess. Poor mum had to dig a hole to bury him because, as usual, Dad was away for work. He's got a job with a pharmaceutical company.' She rolled her eyes.

'At least your dad is still around.' Liv bit her lip.

'Not much.'

'Let's get the homework done so we can muck about.'

Jodi led the way to a corner of her bedroom's floor to ceiling, built-in desk and shelves, big enough to fit four students. They rushed through their homework then sat cross-legged on Jodi's massive king-sized bed. 'So, what do you want to know? I've been at Blueshell Beach since kindy. That's when Mum decided on the seachange even though Dad still works in Brizzy.'

'I guess it's why you have so many friends.' Liv smiled. She liked Jodi, the only girl to show friendship during her first days at school. It made things easier, especially since Ross was a grade up from her.

She'd barely seen him the last couple of days.

'You've been hanging with Ronson's Crew. You have heaps of friends already.'

'Don't think I'd call them all friends.' Liv rolled her eyes. 'None of the surfer chicks talk to me, and the guys are a bit sleazy—except for Ross, of course.' She craved female companionship, girly talk and shit giggles.

'Reckon, the chicks are only jealous because you're so pretty.' She touched Liv's hand. Liv's eyes flicked to Jodi's. Something odd flashed. She pulled her hand away. Jodi laughed with her head thrown back. Platinum bleached hair in an old-time Suzi Quatro mullet splayed on the bed as she tried to contain the laughter. 'Liv, chill. I'm just being a mate. Yes, I do like both girls and guys, but it's no issue. Anyhoot, I know you have the serious, big-time hots for Ross.'

'It's so obvious?"

"Fraid so."

'I'm sorry. I didn't take it the wrong way, but that girl they call Slash said stuff to me.'

'She doesn't want you to like me because I'm different?' Jodi said, frowning. 'She's so narrow-minded. I'd watch her if I were you, though. She's got a thing for Ross.'

'She told me to keep away from you. Didn't say why, but it was the way she said it. Kind of like a warning. Sorry.'

'Don't be. You're being nice enough to be honest with me. Few people are, least of all my effed up parents. Anyway, I don't want to talk about Slash. What's Romeo Ross been up to?'

'They call him Romeo?' Liv blinked, her heart shrinking.

'He had a reputation when he was younger. He's not so bad now. I think though, this town being so effing small, people never forget things. Top it off with his dad being in the slammer—'

'Why is that?' Liv cocked her head.

Jodi picked at a toenail. 'Bashed a teacher when Ross got a C grade. Went home and punched Ross, giving him a black eye. When his mum tried to stop it, he grabbed her neck, trying to choke her. The police came knocking on the door.' She took a deep breath. 'Found Mrs Ronson almost dead in Mr Ronson's grip. Her eyes were, like, bugging out!'

'Jesus, that's horrible.' Liv shook her head.

'Lucky, a guy was jogging past the house. Paramedics weren't there yet, and the police had a fight on their hands with Ross's dad. He went off, kicking and punching them. The guy performed CPR and saved Mrs Ronson's life. Don't know how he did it. I was holding my breath.'

'Were you there?' Liv's heart ached for Ross. *How could a father do that?*

'I was watching. We lived next door to them. Way before Dad's corporate job took off, and we moved to Brissy for a bit before coming back here.'

'You saw it all.' Liv's mouth fell open. 'Who was the good samaritan?'

'Ah, there's the odd part. It's Mr Silent. The smoking-hot guy who lives next door to you.'

'Keegan? How would he know how to help her?'

Jodi rolled her shoulders. 'It's a mystery, isn't it. Rumour is he killed someone, and then he goes saving her. Weird.'

'He's a super nice bloke. Can't imagine him killing someone. You know it was probably when he was in the Air Force. I reckon he must have been in bomb detection or something because his dog, Gus, is a failed recruit.'

Jodi laughed, loud and hearty. 'Serious. It's a malinois, right? How could it fail?'

'Too friendly.'

'Lick the enemy to death!'

They both rolled on the bed in fits of giggles. *I've made a friend.* Liv figured as long as she had one good friend and a boyfriend like Ross, she wouldn't have time to think about how much she missed her dad.

***

The diary's leather cover smelt of musk, aged paper and Pandora's box. Pepper leant over the kitchen table, staring at it, taking deep, ragged breaths. *You opened the garage. Open the damn book.*

Curling her fingers around the stem of a half glass of wine, she took a long swig until it was empty. Wobbling the stem before straightening it, she placed it on the table—*false courage.* Delaying further, she grabbed the glass, took it to the sink, and rinsed it. She glanced over her shoulder at the diary. She'd left it unopen, but somehow the cover flipped open. The pages moved like an accordion, probably from the end-storm breeze whipping under the window sash. She pulled the kitchen window closed and glanced towards the shed to survey any damage.

The storm was brief. Puddles pooled but were already drying as the sun set in the west, casting a dramatic orange reflection in them. She didn't bother putting the timber and tools away. Hopefully, none of the skirting boards would bow, but they were the least of her concerns. The kookaburra returned. Its wide-winged shadow brushed the ground before it landed on a gum tree in front of the sunroom.

She turned to face the diary. *Just do it!*

Returning to the table, she pulled out a dining chair. It screeched on the new floorboards, making her wince. She sat, leaning on her elbows. The book taunted her like a ghost with a curling finger. With a deep breath and trembling hands, she flipped the pages to the beginning. The distinctive cursive handwriting of her father filled the yellowed paper.

They were challenging to read, not only because of the story he wrote but also the writing was old-fashioned and hard to decipher curls and flourishes. He chronicled arriving in Vietnam, how invincible he felt—*a real man*. He missed his young family, his little princess in particular. The first pages were a homesick young family man Pepper loved and knew—*a long time ago*.

A third the way through, the writing grew messier, the stories harrowing. Drops of blood stained some pages and other things, perhaps his tears. *Bombs, shrapnel, men dying, scared to be next, anxiety, dread, wanting to go home.* Pepper shut the book, unable to continue further. *Poor Dad.*

With a balled tissue, she wiped tears from her cheeks, thinking about the other bottle of wine in the fridge but didn't get up. Folding her arms on the table, she rested her head down, closing her eyes. Images of her father's time in Vietnam flicked through her mind like an old black and white movie—only splattered in blood.

She woke in the same spot, and the lights were on. The clock on the newly painted kitchen wall showed 3 am—*1 pm New York time.* Clicking her neck, she stood, stretching her arms, yawning. A light was on at Keegan's. *Feeding kittens, probably.*

Lifting the mobile phone to her ear, she waited for Rob to pick up.

'Hey, sis. You're up early. How'd it go?'

'Shaky to start with, but I got there.' Her bottom lip trembled. It would have been better if Rob was not so far away. She could do with his big arms around her and his unquestioned brotherly love. She hadn't seen him since her mother's funeral five months ago. If Keegan hadn't come to the garage, she could have been in a worse state.

'You went in. Yay, you.' Rob chuckled.

'Yeah. I feel better. Well, I did, until—' She blinked down at the diary on the dining table.

'What, Pep? You still there?'

'I read part of one of the diaries. The first one.' She gulped.

'Really? Mum, read them, you know. Years ago. I didn't think you would. I don't care what he says. It doesn't change anything for me.'

'But, Rob. What if it does? What if it changes everything? He was a young family man trying to cope with the horror of it all.'

'There's still no excuse.' Rob's voice took on an edge, and she knew not to push him further. With unsaid words, his thoughts would be on their brother, his twin, Tim.

'Just wanted to let you know, I'm okay.' She glanced at the diary. Rob needed to read it one day, perhaps not so soon after Mum, but one day.

Through the phone, a siren sounded. A horn blasted. The city noises made it difficult for her to hear him. 'Thanks. I'm glad. Hey, I've got to go. My train's here.'

'Thought it was a little loud. Look after yourself, Rob.'

'Always do.'

'Love you.' He'd hung up before the words were out.

A shadow moved behind Keegan's window drapes. The curtains parted. He appeared, not seeming surprised to see her in the light. He held a book in one hand and a smile on his handsome face. He waved. She waved, smiling too, heart thumping at the sight of him. He mouthed the words 'are you okay?'. She nodded.

Go to him. The urge to have his arms around her tugged. *What if he knocks you back?* But she lacked the energy for rejection. Instead, she switched the lights off and went to bed, even if she would need to rise in only an hour.

Blood, guts, body parts. She woke from a bad dream. She stilled, shaking shoulders with her hands and squinted around the room, getting her bearings. No wonder Dad was unable to shake his nightmares. Reading the diary etched her mind with the images, but he'd lived it, endured it—survived it—for a while. *I'm so sorry, Dad.*

***

After observing Pepper was okay, Keegan slept through until eight am. Not a single dream or nightmare pulled him from a deep sleep. He felt the weight of Gus on the bed beside him and wished Pepper filled the space instead. And Joe in the special kid's bed in the spare room—*Joe's room.*

He sprung off the mattress, forgetting the stitches in his foot until the pulling of skin stung. No surfing yet, but he didn't care. *Today will be great.* With a clear plan formed, he dialled Sherry's number.

'Hi, Sherry.'

'What do you want? I'm late getting Joe to school,' she said, impatience in her high-pitched voice.

'Just a quick call. How's Joe?'

'Fine.' He pictured her raising her precisely drawn eyebrows.

'I'd like to meet with you sometime next week. We need to talk.' He tapped on the side table, waiting for her reply. He liked she was off guard.

'If you're going to deny the grog again—'

He cut her off. 'Don't need to. I have proof, and, Sherry, I have every right to Joe as you. You cannot block me out of his life anymore. I know where I stand, and it's about time you found out too. And, don't go getting defensive. It's in Joe's best interest to have both parents in his life—equally.' He dragged the last word, pushing his point.

'Right. Um—Tuesday?'

'Great. I'll come down to Mooloolaba, and we can meet at a café. I'll book one and text you the details. See ya.' He hung up before she could argue. She was sure to want to pick the place, but he wanted control of the situation for once.

Gus sniffed like a vacuum at something near the bedside table.

'Hey, boy. What you got?' He leant down to find the tuft of fur he'd found in Pepper's shed. It must have fallen from his side table. He lifted it to the window light, studying it. While he waited the six days until he could meet with his ex-wife, he might as well use the time to look into the mystery of Meg's missing cat and where the new mother cat was.

A cat with a litter of kittens wouldn't be far from her babies, so maybe it protected them and got injured. He heard a fox in recent nights. A dingo pack sometimes came close to the beach scavenging for scraps. Could be either predator or even as simple as a car clipping the pet and injuring it. The sooner he found out, the better it would be for Pep to put the shock of the blood in the garage behind her. He was still baffled by her family history. *What happened to the other brother?*

Chapter Sixteen

School seemed a whole lot better with Jodi as her BFF. They sat side-by-side in the classroom, hung out at lunchtime, gossiped and giggled endlessly. Ross was aloof, hanging out with his own age group on the far side of the concrete quadrangle.

Leaning over a bubbler, Livia swallowed water, easing a thirst born of another thirty-degree day. She turned, wiping her mouth with her arm, to see Ross. 'Hey, babe. Sorry I haven't seen more of you,' he said, glancing around before pecking her cheek.

She flashed him a look, trying to call his bluff. 'I'm too busy, anyway. It's fine.'

'Don't be mad.' He stepped back, allowing a boy to use the bubbler. 'You know what school's like.'

'No, Ross. I don't. Tell me.' She placed her hands on her hips. Jodi strolled over with an icy pole in each hand.

'Doesn't matter. Will I see you over the weekend?' he asked, giving Jodi a slight nod.

'Maybe.' Her heart quickened. *Yes, definitely.*

Jodi cut in, passing her one of the lemonade iceblocks. 'She's going to a party with me.'

'Hunter's?' He rolled his shoulder as if it were no big deal, but he raised his fair eyebrows at Liv.

'Change of plans. My parents are away. It's at mine. You coming?' Jodi asked, winking sideways so only Liv could see.

'Only if Liv is. Are you, babe?'

'I'll have to ask my mum.'

'You didn't ask the last party,' Ross distanced himself slightly when members of the Rugby League team strolled by, passing a footy between them and bumping broad shoulders.

Liv glanced at Jodi. 'Yeah, well, it was a one-off. I don't like lying to Mum. I might go. We'll see.'

'I hope so,' Ross said, shooting Jodi a narrow gaze before running towards his surfy gang. Slash, the tanned surfy chick with messy blonde hair, smiled when he approached. She glanced over her shoulder, staring at Jodi and then Liv.

'What's her problem with you?' Liv asked Jodi.

'Duh! I think that glare was for your benefit, Liv. She's had it hot 'n' heavy for Ross for years. She'd be glad we're in a lower grade and can't hang out with them.'

The look from the older girl made her question Jodi's answer. It wasn't a jealous look, more like an observation, and she wondered why. At least Ross wasn't totally ignoring her, and he'd come to explain the school dynamics. She touched her cheek, where his lips brushed. It felt warm, and she smiled, wanting more of his affection and feeling the butterflies take flight in her stomach.

'So, you comin' to the party or what? You can say you're staying at mine, and your mum will be none the wiser if we have a party.' Jodi snapped her out of Ross thoughts, clicking fingers over her eyes.

'I don't know.' Liv's shoulders slumped.

'What? Come on, spit it out.'

'My Dad's supposed to phone me Saturday night. I don't want to miss the call.'

'Easy fixed. You have a mobile. He can call you on that.' Jodi pointed to the bleedingly obvious answer in her school bag. It wasn't only about the phone call, which she didn't want to miss, but because the previous party was weird. She didn't like feeling out of her depth and had a suspicion those things could get out of control.

Jodi draped her arm over Liv's shoulders. 'Come on. You know I won't have it if you don't come. Pleeeease.'

Liv weighed it up. Ross would be there, and she'd be dying to see him by the weekend. Jodi ensured she'd be more comfortable than the last party. At least there would be one girl to talk to. 'Maybe, it won't be so bad—but Jodi, I need a favour.'

'What? You name it.'

'How do I go on the pill?'

Jodi's mouth opened wide. She clamped it shut, grinned, and nodded. 'Sorted. My dad's in pharmaceuticals, remember.'

***

Tuesday hadn't come soon enough for Keegan. He waited at the café in Mooloolaba, watching across the road to a happy family on the beach. The guy patted his wife's bum and kissed her cheek before chasing two toddlers around their sandcastle as they giggled, delighted.

Keegan's shoulders slumped. In a perfect world, that would be Sherry and him with indulgent looks watching Joe play—sharing his accomplishments, applauding and proud. Instead, they were about to discuss how to co-parent in separate households and unaligned views on parenting. The conversation wasn't going to be easy, but he had a plan.

She strolled in like a runway model, tossing her slick dark hair over her shoulder. Why she did so, he had no idea because it was hairsprayed to within a millimetre of every strand. It didn't even blow in the ocean breeze. Her dress was some sort of flowery flowing thing, but it did nothing to his libido the way Pepper's had at the barbecue. He pushed Pepper to the back of his mind, standing to face his soon-to-be-ex-wife.

'Sherry, hi.' He edged closer to peck her cheek, but she turned her head, dumping her handbag on the table and sitting before he had a chance to pull out her chair.

'Stuff the formalities. You know I'm not happy about this. I've talked to my lawyer too.'

A tic formed on his cheek. 'I didn't talk to a lawyer.'

'You said you'd done your research or know your rights or something.'

'Didn't mean I got lawyers involved. Jesus, Sherry, they're just like chucking money down the toilet and flushing it away. We can sort this without them.' He flipped open a large notebook. A waiter neared to take their order. Keegan shook his head, and the young guy nodded and hurried back behind the counter. 'Here.' He passed her a piece of paper. 'I've drawn up a calendar of our weeks with Joe. You can take it home, put it against your plans and see where we need to change it. I'm happy for it to be fluid, but I want him to live with me every fortnight or close to.'

She glanced at it blinking. 'You expect me to agree to this?' She flicked the paper in the air.

'Not from that alone.' Fingers trailed his neck, stroking the length of the scar. He sucked in a deep breath, plunging ahead. 'I have a copy of my mental assessment. It's from the psychologist, drug screening and alcohol testing.' *Proof!*

'Seriously?' She raised perfect eyebrows, frowning.

'And these.' A copy of his letter of employment with QFES, two character references, a recommendation for shared parenting from the Blueshell Beach Courthouse and a heartfelt letter he'd written to convince her he was capable of looking after Joe.

With cloudy eyes, she scanned them. The mental assessment was first. She nodded as she read it.

'You can read them all later. Take it all in. I'm not rushing you, Sherry.' He sighed. 'I've waited long enough as it is. A couple more weeks won't kill me.'

Wiping under her eyes, she read the letter of employment. A small smile tugged her ruby-red lipsticked lips. 'If I were still your wife. I'd be proud of you for this.'

He grinned, feeling melancholy tug his heart. 'You can be proud as my friend. We'll always share Joe, Sherry.'

'I know that.' She reached for a tissue in her handbag and waved over the waiter. 'A glass of your best red and a chicken pumpkin salad,' she said without looking at the menu. He should have known she'd dined at the café before. It's all she seemed to do, cafes, restaurants, gym, beauty parlours and art galleries.

The waiter held his pencil aloft. 'You, sir?'

'Double flat white. No food, thanks.' He passed the menus to the young man, who walked away, shaking his head.

'I may disagree, though. I don't doubt you'll have a relapse.' She crossed her leg, exposing her thigh.

He ignored the flash of panties. Something months ago, he couldn't have done. She no longer had a physical effect on him. 'Oh, yeah, great. No matter what I do, it's not friggin' good enough. You know deep down how hard I've tried. Now you're just being a bitch.' *Ouch!* He'd said it but immediately regretted it. Getting into a slinging match with her was not going to help.

'And, you don't think you stopping work to deal with your mental issues didn't upset me and put pressure and stress on us?'

'I know it did. It was a tough time, and we didn't get through together. I'll warrant that, but it's not like I asked to be stabbed and nearly die or to see the things I did.'

'You always wanted to be a rescue paramedic and take risks. Right from when we were young, it was firefighting, ambos or helicopter rescues. You had your career goals set.'

'At least I wanted a career. Maybe I was too idealistic and believed I could help people. At one point, you found that damn attractive.' He clenched his fist in his lap.

'Mmmm. Maybe once. Now I'd prefer a man who can provide for his family.'

'Seriously, I always managed that no matter where my head was at.' He shook his head, staring at the crystal waves rolling into the sandy beach of Mooloolaba. He wished he was out enjoying the surf instead of having the conversation.

'A woman deserves to be looked after.' She pouted.

'No. She deserves respect and love and can look after herself.' *Like Pepper.*

'You always knew I wanted things in life.' She lifted a compact from her purse and checked her flawless reflection, pouting shiny lips.

'I'm sorry I wasn't the man you wanted, Sherry, but let's face it, you let me down too.'

'Bullshit.' She glared at him with narrow eyes.

'One day, you'll admit it.'

'Doubt it.'

'Fine. Let's just be civil and parent Joe.'

'How will it work?' Sherry asked, stuffing the unread letters in a handbag so large a full-grown cat would have fit in it.

He thought of missing cats and deadends before he answered. 'We'll make it work like two adults who love their son more than their own egos.'

She flashed a half-smile. 'I guess that's fair, which I haven't been lately. But I can't make any decisions or agree yet. I have to think it through. For Joe's sake.'

'Joe wants both of us. He'll get used to two homes.'

'But he's started school down here.' The waiter placed the wine and coffee on the table.

Keegan said, 'Thanks, mate.'

Sherry ignored the waiter, lifting the wine to her lips. It bugged him she could be rude without even knowing it.

'I'll get him to school. Yeah, it will be a longer drive by twenty minutes, but we'll just get up earlier. It's all doable.' Her admitting to being unfair stunned him, but was it enough of an apology? He waited, hoping more would come but wasn't surprised when she sipped her wine and dropped her eyes, fiddling with her mobile phone beeping with messages.

'That's my boyfriend. The one who can provide for me,' she said, tapping the phone's face.

'The one who bought you the new car?'

'So what? He buys things for Joe too.'

'Joe doesn't need stuff. He needs love. His father's love.'

'I do know that, Keegan.' She plopped the phone inside her handbag.

'Yeah, well, sometimes I wonder. You can be a bitch to me.'

She raised her eyebrows. 'You piss me off too.'

He pushed the coffee aside, no longer able to palate it. 'I've got to go. Enjoy your meal,' he said, standing and scooping the notebook under his arm. 'Call me when you've thought about it.'

'Okay.' Her eyes lifted to his, holding for a moment with unsaid words. Was it possible she was having second thoughts about them? If only she'd had them months ago before he met Pepper. Though he knew deep down, with or without Pepper, Sherry was no longer his soulmate, and perhaps she never was. Material things weren't important to him, but they were her life.

He strode without a backward glance with a spring bouncing his feet. As if Sherry climbed off his back, a weight lifted from his shoulders. He rolled them loosely. The future looked brighter, the sun shinier, and he lifted his face to it in thanks. He knew he'd given Sherry enough proof for her to agree to shared custody. She had no choice. Warmth seeped into cheeks hurting from grinning at the sky.

There was one thing niggling him—the fight seemed out of Sherry. He'd expected a brawl, had his defensive stance ready, his fists up, but she hadn't even thrown a hook shot in the end. His brow furrowed as he pondered it.

He almost stepped from the kerb without looking, and a truck barrelled past, tooting a horn. He jumped backward with a thumping heart, reigned his mind in, and walked to his car more mindful of his surroundings.

***

'Stuff you, Pepper,' Ian shouted. 'You have no right.'

'Calm down, Ian. I have every bloody right. Not only for me but Livia too.' She paced outside the garage, counting stacks of tiles in her head, mind still on the renovations, not Ian's latest rant.

'I own part of that house. You can't renovate it without consulting me,' he said.

'Seriously. Okay, so if your mum passes away, I get half of her mansion at West End or the unit at Toowong?'

'No—I. It's just I have no income. What do I do?'

'You have plenty to last you until you find a job unless, of course, you've gambled it all away. I paid out your company share before you sent us bankrupt. It's me who's behind because of your betting and women. You have more than enough. I'm sick of you whining about it.'

'I can't work for someone else.'

'Oh, you're too proud?'

'I was the boss.'

She rolled her eyes, tapping a half carton of tiles with a pink boot. 'Not a very good one.'

'You reckon you'll thrive? It's a man's world, construction. You don't stand a chance.' The statement riled her more than she would have let on in years past. When they were married, she'd protected him from how she felt. It wasn't necessary anymore.

'I do. I'm already succeeding, Ian. The business is up to twenty percent profits from last year's, and that's with me being on leave and only overseeing from Blueshell. It's not a man's world anymore, and perhaps the whole industry would run better with more women making decisions. I'm proud of what I've achieved, and I'm sick of being told I need to be a guy to do it. That's the reason you didn't cut it. You always thought you could do less because you're a bloke, where I worked my arse off.' She took a breath. A sob sounded at the

109

other end of the line. 'Ian? What? Are you okay?'

'Nope. Stuffed up, haven't I?' It sounded fake.

'It's okay. You'll get back on your feet.' She rolled her eyes and rubbed her forehead with her free hand.

'I don't want the divorce,' he said it slowly as if he's was trying to make it sink into her.

She ignored it. 'Your mum loves having you home. Enjoy being looked after by her until you find your feet.'

'We can be a family again. You, me and Liv.'

She kicked the tile stack, then paced the driveway, tugging at the tight ponytail at the top of her head. 'Stop it, Ian. It was over before the business almost collapsed. I can't forget the women—and I doubt you have—or will, either. How many was it?' Her voice rose, and she was grateful Liv was at school. 'Four? Seriously, one would have hurt enough, but four?'

'I'm—sorry. I am. It will never happen again.'

'Dalmation can't change its spots, can it?'

'I promise I can.'

'You know what, Ian. I know you're only saying it because I have a good life without you. It's not because you want to share it with me. You only want the spoils. The only reason we are even talking is that we have to be civil sharing Liv.' She pulled the ponytail so hard it hurt. 'Don't forget to phone her Saturday.'

He coughed as if holding back a sob. 'I blew it, I know. I didn't mean to hurt you or Liv.'

She didn't want to feel sorry for him after all he'd done to her, but there was always compassion in her heart, whether she liked it being there or not. 'I know you didn't. It's just the way you are.' *Dick for brains.* 'Look, I've got a load of stuff that's arrived for the house.' She lied.

No truck was pulling up the driveway, but one extremely handsome guy was strolling from his house to hers. Her breath hitched. She hung up on Ian without further thought. Her eyes focused clearly on the only man she wanted in her life—Keegan Dallas. *If only he wanted that too.*

Chapter Seventeen

'I thought I'd check how you are after the shed stuff,' Keegan said, black eyes transfixing her, before glancing towards the open garage. His smoothly-shaven jaw twitched.

'Sorry, I was melodramatic,' she said, shrugging her shoulders. Placing her phone in a back pocket, she picked up a pair of work gloves, slipping them over her hands. The rough-edged Keegan was tempting enough, but clean-shaven, nicely dressed was just as appealing. His buttoned shirt could have had fewer buttons undone to reveal his hairy chest and muscle crevices. *But who's complaining?*

'Not at all. You had every right to be upset. The place held memories that hurt you. I'm glad I could help you through it.' He stepped closer until he was looking down at her. A faint smile turned his lips, and the smile met his eyes, where they crinkled at the corners. *A real smile.*

Wow! Finally.

'I'm embarrassed by it.' She admitted. 'I try to keep composed, but the memories came back so vividly. I guess because Mum hasn't been gone long, it still makes me tear up. And, I scared you away by overreacting.'

The way he looked at her didn't show signs of running. 'Don't be. I thought I'd leave you to your thoughts.' He glanced around the yard. 'Do you want help moving this in the garage? I noticed you seem to be kicking the boxes more than moving them.'

She tilted her head. 'Yeah, actually I do. I need them stacked with the others in there. Thanks. But what about your shirt?' She hoped he'd take it off.

'Won't need it again.' Rolling the sleeves, so they bunched over his biceps made the stuffy shirt less stodgy and way sexier. With little effort, he picked up four packets of heavy tiles.

'You look happier.' She nodded towards a stack already forming on the right side of the garage. The desk and her mother's painting area remained as they were, for now. She'd scrubbed peroxide over the bloodstains to remove them, and the smell of it lingered on the concrete. If Keegan noticed it, he didn't give any indication.

'I am happy.' He grinned wide. Another full-blown grin. What had got into him? It lit his face and made him decidedly more handsome—*if that were even possible.*

'What happened?'

'I stood up for myself, and I proved a point.' He bent at the knees, stacking the tiles, and strolled outside for more.

She picked up tools and other supplies, not caring what they were because she was too busy watching his body. Sweat pooled on the shirt, clinging over his chest and under his arms. His biceps bulged when he lifted the tiles. What would those firm guns feel like in her hands? 'What point were you proving?' she managed to ask, a little too high-pitched.

'I can raise my son.' He flashed another grin, revealing a small dimple in his chiselled chin. She'd never noticed it before. Maybe the usual three-day growth covered it.

'Looks like a load is off your shoulders. Good for you.'

'Except for these heavy tiles—yes.' He laughed.

'Are you going to divulge more information on it?' She lifted a hammer, twirling it with one finger. 'You know your conversation skills have improved, but they're still not up to par.'

He raised dark eyebrows. 'I'll never reach your standard, Pepper Have-a-Chat.'

She brushed past him, elbowing him in the ribs and almost tripping on his feet. 'Ehhh! I'm not that chatty.' She giggled, dropping the hammer where it almost hit her booted feet.

'Alright!' He grabbed her hand before her face planted on the concrete, pulling her up in one motion. 'It'll bore you, though. It's just family stuff.' He left her to carry timber inside. The warmth of his touch lingered.

'Try me. I'm not easily bored.' *Especially when you're around.*

'I met up with my ex-wife.'

O-Oh, here we go. He's getting back with her. She held her breath, thinking of childishly sticking her fingers in her ears so she wouldn't hear him.

'We discussed Joe and co-parenting. I'll have him every two weeks.'

'At your place?'

'Not at hers, that's for sure.' He rolled his eyes.

'So, she said yes? I mean to sharing Joe.'

'No, yeah—kinda.'

'Well, considering how great your negotiating must be. I'm surprised she gave you an answer at all.'

'For once, my speaking skills were on par, but mostly I gave her evidence she couldn't argue with.'

'Of what.' Again, drawing him out was difficult. No matter how much happier he seemed, he would never be a have-a-chat.

'Let's just say I convinced her I'm a new man and leave it at that.' He dumped the last of the supplies and brushed his hands together. Black smudges dirtied his forehead, and she wanted to lean closer and rub them off. *Licking them off would work equally as well.*

***

Pepper stared at his head with her big violet eyes. 'What?' He flicked hair from his forehead, touching it, then checking his grimy fingers.

'Nothing,' she said, with coloured cheeks. 'Bit of dirt is all.'

'Yeah, those tile boxes must have been gathering dust and grime in a warehouse before you bought them.' He glanced down at the shirt, now dirty and not so flash. He'd only worn it to show Sherry he was serious. It didn't matter if the stains didn't come out. They represented the sherry stain of his life.

'Thanks for helping me. I really appreciate it.' Pepper sounded formal instead of funny. *Prefer funny.* He was terrible at reading her signals. A blush usually meant some sort of feeling, even if it was only embarrassment. Her cheeks were flaming. And she was smiling.

'Happy to help.' He scratched his neck scar.

Her sweet lips moved as if she wanted to say more. When her pink tongue slid over ruby lips, he could swear the signal was of longing. He scratched his head but would have rathered shifted his nuts. When it came to Pepper, he was clueless. *But damn, she was cute.* Dirt smudged her nose dark like a little snout. The t-shirt bunched at her waist, revealing a fit, curved stomach, gave him pictures of what delights her jeans hid.

'Liv said you were looking into the finding Mum's cat,' Pepper said, moving to the side, fiddling with some hammer gun contraption that looked deadly.

'Yep.'

'Find out much.' She scuffed her pink boots on the driveway, not meeting his eyes.

'Maybe some tracks in the sand were showing Dingos getting too close. Any reaction from the brochures?'

'Nothing helpful. Want to come inside and get a drink and talk in the shade? I'll show you the cottage renos.'

'Sure.'

He followed her sexy little arse, swathed in tight Levi denim. *Hot damn, what a spectacular view*—and he was not glancing at the ocean. In the kitchen, she passed him a cold bottle of water. He looked around, liking what he was seeing. She'd kept the original beach-cottage vibe with white walls, panelling and shutter doors. It still looked quaint but modern. *Great job, Pep.*

Pointing to the ceiling and the gap over the back end of the sunroom, she took a swig of water. 'Mostly done, down here. The top-level goes up next week.' She grinned, clearly proud of the refurbishment.

'Wow, that will be some awesome view.'

'Yeah, I realised why Dad probably never thought of it. Back then, the bushland wasn't as dense or as high. As a little girl, I could see more of the beach from my bedroom window. Now there's only a snippet. The only way to get the same view I had as a kid is to go up.'

'Make's sense.'

'Want to see?' She grinned like a little kid. But all he wanted to do was kiss her lips. Damn, she was setting his nerves on fire.

'Sure.' He sculled some water and placed the bottle down on the sink, once again quite happy to follow her, especially since now she was climbing a ladder, and the view was even more nerve tingling.

She glanced down as if sensing his thoughts. 'I've got a ramp outside to get supplies up, and stairs will go in once I can secure the staircase top to bottom.'

God, she was so damn capable and hot as the summer day sweltering outside. He reached for a rail, letting his hand trail her bum. *Sorry, not sorry. Nice!*

She shot him a look that was neither annoyed nor happy, but her cheeks flushed pink, making him grin. On the roof, the heat hit like a front-rower, but it was nothing like the boil of his blood. Every second spent with Pepper made him think of bedsheets and two sweaty bodies—*his and hers.*

Holding his hand to his forehead to shield the sun, he scanned the area. Two frames stood, proud and straight. A couple of dozen floorboards were down over the sheeting covering half of the bottom floor's ceiling.

'Careful where you step,' she said, tripping over her own feet as she said it. She landed with a thud on her hip. Rubbing it, she frowned.

Reaching her in two steps, he took a deep breath. 'You should be careful too.' He offered his hand.

She took it with a shrug of her slender shoulders. 'Fuck, I need to watch what I'm doing.' Her head shook, sashaying the cute ponytail.

He laughed, still holding her hand. 'How are you so clumsy?'

'I know. Weird, huh? It's usually tall people.' She let go of his hand to twist and check her hip. She undid the top button of her jeans to try and edge them down. Still unable to find the bruise, she unzipped the fly, sliding one side of her jeans to reveal the purple bruise on her hip.

He couldn't avert his gaze. 'Are you okay?' The words tripped.

'Only a bruise. I'll live.' Her gorgeous eyes met his. She must have realised she had her pants half down. Her mouth gaped.

He made light of it. 'Don't mind me. You can take them all the way off if you like.' He winked, hoping it came off sexy, not sleazy.

The jeans slid up with a wiggle of her hips. She turned her back to him as she zipped them up. 'It's too hot up here. Let's go back down, and you can finish telling me about the cats.' She stepped down the ladder.

A bushfire up here. He followed Pepper down. With a bottle of water already in her hands, she waved it around. 'Cat story. Start now,' she ordered.

The pink of her cheeks could have been the heat, but he doubted it. To test his theory, he stepped close, reaching behind her for his bottle of water. The movement brushed her arms and trapped her against the sink. Her tongue trailed her top lip. He dipped his head to her, seizing her lips in his. Teasing them apart with his tongue was like entering heaven. She was compliant and as hungry as him—the kiss—deep—intense and pushing every button on his body to a high-desire alert.

Her tiny body sunk into his, so he could feel her breast against his stomach. Arms wrapped around his waist, hooking in his trousers, pulling him closer. His erection butted her hip, making her yank from the kiss, saying, 'Ouch!' But thankfully, it didn't deter her. Tilting her head to him, she smiled. 'When we fuck, just be careful of my bruised hip.'

Her words spun him into a vortex of desire. 'When we fuck?' he asked, unable to breathe. He kissed her deeper, broke from the kiss and placed a gentle hand over her bruise. 'When are we fucking?' He raised his eyebrows. *Hopeful.*

'Now.' She trailed her hand around his hips, under his shirt to the front band of his trousers. Her fingers teased the hair trailing down.

'Liv?'

'At a friend's.' She undid his shirt buttons, puckering her sweet lips over his nipples. His legs almost buckled.

***

'Thank Christ!' Keegan said, lifting her in one smooth movement, hands cupping her bottom.

Thank fuck, more likely. Pepper couldn't wait a moment longer to have Keegan's hot body blending with hers. Not to mention the bulge she'd felt through his trousers. She tilted her head towards her bedroom. *Was the bed made, linen washed, stuff off the floor? Had she shaved down there? Was she sexy enough for him? Would he notice she's not perfect?* She couldn't remember about the bed. Wasn't planning. *OMG*, he kissed her deeply, drawing his tongue in and out like a cock, as she pressed her breast to his warm skin. Everything tingled. Her thighs were slick—*nothing to do with the*

116

summer heat.

Bumping the ajar door with his hip, he carried her to the bed, laying her gently. He stood over her. Black eyes raked her like a scanner as if she were already naked. Kneeling each side of her legs, he curled the shirt at her waist with his fingers, tugging it over her head. His large hands smoothed over her shoulders, sending tingles. He reached for her breasts, cupped each one, in turn, leaned in to kiss and tease the nipples until they peeked. She pushed forward, needier with every touch. *Need. Want. Desire. Keegan.*

'Mum, Mum,' Olivia screamed from somewhere outside the house.

Pepper sat up, konking her head on Keegan's.

'She sounds hurt or something.' He pulled her from the bed, passed her the t-shirt. 'You dress. I'll go.' He ran toward the sound of her daughter's cries, shirt flapping behind him.

His broad arms had wrapped Liv by the time Pepper stumbled down the stairs.

'What, Liv? Are you hurt?' She couldn't see Liv's face until Keegan turned around. She didn't know if her rapid heartbeat was from the interlude with Keegan or fear for her daughter. It was like waking from the best dream to a nightmare of reality. Everything was foggy.

'She's fine, Pepper,' Keegan said, stepping aside so Pepper could envelop her arms around her daughter.

Tears streamed down Liv's face. Her school backpack was on the ground at Keegan's feet. Pepper wiped the hair from her face, looking her over. 'Tell me, sweetheart.'

'Her dad. Jodi's dad.' Liv gulped, resting her head on Pepper's shoulder. 'He got angry with Jodi and didn't like I was there. Told me to leave. Yelled at Jodi and pushed her real hard. I was scared.'

Keegan punched a fist in his hand. 'What the hell! I'm going over to have a word.'

'No, you can't,' Liv said, turning her head to him. 'Jodi did something stupid. Her dad has a reason to be mad. I just wish I hadn't been there.' Liv bit her lip, dropping her head back on Pepper's shoulder, where damp tears soaked her t-shirt. Patting Liv's slender shoulder, she sent Keegan a longing look. *It's not over. I want you.*

'Let's go inside and have a cold drink or a cup of tea,' she said to

Liv, leading her towards the stairs, glancing back at Keegan, whose shoulders slumped. 'I'll be inside in a sec, Liv.' She urged her daughter through the door. Stepping towards Keegan, her heart lurched. They'd been so close to—*sex*. The loss hit her like a punch.

He shrugged his broad shoulders, shoving his hands in his pockets. 'Our kids must come first. Sorry.' His dark eyes hooded.

'I agree, but I'm not sorry about what we were doing.' She smiled, reaching to touch his broad shoulder.

***

"Close call." Whatever lust was between him and Pepper was a burning fire. But of course, their kids must come first.

'She didn't suspect we—' Pepper glanced inside.

'I doubt it. Maybe the universe is telling us something, Pep.'

There was a slight movement to her bottom lip. She blinked her eyes rapidly. 'Telling us what?'

'The timing is wrong.'

'It's not, Keegan.' Her hand rubbed his arm, sending the tingles that hadn't died into overdrive.

Feeling the bottom of his pockets was better than igniting the fire again. He shouldn't be risking his heart yet when he needed to give his all to Joe. 'I'll leave you to talk to Liv. She needs you.'

'But—.'

He hated Pepper was biting her lip and holding back tears. It was better this way. She could concentrate on a clearly troubled teenager, and he could fix things with his son.

'I shouldn't have started—.' He ran a hand through his hair. 'I have to concentrate on Joe until I know the custody thing will work.'

She nodded.

'You have enough going on with Liv. She needs you.'

Glancing to the house, she nodded again. 'Okay.' Trudging up the stairs, she didn't look back.

And what he'd said was true. He couldn't give Pepper his all when he was fighting for custody of Joe. And, though he and Liv were close, he doubted she'd like another man in her mother's life so soon after her dad. He couldn't think of what her face would have looked like if she'd discovered them in bed.

He glanced down at his bulging trouser, cursing his body,

118

betraying him with the need for a woman. *Pepper.* She'd cast him in a spell.

Chapter Eighteen

Maisy strolled beside Pepper, picking up shells to study them in her freckled hands.

'Mum used to do that, stare at a shell, weigh up whether it was a keeper,' Pepper said, watching Maisy pocket two and toss another back to shore. 'She would find tiny ones and glue them on matchboxes. I called them my fairy jewellery boxes.'

'This kind?' Maisy lifted a small clear bag revealing a dozen or so. 'Dove snails, tiny ones.'

'Yes, there used to be so many more on this beach.' She glanced out to the surf, shifting the sunglasses over her eyes. Keegan's slick tanned back was visible as he paddled further out, his broad olive shoulders glistening with water.

'He's been out there for hours. Is he avoiding you?' Maisy asked.

'It seems so.' She kicked the sand with bare feet, picked up a piece of driftwood and flung it into the surf. 'One minute, we're heading to my bedroom. Next minute it's the big freeze over.'

Maisy grabbed her arm. 'What? Wait, what did I miss? Bedroom?'

'Oh, yeah, that place where you should have wild, rampant sex with hot men.' She shook her head. 'Nah, that doesn't exist at my place.'

'But you're staring at the damn sexy man right now. What happened?'

'Liv came home.'

Maisy clamped a hand over her mouth then lifted it. Her eyes twinkled. 'She caught you.'

'Nooo!' She chucked another stick further to where the waves were breaking. 'Didn't see us but certainly broke the spell.'

Maisy raised her eyebrows, pocketing more shells. 'Are you going to fill me in? Come on. I need details. And you look sad. I want to know why.' She nudged her gently with an elbow.

'Keegan and I somehow ended up getting hot and heavy in my kitchen. We only planned to talk about Mum's cat.'

'Cat?'

'Mmm, anyway, it happened. Another endless kiss, then me telling him I wanted to fuck him.'

'You said fuck?'

'Yep. Well, I did badly want to fuck him.' She sighed. A plover screeched at them from its nest in the sand. 'He picked me up, carried me to my bedroom. We got as far as starting to undress and hear Liv screaming. She sounded so upset, so of course—God, it was such a letdown. Fuck!'

'Mmmm, I bet you wish you were. Was Liv okay?'

'Yeah, fine. Teenage stuff.' She glanced at Keegan, who was sitting on his board, watching them. 'There was so much promise in it.' He turned the board to wait for the next set. 'Anyway, he won't even talk to me now. Said he has to concentrate on getting his son back. Understandable but—'

'And how long will that take? Months? Years?'

'God knows.'

'You know what you need.' Maisy grabbed her arm.

'What?'

'Distraction. Strap those sandals back on your feet. We're heading to the pub.'

'I'd better check on Liv first. She wanted to stay at Jodi's again since her dad's away, so I guess I should say yes, rather than her being home alone.' She followed Maisy back to her house, ignoring the urge to take one last look at Keegan.

***

Keegan rang Officer Wright and waited for the young constable to pick up. 'It's Keegan Dallas. Yeah, mate, how are you doing? "

'Fine, mate, you? You enjoying the beach life?'

'Better than the city.'

'I wanted to meet up and show you something I found.' He watched Maisy's car leave Peppers. Both women chatted, not glancing his way.

'What?' Dane Wright asked.

'Something I think the police should know about.'

'Righto. Text me the address, and I'll meet you there.'

'Meet at Shute Beach carpark. It's a walk around the cave end.'

'You think I'm a mountain goat? No one goes there.' The officer sighed as if Keegan were wasting his time.

'It's on the goat track, not near the cliffs. You'll thank me. We'll have to move quickly before sunset, but I'll bring a torch in case.'

'Yeah, you can shout me a beer after. It's bloody Friday, and I'm aiming to knock off early.

'Righto. Thanks, mate.'

Keegan arrived before Dane, who pulled up in an unmarked car only minutes later. Keegan reached out his hand. Dane shook it firmly with a smile. 'Nice to see you out and about more,' Dane said. He'd been stationed to Brisbane City when Keegan had been with the ambos. 'You doing okay?' he asked, following Keegan down the track.

'I am, mate. You?'

'Some days are better than others. This town's nicer, though. It was good to get out of the city. At least not so much shit goes on here. The ice problem hasn't hit, thank fuck.'

'That's a blessing, but something else has.'

'Damn, really? Funny to both end up here, isn't it?'

'Serendipity or something.'

They walked in companionable silence until they were about four hundred metres along the winding track. The outcrops dropped down to the beach like shark teeth munching on a seal. 'Anyone could miss it, but look at that scuffed bush.' He pointed. 'Behind it, you'll be surprised.' He led the way.

'Why were you bushwalking here?'

'Looking for my neighbour's cat. I figured the dingos might have attacked it. While looking, I found pawprints, but they ran out about here and then I saw this.' He flourished his hands towards a pile of bush branches over what looked like a hole in the sand.

Dane let out a whistle. 'A stash. Didn't hide it too well, did the dumb crooks?'

'You'll see. I haven't touched anything. Didn't want to disturb your evidence'

Dane picked up a plastic bag poking through one of the branches.

'Drugs is my guess. I'll take photos before we have a better look.'

'I already did that. I'll send them to your phone.' Keegan passed his camera to Dane.

'You only found it how long ago?'

'Twenty minutes, tops.'

Dane held the small bag to the subdued light from the sinking sun. 'Does that look like a cat to you? It's stamped with a cat.' Dane scratched his head, eyeballing it.

'That would be ironic since I was looking for a cat,' Keegan said.

'I don't get what it has to do with cats, but it could be something to do with the drugs. A could stand for Acid. The manufacturers make up all sorts of names.' Dane crouched to pick up another empty tiny zip-lock bag.

'You scrolled through all the photos?' Keegan flipped through his phone images.

Dane tilted his head. 'Yeah. So let's have a better look!' He moved branches aside.

'Wow! Could be fifty pills.'

'This is not a private load. Someone's selling this shit. I'll have to call it in and secure this area so I can get a thorough search. Could pin it on kids, considering the location, but how would they get their hands on this, whatever it is? I'll have it tested.'

'Hallucinogens? Meth? What?' Keegan placed his hands on his hips. Whatever it was, it was no good having it in their town.

'Who knows. God, I hope it's not like ice. I'll call it in.' Dane reached for the phone in his pocket.

Keegan continued to search while Dane spoke to his sergeant, explaining how to reach the spot. Twenty minutes later, they saw torches in the failing light. Uniforms greeted them, saying they'd take over.

'You seen enough, Dane? I'll shout you that beer,' Keegan said, glad the drugs, whatever they were, would be off the streets. He'd dealt with enough drug incidence with his job to know how badly they ruined lives, let alone his own substance abuse.

'Yep, Sarge, okay if I knock off?' He asked a tall policeman hunched over the hole.

'No good doing overtime on our budget, son. We'll take it from here. And you, Mr Dallas, will have to give a statement tomorrow.'

'Sure. Will do.' Keegan gulped, knowing like any other suspect they'd investigate him. His heart froze—*nothing to hide.* But, with so much on the line with Joe, he didn't need the hassle.

***

A bottle smashed over the entry tiles, falling from the hands of a boy carrying three tallies of beer in each hand. 'Oi, duffus. Parties only just started,' someone yelled. Liv searched the broom closet. Booming base and music of Kygo pumped through speakers. Voices rose above the music, laughing and yelling.

When Liv returned to sweep up the mess, Jodi seemed unconcerned, showing the boy inside and rolling her eyes. 'There's always one.'

'Jodi, your mum will find out if they make a mess. And what about your neighbours?' She felt uneasy about Jodi holding the party with her parents away.

'Nah, I have the cleaner to come in and fix it before Mum gets back from the concert in Brissy. The neighbours will only assume it's Mum and Dad. They party every time he comes home.'

'Really.' She noticed another shard of glass glinting in the light and swept it into the pan. 'What's she seeing?'

'Dunno, something old school, Elton John, or someone. Dad's over in NZ for a two-week conference. Yay! I can do without his angry bullshit.'

Liv glanced at her phone. Still no call from Dad.

'Hey, lookie, here comes Romeo Ross and his hangers,' Jodi took a swig of the rum and coke. The most underage kid, probably twelve, carried a tray full of the spirit in plastic cups. Where did his parents think he was?

Liv stilled her heart before looking towards the driveway. A dozen more people, led by Ross and Hunter, arrived at the party. There was something about the narrowed look Hunter shot her that made her uneasy. Ross smiled as handsome as ever, but Liv still

124

wanted to be anywhere else.

'Nice, you'd take on the party, Jodi,' said Ross, kissing Liv's lips.

Hunter cocked his head. 'Not if she's the one who derailed mine,' Hunter said, tilting his head close to Jodi. 'You'll pay for this, Blondie. I prefer my party place.' He bumped his shoulder, pushing Jodi a step back, before sauntering inside.

'Yeah, well. It wasn't safe anymore since those neighbours called the police. So count yourself lucky I could have it here,' said Jodi, shooting a daggered gaze to the back of his head.

Though Ross took her hand, Liv felt cold. Something bad was going to go down. Goosebumps pricked her spine and shot down her arms. She whispered to Ross, 'I want to go home.'

'Chill, babe. What could go wrong?'

She followed him inside, watching a drunk girl puke in a fancy pot plant. *Everything.*

Chapter Nineteen

The Blueshell Beach Tavern beer garden was cacophonous of chatter, laughter, clinking drinks, and music. A duo, straight out of Nimbin with dreadlocks and rainbow t-shirts, played folk acoustic ballads on a small stage. Five middle-aged women danced out of time, the beat irrelevant. Fairy lights blinked, trailing over the open rafters. Above them, the stars were even brighter.

Dane raised his glass to Keegan with a grin.

Keegan took a long swig, enjoying the refreshing beer. He hadn't had a drink in months. He didn't have a problem with beer, but it changed his mood to sullen if he drank spirits. He hadn't touched bourbon in over a year. 'Cheers.'

'I wish this humidity would ease up. Doesn't even look like we'll get a storm to make up for it,' Dane said, pulling his t-shirt neck to let air in.

'Looks like the whole bloody town's out tonight.' Keegan spotted Pepper at a table with Maisy, Trev and the friggin' Kiwi school teacher. They were laughing, and Tui was sitting too close to Pep for his liking. Keegan took a deep swig of beer.

'Did you see anyone near the site?' Dane scratched his blonde head.

'A couple of joggers, but they didn't look suspicious?'

'Mmmm. It's a worry. We've had a few kids caught with weed, but these sorts of pills don't need to be in a small town like Blueshell.'

'Thought's crossed my mind.' Keegan turned his attention to Dane, avoiding the pain of watching Pepper enjoy another man's company. Not usually the jealous type. He felt it now. A big green-eyed possessiveness he wasn't entitled to feel. He hated the emotion, but it wasn't going away with her so close but so far away. 'The Crichton case stays with me.'

'Shit. Yes. The guy who killed his wife's dog. Said it was an accident. His wife believed him. Two weeks later, he tries to top her when he's high on ice. I can't blame you for defending you and Renee.'

'He was, like, superhuman in strength. It was one you never forget.' He shook his head, forcing the image from his mind.

'Yeah, oh shit, man. He came at you too. What else could you do? They kept that fact out of the media at least.'

Keegan rubbed the scar on his neck, again forcing the memory to the back of his brain. 'I'm over it. He was off his tree. Ice and psychopaths don't mix well. If he hadn't stabbed me, I could have saved her without hurting him. The only way was to get the knife off him.' He rose his eyes to the sky even though he sure didn't believe in heaven.

'Mmm. It wasn't your fault that it went through his heart. You were cleared. Self-defence. It was heroic saving Renee and that woman. I was on scene, remember. You can't dwell on it, mate.'

'I guess. Doesn't help me live with the guilt of killing a bloke, though. I'm supposed to save people.'

'I get it, mate. I've had to make that call.' He held a hand on his heart before gulping down some beer.

'Back to what I found.' Keegan rubbed the scar along his neck and pushed aside thoughts of that day. Glancing at Pepper brought him back to earth but with a thud. Damn, that bloke needed to give her space.

'So what's a drug stash doing in a place us cops would never think to look? Drug dealers don't go that far because they're usually cocky little shits and hide it in their homes.'

'There's a few bikers in town. Them or kids?' Keegan leaned in towards Dane, placing his phone between them. He scrolled through the photos. 'See the smaller footprints.'

'Yeah. I noticed. But can't figure where kids would get the drugs from. Or bikies are recruiting to get into schools.'

'Could be an adult, though?'

'It's worth looking into.' Dane lifted the phone, scrolling through and studying the photos, a perplexed furrow to his brow.

'I just want whatever it is off our streets. I like the serenity of this little town, and I'm feeling pretty pissed off someone is messing with it.'

'Mmmm. I'll get to the bottom of it, mate.'

Keegan sipped his beer, trying with difficulty to avoid glancing at Pepper. 'I guess whoever it is, has their fingerprints all over the bags or at least has slipped up in some way.'

'Most likely.'

'Forensics will analyse it and get back to you?'

'Yep. You said some kids were taking drugs down the beach near your place. Could it be what we found?'

'Yeah. It's possible. But I could smell pot. Perhaps that's all they had. It wasn't an out of control party, not like the ones we faced in the city.' He glanced towards Pepper, who was looking his way. His heart squeezed.

'I'll get us another beer. Back in a tick. Hold that thought,' said Dane, strolling to the bar.

Pepper stood and ambled his way, so he turned his back to her. The touch of a warm, gentle hand on his shoulder was welcome but confusing. 'Keegan, are you ignoring me?'

'Nope.'

'Why don't you and your friend join us?'

'We're fine. You have enough company with the big kiwi fella.' He exaggerated his voice in a Maori accent. It was childish, he knew, but he couldn't help it.

'He's just a friend.' She tilted her head.

'None of my business.'

'Don't be like that.'

'You went out with him once, right?'

'I pulled out at the last minute.' She lifted her chin, her hair flicking over her face like a silk curtain. She wore a pretty yellow dress with a red hibiscus flower pattern. It hugged her curves. Tanned skin glowed like an aura surrounded her. *Hotter than a summer's day.*

He shifted in his seat. 'Go back to your friend.' It was a risk sending her near the guy, but with the weird drug shit and organising custody of Joe, he couldn't face what was going on between him and

128

Pepper. *Better to ignore it.* If there were anything of substance, it would still be there when he had the energy to face it. At least he hoped so.

Her pretty violet eyes held his. 'Have you heard from your ex?'

'Not yet.'

'So, once you know—.' She cocked her pretty head.

'I need to concentrate on Joe.'

She twisted shiny, pink lip-glossed lips in a half frown. 'I get it. I'm patient. You're not getting away with nearly bedding me, you know. There's so much more to it—to us.' She leant close, brushing soft lips to his cheek.

He held back the grin inside him, knowing giving in to her would force his mind from his precious son. *But, damn, her lips were soft.* 'Later, then,' he said, feeling his heart shift when she strode back to her friends. Tui shot him a glance of contempt. He ignored it and reached for the beer Dane placed on the table.

'Bloody long line up,' Dane said. 'Gave me time to ponder the case, though.'

They talked about different scenarios but went around in circles. Keegan couldn't keep his mind on anything other than what Pepper had said. *Us.* Glancing at her table didn't help his concentration because Tui wrapped his friggin' big arm around Pepper's shoulder and squeezed, whispering something in her ear. She giggled but at least shifted his arm from around her. *Sucked in, mate.* He lifted his glass.

Dane raised his eyebrows. 'What's going on over there?'

'Nothing.' Downing the last of his beer, Keegan stood. 'I'm beat, mate. Gonna head home.' He never liked having more than a couple of beers anyway.

Dane stood too. 'Yeah, I need to check with Sarge and see if they found anything else. I won't be able to sleep thinking about the possibility of these drugs out on the streets.'

Keegan could have shared an Uber with Dane but instead decided to walk off his anger, jealousy, whatever it was that wound him tighter than the inside of a pen. The air was thick with humidity. Cicadas buzzed in a loud chorus, almost drowning out the booming surf. An owl hooted somewhere high in the trees like an ominous sign. Barbecue steaks, sausages and onions wafted in the hot air from nearby homes.

The concrete mansion on the rise was lit up like a Christmas tree, lights flashing in time to boom-box music. A party seemed to be in full swing, but he couldn't see past the massive rendered fence surrounding the property.

He looked forward to Gus's enthusiastic welcome and checking on the kittens. The damn little cuties had claimed a place in his heart. He wondered how the hell he was going to be able to give them all away, especially Oddball. He'd always been a dog person, but he'd warmed to the little balls of fluff and their individual personalities.

Two teenagers ran past, hand-in-hand, giggling. 'What a weird party,' the skinny young bloke said to the girl.

'Are you buzzed? What—' the girl's words floated and were lost.

Keegan glanced at the mansion. He hoped the kids weren't on the drugs they'd found in the hole. *Not my problem.*

***

'Don't go in the garage,' Slash warned Livia, leaning against the pergola beam with one foot raised against it. Her messy blonde hair covered one green eye. She dragged slowly on a joint, offering it to Liv, but she refused with a shake of her head.

'Why?' Liv asked, wondering where some of the party-goers had disappeared to. *The garage.*

'Hunter. He's messed up because of her.'

'Who? Why?'

'You're stupid BFF. You have no idea, do you? You're such an innocent.' Slash glanced at Ross, who was fishing beers out of an esky. 'You know he's telling everyone he's shagged you.'

'No, he hasn't.' Liv glanced at Ross, not wanting to believe he would do that to her.

'It's a guy thing: Bravado and all that shit. Just tell him to shut his trap, or he'll never have a chance to get in your pants. Dumb ass.' She blew pot smoke away from Liv, but she still got a massive whiff of the sweet herb. 'Got you,' she said with a smile.

'So, he didn't say it?'

'Say what?' Ross asked, striding over with two beers in his hands. He passed one to Slash and sipped the other. Her real name was Nancy Wells, but she was a champion surfer, so they called her Slash because she slashed through the waves. Liv was beginning to like the surfer girl, even though she still didn't trust her and didn't get her warped sense of humour.

'What's going on?' he asked, wrapping his free hand around Liv's waist.

'Shit, again.' Slash rolled her eyes. 'Don't know how Jodi hasn't been busted.'

'Busted for what?' Liv wished people would just explain things to her.

'Drugs, luv. My drug is the ocean and a tiny bit of harmless pot. I don't get that heavy-pill shit.' Slash strolled off.

'Jodi sells her father's drugs. I thought you knew,' said Ross. 'She figured out his safe lock and took his samples or something. Not sure how she gets away with it. Anyhow, Hunter controls the parties, but she brings the drugs. He's pissed off the hidden stash was discovered, and we couldn't go to the old hangout. But it was in a shit spot, and I didn't want to take you there anyway.'

Liv clamped a hand over her mouth. 'What party place? Where?' She glanced inside the house and whispered, 'Hey, that's why it was so easy for her to get me the pill.' And why her father was so angry when he found her in the garage near his drug safe.

Ross raised his eyebrows. 'The pill?'

Liv gulped at what she'd said. It was too late to backpedal, so she told him the truth. 'In case, one day, not yet, we—.'

He squeezed her to him. 'No pressure, babe. Nice to know you've thought of protection, though.' He laughed, obviously chuffed.

'Doesn't mean you wouldn't need some too. Condoms will be mandatory,' she said, kissing his lips and feeling so grown up, speaking the words. Gosh, he tasted good, like beer but sweeter. *Hot, charming boy. All hers.* But was she ready to lose her virginity to him? She was still a bit on edge about that. *But God, she loved him so much it hurt.*

'Of course.' He nodded.

'You don't use any of the drugs, do you?' she asked, holding her breath.

'Sometimes. Not as much as Hunter.' He shrugged his shoulders. 'Who needs pills where you're the only drug I need.' He kissed her lips. 'I'm addicted to you, Liv.'

131

She giggled. 'So corny.' She kissed him. 'Can we go now?' She took his hand, tugging.

'Thought you were staying here, Liv. Weren't you doing the sleepover with Jodi?'

'No, not with drugs going on. I'm going home. I'll get my bag. You'll walk me, right?'

'Of course.' He sculled the rest of his beer, ditching the bottle on a table.

Liv walked up the long hallway to Jodi's bedroom. She opened the door, picked up her bag, and turned to go when she heard voices in the ensuite off Jodi's room.

'They were into it, don't you think?' It was Jodi's voice.

'Maybe. You have to be careful, though. Now the cops found some it could get traced to you. Don't have another party here, okay?'

She couldn't decipher the second voice, a bit deeper. Maybe a boy. What were they talking about? Something to do with the drugs. She grabbed her bag, slung it over her shoulder and was stepping out of the room when she heard the ensuite door open.

'Liv, don't go,' Jodi said, her eyes wide. 'Join in the fun. You're my best friend, remember.' The other person or people remained in the ensuite. 'Are you going home?'

'Um, yeah. Mum called, um needs me at home.'

'Okay, chickie. See you tomorrow.' Jodi winked.

By the time Liv reached Ross, tears were streaming down her face. She wasn't sure if it was shame, disgust, fear or fascination that her friend could be a drug user.

Chapter Twenty

Tui grabbed Pepper's hand under the table, squeezing his large fingers around hers. He was a sweet man, intelligent and confident, and she'd warmed to his company. At least he could hold an interesting conversation—*unlike Keegan.*

The tingle of kissing Keegan's cheek still lingered on her lips, like a tic—but a nice one. Reminding her, he was the only guy who could make her feel horny as a porcupine. But, an attentive, handsome man was paying her attention, and his intentions were clear. Brown eyes gazed into hers with an I-want-to-fuck-you look.

'I'm heading to the bar, my shout,' he said, standing. 'Same again, everyone?' He strolled to the bar, but Pepper's eyes didn't linger. Why had Keegan left? She was hoping he would join them.

In her peripheral vision, a woman neared. 'Is that you, Pepper Cassidy?' the woman asked. She leaned against the table, clearly drunk, slopping a full beer. Her legs wobbled like gummi bears.

Pepper squinted at the skinny woman trying to figure out who she was, but the hazel eyes held hers. 'Judith Simpson?' She stood, putting her arms out to her old friend.

'Ronson now, but yes. What's it been thirty years?' Judith did not return the hug.

Pepper stepped back, worried at how skinny Judith was. Pepper once envied Judith's curvaceous body. She tried not to look stunned. Was Judith sick? 'How are you?'

Judith glared at Maisy, top lip curled up. 'Be better if this bitch didn't steal my house.'

Reaching gently for her arm, Maisy said, 'Come on, Judith, you know the bank foreclosed on your parents. It's not our fault we bought your old family home.'

Judith shrugged her away, turning her back to Maisy and Trevor. 'Shut up. Seems you've also stolen my best friend.'

'Judith, do you want to sit. Catch up for old time's sake.' Pepper tried to appease her. 'Or why don't you call over the beach house for a cuppa sometime.'

'Right, of course, you got your mother's house, didn't ya?' Judith lifted a beer to her lips, glaring over the top of it. 'As always, you have every fuckin' thing. Nice house, cute kid, friends, guys drooling over ya. And what do I have? Fuckin' nothin'.'

'Come on, Judith, luv. I think maybe you've had a few too many schooners and aren't thinking clearly,' Trevor said, glancing around as if hoping the publican would kick her out.

'Nah. Piss off. I'm right as rain. Where's your rich husband, Pepper? Surely he's not the big Kiwi or that Italian guy.'

'No. He's a friend.' She pointed to Tui standing at the bar. 'I'm in the middle of a divorce. Things didn't work out with Ian.' She knew not to ask about Bobby, knowing he was in jail, and it was bound to be a touchy subject.

'Guess you heard they didn't work out with Bobby 'n' me either.' She sculled some beer as if it were making her problems go away. 'Still married to the dickhead, though. At least he's locked up for a few years.'

'I'm sorry, Judith.' Pepper meant it.

'It's alright. It is what it is. At least I have my boy.' She glanced away. 'Hey! I might take you up on calling in one day. See ya,' Judith said, staggering away with a barman following her.

He stopped Judith and asked her to drink water from now on. She spat beer in his face, which gave him no alternative, but to banish her from the beer garden.

'Jesus, what was that?' asked Tui, returning with beers and wine.

'An old friend,' said Pepper frowning. 'She's had a tough time of it.'

'Pepper, I know that look. You cannot go fixing her,' said Maisy.

'We used to be close. I can't believe she's let herself go so much.

She used to have so much pride in her looks. It's sad to watch.'

'Just be careful, luv,' said Trev. 'She's a bit of a loose cannon that one. Bobby used to beat her after he lost his job. The poor woman hasn't acted like herself since.'

Pepper's heart ached for her old friend. If only Judith would have let her hug her and help her through her turmoil.

Maisy and Trev called it a night, but she stayed chatting with Tui late into the evening. She'd drunk too much wine and was feeling sorry for herself over Keegan's rebuff and worried for Judith and the son who was dating Livia.

It wouldn't hurt to let a bit of the libido out of her system with Tui. A one night stand at her age, though? She had better morals than that. But, Tui's hand trailed her inner thigh, sparking a fire. Keegan may have ignited it, but Tui took the flame and ran with it. Tui's fingers edged the elastic of her underwear. She sucked in a breath, slapping his hand.

'I want to bed you, Pepper.' His deep voice whispered in her ear, melting her resolve. *Sex was just sex, right?*

She wobbled to her feet. 'You can walk me home, but that's it,' she said, trying to avoid his fuck-me gaze.

'Sure. Come on.' He took her hand, leading her away from the tavern.

He tried kissing her on the way home. She resisted but let him hold her hand, and even that felt odd. She leant on his arm, feeling fuzzy with booze. A slight headache formed on her temple, throbbing, intent on worsening. She needed water and a bed—not a man who was hoping for a bounce between the sheets.

Tui walked her up the stairs. The regular kookaburra sat on the rail staring at them. 'A bit tame, eh?' he asked. Before she had time to answer he waved his arms around, shooing the bird.

Pepper took three goes to insert the key in the door, finally flinging it open. Turning to say goodbye, she realised Tui was in the doorway, trying to kiss her neck.

Switching the hall light on, she blinked in the glow, ducking out of his grasp. 'Do you want a water before you go? I'm thirsty.' She wobbled to the kitchen, leaning heavily on the bench, before reaching for the fridge. Passing him a water bottle, she took a swig of hers, remembering Keegan reaching around her and trapping her against the sink. Her heart was elsewhere, not with the man in front of her.

'I'm sorry, Tui. This is not going anywhere.'

He stepped close. 'Why? You're giving me all the signals.'

'I'm not. I've drunk too much.'

He raised his eyebrows. 'Not so much that we couldn't still do it.' He trailed a big hand over her shoulder.

'No.' She said it firmly, but he moved into her personal space, dwarfing her.

He leant in to kiss her. The front door slammed.

'Really, Mum?' Liv screamed. 'How could you? And a teacher too.'

'I'm not—.'

Tui at least looked guilty. 'I'll see you, late-a.' He strode out the door, slamming it as well.

Liv stormed to her room, slamming that door also. Pepper's headache took full hold, like a nail hammered into her head. She clutched it, leaning on the bench. Glancing out the window as she reached for a box of Nurofen, she caught a glimpse of Keegan on his verandah, the dog faithfully by his side. He watched Tui walk up the road before casting his eyes her way. He shook his head and went inside. Gus followed.

Pepper clutched her stomach, not knowing whether she wanted to throw up because of the alcohol or due to her heart breaking. Keegan would assume, especially, because it was past 1 am, that she and Tui had—

She slumped her head in her hands. Keegan would have every right to think it. What if he hated her? Had she ruined their chance? *And, what was up with Liv?*

Chapter Twenty-One

Sherry reluctantly conceded, agreeing to Joe staying for the next two weeks.

'Thank you,' Keegan said to her. 'You won't regret it. I promise.' He dropped his phone on the table, shot a namaste prayer to the blue sky, and performed a happy dance.

Gus yapped his approval before taking up a soldier position in front of the kennel, where fat, full kittens slept on top of each other like tumbled washing.

With a grin on his face, he drove into town to shop for special things for Joe. While there, he'd give his statement to the police. He'd pushed Pepper's betrayal to the back of his mind, but it kept floating to the surface like a cork, bobbing in front of his vision no matter which way he looked. Slamming his fist on the steering wheel did nothing to release his pent-up annoyance, but he knew better than to let things bottle up.

After giving his statement, he realised with relief; he wasn't a suspect. The police traced the drugs and were close to putting a case together. Of course, they didn't divulge any further details. It was Dane's day off, so he couldn't push him for specifics either.

At the local Coles, he bought enough food to feed a footy team. Being unsure of Joe's favourites, he couldn't leave anything out. The toy store was just as baffling. Did Joe still like dinosaurs, or was he into superheroes now? Or would he rather colour-in or play football? With a sinking heart, realising how little time he'd spent with his son in recent time hurt deep.

He was about to drive home but walked past the pet store and decided to go in.

'Hi,' he said to the young girl at the counter.

'How can I help you?' she said with a smile, petting the bird on her shoulder. 'He's a cockatiel. Scooby is his name. Do you like him? We have more.'

'No, actually. I have kittens. Seven of them.'

'For sale? Are you a breeder?'

'Nope. Giving them away.' The bird pooped on her shoulder, green and slushy.

'Why?' She didn't seem to care about the bird shit.

'They were abandoned. They're not even mine.'

'Oh, I see. I can put up a notice and see if anyone is interested. Did you hear about cats maimed by the dingo pack?'

'Yeah, I guess that's why these kittens don't have a mum.'

'Oh, right. At least the rangers have moved the pack on, so they're not so close to town.' She picked up a pen. 'How many male and female?'

He scratched his head.

She grinned. 'Never mind. How many?' The bird repeated her. *Never mind. How many?*

'Seven. No. Make that six.'

Six, six, six, the bird said, repeating it like a broken record.

'Aww, you got sucked in, and you're keeping one, right?'

'Yeah.' *Oddball.*

The girl promised she'd give him a call if there were any interest, wiping shit off her shoulder with a paper towel.

He left the pet store. Perhaps those who'd had their cat killed by the native animals were looking for a new kitten to replace their beloved pet.

Once home, he made up the single bed, placed toys on top and stared at the room, his heart thumping. He'd painted it red, white and blue, the colours of Joe's footy team, The Roosters. At least he still hoped his son barracked for them. Funny that a kid from Brissy didn't want to support the Broncos, but he liked how Joe was already an individual, making his mind up with no persuasion from others, even his mum, who was so die-hard Broncos you'd think she'd actually played Rugby League. She loved the fact women now played, not that she'd break a nail to give it a go herself.

That afternoon, he sat on the deck waiting for Sherry's car, drumming his fingers on the table where a textbook lay unopened. By sundown, he was angry. By dark, he was worried.

He put off ringing Sherry, not wanting to distract her driving, but the phone sat heavy and unringing in his hand. When Dane's marked police car pulled up, he was terrified. He wanted to slam his hands over his ears. *No! Police arriving when someone hadn't come home always spelt—*

Dane in uniform and a female officer walked towards him, taking their caps off and placing them over their chests. He stood on wobbly feet, walking down the stairs to greet them on the driveway. *Not Joe. Please, not Joe.*

'Keegan, I'm sorry,' said Dane.

His heart stalled, totally stopped beating. *No, no more words.*

The woman nodded at Dane encouraging him to speak.

Dane gulped. 'Your wife, Sherry Dallas, was in an accident. A driver t-boned—

Keegan hunched over, his head in his hands. 'No, shut up!'

'She's—um—didn't make it. Your son is injured but alive.'

Keegan raised moist eyes. 'Dead?' he asked. It couldn't, wouldn't sink in. Not beautiful, vibrant Sherry. For the pain in his arse that she was, he couldn't picture her gone. *So young, beautiful—gone.* His fists clenched and unclenched while tears brimmed in his eyes.

'Yes,' the female officer said with a frown, touching his shoulder. 'It was instant.' *As if that made any fucking difference.*

He shrugged her hand off, stepping away and pacing. 'Joe, where is Joe. He'll be scared. Oh, my God, my son. How can he get over seeing that? Having that fear? Is he okay? He needs me. This is wrong, so wrong—' Keegan sobbed into his hands.

'We'll take you. Chopper's ready to fly Joe to Queensland Children's Hospital in Brisbane.'

Keegan stood, shook himself. Get together for Joe. 'I'll grab some stuff. He ran inside. His fingers were shaking when he stuffed Joe's clothes and new soft toys in an overnight bag. He couldn't yet face what shape Joe might be. *My precious, beautiful child.*

***

Pepper saw the police cars in Keegan's drive, and her stomach lurched. She ran from her house to Keegan's with Liv behind her.

'What's happened? Is Keegan okay?' she blurted mid-stride.

Dane frowned. 'It's his estranged wife and son.'

'What?'

'Sherry Dallas died in a car accident half an hour ago. Her son, Joe, is being choppered to hospital. He's critical but stable. They believe he'll pull through.'

Liv stopped, eyes wide in disbelief. 'Oh, my God. Poor Keegan.'

Tears sprung from Pepper's eyes. Her heart split, twisted and ached. *Keegan.*

He ran from the house with a full overnight bag over his shoulder. His beautiful eyes were moist and darkly haunted. She ran to him, flinging her arms around his waist. 'I'm so sorry. What can I do?'

He passed her his key, the tic in his jaw was evident. 'Look after Gus and the kittens.' He kissed her forehead, looking pale in his olive skin.

Her heart broke for him. 'I will. Ring me when you get a chance. Cry on my shoulder. Whatever you need.'

'Me too,' said Liv, walking towards the kittens and Gus, tears trailing her young cheeks.

'Thanks.' He squeezed Pepper to him as if drawing strength, then let her go. He reached down to ruffle Gus's fur as the dog whined. 'Stay.'

Pepper knelt beside the dog. 'He'll be home soon, boy.'

Keegan followed the police to the waiting car, glancing back with harrowing sadness in his dark eyes.

The dog barked, trying to pull towards the police car.

Keegan's life changed in the blink of an eye, and there was nothing Pepper could do to comfort him. Tears trailed her lips, salty and bitter. She watched them drive away while his dog howled into the starry night sky until the dingos in the bush joined in.

Chapter Twenty-Two

Squeaks of rubber shoes on linoleum echoed up the hallway along with the clatter of trolleys holding linen or food. Machines attached to Keegan's tiny son beeped and hummed. He wanted to pull every friggin' piece away from Joe, his perfect child, but knew his little body needed them all to heal. It was the most distressing thing Keegan had ever seen or suffered. *Hell.*

He'd been a paramedic for over fifteen years, but nothing equated to the misery he was in, watching his defenceless baby. He felt useless, inadequate, and shameful. How could he have ever said a bad word about Sherry when life was so fragile?

Dropping his head on Joe's stiff bed sheets, he let the tears flow, clutching Joe's tiny, cold hand, willing strength into his body. *Don't die on me, Joe. I can't live without you.*

His mind scrambled with what their future held with no Sherry. Joe, motherless. It was incomprehensible. He took a deep breath, reached for his phone and made the call. 'Danny, bro—,' Keegan stammered before the tears took over.

'Keegs, are you okay? What's wrong?' his brother asked. The deep concern in his voice was like a hug over the phone.

'Not me, Dan. Sherry—she—she's dead. I'm at the children's hospital with Joe.'

'Fuck, man. Jesus! Fuck. Joe's alright though, yeah?'

'They haven't said much yet, but I checked his chart. They induced a coma to stop fluid in his brain due to cerebral edema. He's cut and bruised, busted ankle too, but my guess he's going to be okay—at least physically.' His fingers shook, holding the phone.

'Good. A relief. Right, um. I'll get to you soon as I can. Have you rung Mum and Dad?'

'Nah, can you? I can't. I'm in shock. Still compartmentalising it all, so I don't go off the rails and end up no bloody help to Joe. Dan, it's hard to keep it together.' His brother, the Navy vet, was one person who understood the way PTSD distorted the world and sent you within warp speed to a dark place you never planned to be in but somehow found yourself there.

'Will do. I'll be there soon. Hang in, Keegs. Love ya.'

Keegan dropped the phone on the bed. He woke to it, beeping in his ear. Disorientated, he glanced at the monitors, then at Joe. *No change.* His tiny bare chest rose and fell, machines beeped incessantly, graphs and numbers shining from the screens, keeping a check on his vitals. Keegan remained in the nightmare. He shook his head and glanced at the phone, noticing a missed call. It went to voicemail but he didn't bother listening. Instead rang her.

Pepper's voice was soft and comforting. 'How are you doing, Keegan? Noone's heard. Everyone's worried.'

'Sorry—I don't know what to say.' He rested his head in his palm, leaning on the bed with his elbow.

'You don't have to. Just know we're here for you.'

'I feel this massive guilt. I don't know if I can ever shake it.' He confessed, trying to stem the tears and sick of himself for shedding so many.

'It's an accident. There's nothing you could do.'

'Yep. I know. It's not that. It's some stuff I said I can never take back now. It's too fucking bloody late. Sorry.'

'What, you're apologising for swearing? Swear away. I always do. And I say the F word a hell of a lot more than you. Swearing gets the shit out of your system like nothing else. Scream it to the high heavens if you need to.' He heard her take a deep breath as if she were scared to ask. 'How's Joe?'

'Stable.' He glanced at the angel on the bed, stroking his face. 'He'll be okay. Just needs to let his brain shrink back to normal size, and thank fuck he'll make a full recovery.'

'Oh, gosh, that's so good to hear.'

He chuckled. 'You said gosh, and I said the F word. That is so unlike you, Pepper Cassidy.'

'I'm trying to be a supportive friend, and not using expletives every second is a good thing, right?'

'You just told me I should swear.'

'You, not me. I'm trying to kerb it. A woman my age shouldn't curse just because she runs building sites and needs to act like the men and intimidate them where necessary.'

'You intimidate me without swearing.' He chuckled and realised he hadn't done that since the accident.

'Really?'

'Pepper, you never needed to swear to get men to work for you.' It was nice to be distracted by her voice. 'You only thought you had to become one of them. You have enough swagger to do what you do without swearing.' He squeezed Joe's hand, hoping for a response.

'Swagger? I never knew I had swagger. How did we get on this subject? I believe you're shifting from how you really feel, Keegan Dallas.' He heard her sigh. 'I'm worried about you.'

'I'll be okay.' He glanced at Joe's angelic face and knew it without a doubt. *Joe.* Joe was relying on him. 'How's Gus and the kittens?'

'We've moved them to my place. They're on the deck near Liv's room. She sneaks them into her room. I don't care. She's obsessed with them, nearly as much as Ross Ronson.' He pictured her rolling her eyes.

'Ross isn't so bad, Pep. Give the kid a chance.'

'Really? He's the Romeo of Blueshell Beach. I've heard the talk. And, with his dad in jail, how is anyone keeping the kid in check? Judith doesn't seem up to the task, poor girl.'

'Pepper, he's okay. Some of the other kids Liv hangs with; I'm not so sure.' A knock and the door to Joe's private room opened. 'Gotta go, my brother's here. Thanks, Pep. It means a lot.' He hung up on the love of his life and stood to let his brother hug him. Dan's wife, Trudy, stood back, holding a slightly engorged belly. Tears pooled in her eyes when she stared at Joe. They were yet to have children but, after two IVF bouts, were desperate to start their family. Trudy's emotions about her beloved nephew, Joe, spilled over in tears trailing her freckled cheeks.

She moved to Joe's bedside and leaned to kiss his forehead. 'He looks so tiny,' she said, swirling one hand over her stomach.

'You're pregnant, Trude?' Keegan asked, hoping it was true.

Dan grinned, taking his wife's waist and kissing her cheek. 'Finally, yes, we are. Haven't told anyone yet, waiting on the next scan.'

Trudy nodded, smiling through her tears. 'We're happy but are so worried about Joe. Tell us the truth, Keegan. He's going to be okay?' She reached for a tissue and wiped her tears. 'Sorry, it's the pregnancy hormones.' She blew her nose, and Dan squeezed her tighter.

Feeling dog tired, Keegan yawned. 'Yeah. I'm sure he is. He's breathing on his own. He'll wake soon. I need coffee.' He rolled his shoulders.

'I'll get it.' Trudy offered. 'You'll want a pep up before your folks arrive. Have you eaten?'

'Nah, haven't been able to stomach it.'

'You need to eat. I'll get you something.' Once she left, Danny ran his large hand over Joe's angelic face. Danny was taller and broader than Keegan, but they had the same olive skin and dark hair, though Danny's was more salt than pepper and cut short as if he were still in the military.

'Man, I don't know how you can watch him like this.'

'Barely can, but I'm all he's got now.'

'So weird to think of Sherry as gone, eh? Boy, she was a pain in the ass.' He chuckled. 'But she had sass that girl.'

'Mmm, attitude in buckets. Her dad's headed to the university hospital, where they took her—body. He's pissed off Joe couldn't go there. I told him this hospital is best for Joe with the paediatric specialists.'

'He blaming you?' Dan asked what Keegan assumed. They'd always been in sync that way.

'Probably.'

'Not your fault. Don't ever think—.'

'She was dropping Joe at my place. It's hard not to.' Antiseptic and peroxide wafted in the stuffy hospital suite. You'd think he'd get used to those smells, but he never did. It was preferable to smelling blood though, it always got him worse and pushed the panic buttons he'd only recently been able to control.

'Don't go down that road, bro. You've only recently got back on track. Hey, when does the new job start?'

'Supposed to be in a fortnight. I can't even think about it with Joe in here.'

'I'm proud you got it.'

'Thanks.' He glanced at his beeping phone. Messages from Trev, Liv and Dane. 'Hopefully, it will lead back to rescue work.'

'Yeah, I can't picture you in an office environment for long. You'll get there.'

Joe's eyes blinked. Keegan dropped the phone on the food table and stared. 'Joe, son? Hey, Dad's here. Uncle Danny too.' He pressed the call button above the bed to let the nurses know Joe was out of the coma.

A tear slipped from Joe's eye, down one pale cheek. How the hell was Keegan supposed to tell him about his mum? 'Daddy, I'm scared,' Joe said in a tiny, scratchy voice. It broke his heart, but Joe was awake. Keegan had to be strong. *Falling apart but staying together.*

He stroked Joe's forehead and leant in to kiss his cheek. 'I'm here for you, Joe. I'm not going anywhere.' Glancing at Joe's heart rate and stats, Keegan knew his son was on the mend, at least physically. Dan was there, and his parents would arrive within the hour to lend their support, but Keegan had never felt so alone. *Just Joe and I now.*

He'd wished for it, but not like this. Without Sherry, it was bittersweet.

***

A cool breeze gusted from the Pacific Ocean with the promise of another storm. Dark clouds built in the west, rolling and groaning, and the humidity dropped along with the temperature. Enough for Liv to grab a long-sleeved shirt to throw over her singlet top. It curved over her blossoming body showing too much pert breast. Pepper frowned, knowing quite well what Ross Ronson saw in her lovely daughter. But she hoped he also loved Liv for the sweet girl she was. *If he took advantage of her, he was toast.*

Liv's veggie garden needed rain, but she wanted to cover some fragile vegetables in case the storm was intense, as was often the case in the near tropics. Liv ran to the garden with Gus following at her heels. He let out an enthusiastic bark, wagging his tail as they rounded the house.

Pepper sat in the sunroom thinking about Keegan. *How was he coping?* Was he grieving his ex-wife? How would he manage as a single parent? Was his heart so broken he'd never get back to the cheerful Keegan, who only so recently emerged? *A lot of bloody questions.* If only he'd answer her phone messages. She glanced at the phone, willing him, but he was probably busy talking to doctors, and his family had arrived to rally around him. He probably didn't need her phone calls as much as she needed to talk to him.

Trying to figure a way to help, she lifted a cup of tea to her mouth. Yes, she minded the pets, but surely there was more. Liv ran towards the house with raindrops the size of ten-cent pieces plopping on the ground, splashing up dirt with the water. She held the shirt over her head, bolting inside from the quick downpour. Wet clothing plastered her young body.

Keegan's dog's muddy paw prints trailed into the sunroom. Gus paused, shook himself like a wet sponge and sprayed dirty water over Pepper's feet. 'Gus, you have better manners, surely.' Pepper stood, almost spilling the tea. 'Out on the back deck with the kittens, now!'

Liv giggled. 'He didn't mean it, Mum.'

'I know. I can hardly get mad with him. He's such a sweet dog.'

'Can we have one of the kittens?' Liv asked. 'I'd keep it safe so the dingos or foxes or whatever wouldn't get it. It would be an inside-at-nighttime cat.'

'Yes, you'd have to. Our native wildlife don't need cats in their territory any more than we want them in ours?' Pepper said. Her poor mother's cat. Mum would have been distraught about her pet's fate and wondering where she was. Pepper shivered. 'I hope Chloe turns up soon. Come to think of it.' Strolling into the kitchen, she placed the teacup on the sink. 'Keegan wanted to tell me something about it.'

Liv's eyes grew wide. 'Really. He didn't find her, though?' Liv's gaze dropped. *A sure sign she's hiding something.*

'Not sure. Did you talk to Mum's friend Mrs Walters when you dropped the brochure off?'

'She didn't seem to be home. I could hear her cat meowing,

though. For a lady who wrote you a nice note of welcome, she hasn't been all that friendly. I'll secure Gus and the kittens, and then I need a shower,' she yelled as the storm intensified and rain slammed onto the tin roof.

Pepper glanced up at the second floor, checking for leaks through the ceiling. Thankfully she'd secured the sheeting earlier in the day with the help of some tradies. The unfinished areas were tarped and tied off in preparation for another summer storm. Pausing her hand near the new staircase shining wet with paint, she smiled. It reminded her of Keegan following her up there, touching, catching her, kissing, almost—'

When Liv emerged fresh and sweet in short cotton pyjamas, Pepper hugged her tight.

'What's that for?' Liv squirmed out of her hold.

'I'm happy you're safe. Poor little Joe.'

'And Keegan,' Liv said. 'Can you imagine?'

'Not really, and I never want to. He must be scared for Joe's future. It's got me thinking we should drive to Brisbane over the weekend. Maybe take you out of school early on Friday and head down. We'll see if your dad is free to see you for a few hours.'

Liv rubbed her hands. 'Could we? Dad didn't ring on Saturday, though. Do you think he'd want to see me?' she asked, with a frown, but Pepper sensed there was anger in the question too.

'He's your dad. Of course, he will.'

'I know you don't like me on my phone before dinner, but can I at least ring Ross and tell him I won't be here this weekend?'

'Sure. Be quick.' She wondered why Liv was staying home more and avoiding Jodi's house. There seemed something odd about the wealthy family high on Moon Beach. It was disappointing because Pepper pinned her hopes on Jodi, distracting Liv from Ross, at least a little. *Young love.* Who was she to mess with it? She remembered the thrill of those first loved-up feelings.

The same sentiments were brewing for Keegan. But would he have the energy to fit her into his world after the accident? *Life had a way of switching in an instant.* There was no point in feeling sorry for herself. Keegan needed a friend right now, and that's all she could be.

On Friday, they left Blueshell Beach at midday, hoping to arrive in Brisbane before two pm. A truck rollover unhinged that plan. Liv slept with tiny snores escaping her lips during the traffic crawl.

Pepper lifted and stretched her shoulders, trying to relax. There was nothing she could do about the delay. When they finally neared the accident, she jolted with realisation. Under the truck, a small red car wedged in the middle twisted like a bloody wound. Firefighters and paramedics seemed in slow motion, trying to save the unfortunate people inside. One gurney rushed to a waiting ambulance, a bloody and bandaged figure on board. Pepper looked away, goosebumps spiking her arms.

Only two week's ago, Keegan's family were the casualties on the side of the road. 'Fuck, slow down, people,' she said, under her breath, banging the steering wheel. Illness rested in the pit of her stomach like shifting jelly. The only consolation—the traffic hit one-hundred kilometres, and they'd be at Ian's mother's West End home in twenty minutes.

Pulling up in front of the substantial old brick cottage in inner Brisbane, she shook Liv's shoulder with her hand. 'Livia. We're at Dad's. Wake up, sweetie.'

Liv lifted one eye, looking around, getting her bearings. She yawned, stretching thin arms. 'That was quick,' she said.

Pepper rolled her eyes. 'Except for the hour wait to pass a major accident.'

'Really. You should have woken me.'

'You didn't want to see it. I promise.' *And neither did I.* 'Did you get an answer from Dad?'

Liv checked her phone. 'Oh, shite. He said he's not at Nan's. He'll come get me from the hospital and take me out to dinner. Somewhere fancy, he says, with a smiley face.'

'Oh, really?' *I hope he turns up for your sake, Liv.* 'Let's go to the hospital now. We'll grab a coffee and head up to see Keegan and Joe.'

'Does Keegan know we're coming?' Liv's eyes clouded. She stared at her father's house, chewing her nails, clearly annoyed he'd changed plans.

'Yep.' Didn't want us to come. *But we're coming anyway.*

148

***

Keegan asked the neurosurgeon, 'So why do you think he's not talking. Will his speech come back and when?'

The tall, skinny man's spectacles nearly fell from the brim of his nose. He looked across the top of the chart with a slight frown, righting them. 'As I said, the brain is an amazing thing. Being so young, there's more bounce to Joe's brain than in adults. His last scans showed nothing abnormal. There's no cerebral edema. The reason he's mute could be either neurological or mental. He's possibly grieving and can't or won't articulate it. It's called psychogenic mutism.'

Keegan nodded. He'd come to the same conclusion. 'It's frustrating. I don't know how to help him. With Joe only just starting school, I can't even get him to write what he's thinking.' He glanced towards the bed where Joe lay sleeping peacefully. His tiny, pale body no longer had anything attached to it. And it was a relief, but Keegan longed for his child to speak again. On one side, the blankets bulged where the moon boot covered Joe's broken ankle to mid-calf.

'He spoke when he woke up—just one sentence.' *Hope.*

'Yes, it's in the notes, so a good sign. More than likely, Joe's muteness is temporary, maybe even selective. I've arranged a psych counsel.'

'Okay,' Keegan said, taking a deep breath. He knew about selective muteness. It was part of his experience with PTSD. 'What after that?'

'You'll have to take it day by day until his speech returns. Limit his movements for a few months to let the brain heal. The broken ankle may be a blessing in keeping him less active. No jumping, contact sport, running, trampolines, wrestling.

'Okay. I know.'

'He can go back to everyday life, return to school and play soon after. There will be check-ups. He's a very lucky boy.'

Yeah, really? He just lost his mother. Keegan shook his head.

The doctor scribbled on the chart, latched it to the end of Joe's hospital bed and strolled to the door. 'You'll need to keep him occupied with new activities. Introduce him to new people who won't remind him of the event.' He said it like the accident was a rock concert, not something that had tragically killed Sherry. 'I'll pop in next week. Hopefully, we can discharge him then.'

Keegan's heart skittered. *Joe home. Thank God.* But the new job started Monday. He had no idea how he was going to wing it. Joe needed him, but the job meant more than just a career—*it was lifeblood, redemption and healing.*

Mum offered to come and stay, of course. Perhaps it was the only way he could get through the first few weeks of being a single dad with a shiftwork career. But, his mum, God love her, was hard work. Yes, loving but such a controlling fusspot. She'd rearrange his house, diet, lifestyle, and before long, she'd drive him bonkers.

He paced the linoleum floors trying to find a solution. Dad wouldn't know how to look after Joe, let alone a dog and seven kittens. Danny and Trudy were expecting their first child. He couldn't disrupt their special time and didn't want to. There were people in Blueshell Beach he could rely on, surely. *Maybe, maybe not.* He'd only been in the town a year. Was it too much to expect of people?

His train of thought drifted when Pepper and Livia knocked on the open door and strolled in. Liv held a big blue bear attached to a helium balloon in one hand and her ever-present mobile phone in the other. Pepper wore a grin and a snug-fitting jumpsuit that looked stylish, but he found hot-damn sexy.

'Hey, you two,' Pepper said, singsongy and bright as the sun. He'd missed her and her friggin' optimism.

'Hi.' He stood, not knowing whether to hug them or shoo them away.

***

Keegan smiled, but his handsome face showed lines of fatigue, grief, and shock. Dark eyes clouded with old tears were—*haunted*. The three-day growth on his chin and upper lip were probably closer to five and an almost-beard. It nearly covered the hollow of his cheeks but not quite. Pepper could no longer make out the dimple in his chin.

'You haven't eaten for days. Have you?' she said, not waiting for an answer. She wrapped her arms around him, feeling ribs. 'I'm so sorry this has happened to you and Joe.' Tears brimmed, but she tried holding them, knowing he needed other people's strength. His slighter weight leaned into her, large arms circling her shoulders. His fingers gave a brief squeeze as if thanking her.

150

Keegan let go and strode to Liv, who cuddled into him, her cheek resting on his chest, the balloon bobbing above them. He glanced at Pepper over Liv's blonde head with a look saying, I think she likes me. *Probably more than her father.*

'Thanks for coming,' he said, taking the bear and resuming the seat beside Joe's bed. He placed the bear on the shelf near Joe's head. The balloon moved up and down for a while before settling. 'I told you not to, Pepper. It's too far to come.'

'Not really. Liv's seeing her dad. He lives at West End.'

He glanced at Liv. 'That's good. Are you staying with him?'

'Doubt it, not with Nan.' She pulled a face. Unfortunately, she'd never bonded with her overbearing paternal grandmother. 'Mum booked a motel, and I'll stay with her, probably. Dad's taking me to dinner at some swanky restaurant. He thinks he can spend money on me to make up for stuff.'

'I'm sure he means well. He'd be keen to see you,' Keegan said kindly.

Liv shrugged her shoulders. 'How's the little fella doing?' she asked, tactically changing the subject.

'Good. He should be awake soon.' Keegan smiled down at his angelic child. Love shone from his dark eyes. He explained Joe's brain injury and how well it healed. Kids were resilient. Pepper nodded, only taking in the fact Joe would recover. 'So, it's a relief after everything we've been through in the past two weeks. I just wish he'd talk to me.'

'Doesn't want to speak about the accident? It's understandable,' Pepper said, twisting her hands together to avoid reaching out. She wanted to touch Keegan—*give him strength.*

'No. Joe isn't talking at all.' He shook his head.

Pepper baulked, touched her cheeks with fingertips, steadied her wobbly legs and found her way to a chair at the foot of the bed. *Psychogenic mutism.* Could she confess her own story of muteness?

'You okay, Mum?' Liv asked.

Keegan's eyebrows furrowed.

'Fine. Just hate hospitals. It's overwhelming.'

'Dad's downstairs,' Liv said, turning her phone to prove it. 'I gotta go. I'll get him to drop me at the unit later. See ya, Keegan. Love ya, Mum.' She planted a kiss on her cheek.

'If he's drinking, give me a call, and I'll pick you up,' she said, glancing at Keegan. The thought of the drunk driver who killed Sherry was on her mind, and probably Keegan's too.

Chapter Twenty-Three

'The funeral was Wednesday, right? Did you go?' Pepper asked. She was standing on the other side of the bed staring at Joe with moist eyes, trailing her hand gently down his small arm.

'How did you know? And, no, I couldn't leave Joe when the service was on the Sunshine Coast.' Pepper's presence in Joe's hospital room gave him the strength he didn't know he needed from her.

'It's been splashed all over the papers—you know about the guy, right?' She glanced at him, new concern flashing across violet eyes.

'Yeah, she said she had a boyfriend.' He squeezed Joe's tiny hand. 'Joe didn't like him. And I didn't care.'

'Erol Fitzgerald, you know the mining family, very rich. He'd bought her a house at Mooloolaba, a unit overlooking the Storey Bridge and jewellery, other things. He's acting like her saviour.'

What? Sherry never said. 'Doesn't matter now, does it?' *It does explain the Land Rover, though.* And it was probably the reason she didn't fight him over Joe living with him every fortnight. She'd wanted her freedom to date some rich snob.

Joe's eyes fluttered 'Joey.' Big adorable dark eyes stared first at him and then at Pepper. He blinked faster, lifting his hand to touch hers.

'Hi there, Joe. I'm Pepper, a friend of your Dad's.' Her voice softened, kind and patient. 'Are you feeling better? I hear you went for a ride around the wards in a wheelchair yesterday. That's awesome, huh. You're a brave boy.'

Joe's eyes widened. He glanced at Keegan as if asking how she knew. Keegan nodded, feeling grateful his son was alive. 'And, you'll be able to put pressure on the moon boot soon and get out of the wheelchair. You'll be running around before you know it, son.'

Joe nodded, reaching for Keegan's hand. He squeezed it with his little fingers, glancing at the door and back a couple of times. Was he wanting to know why Sherry wasn't coming, or maybe he knew what had happened. It was difficult to tell when Joe wouldn't speak. Keegan gulped, unable to find the words to comfort him. Maybe if they both never talked about it, it didn't happen.

Pepper sighed. 'Joe, when I was a bit older than you, something scary happened to me.' She gave Keegan a small crooked smile. 'I was so upset and shocked. I guess I didn't talk for a bit. Like you, I needed to keep it inside. Is that how you feel, sweetie?'

Joe nodded with his bottom lip wobbling. He tried to sit, pushing his hands against the mattress. Keegan pressed the button to ease the bed to a sitting position. He shifted Joe's pillow to make him more comfortable while tears stained his cheeks. 'Do you want to hear more about Pepper not talking, Joe?' He asked, shooting her a thank-you look.

Joe nodded, staring at Pepper. He was usually timid around strangers, but her aura oozed safety and protection. She probably didn't even know she did it, but it made her even more appealing. He smiled despite the situation. Joe reached for Pepper's hand, curling his tiny fingers over her's.

'I—well, you see, Joe. I saw something I didn't want to see. Something frightening, and being little, I couldn't understand it at all. So the doctors tell me my brain wanted to forget it. But because people needed to know about it, they kept asking questions I couldn't answer. My voice disappeared, and I didn't mind that I couldn't speak of it. It's like the brain protects you for a while. When you're ready to talk, you will but not yet, and that's okay. You don't have to stress about it. It's a normal way to cope. Okay?'

Joe turned to Keegan, grabbing his hand, squeezing as if to say, Dad, see, I don't mean to not talk to you. 'It's okay, Joey. I know you need to heal. It's like when I moved away. It wasn't because I didn't love you. It was because I'd seen scary stuff, too, at work. My brain needed to get better, as well. I didn't stop talking, well much anyway, but it's the same thing.'

154

'What? You hardly ever talk,' Pepper said, winking at Joe and laughing. 'It's like pulling teeth.'

Joe nodded, a tiny smile tugging his lips, but he didn't utter a word.

Keegan shook his head but grinned at them. 'You talk when you're ready, Joe, but as I always told you, sometimes it's not words, but actions that speak louder. Like when I hug you tight, I'm showing you how much I love you.' Joe leaned his head to kiss Keegan's hand, like a butterfly landing. It made his heart burst, knowing Joe understood everything he said. His brain healed, but now he needed to work on his broken heart.

Soon after, Joe fell asleep, and Pepper shifted her chair nearer to Keegan's. She rested her head on his shoulder and reached for his hand. Joe slept with little slurpy snores escaping his sweet lips.

'That was about your dad, right?' Keegan asked her.

'Yeah, the garage stuff. I was ten, and I didn't talk again for six months. When I could speak, I asked to go to a boarding school because I couldn't see our garage every day. Mum, though heartbroken herself, complied. I'm sure she missed me, but she must have realised I needed that time. I came home during school holidays but avoided the garage. It was like a black hole that didn't exist to me.'

'I get it.'

'Not talking helped me cope. I internalised it but somehow healed when my brain could finally wrap around the horror of it.' She sighed. 'Then, when I was eighteen, my brother, Tim, suicided too. He was obsessed with what Dad did and talked about it all the time, morbidly. A huge contrast to me.

His twin, my brother, who lives in New York, never forgave Dad for what happened to our family. It's why I have the house. Rob didn't want anything to do with it.' She took a deep breath. He squeezed her hand, lifted it and kissed it, then wiped the tears off her cheeks.

***

She glanced at Keegan feeling his pain and confusion. 'I think Joe will stay silent as long as it takes. Just give him love. That's what Mum did. She'd talk to me like I was answering her. I finally couldn't do it to her anymore. She's the reason I spoke again because she loved

155

me enough to never give up on me.' *Dad gave up. He never even knew I beat the ocean's rip.*

Keegan leant in, warm breath caressing her face. His lips touched hers, soft, perfect. After avoiding the temptation all day. *Bliss.* During the afternoon, he'd been so close she could smell coffee, aftershave and male. *Irresistible.* Their lips melded. Tongues twisted. Sparks ignited. She pulled away breathless and said, 'Just love Joe. Love is the only thing, Keegan.'

'It is,' he said, kissing her again. 'I love you, Pepper.' *What?* Her thudding heartbeat quickened further. *Had he really said—love?*

She smiled, lifting her lips from his. Rubbing a finger along her bottom lip, she glanced at Joe, trying to keep her composure and not happy dance in front of them. 'You need to love Joe right now, not me. Use your energy on him.'

'But later?'

'I'll be waiting.'

'No, Tui? I saw him leaving your house.'

'Never was. Tui walked me home and thought he had a chance. He never did. My heart belongs to my silent, caring, kind and handsome neighbour.' She giggled, feeling her face flush with delight and, yes—*love.* 'That's you, you know?'

'I figured that much at least.' He smiled, and the smoulder in his eyes was so Antonio Banderas but sexier.

***

His heart floated in his chest, hammering like the nail gun she used with such skill.

'Yes, Keegan. We have something I can't deny, but I have a teenager who has problems with her father, is hanging with the wrong crowd, has a boyfriend and asked me about the pill. You have a son who lost and is grieving his mother and a lot of adjusting to your new life. I think we need to concentrate on our families for the time being.'

'I know you're right, but while Joe's asleep, do you want to fool around?' He grinned, and it widened when she returned it with a sweet smile. She lifted her lips to his, and the kiss intensified, pushing his pulse and sending it straight to his cock. Pepper had no idea of the total effect she had on him, which was the biggest turn-on of all. She possessed power, but she wouldn't use it because she was full of love, cheerfulness and brightness like a star that didn't try to shine it just sparkled.

***

The following day Liv returned to the hospital with her mum, she felt cheerful and chatty, but deep down, she was peeved with her dad for not being attentive. 'Dad said I could get the bus down and visit any time. He was sorry that I couldn't stay because Nana said the house is too crowded already. But she goes to Europe next month. It's such a long bus trip, though, and I'd miss Ross,' she said.

'Maybe just for a weekend. It will be good for you to see more of your dad.' Her mum tilted her head with questions in her eyes.

'I guess. So how was little Joe when he woke.'

'Sweet but not talking. Keegan said they'll discharge him next week. I think we should offer to help. It's going to be a tough adjustment for them both. You head on up to the room. I've got to go to the ladies.'

Liv strolled to Joe's hospital suite finding Keegan sitting on the bed, smiling with pride. Joe was taking his first tentative steps with crutches. She clapped and said, 'You're like a superhero.'

Joe beamed in delight, taking further steps and glancing her way with big black eyes. 'He's got the knack.' Joe wobbled. Keegan put out his hand to steady him. 'Almost.'

The physio nodded. 'Great job, but let's go up the hallway.' He put a hand up to Keegan to stop him from following.

'Where's your mum?' he asked Liv.

'Coming. She's gone to the loo.' Liv shrugged her shoulders. 'Hey, Keegan?' she asked, 'have you heard about the drugs that were found?'

'My mate, Dane's on the case. Still not solved?'

'Why?'

'I–um, my boyfriend told me something. You can't tell anyone.' She glanced to the door, not wanting her mum to hear.

'My lips are sealed.'

'He reckons, and I don't want to dob, but I'm afraid for the kids taking it. I know who sells it.' She paused. Dobbing on her best friend didn't seem right.

'Which kids? And will you tell me who?'

'That doesn't matter.' God, why had she brought it up? Keegan

157

would dig until he got something. Was it so wrong to tell him? Surely it would save Jodi in the long run.

'Mmmm. Can I ask you, Liv? Was Ross or Hunter taking these drugs?'

Liv shrugged her thin shoulders but didn't deny it.

'And what about the rumours about you and Ross?'

Her gaze dropped to the floor. Keegan's scrutiny hurt. Like a dad sort of thing, she didn't want him to think bad of her. 'Untrue. Ross hasn't—we haven't. I don't know how it got around town. It's why I was happy to avoid people this weekend.'

'It's a small town, Liv. Things come out.'

'I asked Ross, and he didn't start it. I'm not sure who did, but it's horrible. Has Mum heard the rumour?' Her heart thumped as she waited for his answer. She knew how close Mum and Keegan were, even though the two adults were at pains to hide their feelings. She'd never seen her mum happier than in Keegan's presence.

The thing was, Livia liked him too. He was kind and compassionate with animals and had such a slow, thoughtful way it was impossible not to like him. Even Ross said he thought he was an okay dude.

'I don't think so.'

'Don't tell her—'

***

'Tell me what?' Pepper asked with a smile on her face. 'Joe's doing great out there.' She poked her thumb behind her shoulder towards the hall.

'He is,' Keegan said, his voice catching with pride. 'Pepper, I start a new job Monday. Wednesday Joe's probably coming home.'

'We'll help,' said Liv.

'Definitely.' Pepper smiled, touching his shoulder, sending sparks.

Maybe everything would work out after all. But what Liv revealed so far sat in his guts like lead. *Which of her friends was the drug dealer? It didn't make sense. And now, not only did he have Liv and Pepper to protect from the town's drug problem, but he also had Joe.*

Chapter Twenty-Four

Keegan's mum insisted on staying for the first week, but with his dad's help, he convinced her he could cope—*just Joe and him.* There was no way of getting Joe in a routine with his well-intentioned Greek mother interfering. He always felt more Australian than Greek, being the fourth generation and his dad being Australian, but his mum still held on to the traditions, particularly family gatherings. The fact that he'd married a good Greek girl like Sherry had always held favour, but in hindsight, it was probably more her decision than his.

On Sunday after dark, they arrived home from the hospital with the surf booming and cicadas humming under the gum trees. The sky was full of stars and a quarter moon. *Home.* But was it Joe's?

Joe was asleep in the back booster seat, head lolling with tiny lips half-open. Keegan opened the back door staring at his sleeping angelic child for moments before he could move. Slowly and as silently as he could, he unclipped Joe's seatbelt, reached in and lifted the precious child to his shoulder, careful of the moon-booted foot. The moment burned in his memory forever. *I'm a single dad.*

He carried Joe inside, greeted by Gus's wagging tail and happy bark. Pepper wanted to ensure everything was as normal as possible for Joe's arrival. She returned Gus and the brood of kittens some time during the day. *Sweet. Kind. Dependable.*

Joe stirred on his shoulder, tightening his fingers and clinging to Keegan's neck as if his life depended on it. Keegan patted him, trying to soothe whatever anxiety was surfacing. At Joe's bedroom, he paused, taking a deep breath.

Joe was home. Yeah, but how would he feel when he realised he wasn't back to the house, he called home? *With Sherry.* Keegan's beach cottage was not yet Joe's. The poor little kid was straddling two worlds. Thrust straight out of the one he knew as familiar to a different unusual place he had no choice over—living with Dad instead of Mum.

No more maternal stuff. Now it was up to Keegan to be both mother and father. It wasn't fair to Joe, but somehow Keegan must manage and aim up. He would find a way to make up for the fact Joe's mum was no longer in his life—*ever. How?* He had no idea. Death had a way of making things permanent. *There was no choice.*

Joe shifted on his shoulder, glancing at the room. One fist rubbed the sleep from his eyes while he took in the surroundings. Keegan kissed his cheek. 'This is your room, buddy.' Gus padded the floorboard, letting out a yelp of happiness, having two favourite humans so close. He circled before curling into a furball in the corner of Joe's room. It was as if the dog knew his role. *Protect the kid.*

Kittens meowed in protest on the deck, but they were fat and healthy now and did not need a surrogate doggy daddy.

The toys Keegan bought for the day, supposed to be the start of his shared care. A fortnight on, fortnight off. *Not forever.* The gifts lay on the bed and the shelving like tokens, not the sign of love he'd wanted them to be. Nothing could make up for losing Mum. *Toys were just stuff—shit!*

Keegan wiped them off the bed with his arm before placing Joe down on the mattress. Joe's eyes held the plush kangaroo on the floor near Guss. A toy Keegan thought was too young for his five-year-old son but bought it because it was Aussie, cute and soft.

He glanced at it and back at Joe, who nodded mutely but enthusiastically. Keegan picked up the toy, passing it, catching the soft, warm skin of Joe's fingers and relishing the touch.

Little Joe clutched the fluffy toy to his chest, rubbing his cheeks into the plush fabric. If it was his security for the time being, so be it. Keegan lifted the bed covers. Joe shifted his broken ankle and curled the other under the sheet. Keegan helped the bad leg gently under the covers, pulled them up to Joe's chin and kissed his lips.

'I know you're scared, buddy, and you're in a world of pain, but I'm going to do everything in my power to make your life good, happy, wonderful—,' he trailed off, the words he needed eluding him.

Joe snuggled into the toy, glancing up with moist eyes, and nodded.

'Do you want me to stay with you for a bit?'

Joe nodded, and Keegan sat on the floor, shoulder against the bed, facing Joe. He reached his hand to Joe's arm, holding, squeezing, giving strength, support, love and anything else he needed. If he'd bought a bigger bed, he'd have curled up beside his child and never let go. It didn't take long for Joe to fall asleep.

Dog-tired himself, he found his head lolling to his chin. He stretched and stood, glancing back at his angelic child, feeling sincere gratitude and mixed emotions—*guilt* for having Joe when Sherry would now miss out on the milestones. Primary school. High school. Girlfriends. Sport. Hobbies. Jobs. Marriage. *Hell, she's going to miss so much, and how do I do that alone?*

***

The morning alarm of the wattlebirds rang through the bush, *poop-kack, poop-kaaaack.* Keegan watched the little khaki-green birds with yellow bellies flit from bush to bush. He sipped coffee from a mug wondering how the hell he was going to cope.

He glanced towards Pepper's home, where she was standing on the top level ordering workmen, pointing, shaking her head, hands-on-hips. He grinned, then frowned, running a hand through his hair. Why had he told her he loved her? She was only being kind. Did it mean as much as he hoped? The kisses were incredible, but she'd said they needed to wait. Was she only putting him off forever?

So much had gone on he couldn't recall everything they'd said. Were they going to be a couple once the dust settled on their lives, or was Pepper just kind-hearted and telling him what he wanted to hear so he could get through it? But, the chemistry was undeniable—*wasn't it?*

A smash inside alerted him to Joe. He placed the coffee cup on the table and ran inside to see him standing in the kitchen, glancing down at a broken ceramic bowl shattered on the floor. His bottom lip trembled when he glanced up with sorry eyes.

'Hey, buddy. Doesn't matter. Just a bowl, no big deal.' Keegan reached for Joe's hand.

Joe took it with tears brimming in his big beautiful eyes. He shook his head.

'Really, it's nothing. Were you trying to get breakfast? Coco Pops?' He noticed the packet on the dining table. 'I'll get the milk. You take a seat.' He gently eased Joe towards a dining chair.

Joe limped over with one crutch under his little arm and sat. He dropped the crutch to the floor, though he'd tried to lean it against the dining table and gave up. Frowning at Keegan, he twisted his fingers together in an anxious gesture.

Keegan brought the bowl to the table and sat in the chair next to Joe. He smiled. 'Do you want to pour, or shall I?' Lifting the box of Coco Pops in a movement of pouring, he raised his eyebrows to Joe.

Joe nodded, and a half-smile creased his lips.

'Righto, here you go, buddy.' He pushed the bowl Joe's way, lifting the bottle of milk to pour over the crackle-popping cereal.

Joe twisted the spoon in his hand before digging in. He took a big mouthful, munching loudly.

'Why so worried about dropping a bowl, buddy?' he asked.

Joe shrugged his tiny shoulders.

His jaw twitched involuntarily. It was difficult negotiating Joe's mute world. *Love.* That's what Pepper said. Just keep loving him and never give up.

While Joe munched with renewed appetite, Keegan spoke, 'Righto, the rules here are no one ever raises their voice.' He chuckled. 'And I guess, for you, that will be easy right now. And for me, super easy too because I love you and will never raise my voice, even over broken plates. Broken people are way more important, son. Okay?'

Joe nodded, with chipmunk cheeks and big wide eyes.

'So today, we sort out how our new life works. You'll be meeting some lovely people who are going to help us. Maisy and Trevor, and you already know Pepper and Livia. Are you cool with that?' His voice caught.

Joe nodded with a milk moustache.

He wiped Joe's top lip. Joe took his fingers, smiling, kissing them, as if to say 'thank you, Dad' but still no words from his lips.

'Right.' Keegan scratched his chin. 'Um, so today we explore Blueshell Beach, obviously where we can.' He pointed to Joe's crutch. 'Then we figure out a routine. You know I have to start my new job Wednesday, that's two days after I was supposed to start. It's night shift, so you'll be sleeping when I'm gone, and people will be here. Are you going to be okay with that?'

At first, Joe shook his head, and then he dropped his chin before looking Keegan deep in the eye, taking his hand and nodding. His tiny fingers squeezed.

Keegan gulped and took a deep breath. *This was too hard.* How could he leave his fragile son? *No.* His mind twisted with what to do. He needed to work, but the timing sucked.

Joe's fingers trailed Keegan's arms to his face, pressing his lips.

'What, son? I don't know what to do?'

Joe opened his mouth. *Go.* He mouthed it, but the voice still didn't carry. *Go.*

'Okay. We need me to have a job. It will be good for both of us. I promise.' Keegan crossed his heart. It felt heavy with gratitude for his beautiful boy, who couldn't speak but communicated through love.

Joe smiled. Gus barked. Kittens meowed, and Keegan realised love would get them through.

Chapter Twenty-Five

'I'm annoyed, alright!' *Pissed off was an understatement.* Pepper was ready to throw her mobile phone from the top floor. 'You are telling me someone read my order wrong? You cut this cladding to run portrait instead of landscape? It won't work. This is a beach cottage.' She paused, pulling her ponytail so tight it hurt as she listened to their excuses. 'No, you will not. I expect the correct delivery tomorrow. I spend a shit-load of money with your company.' She didn't yell because it was a business negotiation, not a slanging match. *But hell, I want to scream.* Finally, they apologised for the mistake and promised they would remedy it. They hung up. 'Fuck!' she swore, squeezing the phone and spinning towards the staircase.

At the bottom, Keegan stood with his wide-eyed adorable son, leaning on a tiny crutch. 'Hey, Pepper.' Keegan half-smiled.

'Sorry. A slip of the tongue. Dealing with some difficult suppliers. How are you two?' She stepped down, grabbing the railing when her feet slipped. Letting out an angry ragged breath that lifted her fringe, she steadied herself and continued down.

'Bad day?' Keegan asked, dark eyebrows raised.

'Sort of. Sorry, I can't complain. How are you doing?' She glanced from child to man, trying to determine how they were coping. They seemed happy in each other's company, though clearly, Joe was still mute. 'Are you liking Blueshell Beach? It's certainly turned on a beautiful sunny day for you.' She glimpsed the aqua ocean from the window. *A swim would be nice right now.*

Two beach towels draped over Keegan's bare shoulder. His left bicep bulged as he held them in place with a plastic bucket and spade.

'Yeah, I've shown Joe around the main street, now we are heading to the beach. Thought you might like to join us.'

Her breath hitched. A day watching half-naked Keegan frolic in the sea was a no brainer. 'Sure, I've had enough of this place after that phone call anyway. I'll change into my swimmers. I'll meet you down there.'

Joe nodded, a little grin changing his solemn face to absolutely adorable. They strolled off, with Keegan urging the little boy to be careful on the goat track. A memory hit, making her gulp.

Dad followed me on one crutch, the broken leg wrapped in a white plaster cast. He grumbled about being incapacitated, but he followed to watch me swim. My heart pounded with pride and hope. There was always the chance old, happy, and kind Dad could escape from the shell of the dad he had become. He was going to watch me swim, and coach me, he said. Showed that he cared, I reckon. I'd been practising for weeks perfecting my strokes, while he was away at work. I needed to show him I'd listened. I was a good girl, strong and capable. Be proud of me, Daddy.

Shaking her head, still staring at the empty goat track, she pushed the memory back, as well as the lingering tears. Maybe it was time to read more of his diaries—finally purge his ghost once and for all.

But first, a swim with Keegan and Joe to clear the head. Not that it would solve the heat rising each time she was near Keegan even if the water was cool. Keegan set her temperature boiling no matter what. When he was quiet—*smouldering*. If he talked—*smoking hot*. And, when he was happy and in the company of his child—*adorable. Damn that man!*

She tried on four sets of swimmers. One too skimpy, two the wrong colours, three too daggy, four was a maybe. Tucking in her bits, checking herself over in the mirror, readjusting her boobs, sucking in her stomach, she was finally ready for the beach. Grabbing a light sarong, she tied it around her waist, hoping for the sunkissed goddess kinda-thing but knowing she was well short of that. A wide straw hat and sunnies completed the look, but her heart faltered when she neared them.

She needn't have worried. Keegan's dark eyes trailed her body with a 'wow' look that lingered at her breasts a moment too long before glancing away at Joe playing on the sand. When she unwrapped the sarong and placed it on the ground to sit, Keegan's eyes did a double-take, and his Adam's apple bobbed.

He whistled softly, but it seemed sweet music, unlike a worksite wolf-whistle. 'Not many women your age get away with a bikini, but you are not like other women, are you, Pepper?' He lifted his towel to move it closer to hers, sat, and bumped her shoulder with his. 'Thanks for coming down here. Seeing you in that swimsuit has certainly cheered me up.'

She touched her flaming cheeks. 'Did you need cheering up?' she managed to ask, edging her fingers towards his.

He sighed. 'I told Joe about Sherry.' He glanced at his bare toes, wrapping his arms around his knees. *Chance gone.*

'Oh, dear. How did it go?'

'Strangely.' He waved to Joe, who edged too close to the shore, dipping a bucket. 'Back near the sandcastle, buddy. Only go in the water when I'm with you.' Joe grinned, strolling with a limp back to the massive sandcastle he was constructing.

'He could come work for me when he's older.' She joked.

'Joe tends to do things big.' Keegan chuckled. 'Anyhow, I asked again if he could tell me what happened. Of course, he said nothing, but his eyes told me so much.'

He dropped his knees, his hand moving near hers. She reached for it, squeezing. 'It's okay. You'll both get through this.'

'Mmmm.' He pressed her hand. Warmth swept through her veins. 'The doctors said to give him time, but I had to know if he knew. So I said, Joe, I know you can't talk yet, but I have to tell you something. He nodded his head with tears slipping down his cheeks. I wiped them off, and new ones came.' Tears pooled in Keegan's eyes as he spoke.

'It's always hard to see your child upset.'

'Yeah, so hard. I asked, did you see Mummy? He nodded. Did she say goodbye? This time he nodded so slowly, like yes, but he didn't want to acknowledge it. I totally get why he's not talking.' He shook his head, lifting her hand, turning it over, but staring at Joe. 'Finally, I came out with it. Joe, do you know Mummy is in heaven? But he shook his head—he mouthed the word 'Hell'.' The scar on

Keegan's neck seemed to redden as he spoke. Again, she wondered how he had got it. And, why did dear little Joe think his mother was in Hell?

Pepper squeezed Keegan's hand. She didn't want to make light of his feeling, but it was the most words he'd ever said to her. The usual urge to joke with him was there, but she resisted it. If he trusted her with so much of his thoughts, she needed to honour that. For once, she was at a loss for words. Instead, she laid her head on his shoulder. They sat in silence, staring at Joe building the biggest sandcastle on Blueshell Beach.

'He knows it's just you and him now?'

'I guess.'

'Did you speak to your bosses?'

'Yep. They are willing to work around my situation. Once they have a spot at the creche in the Freebank building next door, I'll have Joe there sometimes, depending on my shifts. Hopefully, I'll only do nightshift for a few weeks and get on days to work around Joe and schooling.'

'Good, so they should help you. You deserve a break.'

'Are you and Livia still okay for this week?' His lovely eyes held hers.

'Of course. As long as you need us. Plus, he knows us a little; hopefully, it will make it easier on him. I'm going to get a closer look at his sandcastle.' She stood, glancing back with a grin, rubbing sand from her pert bottom, and strolling over to Joe.

'Great construction work, there, Joe.' She pointed up at her house. 'See my house up there. My dad built it a long time ago, and now I'm rebuilding it. You'll notice the extra work at the top and how I've added a floor? Like your sandcastle, it's all about laying the foundations.'

Joe nodded, looking pleased with his sand sculpturing efforts.

***

Keegan watched Pepper with Joe. She crouched down at his level, talking to him like he was a person, not a child. Joe seemed relaxed in her company. It made Keegan unwind a little, too, though part of him remained wound tight. If he stopped, he would flick out the other way and smash into something.

Sherry's father, Ron, phoned two days ago to tell him how the

167

funeral service went. For once, the man didn't blame Keegan. Instead, he said he understood why they broke up and was glad Joe had a father like him. Ron confessed he told Sherry she was too hard on Keegan and should have been more understanding of the PTSD. It was like the man was purging himself. He even said he was proud of Keegan's work as a paramedic, something he'd never mentioned while they were married.

Keegan hadn't agreed about Sherry needing to be more understanding. He told Ron, Sherry could only take so much before walking away, and he understood it. He'd promised to bring Joe for visits with his maternal grandfather. They'd left it on a guarded, though good note.

Soon after, Sherry's boyfriend, Erol Fitzgerald, called. That conversation did not go down well. Keegan's opinion of the man went from zero to fuckwit in five seconds. Fitzgerald wanted the two properties he brought Sherry, but they were in her name. Erol Fitzgerald had no right to them. Technically, since Sherry and Keegan never got around to divorcing, it meant the properties went to him. The bloke was livid, even though Keegan didn't want the properties. He told the bloke he had enough to deal with bringing up Joe, and the guy could send him the paperwork, and he'd sign it, possibly.

Pepper returned from the sandcastle. 'I'm going for a swim,' she said, grinning.

'You go in. I'll watch Joe.'

'You can have a dip when I come back.'

'Sure.' He watched her cute ass, knowing the grin on his face would not hide how he felt for her. He'd asked Trevor how old she was. *Almost fifty. Wow!* Yeah, she wasn't smooth, skinny, silky 20-something, but her curves were more womanly, and she carried them with pride and dignity, so comfortable in her skin it almost made him jealous. She was ten years older than him but somehow possessed youthful energy and spark. He felt older and jaded. Maybe it was what drew him to her—the exuberant spark she seemed to emit in every direction, like a lighthouse urging him to safe waters.

Shifting his eyes between Joe and Pepper, he watched her swim with smooth, confident strokes. Returning towards the shore, she caught a wave, and even from where he sat, he could see the broad smile on her face. She waded in and then ran towards him, sitting beside him on the sarong.

'Do you want a towel?' he asked, lifting a Superman towel towards her.

'Nah, I'll drip dry. It's such a lovely day.' She tilted her pretty face towards the sun with salty water dripping from her hair, trailing down her forehead and nose.

Tearing his eyes from the goddess beside him, he watched Joe edging closer to the water. He stood, striding to his son. 'How are you going, buddy? Want to go for a swim?'

Joe nodded, running into the water beside Keegan. He grabbed his hands, edging him towards a small wave. 'Take a breath, one, two, three.' Joe's little head went under the water. He surfaced with a wide grin, spitting. 'I told you to keep your mouth shut.' He laughed while Joe clung to his neck, clearly happy in the ocean. 'We'll have you swimming in no time.'

It was another one of the issues he'd raised with Sherry. He wanted Joe to have swimming lessons as a baby. Sherry disagreed, saying he was too little. He'd tried to convince her the earlier, the better, but she wouldn't have a bar of it. It was only good luck that Joe loved the water because he could have just as easily been terrified by it.

When they returned to the towels and Pepper, she was lying on the sarong with closed eyes. He shook his hair over her, making her sit up, opening one eye. 'Hey, smart guy,' she said with a giggle. 'Oh, that cooled things off. The sun is hot today.'

'The water's perfect, isn't it, Joe?' He handed Joe the Superman towel and lifted his from the sand, shaking it away from Pepper. Joe nodded, slipping the hooded towel over his head, wobbling on his injured leg.

'The moon boot's waterproof?'

'Yeah. Specially designed for kids. Can you imagine a summer without swimming?'

'Nope.' She glanced towards the northern rocks with a faraway look. He followed her gaze, wondering what she was thinking. 'The sand's changed over the years. It leaves and then comes back. Over there was a blowhole, but now there's a beach in front of it.'

'Trev told me about it. He reckons it returns every time there are king tides and heavy swells.'

'Probably. It's strange not seeing the water shoot up.' She rubbed her arms. Her eyes took a faraway look.

Joe limped back to the sandcastle. He was walking better without the crutch in the sand. Kids were so bloody resilient. 'You said you almost drowned the day your father died. Was it over there?'

'Yep.' She trailed her small hands in the sand. 'The blowhole didn't suck me in because the rip was too strong. I got swept past it before it sucked me under the rocks. I ended up at Moon Beach. I assume Dad—well, I guess he thought the blowhole got me. That's what Mum believed. She reckoned he would never have done it otherwise. Um—'

'You don't have to say anymore,' he said, patting her hand, feeling sand and soft skin. *Heat.*

She half smiled, nodding.

'Now who's not talking.' He nudged her with an elbow. It worried him when she didn't talk because chatting seemed such a big part of her personality.

Flicking a damp strand of hair from her face, she stared at the rocks. 'I'm going to swim around it when the king tides come in,' she said, tapping a finger on her lips.

'Why?' He raised his eyebrows.

'Because I need to.'

Chapter Twenty-Six

Joe ran to his father, tugging on his boardshorts, without words. A crab scuttled sideways in front of the sandcastle. Joe pointed to it, grinning, urging Keegan to follow him.

'Okay, buddy. I'll come see your crab.' He stood. Pepper did too.

'I'll head back home. As lovely as this is, I have work to do. See you, Joe.' Pepper waved. 'We'll come over to babysit Joe at six-thirty on Wednesday. It will be easier for him at yours, don't you think?'

'That'd be great. Thank you. Hopefully, he'll sleep right through, but won't you be tired? I won't finish my shift until three am.'

'We'll manage. I'll read and doze, but don't worry, Joe will be fine. Bye, Keegan.' She wrapped the sarong around her waist, turning from him, not wanting to leave them but knowing she had to.

Something undeniable was building between her and Keegan. The spark was so bright. Dizzy with its delight, she had not felt something so deep, profound and heartwarming since teenage first love.

She cast her eyes over her shoulder to see him huddled next to his son, holding the crab in his hands. The man was a contradiction. How could he have fought in war the way her father had? It didn't make sense. In all the conversations they'd had, he never let on what he did for a living. Even with the new job, he was vague.

A kookaburra laughed as she approached her deck. More birds in the distance answered its call like an echo. It was an adorable cheeky bird eyeing her with unblinking eyes. 'No food for you today, mate.' She shook her head, and the bird flew off. Livia should never have fed the bird leftover steak; now it would think they'd be offering it smorgasbords.

Inside, she poured a glass of coconut water, picked up her laptop and strolled out to the sunroom. Opening the computer and waiting for it to boot, she could just make out Keegan and Joe on the beach. Searching Google maps, she came across the place she was looking for. Next to the Freebank building was the QFES response headquarters. *Night shift?* What was Keegan doing at Queensland Fire & Emergency Service?

They strolled from the goat track, waving as they passed with Joe barely limping in the moon boot. She snapped the laptop shut with guilt. Snooping on Keegan wasn't right, but why wouldn't he tell her what he did for a living? *What was the big deal?*

One of her father's diaries lay unopened on the table. The whole confession to Keegan about the blowhole and the fact she wanted to swim around it, made the journal seem to jump out at her. It beckoned her to turn its pages.

Much like she was in a trance, she lifted it, sniffing the old leather and paper, opened it, read the words as they tumbled from the pages into her mind. She saw the war through her father's eyes, and then a passage caught her attention.

The child was dead—a little girl. Yes, Vietnamese, but what did it matter? She was a child of Pepper's age, one I loved like my own. The other guys said I shouldn't go soft on the orphans, but how could I not? They were alone in this horrible war with no one to protect them. And here I was crying over a child I didn't really know. She couldn't speak English, and I knew little of her language, but somehow we'd forged a bond. The poor little kid was dead because of me. Followed me into the bloody thick of it and I never saw her shadowing me. The medics took her, with half her body gone, the rest twisted mangled blood and bone. The grenade clipped me too, shrapnel slicing my shoulder and arm, but I lived, and she didn't. A cruel fact. Cruel as life is death. Cruel as life, at least the one I'm living. I vow I will never let another child die because of me. I don't even think I can get close to anyone again. It hurts too much to feel these things. What are they? Grief I guess, but today I only feel numb, like that's the only way I can exist anymore.

Pepper wiped her eyes, reading on, able to fathom the depths of her father's despair. Weeks later, he wrote:

Our pastor told me it was heartache, making me ill. Maybe it was, but I am jolly sick and tired of the bloody war. I'm cynical. I don't care either way. I feel dazed as if I am no longer me but a shell of the man I was. Like when Randle Clark passed me a cigar when we got over the high ridge to spy on the Congs, I refused it. I used to crack jokes and be the lad, but I couldn't be his mate. What if he died like Joey, like the little girl who reminded me of Pep? I don't talk much anymore.

There are too many images in my head haunting me not only in my sleep, but when I'm awake also—every bloody moment. I jump at shadows. My Corporal told me to toughen up, which pissed me off. He didn't have kids. How could he understand it? I had nothing left to say to any of them. It makes me wonder if I'll have anything to say when I get back home. How do I protect my family when I no longer want to live a life of tortured nightmares? Sometimes I wonder if it would just be better for everyone if I stepped on a landmine. I almost did today. I knew it was there, but I told the platoon because I know Randle wouldn't have handled me blowing the fuck up in front of him. There's more guilt in that too.

Pepper closed her red-raw eyes, gulping back the sobs escaping her lips. She pictured her mother reading the diaries and how she would have felt knowing her husband suffered the war more than most because of his compassion and kindness. It was too sad even to contemplate what the war took from him, changing him so much on his return. She shut the diary. There was one more, but she didn't have the energy to read it. *Poor Dad. My dear poor dad.*

She could see into Keegan's yard. Joe sat on the lawn with kittens and the dog surrounding him. Keegan hung clothes on the line, eyes often sweeping to his son. Pepper smiled. A man with PTSD but coping, remaining calm and kind. But maybe he hadn't endured anything like what her father had. It was different times too.

Back then, men didn't ask for help. Dad wouldn't have any more seen a psychiatrist than run naked through the main street. But Keegan admitted to seeing one when they spoke at the hospital. He didn't let on why. She wished her father had, but after reading his diaries, it seemed pretty evident he was far too damaged. The slightest thing could have led to suicide, not just a little girl swimming in the ocean of her dreams.

The phone rang on the table beside the closed journal. She glanced at the screen, not knowing the number. 'Hello.'

'Pepper, hi. It's Judith. Sorry about the other night. I'd had too much to drink and was in a foul mood. I'd like to catch up for a chat. You know it's been so long.' There seemed a desperate edge to her voice, and Pepper's heart went out to her old friend.

'Of course. The invitation still stands. I'd love to catch up. When are you free?'

'Anytime through the day. I work at the nightclub at Whalebone Beach, so days are best.'

'What about Wednesday lunch? Come over about 11.30.'

'Perfect. See you then.'

Pepper hung up, wondering why something didn't feel right. The conversation was normal enough, but something was bothering her about Judith's tone.

Did Judith have ulterior motives in contacting her? Did she know her son was seeing Livia? Only one way to find out, and that was going through with seeing her.

Chapter Twenty-Seven

Pepper poured Judith a cup of tea. Steam curled, joining the ocean breeze wafting on the deck. She placed the teapot on the table, glancing at Judith, unsure what to say.

The cup and saucer rattled in Judith's shaky fingers. 'Thanks,' she said before taking a sip.

A kookaburra landed on the verandah rail and tilted its head to Pepper. 'Our regular visitor,' said Pepper, trying to break the silence.

'Bloody pests, I reckon.' Judith put her cup down and shooed the bird away with both hands. It flew off to perch on a branch of a nearby ghost gum, cackling as if laughing off Judith's rebuff.

'How are you doing, Judith?' Pepper leaned her head. 'I know I asked you at the pub, but it's only us now. You can be honest.' It was bizarre sitting with a friend once so close she could talk about boys, menstruation, sex—anything. Now they were strangers.

Judith shrugged her shoulders. 'Better with Bobby in jail. At least we feel safer. How'd your *perfect* marriage fail?' Her thin lips twisted. She was changing the subject, perhaps shifting her problems to the back of her mind.

Whose marriage was ever perfect?

'Ian thought it was okay to have a wife and girlfriends, was one reason. There's plenty of others.' Pepper shrugged her shoulders. Despite saying it like it didn't matter, it hurt deep.

'Women? Hah! I guess Bobby had plenty. I never asked. Didn't want to know.'

'Hurts, doesn't it? At least Ian was a good father to Liv, until recently, anyway.'

'Bobby wasn't even a good dad. Not ever. That's not fair to Ross.

Sometimes I wish I had let Bobby choose you.' Her eyes held Pepper's for a moment, then narrowed. She picked up the teaspoon, adding more sugar to her tea.

Three spoons already.

Pepper blinked. She sipped her tea, rolling an answer on her tongue. 'I never felt for Bobby in that way, Judith. You know that, right? I don't know what he told you, but I didn't like him, plus I would never have betrayed our friendship.'

'So why did he always talk about you? Even when he married me. Everything I did he compared to Perfect Pepper.' Judith twisted her mouth then looked out to the billowing ocean. 'Perfect Pepper got her building licence. Perfect Pepper never ages. Perfect Pepper would be a good root. He said that, ya know?'

'I'm sorry.' Pepper sipped her tea, feeling ill, watching Judith closely. Her skin was sallow and hung around her face like a hound dog. Lank greying hair, cut in a spiky, pixie cut, gave her angular face sharp edges. She looked closer to 60 than 49. Time had not been gentle to her. Pepper couldn't figure out whether it was due to bad health, abuse or mental fatigue but noticed the nicotine stains on her fingertips and smelt stale cigarette breath over the hot tea. Maybe it was the stress of having a husband in jail. At least Judith seemed to be trying to raise their son well.

'Don't matter now. I've got Ross. Kid's turned out nothin' like his dad at least. He's a good kid. Looks after his mum, he does.'

'He's the spitting image of Bobby, though, isn't he? Must be a constant reminder.'

'Sure is. It's hard not to see it. Ross is softer. Kind even. Not a bastard like his father.'

'That's because of you. I'm sure.' And she meant it. Judith used to be a nice, happy, bright person. It was sad seeing her so bitter. A little flattery wouldn't hurt an old friend.

Judith's face lit up. 'I hope so. I've tried. Bobby thinks he's a sook, but I like Ross being like that.'

'So, you should. There's nothing wrong with kind, young men.'

Judith narrowed her gaze. 'You know he's dating your daughter?' Judith said it like she was the only one privy to a secret.

'I do.' Pepper didn't want to get into a discussion about the young sweethearts. She wanted to tell Judith to make sure her son never hurt Livia, but Judith looked defensive. She let it be.

'Like father like son, falling for those violet eyes.' Judith placed her cup so hard in the saucer. Pepper thought it might have cracked.

Pepper couldn't find words. Judith seemed embittered, but Pepper felt sorry for her and partly responsible even though that seemed absurd.

'You think I didn't recognise her loitering around the garden shop flirting with Ross, twirling her goddamn flawless blonde hair.'

'You knew she was my daughter?'

'Put two and two together since the whole town knows you came back here with a sweet little daughter in tow.'

'The town does talk as always. Livia's got her father's blonde hair.'

'The typical beach girl who doesn't surf. Ross says he's going to teach her.'

'Does he talk about her to you?'

'All the fuckin' friggin' time. It's like a broken record. I guess it's the rose-coloured glasses of first love.'

'Hmmm.' Pepper doubted it was the first love for Ross, but it was for Livia. With a nickname like Romeo Ross, his reputation preceded him.

'Remember when I first saw Bobby at the skating rink?'

'Yeah. He was with Trev's older brother and wearing a leather jacket in the middle of summer, smoking a cigarette. You couldn't take your eyes off him and said you'd marry him.'

'Should've known he was trouble. Got my wish.' Her eyes darted around like they were twitching. It seemed odd to Pepper.

'Yeah.'

'Careful what you wish for, right?' Judith stood. 'Well, it's been nice, but I've got to get ready for work. You tell your Livia she's welcome to visit Ross anytime.'

Pepper's eyes must have betrayed her worry.

Judith put up a hand. 'Don't worry. They won't be allowed near the bedroom. She's too bloody young, anyway.'

'Thanks for coming, Judith. I've missed our friendship.'

'Me too,' said Judith, but didn't hug Pepper or look back, just strolled down the steps and across the driveway.

Pepper rubbed her forehead with straight fingers. Something didn't sit right, but she'd seen hints of her old friend, mainly when Judith talked about her son. *What was the conversation about resuming friendship or some sort of scrutiny?*

Chapter Twenty-Eight

Tears rolled down Joe's little face like pearls. Pepper held him in her arms, encouraging Joe to wave by lifting his hand. Liv stood on the other side, trying to distract Joe with a kitten. Keegan's gut twisted, but he turned on the ignition and reversed out of his driveway. *Joe would be fine. Joe would be fine*, he repeated, trying to ease the fist turning in his gut. He wound down the car window. 'Love ya, buddy,' he called, pressing his foot on the accelerator and trying not to look back.

Jacarandas lined the new area of Brigemeadow's streets and housing estates with beach-style modern homes. The town centre's buildings shone with orange reflected glass as the sun sunk in the west. He drove into the underground car park feeling nervous energy. Climbing the stairs instead of taking the elevator, he arrived on the fifth floor with fifteen minutes to spare.

People sat at partitioned desks in a massive room half a football field size. They spoke into headpieces and stared at multiple flashing computer screens. A large man with the confident bearing of a policeman strolled towards him with an outstretched hand. 'Keegan Dallas?' he asked in perhaps the most resounding voice Keegan ever heard. He could have been an opera singer or a front-row forward.

'You must be Josh O'Halloran,' Keegan took the big man's hand, feeling his fingers crush. 'Thanks for the opportunity.'

'Are you kidding? Someone with your expertise will be an asset to first responders. Thank you.' Josh led him around the room. 'Too many people to remember, but we all have name badges, so you'll figure it out eventually. The lunchroom is through there.' He pointed to glass doors and a plush lounge room with coffee and a vending machine. 'My office is over there if you need to ask anything.' O'Halloran pointed to a partially open door with *Josh O'Halloran, Supervisor,* etched on a metal sign.

O'Halloran ushered Keegan to a desk where a plump woman with a kindly face and deep-set green eyes looked up with a smile. Her hair was a floppy wave of 80s perm-style. 'This here is Sally. She'll be your trainer, but from what I can see from your results and reports, you'll nail it pretty quickly. Most of us have backgrounds in nursing.' He pointed to himself, barely taking a breath. 'I was from policing. Having someone like you, a rescue paramedic, will be beneficial because you have experience as a first responder. So welcome aboard.'

Keegan settled at his desk with the three computer screens and Sally sitting so close he could smell the mints on her breath. He pushed down a rising panic. Sally tapped his shoulder gently. 'Hey, you'll be fine. I know all these split screens can be a little daunting.' She leant over him, pointing to the left screen. 'This shows the calls. Once you take a call, assess the patient, type in the code you believe them to be.'

'Yep, all good with that.' His mind boggled.

'Maps are here.' She pointed. 'You can see the responders locations. Ambo, Fire, Police and others. See that one's the Careflight chopper flying over Noosa National Park.' Sally continued with the instructions. 'We take all calls from Bundaberg to Caloundra, so it's an intense job but so rewarding. Okay, call coming in now. See.'

Keegan nodded, fingers poised over the keyboard. 'Triple Zero. What is your emergency?'

'I have a cold,' said a man before sneezing.

Sally sliced her fingers over her throat, shaking her head.

'This is an emergency line, sir. Could you see your GP?'

'I don't want to. She's mean. Says I'm a hypochondriac.' The person whined.

'Okay, Sir. I have an urgent call coming through. Please visit your local chemist, and ask for some cold medication. If that doesn't work, book in to see your GP.'

He took the next call. 'Triple Zero. What's your emergency?'

'My son's up a tree,' said the lady.

'How old is your son?'

'Eighteen.'

Sally rolled her eyes. But Keegan sensed something in the caller's gasping tone.

'Keep calm and give me your address.' She did. 'Is he injured? Do you think he will fall? Is anyone else in danger?'

She rattled off the address. 'No, but—he's meowing like a cat and spitting at me. I'm afraid he'll fall. He hasn't been himself lately.' Keegan typed the address, glanced for a firetruck close to the address. 'Help is on its way. Just keep talking and keeping him calm. Has he taken any drugs?' He asked, assuming he already knew the answer because the address was at Blueshell Beach.

'I guess. He didn't say." She shrieked. "Don't move, Randle. Help's on its way, honey.' Keegan scanned the computer screen, noticing a cop car nearby and typed for it to respond also.

He could hear a siren in the background. 'Can you see the fire truck and a paramedic is following?'

'Yes, yes, oh, thank you.' She hung up.

Sally shook her head. 'Thought she was a nutter to start with. We get plenty.' She laughed. 'Good job. I'll leave you, but I'll just be at the next desk if you need any help.'

He continued the first part of his shift, answering the odd irrelevant questions, giving advice, keeping people calm and saving at least one life. At first, he didn't know if he was saying the right things, but it was like being in the ambulance talking kindly to injured people, calming and aiding them. *Natural.* He felt a satisfaction he hadn't felt since his PTSD diagnosis.

During the break, he found a huddle of women gathered in the lunchroom. They stopped talking when he entered. He shot them a weak smile and said, 'Hi,' before making himself a coffee and sitting at a chair facing the switchroom, studying how the team worked.

'He's divine,' one of the women said. 'Sally, you're so lucky to be sitting so close. What's his story?' They were trying to whisper, but the sound of their voices carried to him. He tried to block it out, wondering if Joe was sleeping peacefully under Pepper's and Livia's care.

'Ex-rescue paramedic with PTSD. He had to have a psych clearance to start work.'

'Oh! A troubled soul. I'll put my hand up to soothe that,' said the twenty-something-year-old, giggling.

He took a deep breath. 'I can hear you loud and clear, ladies.'

'Sorry, we—'

He put up his hands, strolling closer, eyeing their name badges. Claudia, about his age, Shenay, the twenty-something. 'Sally, Claudia and Shenay, I'm Keegan, and I'm married.' He lifted his left hand showing the wedding ring, feeling like a hypocrite for doing so. 'If you need any advice on emergency and rescue situations, I'm your man, for anything else not so. Right?'

They nodded, looking contrite, but Shenay's face held a smirk.

'I'm going back to work.' He strode out. Weird how he used to enjoy the attention of women but now it annoyed him, probably half the reason he'd not taken the wedding ring off. The only interest he wanted was from Pepper. He walked to the hallway to phone her and check on Joe.

'Hi,' she said. 'How's your first shift?'

'Good. Different but great. How's Joe?'

'Sound asleep on the lounge snuggled into Livia. They were watching *Matilda*. Every kid loves that movie.'

'I wouldn't have even thought to play that one to Joe.'

'It has nice subtleties of resilience and hope, plus some magic and pretty hilarious scenes.'

'Really? You should be a movie critic.' He chuckled. 'Still no words from Joe?'

'Nope. He was silently laughing through the movie. It will take time for him to talk again; you know that?'

'Yeah.' He scratched his head.

'So what is your job anyway?' she asked.

He knew she would eventually query him, and he couldn't fob her off anymore. 'I never was with the military, like Liv thought. I'm working triple zero calls for first responders.'

'Oh, wow. Why not just tell us?'

'Dunno. Thought the military sounded more honourable or something.'

'I think saving lives is way more moral. It would be a high-pressure job too. Do you have much training?'

182

'Plenty.' He smiled. She was always fishing for more about him, and he liked it. It meant she cared. Glancing down at his watch, he sighed. 'Gotta go. My shift's back on. Kiss Joe for me.' *And one for you too.*

'Will do. See you in a few hours. I will try to put him to bed, but they look so cute snuggled, and Oddball is on his lap.'

He grinned at that. Who would have thought an ugly little kitten could creep into his heart. Only a year ago, even his wife and anyone else who tried to love him couldn't find their way. 'It's okay. Leave him until I get home. Thanks, Pepper.'

'No worries.'

God, the woman was amazing.

The rest of the shift was unexciting until a call from a young girl. 'I'm scared this time,' she said in barely a whisper.

'Scared why and what's your location?'

'My friend is sick, real sick. Please help him.'

'Does he have an illness, injury or taken drugs? What are his symptoms?'

Keegan gave her first aid instructions for the boy. It was an overdose. The address she provided was the mansion on Moon Beach Road. It was Liv's friend, Jodi.

'Help is on its way.'

***

Cicadas chorused in the bush, almost drowning the tinnitus in Pepper's ears. It was nearly the same sound—buzzing and endless. She tugged the left lobe, where it was worse. Served her right for not using earpieces while building. She'd probably be deaf before she was sixty. It made her ponder her muteness when she was young and, of course, Joe's.

The sound of Keegan's station wagon broke through the cicada's and booming surf. She waited, holding her breath, feeling a mix of emotions. What would it feel like for the beautiful man to come home to her? She pretended he was. Imagined greeting him after every shift, welcoming him with a hug, kiss—*sex*. She squashed down her rising libido. If she didn't shag him soon, she'd combust. But did he want it, or was he too consumed by loss and looking after Joe? Could he need her as much as she needed him?

He stepped from the car, strolling towards her as if in slow motion. She gulped, noticing his uniform of navy-collared shirt and black trousers still fitting him like a glove after an eight-hour shift.

'Good first day?' she asked, wanting to kiss him in welcome.

He ran a hand through his hair. 'Bizarre at times, but yeah, good. Joe?'

'Still asleep, and so's Liv.' She opened his front door.

He went in first, stopped and stared. His shoulders rose and fell before he turned to her with cloudy eyes. 'Thank you. It was so hard to leave him tonight, but you and Liv have helped.'

'You're welcome.' She wouldn't tell him Joe cried when she reached out to him. It was as if the gesture reminded him of his mother. There were almost as many tears as smiles, but she didn't want Keegan to worry about Joe when he was at his new job. Joe was grieving, and it wouldn't heal quickly, no matter who's caring for him. 'He's an easy kid and a pleasure to mind.'

He half-smiled. 'Yeah, because he doesn't talk.'

'He kind of does with those big, beautiful dark eyes of his.' *His father's eyes.*

'Yeah, he does, doesn't he. Joe cuddling into Liv looks so cute.' He leant down, kissing Joe's cheek and then did something she didn't expect. He kissed Liv's forehead and cupped her cheek. 'You should be proud of her, Pep. She's a beautiful kid.' It was such a sweet gesture; it made her weak at the knees.

'Thank you.' Had Ian ever been so genuinely besotted with his daughter? Maybe when she was little, but he'd become clueless as soon as the teen years hit.

'No. Thank you. I couldn't have done with without you.'

'I reckon you could. You've got more strength than you realise.' Reluctantly, she yawned. Tired as she was, every second spent with him was priceless. 'I'd better get Liv home. She's got school tomorrow. Hey, when does Joe return to school?'

'When the moon boot comes off. I wanted him to have a fortnight to get used to living here before he starts back.'

'You're using the creche at work then?'

'It's for two weeks. What else can I do?'

'Rely on us. Maisy's got a couple of nights she'll take too.'

'But you have the house to finish and early mornings. It will disrupt Liv's schooling with late nights.'

'We'll all cope for a fortnight. Joe's still fragile. Don't send him to the creche where he doesn't know anyone. I really don't mind. In fact, I love his company.'

Keegan stepped closer. She took a deep breath, willing him nearer still. He wrapped his arms around her. 'You are a treasure, Pepper. Thank you.' He dipped his head to her lips.

Liv yawned loudly, and they pulled apart. She took the kitten from Joe's lap. Keegan bent to pick up Joe, who barely stirred. He carried him to the bedroom.

'Come on, Liv. Let's go home.'

Liv took the kitten outside, and Gus followed.

Keegan returned. 'Thank you both. Hey, something weird happened on my shift.'

'What was it?' she asked.

'A kid up a tree meowing like a cat.'

'Sound like a typical firefighter call out, well if it was a cat, not a person.' She laughed.

'The address was in Blueshell Beach. I dispatched the police as well. I'm going to see if Dane knows anything. Seems the kid was high on something.'

'Oh, that's not good. There were no drugs here back when I was growing up.'

His voice went down a decibel. 'There was a call from Jodi's. Don't tell Liv, but maybe that kid's problems run deep.'

'What was happening?'

'I can't divulge that, but, Pep, just be cautious of the friendship. I'd be worried more about Jodi's family than young Ross. Don't concern yourself tonight. Get a good night's rest. Thanks again. I really appreciate it.'

Goosebumps ran along Peppers's arms. *What happened at Jodi's house, and should she keep Liv away to protect her?*

Chapter Twenty-Nine

Dane stabbed the nose of his surfboard in the sand, grinning at Keegan. 'Man, that surf was good,' he said.

'The swell's only going to get better, mate. The southerly has picked up.' Wind blew his wet hair, whipping it across his face. He wiped it away with the towel in his hands. 'It was great to get out there again.'

'I guess it's difficult with a five-year-old.' Dane flicked his towel on the sand to sit.

'Yeah. I can't take my eyes off Joe down here. He can't swim properly yet.'

'He any better?' Dane asked, concern flashing across his green eyes.

'Some. Still not talking.' Keegan shrugged his shoulders, wiping salt water from his arms and chest. 'Hey, any news about the kid up the tree?'

'We have some leads.' Dane glanced to the ocean.

'And the other one?'

'You know I can't talk about it.'

'You'd never have found the stash without me.'

'Probably not.' Dane faced him. 'Just keep it to yourself, okay.'

'Don't talk to anyone much anyhow.' He half-smiled.

'The kid had taken one of the pills we found. It's not meth but similar to LSD, some sort of synthetic drug we haven't come across yet. But it causes hallucinations, as you could tell when you were talking to the mother who called it in.'

'Bad shit then?'

'Not as bad meth, but yeah, it's certainly something we want off the streets. The other kid had similar symptoms but had passed out, so he probably took a couple of pills.'

'What sicko would be selling it to kids?' Keegan scratched his head.

'Yeah, we have solid leads on the drugs but are putting the evidence together first.'

'Great. It's all I need to hear. Especially now I'll be bringing up Joe here full time.'

'The fewer drugs on the streets, the better.'

Keegan flung his towel over his shoulder and glanced towards Pepper's blue house.

'You know that Tui Himona teacher who recently came to town?' Dane shrugged a tee-shirt over his head, making his last words muffled.

'The bloke is a jerk.' Keegan shook his head.

'Why do you say that?" Dane shrugged his shoulders.

'No reason.' Keegan glanced towards Pepper's blue house. "Why, what about him?'

'I'm keeping an eye on him.' Dane pulled his board from the sand and placed it under his arm. 'There's been a couple of attacks on women, and so far, he's a suspect.'

'Told you the bloke was a jerk.'

'Don't go all half-cocked, Keegs. It's an investigation so far, and I have nothing on him that will stick. I need him to think he's not a suspect and hope he slips up. That's if it is him.'

'So long as he doesn't hurt another woman in the meanwhile. What's this town coming to? First I arrived, and it was paradise.' He glanced at the crystal surf.

'Mate, crime is everywhere, not just in the city. Soon the drugs will be gone, and the bloke assaulting women will be caught, and all will go back to normal. At least that's my plan. I got into policing to keep people safe, and that's what I propose to do.'

'Good on you, Dane. Same reason I became a paramedic. I would never have had to get out if it weren't for one nutter with a knife.'

'How are you going with Joe home?'

'Awesome. I hadn't realised just how much I missed him. Now Joe is in my life full-time, I need to ensure his safety. Anything I can do to help you, let me know.'

'Will do.' Dane turned to leave the beach.

Pepper's house loomed on the rise. Joe was there with Livia for an hour to allow him to surf. 'I'd better head off. Joe's babysitter is probably wondering where I am.'

'Are you getting enough support?' Dane asked.

'Yeah, even more than I expected. This town has good people too.'

'Sure has. And another reason I'm working hard on the cases. Keep things to yourself, though.'

'I will. See ya, Dane.' He grabbed his board from the sand and ran up the goat track to Pepper's house.

Joe and Livia tended the vegetable garden, blooming with health. Gus lay on the grass, tilting his head towards Keegan and wagging his tail on the lawn. Joe shuffled to Keegan when he saw him. 'Hey, buddy. Having fun with Liv? You're walking better. Maybe we can get the moon boot off soon.'

Joe nodded, wrapping his arms around Keegan's leg. Dirt smudged over his cheek, and his fingers were grimy with soil.

'He's a terrific little helper, aren't you, Joe,' said Livia with a grin. She pushed soil under a new plant. 'He's planted strawberries with me. Hopefully, we'll have fruit when it gets colder.'

'Isn't it early for strawberries?' Keegan asked, ruffling Joe's hair.

'Ross said this is a hardier variety. Perfect for the Queensland climate. I love strawberries. Joe does too.'

Joe nodded, big eyes shining. God, he loved his child so much his heart ached with the power of it. He tried to be patient about Joe's muteness, but each day he woke, hoping the new day would give Joe his voice back. They communicated fine without words. Keegan never was much of a talker even before PTSD, so they found their comfortable silences.

Oddball bounced out from the bushes towards them, bounding over the dog, who practically rolled his eyes. Joe scooped the kitten in his arms, kissing its fur and snuggling it close to his face. Another kitten, Rushy, bounded after Oddball, Livia's pet.

The other kittens went to forever homes, thanks to the lovely girl from the pet store. He missed them, but Oddball made up for it, worming his way into their hearts and Gus's too. Though the dog pretended disinterest, the three pets were thick as thieves.

'Is your mum back?' Keegan asked, trying to sound like it was a question more than hope.

'Not yet. You ask about her a lot.' Liv winked. Nothing got past the teenager.

'She's been a good friend.'

'You want her to be more than a friend, right?' She brushed dirty hands down her shorts.

Joe glanced between them.

What to say? 'I—hey, Joe, can you take Oddball to the doghouse, and I'll follow in a sec.' Joe turned, clutching his precious kitten with the dog, following with an excited yap. 'Liv, whatever is between your mum and I—'

Liv reached for her kitten so it wouldn't follow. 'Is none of my business,' Liv finished for him. She grinned, elbowing his stomach. 'Well, my eyes see what they see. You two can't take yours off each other. Mum does dumb stuff around you, which is funny.' She laughed. 'So that you know, I'm fine with it. It would be nice to see Mum happy again.'

Wow, the blessing of Pepper's daughter. His chest swelled, and he gulped down the lump in his throat. 'Thanks, Liv.'

'Joe seemed to be trying to talk today. He was mouthing words more.'

'He's comfortable around you. Thank you for being so kind to him. You're an exceptional teenager.'

She grinned, twirling her long hair in dirty fingers.

'Liv, do you know anyone in Mr Himona's class?'

'Jodi and I have him for woodwork but not history. I'm pretty sure Ross and Hunter are in his class too.'

'What's he like? Does he seem like a nice bloke?'

'He's a bit sleazy. Gets real close to Jodi. Says she reminds him of Suzi Quatro. She said he smells of overwhelming aftershave. I didn't need her to tell me that. He reeks of it.' She pinched her nose with her fingers.

'Maybe he's covering BO or something.' Keegan winked, and she laughed.

'You know he tried to kiss Mum once.'

189

Keegan's fists curled until his nails bit into his palm.

'Oh, right.' It hurt deep in his gut.

'She doesn't like him, though. Why are you asking about him?'

'Um, dunno.'

'Hunter thinks Mr Himona is the bomb. It's the only class he likes. Ross hates school and just wants to surf and work. Don't know what other kids think. I think Slash thinks he's a jerk too.' Word hadn't gotten to her yet that Hunter had the overdose at Jodi's home.

'Slash?'

'It's her nickname on account of being an awesome surfer. You know the blonde, scruffy girl?'

'Oh, right. Anyhow, thanks again for keeping an eye on Joe.'

'No problem. He's an angel.'

And he very nearly was. Keegan counted his blessings every day. The fact Joe was even alive was a miracle. He'd seen photos of the wreckage. Though he'd attended many accidents in his job, seeing a picture of Sherry's car's mangled mess made him want to throw up.

Once Joe was fed and bathed, Keegan told him it was bedtime. Joe put up no resistance, yawning and stretching his arms. He crawled under the covers, grabbing the toy kangaroo, laying it on the pillow beside his head.

'Do you want a story, Joe?' They'd got into a weekend ritual of bedtime stories. Keegan relished every moment, but thoughts of Sherry crept into his mind making it bittersweet. Joe's mum would never read to him again.

Joe shook his head, shutting his eyes, his thick lashes brushing sweet rosy cheeks. A meow sounded under the bed. Keegan bent down to scoop up the kitten.

'What are you doing in here, Oddball?'

Joe opened his eyes, blinking hopefully, tiny hands patting the bed beside him. He'd been sneaking the kitten into his room, probably thinking Keegan hadn't noticed.

'Okay, just tonight.' He placed the kitten beside Joe. The smile on his face was worth having the furball in the house. Gus's paws clipped on the timber floor. The dog performed his nightly ritual of two full circles before snuggling into the pet bedding in the corner, a watchful eye on the child and kitten.

Keegan kissed Joe's cheek. 'I love you, Joe.' Joe's eyes were shut, but his lips curved into a smile. Gus's tail thumped on the floorboards. He leant to pat the dog. 'Good dog.'

He brewed a cup of green tea, inhaling the herby scent before sipping. Placing the cup on his desk, he flipped open his laptop. Logging into the news site, he typed in Tui Himona's name. Nothing on the man. How long had the Kiwi been in Australia? This time he Googled New Zealand newspapers, typing Himona's name into the search engines. *Nothing!* Maybe the guy was just a sleaze and harmless. Either way, he hoped Pepper was no longer friends with the guy.

Lights blinked off at Pepper's. He stood, staring at her house, seeing her shadow move from the kitchen. A light flickered on at the back. Probably the room she'd set up as a temporary office. He pictured her going through building plans, approvals and the million other things requiring her attention. It was a marvel how well she ran her company. He'd noticed many new homes near his work were under Pepper C Constructions.

After driving through the estate, he realised she was no small-time builder. She was a corporation. How she managed it all with a teenager while upgrading her own home was beyond him? He knew women could multitask better than most, but she was a powerhouse of multiskills. *A pocket rocket.*

***

'Rob, you do need to read them,' Pepper pleaded with her brother via a Zoom call on her laptop. 'It's given me some closure. It might do the same for you.'

'Look, Pep. You lost a brother, I know, but I lost my twin. It's half of me gone, and I'll never forgive Dad. I'm at peace with that. I don't need or want to forgive him. You've got your reasons to want to. That's you.' He shrugged his shoulders, frowning. His hair was greyer, and more lines etched around his blue eyes. Rob was a handsome man, aging well, but now the spitting image of his father. She would tell him so, but it would only make him angrier. He didn't want to look like the father he hated.

'You know he was only thirty but looked as old as you now.' Rob, at forty-seven, did not consider himself old.

'Hey, watch the old.' He laughed. At least he was trying. 'Yeah,

I remember. It was probably the rum and cigarettes. I can't ever remember him without a ciggy in his hand or the smell of rum on his breath.'

'They were his emotional crutches. At least he didn't hit us,' she said weakly, feeling defeated, knowing Rob would not read diaries without convincing. For a reason beyond her comprehension, she wanted to share them with him—with someone at least.

'Not with his hands, but the verbal punches hit hard enough. You should know. He directed most of them at you and Mum.' He shot her an earnest look. 'Sis, drop it. I'm happy you're finding your peace with it.'

She sighed. 'I am. I've decided to redo the garage too.'

'Great. I would bulldoze it myself, but good on you.'

'I have big plans. I realise I don't want to commute to the city, so I'm moving my office into the garage. Where Mum did her artwork, I'll set up plan benches and computers. I'm cleaning up Dad's old desk to use as a reception, or maybe it will go in the library in the new section of the house. One side of the garage will be storage, one side office, and up top—'

'The attic?'

'Did you ever look out from it as a kid?'

'Not really. The windows were always grimy with salt. I guess it has a view.'

'It's beautiful. I'm opening it up, adding a mezzanine, and it will be the lounge, lunch area for my staff.'

'Aren't they all in Brisbane?'

'Some. Tammy wants to move nearby to Whalebone Beach. So my accountant is a yes.' She ticked her fingers off. 'Baz, my project manager moved to Caloundra last year, not that he'll be in the office much. I'm looking for a new draftsperson and some locals, so I think it can work. We're doing homes all around the southeast now, so it kinda makes sense to work from here. I'll keep the Brisbane office too but scale it down and put a manager in place.'

'Work-lifestyle balance is good. But, Pep, I had the feeling you'd hate being back there and sell Mum's house.' He shrugged his shoulders, smiling.

'Funnily enough, I love living back here. I think I let Dad's death ruin a beautiful place, and in hindsight, I've allowed it to take over my life when I should have let it go a long time ago.'

'You sound happier. I sense it's not only the house and the beach, plus the fact Liv has found her feet. Ian still whinging?'

'Yeah, sometimes. I'm over him and feeling relieved he won't be the person I spend my life with.'

'Good.'

'Everything is coming together. I'm happy.'

'What aren't you telling me?' He shifted his eyes to the left and scratched his chin. 'I know that look. You had it when you first dated Ian. Who's the lucky guy?' His face moved closer, looking distorted on the screen.

She sighed. 'It's it that bleeding obvious?'

He chuckled.

'He's my neighbour, and it's complicated.'

'Sis, just uncomplicate it. Hey, gotta go. Love ya.'

'Love ya, too.' She blew him kisses as his image disappeared.

There was a heap more things she could work on, but her mind was on something else. *Keegan.*

Switching on the hall light and turning the office light off, she made her way to the kitchen. Pouring a glass of water, she sipped, staring out the window. Keegan was on his verandah, his head back, gazing at the stars. The urge to go to him, curl on his lap, sniff his essence, kiss his thick lips, taste his tongue, and feel his warmth was burning in her like a kettle ready to whistle.

What did he think about as he stared into the heavens? His poor ex-wife, Joe, work? Or was he thinking of her? She hoped so with all her heart because even her brother figured out she was in love with someone. And that someone was metres away watching the Milky Way, oblivious to how deeply she felt for him.

Chapter Thirty

Without looking, he knew she was there. It was the smell of coconut-frangipani soap and feminity wafting in the briney salt air like a tropical oasis. He turned, smiled and patted the lounge beside him. He'd been hoping she would come to him because he would never leave Joe alone in the house. And he needed her. Despite the timing, he needed her now.

'I couldn't sleep and saw you were still up,' she said it like it was an apology.

'I'm glad.' *No apologies, babe, you've made my day, my night, my year.*

'Me too. I have lots to tell you about my plans. I want to run some by you to make sure it's okay. Since you're my neighbour, and it will affect you too.'

'I'm okay with anything you do. Especially now, the house is almost finished.'

She tilted her head, biting her lip. With her fingers, she showed an inch. 'Maybe a teeny bit more renovating.' She shrugged her shoulders, glancing at the garage.

He didn't care what she did with the damn garage. 'Can we stop ignoring this, Pep?'

'Ignoring what?' She sat tantalisingly close—*a leisurely kiss.*

'Us. The attraction.' He turned to face Pepper chest to chest, so close her breath was warm on his cheek. Though he wanted to hold her, he waited for her to catch up with his intentions. Her husband had hurt her, and there were reasons for her seeking him out and then pulling back. So much happened since she moved next door, but none of it mattered. In his mind, it was clear—she was perfect for him. But did she think he was ideal for her?

'I thought you needed to get Joe settled. Our timing isn't right.' Her breath came in tiny rasps. She bit her bottom lip. A lip he wanted to suck, tease open. *Kiss.*

'I don't need any more time. Do you?' He slid his wedding ring off his finger and placed it on the coffee table.

'No.' She sucked in a small breath.

He gave in to the temptation and kissed her. Like the other kisses they'd shared, it was intoxicating, but this time there was more to it— *deep love—at least on his part.*

His tongue teased her lips apart. Their tongues danced, deep and intense, tantalizing every nerve, sparking fire across each vein. She tasted strawberry-sweet and matched his intensity, not breaking for air.

It was as if they couldn't dive deep enough. And, of course, that sparked more desire. He fumbled with the buttons on Pepper's blouse until he exposed pert breasts in a pink bra. Sliding his fingers over the warm curves to her cleavage was like touching heaven. She grinned cheekily, unhooking the bra to give him an eyeful of boobs he'd been dreaming of. Dusky pink nipples peaked at his touch. Slowly, he twirled fingers over them, dipped his head to suck each in succession, hearing her gasp of delight.

Trailing kisses to her neck and back to her mouth, he paused. 'Come inside.' He stood on shaking legs, taking her hand, pulling her up with him.

'I—but, Joe.'

'Sound asleep. Pepper, please.'

'You had me at, come inside,' she said breathlessly, pressing her lips to his upper arm and letting him lead her inside by the hand.

He opened the door to his bedroom. It meant he was opening the entrance to his heart too. A risk, but he was willing to take it. Shutting the door behind them, he took some moments to let it sink in. *Pepper in my room.* He'd dreamed of it for so long he should pinch himself to make sure.

When her lips met his and her hands slipped to his waistband, there was no need to pinch. There were plenty of other things he could think of doing. All involved her on the bed and his hands exploring every inch of her.

***

It was like a dream, but it was real. She was in Keegan's room. She pulled his shirt over his head, staring at the muscles, sliding her fingers along the crevices. Firm hairy chest, warm, masculine and skin the delicious colour of cocoa-latte brown. So enticing, she could have bent to lick his navel just to explore if he tasted like chocolate. 'Mmmm,' she managed.

His hands slid to cup her bottom and lift her to straddle his hips. The movement pushed her against the door with a thud and squashed her boobs into his bare chest. *Closer.*

She stifled a giggle at the noise they'd made against the door, shushing him with a finger to his delectable thick lips. 'Joe.' She narrowed her gaze, mock-angry.

He grinned. Their mouths entwined, hands entangled in hair, only coming up for air long enough for her to say, 'Put me on the bed. I need you inside me.'

As usual, he didn't speak, but his dark eyes burned. They quickly discarded the rest of their clothes—over the bedhead and across a chair. Pepper's lace panties ended up hooked to the spinning fan above the bed. Not that they noticed.

As he crawled over her body, sliding his hands along her legs, over her stomach, to her breast, neck, ears, mouth and lastly to kiss her, she was delirious with desire. But he seemed intent on taking his time. He sucked her nipples in turn, dark eyes intently watching them peak. His fingers left her breasts, teasing down her stomach, edging closer to where she throbbed. Widening her legs, she jutted her hips towards his teasing fingers, letting out a moan. 'Keegan, you're killing me,' she said through gritted teeth.

He said nothing but glanced up with a smile before touching the folds, finding her clitoris with one finger, sending zaps of fire skirting her limbs like a bushfire uphill. His eyes dropped to explore her flesh, touching, caressing, dipping inside the wetness, in-out, in-out until she was on the brink.

But she wanted all of him, not just his amazingly talented finger sending her into spasms of desire. *His cock.* 'Keegan, now, please.'

196

'Babe, I can barely hang on myself. I should beg you.'

She felt him hard as a hammer, and she knew how to wield one of them. Grabbing it, she stroked the smooth rod, found her way to his hairy balls, cupping the weight. He grunted and spasmed. 'Oooh, these guys need some relief.' She giggled, letting them go to hold his shaft again, gliding her hand up and down, feeling already taut skin tighten further.

'My balls have been filling every second I'm near you,' he said, taking her mouth possessively in his. He angled his body above her inching closer until the tip of his cock teased her entrance.

'Fill me then.' She almost screamed it. Her need for him was so great. *Fuck me now!*

He froze above her, leaned off to the side and reached for the bedside table drawer. With fumbling fingers, he grabbed a foil, ripped it open and passed the rubber to her.

'I haven't used one of these since high school. Like a banana, right?' She rolled the condom over his cock. 'God, will it even fit you?' *Impressive.*

He winced, his face scrunched, but it was because rolling a condom did not come naturally on an erection so grand. 'Pep, you're killing me.' He blew the hair from his face.

Once the condom was on, he ensured she was ready, dipping his fingers to feel her moist and eager. She smiled. 'I couldn't be more ready,' she said, grabbing his cock and guiding it back where it belonged.

He needed no further encouragement, dipping into her inch by delicious inch until she felt him to the hilt. They blended like one, meeting each thrust in a timeless dance to the beat of their rapid hearts. He kissed her, consuming her with lips, teeth, tongue, cock and hands. She'd never experienced anything so primal and beautiful at the same time.

When he sped up, groaning deeply into her shoulder, she matched him and then some. Sweat slicked between their thrashing bodies, making them slippery and fluid.

When she neared the peak, she called his name, 'God, Keegan.' Wave after delicious wave of orgasm swept through her, making her shudder and tingle. It was like being sucked into a vortex filled with only her and Keegan.

Seconds later, he was spent too, thrusting, grunting and then panting on her shoulder. When he caught his breath, he kissed her cheek, lips and earlobe.

She snuggled her body into his, feeling protected, loved and needed. 'Wow. God, if I'd known it could be like that with you, I wouldn't have waited this long.' Looking into his eyes, she noted the happiness shining deep in the darkness. A grin slashed across his handsome face. Running a finger along the scar on his neck, she pondered how he got it.

He moved her hand to his chest over his heart, where the thud was rapid. 'This might sound corny,' he curled a finger through her hair and brushed her cheek.

'I'm the corny one in this relationship. But go ahead.' The feel of his warm body against her stirred so much emotion. She was stunned by the intensity of her feelings. Though she'd been married, she'd never loved like this. Even though she knew Keegan hid some things from her about his PTSD, it didn't concern her or ring any more alarm bells.

"I loved you the moment I saw you.' He watched her intently as if he expected her to flee at any moment.

'Oh, that kind of corny.' Pressing her hand to his heart, she said, 'It's not so strange. When your eyes met mine, there was an instant spark. It's not even something I believed in until now.'

'Me neither.'

'You didn't love Sherry at first?'

'Not even after seven years of marriage. My mother, Alexandra, is Greek, and she wanted me to marry a Greek girl. Dad's a true-blue Aussie, so her reasons are unclear. There were moments, especially when Joe was born that I thought I could fall in love deeper, but something was missing.'

'Connection?'

'Perhaps.' He shrugged his shoulders.

'What makes you feel connected to me?' she asked it, hoping she wasn't going to watch him pull away. Why couldn't she just stop being chatty and enjoy the moment? *Shut up, stupid!*

'Your vitality, cheerfulness, loyalty, kindness, and you have no idea how sexy you are.' He trailed fingers over her nipple before reaching down to pull the sheet over them.

'Don't start me on you, Mr Half-Naked Handstand and Adonis Surfer. You've seriously pushed my composure so many times.'

He laughed. 'I took a while to read the signals.'

'Why? You're a gorgeous guy, and I clearly showed my interest.'

'I guess my history.'

'How so?'

'When the person who's supposed to have your back, support and encourage you doesn't—like a wife—it—well, it makes you insecure. To be honest, I didn't think I was worthy of your love. You're too good for me, Pep.'

'I knew you were worth all the love in the world. You should feel valued. You are worthy.' Her hand reached for the cock that was prodding her leg.

'Mmmm. There was you wiggling your butt up the ladder that day. You did that on purpose?'

'Uh-huh!' She giggled. 'Almost worked too.'

'If it weren't for our interruption, I'm sure—.' He groaned because she was stroking him, tugging him closer.

'I was so friggin' disappointed Liv wrecked that. Oh, sorry, the swearwords. Shit, sorry. I'm so trying not to anymore, especially now Joe is around.'

'See, kindness.' He gently placed a finger on her bottom lip. 'You don't have to stop swearing for us, do it for yourself. As I told you, you've got enough power in your work ethic and ability to command your workers without acting like a bloke.'

'You think it's blokeish?'

'Umm, no. I guess plenty of chicks do, but I sense, and from what you've said, it's become a habit that you thought made you one of them. You'll never be one of them. You're above that. Don't treat anyone by gender or anything else, just ability.'

'For a bloke who usually doesn't say much, the most profound words are spitting from your mouth. Now I think your lips need to do other things, like kiss me.' His lips met hers at the same time his cock enticed her other lips open. *I can still say fuck in my head. Fuck, this is good.*

***

They didn't notice when the panties unhooked from the fan and landed on the floor, nor the shadow on the deck.

Gus's inquisitive bark sent the ghost from the past scurrying away like a rat in Pepper's attic but barely made them pause from the heat of their copulation.

It was after one thing—*vengeance*.

Chapter Thirty-One

It was Monday, and Keegan was finally on the day shift. He drove Joe to Maisy's, explaining how the day would proceed. 'So, son, today it's Maisy's because Liv's at school and Pepper has a business meeting in the city. Maisy's planning to let you help her cook today. Muffins, I think she said. You'd like that, right?'

Keegan watched Joe in the rearview mirror. His son nodded before glancing out the window with tears pooling in his eyes.

He wanted to swear at the unfairness of it all. It wasn't fair Joe lost his mum. It was shitty that he needed to work when his son needed him. It was unjust someone could slam into Sherry's car shattering their worlds.

Maisy greeted them at her front door with warm hugs and the aroma of fresh baking. Joe stepped behind Keegan, clinging to his leg.

'Joe, it's okay. Your daddy's got time to stay until you settle. How about I make him a cuppa, and you can have a taste of my first batch of triple chocolate muffins?' Maisy smiled at Joe and shot an it-will-be-okay look at Keegan.

It tore his soul to see Joe, so heartbroken about his mum. He'd do anything to take his pain, but he felt useless because all he could give was love.

As if reading his thoughts, Maisy said, 'Love will get through to him eventually. You're doing such a great job. Don't ever doubt it. Joe, you'll find a toybox over there. Go ahead, play with anything. We're just going over here to the kitchen.'

He lowered his voice so Joe wouldn't hear. 'Thanks, Maisy. It's hard seeing him sad. And without words to tell me, you know—.' His shoulders slumped.

'It's difficult to understand when he can't speak to you. He'll come around. Give him time.' She walked over to Joe with a chocolate muffin on a plate and showed him the lego she'd set up in the corner for him. 'Pepper told me you like building things,' she said to Joe.

Joe nodded with a wobbly half-smile. He sat crosslegged sorting lego into colours, and began constructing a tower.

'I hear you're doing okay in the love department,' she said to Keegan, switching the kettle on and raising her eyebrows.

Without a thought to it, he grinned. It was so natural to be in love with Pepper.

She pointed a finger. 'See. That's it. The look of love if I ever saw it.'

'Pepper's the one thing that makes everything easier.'

'Well, don't you go breaking her heart.'

'Don't plan to. She could break mine, though.'

'No way. Pepper's as loyal as a barnacle on a whale, that girl. She's even giving Judith a second chance. I've never met anyone quite like her. Coffee or tea?'

'Tea, thanks.'

'So. What now?' She dangled a teabag in a mug and pushed it towards him.

'What do you mean?'

'Is it serious?'

'Is this the third degree?'

'I care about you both and want happiness for you. Sorry, I'm inquisitive, but that's just my nature. Plus, I can't get much out of Pepper. She's holding things close, but she keeps getting these faraway dreamy looks and doesn't really listen to me.'

'Does she?' he chuckled.

'And?'

Trevor came in through the back door. He ruffled Joe's head. 'G'day, little mate.' To Maisy, he said, 'Give the bloke a friggin' break, woman. Let the lovebirds alone, will you?'

She kissed Trev's cheek. 'Can't help it.'

Keegan watched the easiness between them, realising Sherry had never been like that. He and Pepper were a different matter altogether. 'Hi, Trev. It's okay. Just be a bit quieter around Joe. It's all too soon after losing his mum. Pep and I are keeping it as discreet as possible. So don't go spreading the word quite yet, Maisy.'

'My lips are sealed. I think it's a beautiful thing. You two look gorgeous together.'

'Maisy.' Trevor playfully smacked her bum. 'Enough.' He shook his head at Keegan, rolling his eyes to the ceiling.

Gulping down the last of the tea, Keegan checked his watch. 'Gotta get going. Thanks for the tea and looking after Joe. Call me if you need to. But I'll ring in at lunchtime and check how he's doing.' He strode to Joe. 'Buddy, Dad's gotta go to work. It's only one more week, and you'll be back at school seeing all your friends. Have fun baking with Maisy.' He winked at Maisy.

Joe nodded solemnly. Tears formed in his eyes, trickling down rosy cheeks. Keegan kneeled beside him and took him in his arms. 'You'll be okay, buddy.' He squeezed him, feeling his fingers clinging to his shirt. Prying them off, he gulped back his own tears to stand. He shot Maisy a helpless look, striding to the door, trying not to turn back to his upset child.

'Come on, Joe. Let's go see my chooks. They'll have a couple of eggs for sure,' said Trevor, trying distraction.

'I need eggs for the other muffins. Could you bring me four, Joe?' Maisy asked.

Keegan glanced back, his heart dropping to his stomach.

Joe nodded, following Trev outside, looking so tiny beside the tall man.

He left before he couldn't. When he got in the car, he rested his head on the steering wheel, forcing tears back from his eyes and calming his breath. *Breathe, mate. Breateh.*

***

Pepper commanded the large room full of project managers, forepersons, planners, administrators, tradespeople—her staff. 'As you know, Ian's interests in the company have been terminated. There will be no more saying you'll ask him when I give you a direct order. Though he stayed on for a while, he is no longer employed by

203

Pepper C Constructions.' She paused, checking her notes but didn't need them. She put them aside. 'I want to thank all of you for the progress we've made in the last quarter. It's your efforts that have us in an excellent financial position and able to fulfil the current projects and take on more as we grow.'

Clapping broke out, and some high fived or patted backs. 'Great work, Boss,' called Robbo from Stafford, a hardworking foreperson.

'Thanks, Robbo. I'm sure you've all had time to read through the memo Amber handed out to you.' She watched the nods and a few who were scanning the pages as she spoke. 'I'd like to reassure everyone, you all keep your jobs.'

More applause and thanks.

'But, now there's always a but, right?'

Stunned silence.

She smiled. 'I'm setting up an office on the Sunshine Coast. Eventually, it may be bigger than here, but this will remain head office. I just won't be here, often anyway. I'll be up there where the new developments are booming. I guess you're all dying to know because I left it out of the memo. Who's in charge here?'

Amber, her personal assistant, stepped to the side of her.

'What?' yelled one of the blokes.

Pepper flashed Amber a conspiratorial smile. 'Amber Jonas is the new CEO of our Brisbane branch of Pepper C Constructions. Please give her a round of applause.'

When the applause died down, and the few annoying protests subsided, Pepper spoke again. 'Amber's been with me from the start. She knows the business inside and out, has a finance background, and a Bachelor in construction completed while learning the ropes. To top it off, she's smart, savvy and extremely loyal. I'm proud to call her my friend and now my CEO. I'll hand you over to Amber.'

She stepped back, allowing Amber to speak. The younger woman did so with aplomb, proving Pepper made the right decision with her choice. Initially, she was swaying towards Robbo. It was something Keegan said that made her choose Amber. *Stop seeing people in your industry by their gender and judge them on their ability, and they'll do the same for you.*

A man moved forward from the back of the room. It was Ian, and though he was clapping in the air, there was anger twisting his face. 'Brav, fuckin'o. Another chick in charge.'

'What are you doing here, Ian?' Pepper nodded at the security guard in the corner, who began to approach Ian.

'Wanted to see the spectacle for myself since a rumour was getting around.' He stood with his hands on his hips, glaring at Amber. To her credit, Amber didn't look one bit intimidated.

'Please remove yourself from the building, Ian,' Amber said.

'Can't work with two women in charge.' Ian glanced around, but he didn't get the support he'd probably expected.

'Cause they can. Look what Pepper's done so far,' said Robbo.

'Bloody oaf, these two are amazing.'

'Get out a here, dickhead. You nearly ruined all our jobs.'

'You're the one who shouldn't be in charge.'

And it went on. The security guard escorted Ian from the room, and though Pepper badly wanted to high-five Amber, she kept her hand by her side. She felt slight pity for Ian, but it was only because of their past marriage and nothing to do with the business decisions.

Later, she reflected on how well it went, but the old sadness kicked in about her failed marriage to Ian. Though she felt sorry for him, the realisation, he betrayed her, sunk in, and she was glad she'd decided to move away from him months ago.

She drove back to Blueshell Beach, singing along to the radio, when she noticed a battered blue car tailing her for over fifty kilometres. It didn't try to overtake, just trailed about two cars back. Goosebumps ran the length of her spine. Was it Ian out for vengeance? But she didn't recognise the car as his.

When she'd driven past the sign saying The Town of Blueshell Beach, the car was no longer in view. She sighed, wiping sweat from her forehead, feeling stupid for worrying about it. It was probably only coincidental. So, why did the chill down her spine remain like ghost's fingers crawling on her skin?

Chapter Thirty-Two

Jodi's father, Lucus Savant, watched the police car pull up in front of their house. 'Wonder what they want?' He glanced to Jodi.

Jodi's eyes grew wide. 'Dad, I have to tell you something.'

'I know, petal. You've taken some of my drugs. I did a stocktake.' He said it calmly, like they were talking about eating the last choc-chip cookie. 'I had a suspicion it wasn't the first time since I caught you snooping around down there when your friend was visiting.'

'You knew?' She was unsure whether to be relieved or terrified.

'Only since yesterday when I had a call from an Officer Wright asking whether I kept pharmaceutical supplies at my home. I said I did and then got to wondering why the question because everything I do with the business is above board.' He shot her a warning glance. 'Keep quiet and let me talk to them.'

'But, Dad.'

The doorbell sounded.

He placed a finger to his lips.

'Police. Please open up,' the officer called.

Lucus opened the door. 'Hi, Officers.'

'Lucas Savant?' The blonde-haired male officer asked.

'Yes.'

'I'm Senior Constable Wright, and this is Constable Rosella. We would like to ask you a few further questions about your business.'

'Sure.'

'We've found these.' Dane Wright lifted the small clear zip-lock packet containing pills to Jodi's dad's face. 'Cats. Ketamine, sometimes called Cat Valium mixed with a synthetic Peyote and something else. Forensics are still trying to figure it out. Quite a combination. Do you recognise them?'

'Please come and sit in the lounge room. I'll explain.' Lucus lead the constables to the room facing a spectacular view of the Pacific Ocean. 'This is my daughter, Jodi.'

Jodi backed out of the room to the kitchen and listened from there, holding her breath. Her stupidity was probably going to send Dad to jail. *What have I done?* Her fingers shook where she clutched the door frame.

'It's a trial drug for use in some major illnesses. We've tested patients in recent weeks with it and a placebo. Of course, it wasn't meant to get out on the streets. Unfortunately, my safe seems to have been broken into. I only realised after your phone call that perhaps I should check it. That's when I discovered stock missing.'

'Convenient,' said Constable Rosella shaking her head.

'You have the necessary paperwork to store?' Dane Wright asked.

'And the stock numbers?' Rosella glanced at Jodi, regarding her with eyes scrutinising every inch of their loungeroom.

'Of course, I have scanned copies on my phone.' Lucus flipped open his phone and scrolled through until he found the documents. 'I can email them to you if you wish.' He passed the phone to Rosella.

'Seems legit.' She sent the documents to her phone.

'Who do you think took the drugs?' Dane asked, glancing towards the kitchen. Jodi stepped back out of view, heart hammering.

'No idea.' Lucus shook his head. Jodi marvelled at his composure.

'We'll need to see where you keep them. This is a huge breach of security in your industry. You may be charged if it's not secure enough.' Dane stood.

'No, no, stop,' Jodi ran into the room. 'It was me. Don't blame my dad. I watched him and figured out the safe combination.'

'Jodi, stop.' Her father stood too.

The constables glanced at each other. 'Jodi, please sit down and tell us what happened,' the male officer said kindly, pointing to the lounge.

'No,' Lucus shook his head. 'It's my fault. I should have been more careful.'

'Do I need a lawyer, Dad?' Jodi asked, wide-eyed.

'You're a minor, Jodi,' Rosella said. 'Let's just find out what you did first. How many drugs did you take from your father's safe?' Jodi sat next to her dad, who placed a reassuring hand on her thigh. She wanted his attention, and she sure had it now. The officers sat too.

'I'm not sure. Maybe thirty the first time. About twenty the second.'

'Twice?' Her father shook his head.

'Did you sell the drugs?'

'No. Never. I gave them to my friends. I wanted everyone to have a good time. I didn't know they could be so dangerous. I didn't mean for Hunter to OD.' Her bottom lip trembled.

'Are you sure you never sold any?' Rosella asked.

'Look around. We're rich. I didn't need the money, just the attention.'

The woman glanced at the authentic Persian rug and ran her hand across the Fendi Casa sofa's soft leather.

'When you took the drugs from the safe, where did you keep them?' Dane spoke softly, making Jodi feel safe to unburden herself to him.

'I dug a hole at the beach. You know that because you found the stash a couple of weeks ago. It was stupid to put them there, but I was a little panicked when I first took them. I kept the rest under Bluey's headstone. There's a dozen or so still there.' Jodi was grateful her mother was shopping. It was bad enough having her father's shock and scrutiny. Her gut twisted with guilt.

'Bluey is?' Rosella's poised her pen over the notebook.

'My cat. He's buried in the backyard.'

'The amount of illegal drugs are an imprisonable offence. Do you realise that, Jodi?' Dane said.

Lucas paled, grabbed Jodi's hand and said, 'Is there a way for her to take a rehabilitation course or community service instead of an arrest?'

'As a juvenile, there are those avenues, but even if payment wasn't exchanged, drugs supply is serious. Imagine if Hunter had died.' Dane paused, lifting kind eyes to her. 'I'm going to have to speak to my sergeant, but since you are both being cooperative, I would think a magistrate would let you off with a warning, but yes, you will have to do a course. All juvenile drug offenders must.'

Rosella scribbled in a different notepad. 'We're issuing you with an infringement notice. You'll have to appear in front of the magistrate.' She tore off one page, handing it to Jodi. Another she gave to her father. 'Now, we'll need to see the safe and where the rest of the drugs are. You'll have to upgrade your security, Mr Savant, or your paperwork will be ripped up, and you'll no longer be able to hold them here. I suggest, since a teenager is in the house, you seek alternative arrangements anyway.'

'Yes, you're quite right.' He stood, grabbing Jodi's hand. 'Come on, petal. Don't look so glum. Being honest is the best thing, and I'm proud of you for that.'

'I'm so sorry, Dad.' Tears plopped from her eyes. He wrapped his big arms around her, something he hadn't done in a long time. *It was worth being in trouble.*

'It's a big lesson in life, Jodi. But you'll be wiser from it.' Rosella smiled for the first time.

Jodi nodded. Why were they so nice when she had totally stuffed up.

'You must realise drugs are not a toy. They can be deadly. The last thing we want in this beautiful town is a drug problem. If you know of any of your friends who may still have these pills, you must tell them to flush them down the toilet because if we find them, they will be charged with possession, okay?' Dane's voice was soft but steely.

Downstairs in the basement near the garage, Lucus showed the officers the safe. They took a few photos and gave some suggestions for better security. Jodi led them to the garden, where she buried her cat. 'Bluey was old, but he was a good cat,' she said, lifting the carved stone in the shape of a cat head over a small mound of earth covered in colourful flowers. There was a small hole under the stone. She leant down, pulling out a dirty calico bag.

Dane reached for it. 'Thanks.'

Her father frowned. 'I'm sorry I wasn't here when Bluey died, Jodi. I know it was hard on you and your mum having to bury him.'

Jodi gulped back her tears. *If he only knew how hard.*

Soon after the police left, Jodi rang Livia. 'Hi, Liv. Sorry I haven't been myself lately. I've got rid of the drugs, all of them. I know that's why you didn't want to be friends, but I promise I'm not doing stupid stuff anymore.' She didn't pause in case Livia was going to hang up.

'Oh. That's great. You don't need stuff like that. You're fun to be around anyway.' She went silent. Jodi held her breath. 'I've missed you, Jodi.'

'Thank God, Liv. You have no idea how much I've missed you. I did some dumb stuff trying to get my father's attention, and it almost sent him to jail, let alone Hunter being so sick.'

'What, Hunter? What happened to him?'

'Oh, Jeezus! The old Blueshell grapevine didn't get to you? He OD'd. Don't worry, he's okay, but it was pretty scary. It made me realise how irrational I was being, and I wasn't a good friend to him by doing that.'

'Ross never told me. When did it happen?'

'Last Friday night. I'm sorry, Liv. I'm sure you're disappointed in me.'

'Chill, Jodi. We all make mistakes. As long as Hunter is okay.'

'He's kind of more than okay.' Jodi laughed. 'He confessed to only taking the drugs to get closer to me.' She giggled, feeling giddy with love for Hunter and regaining her friendship with Liv. 'Hunter asked me to be his girlfriend.'

'Wow, that sure is one way to get his attention.'

'I know, right!'

'Be careful, though, Jodi. Hunter is—well—.'

'Hunter.'

Liv giggled. 'Yeah, you know what I mean.'

'Well, he's best mates with Ross because he's a top bloke and fun to be around.'

'That's true. Hey, guess what?'

'No idea.'

'I'm going to meet Ross's mum. I'm going over there for lunch. I'm so nervous.'

'Don't be. Judy is alright. A bit mad at the world but adores Ross, so I'm sure she'll love you. Have fun. Gotta go. See you at school Monday?'

'Yeah, let's hang out.'

Jodi hung up, grinning. The police arriving still had her a bit edgy, but at least she wouldn't be in court for a while. The police reassured her dad that she had a chance of a good outcome in front of a magistrate. It could have gone horribly wrong, but in a way, she was relieved. Lying to her parents always felt stupid. In fact, the day was almost perfect. Her dad seemed closer, and Liv was her BFF again.

***

Fresh bread wafted in the room, but it didn't mask the odour of cigarettes. The home was a small weatherboard on the riverside of town. It could do with a renovation, but by the state of the clutter, odd ceramic ornaments with a layer of dust, a collection of teaspoons, old doilies and books, it didn't look like Ross's mum was house proud enough to give it a second thought.

Livia smiled at Ross's mum, trying to make eye contact, but Judith was busy placing layers of cheese on a sandwich. 'Thank you for making lunch. It's very kind of you, Mrs Ronson.'

'Call me Judy. Mrs Ronson sounds like I'm a hundred or somethin'.' She laughed a brittle laugh before coughing. 'Should give up the fags, eh Ross?'

'Yeah, Mum. I've been telling you how bad they are for your health.' Liv shot him a glance, knowing he snuck the odd cigarette himself. He sat on the stool beside her, passing a glass of lemonade.

'Help yourselves, then. There's ham, cheese, tomato, whatever you want on the bread.' Judy wiped her hands down the side of a pretty dress. It hung on her skinny body, but Liv imagined she probably looked beautiful in it once.

Liv's hand shook when she picked up the glass of lemonade and sipped. She watched Judy over the rim, feeling foolishly nervous. She didn't know why it was so crucial for Ross's mum to like her. At least her mum finally warmed to Ross and let him come over as long as they stayed out on the deck.

Ross squeezed her thigh under the table. He whispered, 'Are you okay, Liv?'

She smiled. 'Just a little nervous.'

'She won't bite.'

'So, miss Livia Cassidy, are you going to break my boy's heart?' Judy asked in a mumble, her cheeks stuffed with the sandwich.

'No.' Liv said softly.

211

Judy laughed. 'Cause you won't. Wouldn't dare. Ross is all I've got in the world.'

'I love Ross and would never hurt him.' She squeezed Ross's hand. He sent her a doting look.

'And I love Liv too, Mum. Quit with the pressure. Just try to get to know her, please.'

'I'm trying. All I'm seeing is her mother. God, you look like Pepper. 'cept for the straight platinum hair.' She leant her elbows on the table, resting her chin in her palms. Green bloodshot eyes studied Liv.

Liv picked up her sandwich and put it down again. Her stomach lurched.

'Yes, she does look like her mum, but prettier, of course.' Ross bit into his sandwich.

Liv smiled at him. He always had her back. Even when she decided not to see Jodi for a while, Ross got it. Liv twirled hair through her finger, a nervous habit. Her appetite was lost, but she wanted to take a mouthful so as not to offend Judy.

'What do you plan to do with your life? I hear your mum is now a top-notch builder. You going into construction?' Judy's lips twisted.

'No. I think Mum is amazing, but I'm not interested in it, though I do woodwork at school. I'm only fourteen, but I know I want to work with animals. Maybe be a vet or something.'

'You should have a plan. Ross has one, don't ya, love? Gonna win the world title.' She fist-pumped the air.

'No, Mum. I'm not going to be a professional surfer. It costs too much to travel the tour. I'm studying horticulture when I finish school. I want to be a landscaper.' Ross' jaw twitched. Obviously, the conversation about the world surfing championship wasn't new.

Liv turned to him. 'Mum knows plenty of landscape companies. She could help you get an apprenticeship.'

Judy rolled her eyes. 'Of course, she could.' Eating a bite of sandwich, she mumbled the rest, 'Pepper Perfect can do anything.' Some sandwich crumbs dropped from Judy's mouth to the table. A dob remained at the corner of her lips, and Liv wished she'd wipe it away. Judith's green eyes narrowed.

Liv glanced at Ross, but he was busily squeezing more ham in his sandwich. He was biting his cheek in the way he did when he was mad at Hunter for something.

After lunch, Liv and Ross cleared up while Judy went outside in the backyard to smoke a cigarette.

'I don't think she likes my mum or me either,' Liv said.

'Sure she does. They had a cuppa the other day, and Mum said it went brilliant. She reckons they'll be best friends again one day. You know they were at school.'

'I know, but it was a long time ago. People change.'

'Mmm. Mum's had it tougher than most. It's why I always look out for her. Wake her up if she misses her work alarm. Help clean up the place. Ask her to smoke and drink less and look after her health. She listens sometimes, but she says she only does it because of the stress of Dad being in jail. Don't know why she's stressed, though. Our house is much quieter and safer without him here.'

'Do you miss him?' She placed the last dried plate on the bench, turning to him.

He snuck a quick kiss before his mother returned, reeking of nicotine.

'I miss having a dad around, but I don't miss him.'

'Was he violent?'

'Sometimes. Hey, let's not talk about that. How about a walk along the river? We can sneak through the neighbour behind us to get directly to the water. Mum, you want to come.'

'No, thanks. I'll leave you lovebirds to it. Nice to meet you, Livia.' Judy waved them off. Ross said she hated the water anyway and couldn't even swim. Her parents never bothered to teach her.

Livia turned to wave one last time and caught a strange look flashing across Ross's mother's face. *Anger. Hostility. What?*

Chapter Thirty-Three

'OMG, this is so pretty,' said Jodi. She ran a hand along the white walls. 'It's like tropical beach Hamptons. Not that I'm an interior expert like Mum, but this is way prettier than the modern look. Your mum has done an amazing job. I'd love to live here.'

Liv laughed. 'You already went gaga over my room. I knew you'd adore it up here. Look at the view of the beach. It's not as wide as yours, but it works with the environment, don't you think? More trees and bush.'

'Well, I guess that kookaburra on the rail thinks so. It seems it's always here. Hey, Kooka.'

'Yeah, funny that we've aptly named him Kooka.' Liv laughed.

'Wow, I can't believe your grandmother painted that.' Jodi pointed at the family painting, taking pride of place in the dining room.

'She was talented. It looks so real. I feel like the eyes follow me around the house, especially granddad's. Mum loves it. There are more out in the garage she doesn't know what to do with yet.'

More cars pulled up the drive, and some decided to park at Keegan's. Of course, he didn't mind. Liv couldn't believe how nice he was. Though deep down, she'd always hoped her parents would get back together, Keegan made her mum happy.

'I saw Keegan kiss your mum before. Wow, it was like watching a rom-com.'

'Why's that?' It was as if Jodi read her mind sometimes.

'She tripped over the step and fell into his arms. He caught her as if he knew she'd fall.'

Liv rolled her eyes. 'Mum is the absolute clutz when she's in love. It gives new meaning to falling for someone.'

'That's so funny. Let's go and see who else has arrived. Is Ross coming?'

'With his mum.'

'Oh, really?' Jodi tilted her head, sending blonde Suzi-Quatro hair across her face.

'My mum invited her.' The thought gave Liv a chill, and she had no idea why.

***

Judith strolled towards Pepper in a pretty blue dress with pale sunflowers. 'Hi, girlfriend,' said Judith, smiling. It was nearly the smile Pepper remembered—toothy and full.

Liv ran towards Ross and into his open arms. Judith's mouth twitched, and she rolled her eyes. 'Young love, huh!' The teenagers joined other young people mingling near Liv's vegetable garden.

'You look lovely, Judith. That's such a pretty dress.' Pepper smiled, taking her hand because hugging her still didn't seem quite right.

Judith dropped it like she'd been burned and patted the fabric down her skinny hips. 'My boy bought it for me with the pay he makes at the garden shop.' She spun a full circle. 'If only I'd had a husband who was as thoughtful.' She shrugged her shoulders. 'Well, where's the alcohol?'

Pepper showed her to the deck facing the grass where a large esky contained beer, wine, soft drink and water. Most people arrived with booze, but she prepared for the few who would come empty-handed. 'There's beers, mid and full and white or red wine.'

'Beer's fine.' Judith pulled a full-strength from the icy esky and cracked it open with a hiss of foam. She took a full swig. Wiping her mouth with her arm, she said, 'Oh, sorry. Did you want one?'

Pepper half-smiled. 'Not yet. I've got to bring some food out and show a few people around. You're alright here?'

'Sure. Off you go.' Judith gave a shooing motion with her free hand.

In the kitchen, Keegan came behind Pepper, standing at the sink. He planted a kiss on her neck and hugged her waist. 'Everyone seems happy. You should be proud of what you've done, babe.'

'The house or the party.' She turned, kissing his bristled cheek with her hands in dishwashing water in the sink.

'Ah, both. And you're also the hottest woman here. You know that, right?' His lips trailed to her earlobe.

'Stop it. I can't concentrate. I need to get more wine glasses outside. Be useful and find the tea towel.'

He laughed, pulling away, grabbing the towel and picking up a glass. He glanced out the window. ' Jesus, really?'

'What?' She followed his gaze.

'Tui's here. He has a hide.'

'I invited him.' She turned to face Keegan, watching his dark eyes closely for the green devil.

'Why? You're the good Samaritan of Blueshell Beach citizen again, aren't you? First Judith and now Tui.' He vigorously rubbed the wineglass even though it was already dry.

'No. It's just, he's new to town and needs to make friends and put his past behind him. You shouldn't make assumptions.'

He rolled his shoulders. 'Have you given Ross a break yet?'

'He's here, isn't he?'

'You scrutinise the kid, though.'

'I'm only protecting Liv.'

'I think that boy protects Liv just fine.'

'Maybe. Hey, check out Joe running after him. He seems to like the older boys, doesn't he?'

'Younger too. Danny and Trudy called in yesterday with the twins. Coping with two boys, wow, but they're happy.'

'I'm glad to hear it. I wish I'd had more time to see them.'

'Next time. They plan to visit more often. It's nice for them to get out of the city and enjoy the beach.' He kissed her forehead and turned. 'Hey, Judith. What are you looking for?'

Judith glanced around the house. 'Toilet,' she said, eyeing Pepper.

'That way. Oh no, the door's shut. Someone's in the main. Go to my ensuite. It's up the hallway. I showed you where when you were here last,' Pepper said, stacking glasses into a carry crate.

'Thanks.' Over Judith's shoulder, a large yellow bag swayed below her skinny hips. She'd been fishing cigarettes out of it all afternoon. At least she went to a corner of the yard, so the smoke didn't disturb anyone. Two other smokers had joined her.

Pepper, tray in hand, strolled outside. She placed the new wine glasses on a trestle table, picked up a glass. Before she could fill it, Trevor approached with a three-quarter bottle.

'It's about time you drank a glass, love. You've been as busy as a bee on wattle.'

'Thanks, Trev. Did you see where Keegan went?'

'Ducked home to change Joe's clothes after the waterbomb fight the kids had.'

'He copped a lot of the bombs. The big kids didn't let up. Lucky Joe is such a trouper of a five-year-old.' Pepper smiled towards Keegan's house.

'Don't worry. When Keegan was busy, Liv and Ross took him under their wing. I have a new opinion of that young man watching him today. Maybe none of his mother or father rubbed off on him.'

'I guess he's trying to ignore his history and find his own path. My opinion's changed too. He clearly adores Liv.'

'Maisy's waving you over, Pep.' Trevor strolled over to Tui, who nodded at Pepper with a sheepish smile.

She found Maisy talking to Judith. 'You must be proud of Ross,' Maisy said, out of view making a slit-my-throat motion with her finger.

Pepper held back a giggle. That wouldn't have been fair to her old friend.

'He's a goood boy. He bought me this dress.' Judith relayed the story again, but this time there was a slur to her voice.

'It's beautiful. Oh, Trev's calling me. I have to get the cake ready.' Maisy made her exit, leaving Pepper wondering why Judith needed alcohol for a crutch.

What cake? Pepper thought of something to say to her old friend. Keegan strode to beside her, wrapping an arm around her waist and drawing her close. 'How's my gorgeous girl going? Eating enough?'

'I've had a bite or two. Don't worry.'

'We haven't officially met,' Keegan said to Judith, reaching his hand to hers with a kind grin.

Pepper smiled. He was always so in tune with other people. 'Judith, this is my boyfriend, Keegan.'

'Boyfriend? How old are ya? Sixteen?' Judith snickered.

Keegan glanced at Pepper with his jaw twitching. 'We'd say partner, but since it's only new, the term works for us,' he said, running one finger along the scar on his neck.

Judith laughed then coughed. 'Seriously! Pepper Perfect fucks the hottest guy in town. Of course, she fuckin' does.'

'Maybe you've had a few too many wines.' Pepper attempted to pluck Judith's glass from her hand.

'No. I'll drink what I want. I've been eyeing him off myself thinking I had a chance at a roll in the hay. Shit, any bloke would do at this point. I'm so toey.' She poked Keegan's chest with a boney finger. 'But you, man, you are one sexy fucker.'

Keegan's jaw twitched again. 'You know, Judith, the fact is men can be offended by sleazy talk as much as women. How about you cut it out and either stop drinking or go home.' Keegan said it softly but firmly.

Judith stepped closer to him, ignoring Pepper and placing her back to her. 'Only if you come with me, handsome.' She blinked like she thought she was batting her eyelids and wobbled on her feet.

Ross must have noticed the exchange. He ran over and took his mother's arm. 'Mum, don't you have that appointment you have to get to?' He winked.

Judith glanced at him blankly. Ross shot her a secret look, and she slowly nodded. 'Right. Yes, of course. I have to go. Sorry, Pepper. I'll see you another time.' It was as if she snapped into a different person in a daze.

'Tell Liv I had to go,' said Ross to Pepper.

As they walked away, she caught Ross' voice trailing off. 'Mum, stop embarrassing me. I can't keep getting you out—.'

Keegan took a deep breath. 'Pepper, do you really want to keep seeing that friend? She isn't all that nice to you.'

'I think she's troubled.'

'It's obvious, but you can't fix everyone, babe. Look after yourself is all I'm saying.' He chuckled. 'You have the softest heart, woman.'

It wasn't funny. Then Pepper realised where he was watching, and a smile tugged her lips. Joe held both Liv's and Jodi's hands as they swung him in the air. Two kittens and a dog trailed them, plus the O'Shay toddler who fell every three steps but kept getting up to stay with the group. 'Too cute.'

'You are too.' He kissed her lips. 'Now, you need to head this way.' He turned her to face the deck.

A cake the shape of her renovated cottage sat on the outdoor table. It was intricate and beautiful with blue and white icing. 'Did Maisy bake that?'

'Yep.'

'Wow, she is so clever—and kind.'

Maisy tapped a wine glass with a spoon. 'Quiet down, everyone. We wanted to celebrate Pepper and Livia's renovations of dear Meg's old beach house with a special cake. I haven't known the family as long as some of you, but the moment I met Pepper, I found a friend. I wanted to pay her kindness back with this.' She flourished a hand to the cake as Pepper stepped to the deck and everyone applauded.

The dog, chased by two growing kittens and a five-year-old, bounded towards the deck, up the stairs and in front of Pepper's shins. She tripped. Stumbled. Almost righted herself against the rail, but a kitten shot between her feet. With hands splaying, she landed on the soft, spongy, thick-icing cake.

Gus turned his furry head to sloppy blue and white clumps of smashed cake on the deck floorboards. Wagging his tail, he licked them up.

The kittens skidded to a halt, hightailed out of the way and leapt off the deck.

Joe placed hands over his mouth to stifle muted laughter. Sprayed cake dripped from his dark curls.

There was a moment's stunned silence before everyone burst out laughing.

Pepper pushed herself out of the cake with gooeyness covering her hands and dress. She licked the sweetness in her mouth and snorted gunk from her nostrils. She turned, wiping her face, only to plaster more icing in her hair. She curtsied, feeling her cheeks flame red.

Frenzied laughter. Shrieks of glee. Fits of giggles.

Through the side of her mouth, Pepper said, 'Sorry, Maisy.'

Maisy held between her legs with tears streaming down her face.

'No, don't be.' She took a breath. 'That's about the funniest cake face-plant I've ever seen. Actually,' she giggled. 'it's the only one.'

Pepper wasn't seeing the funny side with her pretty dress ruined by the icing. She flicked cake off her fingers towards Maisy.

It landed in Maisy's wide, laughing mouth. 'Oh, yum,' she said. 'I seriously have to pee. Now!' She fled for the bathroom with her thighs squished together, giggling and waddling.

Pepper felt cake hit her ear and turned to find the youngest kids throwing cake at each other. *Okay, it probably is funny.* She laughed, grabbed a big handful and ran over to Keegan. He had the good humour to let her shove some in his handsome face. 'Delicious,' he said before scooping some deep in her cleavage and eating that too with a wicked grin. 'My adorable clumsy Pepper.'

'It wasn't my fault. It was your dog's.'

They glanced at Gus. The dog was lapping up the dessert from the ground like ice cream on a cone. He seemed in doggy heaven.

Other people joined the fun, eating as much cake as they threw so it didn't go to waste. After about five minutes, exhausted from laughing and running around, they glanced at each other and laughed again.

Livia took photos with her mobile phone, trying to duck the sprays of creamy icing. Blue trailed through her blonde hair like streaks. Almost everyone wore some of Maisy's delicious cake. At least Liv shot a photo of the cake before Pepper ruined it.

'I'll help you clean it up,' Keegan said to Pepper, scooping Joe into his arms. 'No more, buddy. You'll end up sick.' Joe, grinning like a chipmunk, had cake smeared over his face and dripping through his dark hair.

'It's okay. I'll get the hose out when everyone goes. I hope your dog doesn't get too sick.'

Gus looked to be in a cake comma, having consumed more than his share.

Joe scraped cake from his stomach and smeared it on Keegan's chin. 'Thanks, Joe.' He laughed. 'Let's get you home for a bath.' Joe nodded. Keegan put him down.

Pepper pushed Keegan's shoulder. 'You go. Joe'll be exhausted. It's been a long day.' She urged.

Maisy, still wearing a wide grin, said, 'Go, Keegan. We have enough people here to clean up. You look after Joe. Plus, it was my cake that created this sticky disaster.'

Pepper giggled. 'It wasn't a disaster at all. No one will ever forget that cake, Maisy. It was brilliant. Could end up Blueshell Beach folklore.'

'You know I wet my pants,' Maisy whispered. 'I've never laughed so hard. I hope that doesn't end up folklore.' She winked.

***

No one noticed Judith's return because they were too busy with the cake fight. She leaned against the smooth bark of a ghost gum, dragging on a cigarette, watching the chaos with narrowed eyes.

When Pepper leaned towards Keegan and kissed him, both with cake covering their mouths, Judith grimaced. She squeezed the lit cigarette, crushing it in her palm, burning a hole. With barely a wince of pain, she wiped the mouldering skin of the ash. The anguish in Judith's mind burned deeper. Vengeance was the only way to ease it.

Somehow harm Pepper and her precious Livia. Hopefully, the oil in the ensuite would do the trick. She wasn't entirely sure why or how she'd come up with the plan. With Pepper gone, the pain of all her abandoned years would go away, just like Bobby had. *Vengeance would be sweet as the cake on the ground.*

Chapter Thirty-Four

The day started brilliantly. Joe was mouthing words, smiling often and hardly ever cried anymore. It was partly due to him returning to school and his friends surrounding him, but it was also partly because of the people of Blueshell Beach. Everyone from the local fruiter to the garbo driver said hello and encouraged Joe to talk back.

And of course, there was Pepper, constantly checking in on them, sometimes bringing food, though cooking wasn't her specialty.

The first batch of cupcakes was slightly burnt on the bottom and gooey in the middle, but it was the thought that counted, *right?* And, Joe loved the green icing, though he'd worn most of it on his cheeks.

Oddball went everywhere with Joe and Gus. If the tiny kitten couldn't keep up, Joe bundled him in his arms. Pepper built him a small fort in the corner of the yard, near Livia's veggie garden. It was constructed with, what she said, was remnant timber, but Keegan held the sneaking suspicion she'd bought bits specifically to please Joe.

And it did make Joe happy. He was playing in it with the dog barking from the outside on the grass.

Keegan performed another yoga pose watching Joe in the fort and the dog seemingly the banished enemy. Keegan stretched up in sun salutation, back down and heard the sound of a car engine. He grinned at Joe. 'Someone's here, buddy. I'm going to check who. You stay playing with Gus and Oddball. Okay?'

Joe nodded.

Rounding the bend of the house, Keegan stopped mid-stride. Surely not. It was Erol Fitzgerald stepping from a white sporty Mercedes Benz. 'Hope you don't mind me popping in,' said the man, in the most annoying put-on posh accent. *What did the bloke think he was British? He was an Aussie farmer, for Christ's sake.*

'So, to what do I own this pleasure?' Keegan asked, feeling it was a stupid thing to say when he'd rather plant his fist on Fitzgerald's pompous face.

'Couple of things.' He reached inside the car. 'I need you to sign these.'

Keegan glanced at them. 'The deeds to Sherry's property?'

'My property.'

'Why'd you buy it for her then?'

'Because I thought she'd be in my life for a long time. They were for our future.'

'You say our. Did that include Joe?'

'Why would it? He's not my kid.' He shoved the paperwork to Keegan's chest.

Keegan took it, glanced down, and it handed it back. 'I don't need to sign them.'

'Technically, you own them as Sherry's next of kin. I want my properties back.' He shoved the paperwork into Keegan's hands.

'Look, mate. I won't be pushed into anything. I have to contemplate what's right by Joe, and considering these are, his mother's, shouldn't they go to Joe? I told you I didn't want them, but I can't speak for my son.'

'Sure you can. He's a kid. Stop being pigheaded and sign. Once you do, you'll never see me again.'

'Nope.' Keegan shook his head. *Like the idea of never seeing you, though.*

'I've lost my girlfriend, a Range Rover, a house and a unit over this. I'm pissed-off already and don't need a low-life like you pushing my buttons. If you don't sign, I'll sue you.'

'So now you're threatening me? The properties are Sherry's. I've spoken to her father, and since he doesn't own property, he wants them to go to Joe. I asked him to decide, and he has.'

'It's not his legacy to give.' Fitzgerald stepped closer. He was a good head taller than Keegan, but he had a beer gut the size of a small car and his muscles sagged rather than bulged.

Keegan tried to keep the angry edge from his voice, but it faultered. 'Joe doesn't have a mum. He'll never have her love again.

He's suffered the most out of this. The least he can have is a legacy from her. It doesn't matter if they were gifts from you. The law says they are hers.'

'I can get the best lawyers on this. You'll never win. Money always talks.'

'Funny that, isn't it? Why would someone so rich be clawing in the properties of his deceased girlfriend? Perhaps you're not as rich as you make out.'

The man's eyes bulged. Keegan knew he'd hit a nerve. 'Shut up. You know nothing.'

'Right, then, as I said in the last email. You keep the unit. I'll sign that away now. But the house remains Sherry's, well mine actually, that is until Joe is old enough to have it. And, I'm pretty sure you would have insured the Range Rover. Being a write-off, I reckon you'll be able to get another one for your next girlfriend.' *Touche!*

Keegan was usually the diplomatic kind, but something about the guy made him want to fight. And he sensed Fitzgerald had never been kind to Joe either.

'Sign this one.' Fitzgerald flicked through the envelopes and handed Keegan the deeds to the unit. 'Here.' He pointed. 'And here' He passed him a pen. Not an ordinary ballpoint, a Waterman. *Expensive shit.*

Keegan signed, handed Fitzgerald the paperwork and turned to see Gus bounding his way, followed by Joe. Joe hid behind Keegan's legs, staring with big eyes up at Fitzgerald.

'Hi, Joe. You remember me? You're mummy's boyfriend.' Fitzerald smiled at Joe, but it didn't reach his hostile eyes.

Joe nodded and looked on the verge of tears.

'Tell me, Erol, why is my son scared of you?' Keegan reached behind to place a reassuring hand on Joe's shoulder. Joe's fingers clung to his.

'He's not. We got on fine. Didn't we, Joe? Speak boy.'

'He's mute.'

'What? No, he can talk fine.'

'Not since the accident.'

It seemed to soften the man's face. 'Oh. I'm sorry.'

Joe's fingers dug into Keegan's. He patted his head. 'It's okay, son. Mr Fitzgerald is going now.'

'Yes, well. Thanks for this, but we'll be discussing the house situation further. This is not over.'

Keegan nodded, turning away from the infuriating man, wishing again that Joe would speak so he could understand why the man scared him. There were so many things he wanted to ask his son. A list was building up, ready for the time Joe could answer.

Another car pulled up as the Mercedes drove away. Keegan turned to the sound and smiled. 'Hey, Dane.'

Dane stepped from the car, grinning. Joe ran to him and allowed him to pick him up. *Now that's a different reaction to a bloke.* 'Hey, there, young Joe. Wow, you're getting so big I can barely lift you.' To Keegan, he said, 'Who was that?'

'Sherry's rich boyfriend.'

'Must be with a ride like that.' Dane whistled.

'Maybe not so. He's trying to get me to sign over the properties.'

'I told you not to.'

'He can have the unit. I have a feeling the bloke's going bust.'

'Could sell that car and buy a small house.' Dane flicked a thumb towards the road where the Mercedes was still in sight. He put Joe down, and the dog and cat circled him.

'I guess it could. Anyhow, what's going on? Want to sit on the deck and get out of this sun?' Keegan strolled towards the deck.

'Sure. It's still hot for Autumn. I wanted to let you know we caught the guy attacking women.'

'Tui Himona?' Keegan sat on the step, and Dane did too. Joe plopped down between them, grinning at each.

'Nope. It was another guy, but I am still keeping an eye on him. I think he's more sleazy than harmful.'

'What about him being a school teacher?'

'I've had a word with him. One false move and the education department will come down on him like a tonne of bricks, not to mention getting the police involved.'

'I guess if he's treating women bad, he'll have his karma one day. Just keep an eye on him. We need to keep the women of Blueshell Beach safe.'

'The other thing is, the drugs are off the streets.'

'Great. I wondered why the calls dropped off at work. The biggest problem I had last shift was a fisherman with a hook embedded in his finger.'

'Ouuch!'

'Yeah, the poor guy was screaming like a racecar. Makes me a bit wary of going fishing with Trev, though.'

'You're sure to catch something. Fish on the barbie is the bomb.'

Joe ran to the dog house and climbed in, followed by the cat. Gus lay on the timber deck snoring. 'Anyhow, how's Joe?'

'Happier. I think he's settled in. Fitzgerald had him rattled, though. He cringed when he saw him. It makes me wonder if he ever hit Joe. What if Joe never speaks again? I want to ask him so much.'

'He'll talk when he's ready. Pepper said she did, remember?'

'Yeah.' He ran a finger along the scar on his neck. 'I'm impatient, is all. I can't wait to have a conversation with him. One that isn't one-sided. I seem to ask him a question and then answer it, and he nods or shakes his head. We communicate, but I hadn't realised how important his words were.'

'They'll come back. I've got to go.' Dane stood. 'I'm sorry I missed Pepper's home warming. It sounded epic.'

'The cake fight was. It was a special day for sure. Joe loved it.' Keegan grinned.

'That's right. You two are joined at the hip.' Dane chuckled. 'Good to see you happy again, mate.'

'Thanks, Dane. It feels good, and it's put the PTSD in its place.' Joe poked his head out of the doghouse, grinning at them. 'Wave to Dane, buddy.'

Joe silently waved Dane off.

***

The paint roller slipped from Pepper's fingers, splattering down the wall and over the drop sheet. 'Bugger!' She climbed from the scaffold to retrieve it feeling proud for not using the F-word. She glanced out the window to Keegan's. It was like he was a magnet, and he always drew her to him.

With a teenager in her house and a five-year-old in his, finding time together was challenging, let alone having sex. Watching him play in the garden with Joe stirred a delicious throbbing between her

226

thighs. She couldn't get enough of him. It's why she was too distracted to paint. She kept picturing him, painting her walls with his precise, slow movements. How she'd loved that day, back at the beginning of their relationship. It had progressed so much further, but she was still unclear of their future. But she was hopeful.

The phone lay on the floor near the paint tin. She picked it up, dialling Keegan's number. 'Hey, you.' She smiled, watching him glance towards her house. Waving like a goofy love-struck nerd didn't dissipate her grin or his either.

'Are you nearly done up there? I can't believe you didn't like the first colour you painted.'

'Yep. Last coat. And, yes, it has to be perfect. Do you think you could ask Trev and Maisy to babysit tonight? Liv's at Jodi's and—.'

'Hell, yeah! I'm aching to stay with you. I'll let you know once I phone Maisy. What time does Liv leave?'

'Gone already.'

'Well, I'd better hang up so I can ring Maisy now. Talk soon.'

She picked up the paint roller, dipped it in the tray and rolled it down the wall. God, she was sick of painting. Maybe Keegan could help her before they found their way to her bedroom. On second thoughts, bedroom first, painting second.

The phone buzzed. She dumped the roller and reached for the phone. 'So?' No voice. She glanced at the screen. It wasn't Keegan but an unknown number. 'Hello. Who is this?' *Breathing. No words. Just breathing.* Then a whisper, 'Watch where you step.'

Pepper hung up. The phone rang again, but it was Keegan. 'All good to go,' he said. 'I'm dropping off Joe in ten. Do you need help with that final coat?'

'I do, but I have something else in mind first.'

'Don't worry, babe. I do too. See you soon.'

She danced a happy dance around the room before glancing down at her paint-stained shorts and t-shirt. Running down the stairs to her bedroom below, she strode into the ensuite, showered quickly, gave her wet hair a quick blowdry, added a dab of makeup and lippy and was about to walk in the bedroom to get dressed. She didn't notice the baby oil on damp tiles. In her haste, her left foot slid, setting her off-balance. Her head hit the corner of the vanity with a crack.

***

227

Keegan called out to Pepper. She must be playing a game. He grinned, searching the rooms, calling her name, 'Pepper, where are you? Are you naked waiting for me?' *I hope so.*

He strode into her bedroom and caught something in the corner of his eye in the ensuite. *Blood.* 'Pepper. Shit. Pep. What have you done?' He bent to her taking her pulse. *Steady.*

She blinked, groaned, reached for her bleeding head.

'Babe, you knocked yourself out. Must have hit the vanity or something. Stay down for a bit in case you're still dizzy.'

He pulled the towel from the rail to cover her nakedness and the handtowel to press on her wound.

'I don't know what—happened.' She glanced to her feet. 'Slippery.' She tried to sit up. 'I'm feeling a bit better.' He inspected the wound while she talked. Not a deep gash and wouldn't need to be stitched but close enough to her temple to be a concern.

'Do you know what day it is?' he asked, gently stemming the blood and wiping wet hair from her face. It hurt him like a screwdriver to the stomach, watching her in pain. He wanted to protect her from everything.

'Sunday.'

'Year?'

'2019.'

'Great.' He kissed her forehead. 'You gave me a scare, Pep.'

She tugged the towel over her breasts. 'I feel sick with embarrassment.'

'Hey, no. Don't do that. I've seen you naked. In other circumstances finding you without clothes would be my kind of heaven. If you weren't hurt.' He shook his head, smiling, reaching for the medicine cabinet to find a butterfly clip or bandaid.

'I'm so clumsy.' She hung her head and groaned when the movement hurt. He gently covered the cut on her forehead, trying not to notice her exposed nipple. She turned him on even in this state, but his need to protect her was more potent.

He noticed a shiny patch on the tiles, ran his hands over it and sniffed his fingers. 'Do you use baby oil?'

'Not since Liv was about five. Why?' She sat up further. 'I think I can stand now.'

'No. I'll carry you. Your feet slid over baby oil. That's why you fell. I'm not having you go down again.' He stepped away from the oil, picking her up. The towel dropped to the floor.

She tucked her head on his chest. He carried her to her bedroom, feeling gratefulness she was okay. A slight turn of her head, and it could have been a worse concussion, even death. *Where had the baby oil come from?*

'This isn't the most romantic way to get you into bed,' she mumbled.

'Well, I like that you're naked.' He laughed.

'Such a clutz.'

'No, you're not. You're adorable.' He kissed her lips before placing her on the bed. 'How's the head feel?'

She touched it gingerly. 'So much better with my own private, sexy paramedic. Hey, why did you keep that from me for so long? Aren't you proud of the work you do?'

'I am. I was.' He lay on the bed beside her, placing his hands behind his head, afraid to touch her while she was feeling unwell.

'You can get undressed,' she winked.

'I thought you wouldn't.' She silenced him with a finger.

'I'm naked. You get butt naked, please.' She smiled, melting him even more than her pocket rocket hot body. While he undressed, she asked again, ' Why aren't you proud?'

'The PTSD. I thought I was weak to have it. When Liv thought I was in the Air Force, I didn't correct her. It sounded more honourable to be a hero than a guy who couldn't work.'

She grabbed his hand, tugging him beside her. He reached for her pretty face, kissing her. 'You told me that, but I guess it goes deeper. And, don't distract me with kisses. You are a hero. Don't you think anyone in emergency services deserves that status? I can only imagine the things you've seen. You should be soooo proud.' Her hand trailed down his back to his arse.

Every nerve ending sparked. But he knew she wanted to talk first. It was probably good for him, to be honest, finally. Without thinking, he touched his scar.

'How did you get it?' This time when her hand trailed it, he let her. Tender, soft fingers explored the pucker from his ear to his clavicle, and he figured it was the most sensual thing she could do.

He shut his eyes, speaking slowly. 'A guy attacked his wife with a knife. My partner and I were saving her. He came up behind me and slit my throat.' He glanced at the ceiling. 'The police got him away but not before I almost bled out. A different crew worked on me in their ambulance during a mercy dash, and I died twice on the way.' He paused, feeling her sweet lips trailing the scar. 'It was—.'

'A nightmare.'

'Yeah. One that comes back. Less in recent times, but it's there, but the worst part wasn't me. I fought the knife off the guy, and somehow it ended up in his heart. I killed him, Pep.'

'No. You can't blame yourself for that. It was self-defence, and you probably saved the lady and anyone else he could hurt with the knife.'

'I should have paid more attention to where he was while we were saving her.' Tears slipped down his cheeks. She wiped them.

'No. You did all you could—and you had to live for Joe more than anyone, no matter how much you would have liked to save everyone.'

'Joe. You're right. I survived for Joe.' He wrapped his arms around her drawing her warmth to him, kissed her deeply. There was a tug where his heart covered with hers. Noone could draw words from him the way she did or listen so intently to every inflection of voice. She soothed, nurtured and loved deep and genuine. If there was another reason other than Joe to live for that day, it was to find Pepper—*his Pepper*.

They talked more in-depth about his past while their hands and mouths explored slowly, building to something so beautiful there were no words. When they did make love, a part of him let go and allowed himself to feel for her the way she deserved. *Totally, freely and openly—no more holding back.*

***

Later, when they'd woken to a barn owl hooting in the bush, Keegan asked, 'Do you think you'd ever get married again?'

'Once I have closure about Dad, I think the right guy could persuade me.' She smiled at his eager face.

He grinned. 'I guess this guy would need his son speaking his approval first.'

230

'Probably best.' To say she was blissful was an understatement but one thing niggled. If neither she nor Liv used baby oil, how did it get on her ensuite floor?

Something didn't add up, but her sore head couldn't comprehend it, especially when Keegan trailed his lips down her stomach and lower, awakening parts of her no other lover had in quite the same way. When his lips and fingers found their target, she tossed her head back and threw all caution and abandonment out the window to the owl.

'Keegan', she called as he pleasured her, but he was far too busy to answer.

***

In the dark of a waning moon, the ghost from the past tossed the quarter-empty bottle of baby oil into the neighbour's bin. Let him take the blame, at least if the plan worked. Strolling up the street and under a streetlight, smoke rings rose above the hooded creature of the night. 'You'll pay,' were the parting words drifting in the breeze.

The owl hooted again as if in a warning.

Chapter Thirty-Five

Trevor fished from the Blueshell River banks, with Keegan standing beside him, a rod in his hands. 'You needed this, mate.'

'It's been a tough few weeks, yeah, but at least Pepper's party cheered everyone up,' Keegan glanced towards the headland. He couldn't see the pink cottage because it was on Moon Beach, the southern side of the river, but he knew Joe was safe there. Maisy was spoiling him with delicious homecooked cakes and ice cream, plus the promise of watching the kids channel. They had Foxtel—a luxury Keegan was yet to set up for Joe.

'How's he settling in?' Trev asked, lifting his rod and testing the line with one finger.

'He's a little champion. Still not talking, but he moves his mouth as if he's thinking about saying stuff.'

'In his own time, right?'

'I guess. But I just want to hear Joe's voice. It's hard to tell how he's feeling.' Keegan sighed. Something splashed out the middle. 'Fish must be over there, not here.'

'Be patient. This is my spot. I always catch a flatty here.'

'My stretch of patience is running thin, Trev.'

'Don't blame you, mate. Did you get all his stuff and close up Sherry's house?' Trev raised his eyebrows. He knew Keegan was avoiding it.

'I did. We had a good day. I tried to keep it light and say he needed his stuff. He wouldn't go inside her room, and I don't blame him. I'm getting a packing team to do the rest. I can't—' He wound his rod, feeling something tug on the line. 'That's some big fish.' With quick rotations, he wound the reel, the rod bowed, but a clump of seaweed was on the end.

'Nice catch, mate.' Trevor laughed.

A small dingy emerged from the dark river, slamming into the sandbank. Those on board jumped into the water and sand and ran. 'What! Oi! That's Ron Furguson's boat. What are you kids up to?' Trevor yelled, dropping his rod and chasing them up the river bank.

Keegan tossed his rod too, following Trevor. 'Do you think they stole it?' he asked, catching up quickly. It didn't seem like they were going to catch fish anyway.

'My mate doesn't have any kids, and no way he'd be loaning it out. Hey, you get over here.'

The kid turned around. *Hunter.* The other in a hood stopped, dropping his head and joined Hunter. It was Ross and a girl, but he couldn't make out her face yet.

'Hunter, your old man, would want to know why you have that dingy. You too, Ross. What's your name, miss?' Trev asked.

'It's Jodi Savant, Livia's friend,' said Keegan, shaking his head. These kids look scared. He glanced at the water. 'Was someone chasing you?'

'Probably. It's not their boat,' said Trevor, clearly not realising the kids looked terrified.

'Drugs?' Keegan asked.

The boys shook their heads.

'Not after what happened to Hunter.' Jodi's eyes filled with tears. 'She's going to kill someone.'

'Who?' Keegan asked, seeing each kid's eyes dart up the river.

They huddled together, shaking either from the water or something more sinister. Trevor glanced at him, a baffled expression crossing his kind features. 'They're in shock, right?'

'Seems it. Secure your mate's boat, and we'll get them up to your place and find out what's happened. I'll ask Pepper to pick up Joe and don't want him at yours when we get them up there. Who knows what's happened?'

'Righto.' Hunter followed Trevor, helping him secure the boat. They trudged up the hill in silence while Keegan phoned Pepper.

'Don't tell Liv. We'll see what the kids have to say first. I'd rather Joe not be there. Thanks. Love you.'

Trevor raised his eyebrows. 'Lovebirds.'

'We're keeping it to ourselves until things settle down, remember. Pep's barely told anyone but Maisy. Maisy already figured it out, anyhow.' He laughed, but he felt far from happy. The kids concerned him. Ross kept looking over his shoulder like a demon was chasing him. Whatever this person threatened the kids with has them spooked.

Pepper picked Joe up, meeting Keegan out the front.

'What's going on?' she asked, taking Joe's hand and leading him to her car.

'Not sure yet. They're spooked by someone but not making much sense yet.'

Pepper kissed his cheek. 'Let me know. Joe's fine with me.' She buckled Joe in, who waved at Keegan, smiling. He always seemed happy to see Pepper. He turned back to Trev's house and went inside.

Once the three teenagers were dried off, wrapped in towels and sipping warm Milo, Keegan asked them, 'What the hell is going on? And who are you talking about?'

Ross cleared his throat, speaking slowly, like he couldn't believe it himself. 'It's Mum. She's taken something and acting odd.'

'More odder than usual. Like batshit crazy,' said Hunter, twirling a finger over his ear.

'What did she do?' Trevor asked.

'Came at Jodi with a knife, saying something like, "you're friends with her too", before turning on Ross.' Hunter's eyes shifted to his friend.

Ross was staring at the ground, tears pooling in his eyes. 'I thought she liked Livia. I thought she understood.'

Keegan's heart lurched. *Livia?*

'It's like Judy snapped or something,' said Jodi.

'She said I'm just like my old man.' Ross dropped his head to hide his tears.

Keegan's heart heaved for the poor kid.

'Judith needs help by the sound of it,' Maisy said.

Jodi spat out Milo and nearly dropped her mug. 'She's scary,' she said in a tiny voice, almost a whisper. 'We were only hanging out there and weren't supposed to hear her ranting.'

'Coincidence? Surely she wouldn't have said such obscure stuff if she knew you kids were there.' Maisy said kindly, passing around a plate of warm scones. 'Come on, kids. Hunter, I'll call your dad. Jodi, give me your mum's number.'

'You can stay here, mate,' Trev said to Ross. 'We'll figure out where your Mum went.'

'My mum won't answer. She's in Brissy—,' Jodi paused, 'never mind. Where's the bathroom, please?' She stood, and Maisy showed her the way.

'What aren't we being told?' Keegan paced the floor, glaring at each boy.

Hunter glanced at Ross, who seemed mute.

Hunter stood, eyes darting every which way. "Said she was heading to the pub, but I dunno.'

Trevor placed a gentle hand on his shoulder. 'Sit down, son. You're not in trouble. We need to act quick. Maybe someone will be hurt by her, but hopefully, she's calmed down.'

'Are you calling the police?' Ross asked, eyes darting to the front door. 'I can't get Mum in trouble.'

'No, no. Just trying to sort this mess out for you is all.' Trevor sat next to Ross. 'One of you has to tell us where exactly she was heading? If we don't get someone out there, something could happen.'

'She whispered something to Jodi before she chased us out, but I'm not sure what,' Hunter said. 'Ask Jodi when she's out of the bathroom.'

Walking back into the room, Maisy shot Keegan a look. *Jodi.* 'She shot through instead of going to the bathroom,' Maisy said. 'I'm sorry, I probably should have kept a better eye on her.'

Keegan ran a hand through his hair. 'I hope she'll be okay. Boys, hurry more info.'

Ross shook his head, glancing at Hunter and twisting long fingers together as if praying. He looked like he were about to be sick. 'I thought at first she meant this bloke she'd been seeing. He'd called it off recently, and he was always at the pub. She didn't say who, but I'm scared I know because she's been ranting for weeks.'

Hunter had the good sense, to be honest. 'Yeah, even when I came around, she'd said stuff about hurting a couple of people.'

'Tell us then,' Trevor said, strolling towards the knock at the door.

Hunter's father glared at his son, shook Trevor and Keegan's hand, nodded his thanks to Maisy and told the boys, 'You'd better have a damn good explanation for this rubbish.' He grabbed Hunter's left ear, pulling him to his feet.

'Ouch! Dad, I promise I'm never doing drugs again. It wasn't drugs. It's a crazy person. Not us. Serious!'

'The kids haven't done anything. They need to clean up a boat they borrowed, is all. Don't worry. Take him home. We're sorting it out from here.' Trevor assured him.

Hunter's dad said, 'Ross, do you want a lift to your Mum's?'

Ross glanced at Keegan with wild eyes. Keegan opened the door wider. 'All good. We'll get Ross home.'

'Let's go,' said Hunter's dad. 'Fill me in tomorrow, Trev.'

When the door shut, Trevor leaned against it. 'Now that was one bizarre night.'

'Hang on, don't know who this call is from,' Keegan said, lifted his phone to his ear, his free hand pointing upward in a 1-minute sign. 'Yep, shit. Shush. Stay calm.' Keegan hung up.

'So?' Maisy asked.

'It was Jodi. She ran to Livia's. Judy has a knife and is threatening them.' Keegan was already opening the door.

'Mum,' Ross raised sad eyes, shaking his head, standing to follow Keegan.

'What?' Maisy asked. 'She'd reconnected with Pepper. They're friends.'

'Mum's pretending. They're more like enemies. We have to hurry, Keegan.' Ross frowned, shaking his head. 'If she's hurt Livia, I'll never forgive her.

'I'll come with you,' Trevor said.

'Hang on. I have a call from Livia. Hi, Liv.' It wasn't Liv's voice, and he could barely make out the whisper.

It was Jodi. 'My phone went flat. I grabbed Liv's from her room when they couldn't see me. I'm at Liv's place around the side entrance. Judy's at the front. I've called the police, but you need to get here.' Her voice squeaked.

'Calm down, Jodi. We're running to the car now.'

'She's lost it. Raving mad. Be quick.'

Keegan didn't need to hear anymore. Sprinting ahead, he opened the car door. Trevor followed, getting in the passenger seat. Ross took the back seat, sliding past the booster to sit behind Keegan. He held his eyes for a second in the rear vision mirror. He could probably tell by the dread in Keegan's face from the colour draining from it. *Joe. Pepper. Liv. His life.*

Chapter Thirty-Six

'Fuck.' Keegan thumped the dash. 'I got Pepper to pick up Joe, thinking he'd be safer there.'

'I'm sorry,' said Ross. 'I should have known Mum would go this far, but I hoped she wouldn't. I thought it was the dude she was most angry with.' His head dropped. 'She's all I've got.'

'Don't worry, Mate.' Trevor turned to Ross, reaching a reassuring hand across the seat. 'We'll sort her out with the help she needs.'

They arrived at the renovated blue house before police were in sight. The siren sounded too far off in the distance for Keegan's liking. Her porch light was on, lighting the front and driveway.

'Don't come any closer,' a shrieking woman's voice warned.

'Judith. Is everyone okay in there?' Keegan said, hands raised in the air. 'We're not the police, just friends. Ross is with us.'

Ross stepped towards her. 'Mum, you don't need to do this. They are nice people.' He pleaded.

'Piss off. Nothing friggin' nice about the bitch.' She stood shadowed in the open doorway, a glinting meat cleaver in one hand at her side.

'Fuck, that could take your whole friggin hand off,' said Trevor, shaking his head. 'No wonder you kids looked like you'd come from a nightmare.'

Ross edged closer. 'Mum, stop this. I only have you. You can't go to jail as well as dad. Think what you're doing, please.'

Keegan squinted, trying to make out where Pepper and the kids were. 'We can help you. Let everyone out, and you'll get the help you need.'

Jodi ran from the side of the house towards them, hugging Ross. 'Thank God you're here.'

'What's going on in there?' Keegan asked the terrified teenager.

'She thinks it's Liv's mum's fault. Something to do with an old grudge about Bobby. Pepper's shielding Liv and your little boy. Judy got cut badly by the knife when Liv's mum fought her off, but somehow she got it back.'

'Fuck! Trev, I've got to go inside.' Keegan took a step.

'Wait for the police, mate.' Trev warned.

'I can't. My boy is in there.' *And the woman I love.* Every instinct told him to run up the stairs and crash tackle the hysterical woman, but what if she lurched for the people he loved? His heart pounded in his ears. Fear mixed with his need to protect them, but something surfaced beyond it—a feeling of control and calmness he had not experienced since before the PTSD.

A year ago, even the mention of a knife would have him in the fetal position, but, sharp as it looked, the blade meant nothing. His loved ones were everything. 'I've talked patients down, calmed them. I can do it with her. She seems just as pissed off with you, Ross.'

'Because I love Livia.'

'Mmm, probably. Trev, if you go around the back, see if you can get inside. While I distract Judith, you get Pepper and the kids out. Jodi, you go with Trev. Ross and I will keep talking.'

'Good plan,' Jodi said.

'Ross, I need more information. What has pushed Judith to breaking point?' Keegan's eyes darted in each window, trying to see Pepper.

Back further in the lounge room, she stood with her arms wrapped behind her, holding Joe between her and Liv. She was talking to Judith and seemed calm. Maybe Pepper could talk her down before he had a chance. *God, he hoped so.* The siren in the background neared, but it seemed blocks away.

Ross whispered. 'Jealousy of a better life. She reckons Pepper has everything she should have had, a house, nice people, popular daughter, boyfriend—that kind of thing.'

'How can I get her thinking away from that? Does she love anyone other than you?'

'I have a little cousin, Kade. The only person she seems to adore.

He's about Joe's age. I think that's why she hasn't hurt them. Your son has thrown her. She probably only expected the two of them.'

'Would she be the kind to hurt someone, or is it just the drugs?'

'The drugs have been a problem. Drinking too. She's so nice when she's not on them. Really she is. But she's sad a lot. She took one or more of the cat pills. You know the type Hunter nearly OD'd on? I'd taken pills from Hunter, and she must have found them. The packet was empty when I saw it on the kitchen bench. Then we realised why she was acting so weird.'

'How many?'

'Two or three.'

'Shit.'

'Judith has serious problems,' said Trev. 'But we'll help her, mate. Don't worry.' He placed a reassuring hand on Ross' shoulder.

'Please do something to help, Liv?' Jodi's voice was high-pitched. Tears dripped down her cheeks.

'Stay on the phone,' Trev said, edging to the back of the house. 'We'll head around the back.' He grabbed Jodi's arm to get her to follow him.

Keegan stepped towards the stairs. 'Judith, I want to talk. I'm coming to the door.' The anxiety pushed back, allowing his protective nature forward. He would do anything it took, die even, to save them.

'I said piss off, mate.' Judith strode to the door, her back to Pepper, whose eyes pleaded him with a mix of fear and bravery.

'I'm not going anywhere. I know Kade would want you to drop that knife, as well as your son. Do it for little Kade and Ross.'

Her eyes bugged out. Blood clotted from the cut on her stomach; some drops stained Pepper's pale timber floorboards. 'Kade?' She glanced back towards Joe, who peeked his head around Pepper. 'Shut up.' She shook her head, lifting the knife. Eyes narrowing at Ross as if he had betrayed her.

Keegan stepped inside only a metre from the psychotic woman. He turned to Ross. 'You know her best. How should we talk her down?'

'She's just as pissed off with me because I'm dating Liv, remember.' He shrugged his shoulders. 'Please do this quick. She looks like she's bleeding bad.'

Keegan gulped. *A bloody big knife. A cut. Blood. Don't think about what happened to you. Focus on Pepper, Liv and Joe.*

He stepped slightly closer to Judith, trying to keep the shake from his voice. 'Drop the knife. We can help you. Really we can. You're bleeding bad.'

Judith blinked, glanced down at herself. 'Soon,' she said with skittering looks back at Pepper.

'Why not now? Don't you want to disappear from this situation? Ross and I will take you away from this house.'

Pepper turned to something behind her. Probably Trevor. He needed to distract Judith—*now.*

'How do you know? Are you reading my thoughts?'

'I've been in your situation where your mind takes over rational thought. It's depression, Judith. I've been in just as dark a place.' She wagged the cleaver, and it glinted in the light, looking way too sharp. He took a deep breath, slowing his heartbeat and trying unsuccessfully to stop his fingers from shaking.

She narrowed her gaze as if trying to read his thoughts. 'You're trying to trick me into dropping the knife.'

'No trick. You don't need it anyway now that you have the power of those pills.'

Ross nudged Keegan. 'What are you doing?'

'Just a hunch. Trust me.'

'You probably even have enough to transport yourself to wherever in the world you want to go.' He whispered to Ross, 'Did she want to travel anywhere?'

'Paris.'

'What about Paris. You could take Ross and Kade with you too. How nice would that be?'

Pepper edged backwards, smiled, blew him a kiss and turned to push Joe towards Trevor's outstretched arms.

Judith noticed nothing, seemingly lost in thoughts. The poor woman was probably delusional, possibly schizophrenic. She needed help. While she stood stupefied, he steadied his resolve, sucked in his fear and reached for the knife. He twisted her thin wrist slightly to take the knife from her hand. He felt a sting of the blade along his arm, but he was in control. Sirens blasted, and red and blue lights flashed, illuminating the clear night sky.

'I'd love Paris. Always wanted to go, even with Bobby back in the day. Is Ross ready to come with me?' Judith said in a monotone voice.

'I'm here, Mum. We'll go to Paris. I promise.' His eyes were wide, moist and pleading. 'Please, Mum, come with me.'

Keegan tossed the knife as far into the yard as he could. Once he knew she'd not be able to retrieve it, he checked Judith's stomach wound. Reaching for the throw rug on the couch, he pressed it to the deep gash.

Judith leaned on Ross, kissing his cheek. 'You're a good son. When do we leave for Paris?'

'As soon as the ambos fix your stomach. You can't get on a plane with an injury like that,' said Keegan, taking the other side of her so they could lead her to a waiting ambulance.

The police arrived first with raised guns and frantic movement.

Dane asked Keegan, 'This is the offender?'

Keegan gave him the shush sign with one finger. He pointed to the knife and said, 'Judith needs to have her wound treated. There's no danger now.'

She narrowed her eyes. 'Why are uniforms here? Are they the pilots?' She furrowed her brow. Glassy eyes scanned the area in the driveway and street. Suddenly she broke from their hold, shaking her head, she screamed. 'No. No. It's Pepper's fault. She made me do it. If only she never came back I—.'

'Mum, you need help. Please let me help you.' Tears streaked Ross' face, but he was calm and kind. 'Mum, we'll get to Paris when you're better. I've been saving all my work money. I'm not Dad. When I promise you, I mean it. You'll get your dream when you're better. And Kade will be old enough to come with us then. What do you think?'

She nodded and didn't seem to notice the handcuffs attached to the stretcher as paramedics worked on her injury and police stood nearby on guard.

Dane came back with the knife in a clear blood-smeared bag. Blood lined the edge like badly tossed paint. 'Everyone else is okay? Only the perp was injured?'

'I think so,' said Keegan, rubbing the sting on his arm. 'Go easy on her, Dane. Those drugs set something off, and she needs a psych counsel before you arrest her.'

'Yeah. I figured as much. I'm so glad you're all okay. When I got the call and knew it was Pepper's house, we got here as quickly as possible after the car accident in town. I'll come in the house for statements in a while. Go see your loved ones.'

'Can I ride with Mum?' Ross curled a finger under his eye. Liv ran up beside him, throwing her arms around him.

'No, mate. Not under these circumstances. Come inside with us, and we'll work something out.' Keegan felt for the young man, now abandoned by both mother and father.

'I'm only sixteen. What do I do?' He stared after the ambulance, standing like a statue, even while Liv tried to get his attention by kissing his cheek.

Poor Judith, trauma must have triggered something deep within her. Keegan hoped she would get the help she needed. After all, he'd been in a dark, anxious place once, and he recovered. She had a chance.

It was only minutes since he'd wrangled the knife, but he urgently needed to get inside and hug Joe and Pepper. 'Liv, bring Ross inside when he's ready. He may need a few moments.'

***

At the doorway, Pepper stood back to let Joe run into his father's arms. She hoped he would speak with relief, but Joe remained mute. He clung to Keegan's neck burying his head under his bristled chin.

'You okay, buddy?' Keegan asked. 'I'm proud of you for being so brave and looking after Pepper and Liv. He winked at her. She couldn't stay apart for a second longer and stepped to him, hugging both Keegan and Joe. Joe grinned. Keegan kissed her lips. 'Thank you.'

'It was you. You know what you did was amazing. That knife terrified me, but you got it off her like some kick-butt superhero.' She'd never felt more grateful for how selfless and caring Keegan was.

'What else could I do?' Joe climbed down and ran to Ross and Liv. 'Everyone I love in the world was being threatened.'

She snuggled into his chest, and his arms enveloped her like a warm blanket. 'I know what it would have taken you to face a knife. It's your trigger. Your demon.'

'I'll confess I was shit scared, but you know what? I reckon I have faced my demon. Weirdly, it feels liberating.'

'Maybe it's time I faced all of mine too.' Pepper glanced to the ocean.

'In time. Let's sit down. It's been a hell of a night.'

'Sure has,' said Trev. 'I just got off the phone to Maisy trying to explain it. She's coming over with freshly baked muffins. Don't know why she thinks food fixes everything.' He smiled, tucking his phone in his back pocket.

'Her cooking fixes most things.' Pepper laughed. 'Unlike my poor attempts.'

'And except for the cakes you fall in.' Trev laughed.

'I will never fall into a cake again.' She crossed her heart.

'I don't doubt that you will.' Keegan kissed her cheek.

They all sat around the dining table. It was a six-seater, but Joe happily perched on Ross' lap.

'It seemed little boys look up to teenage boys,' Trevor said to Ross, who smiled weakly.

Heaven help us!

When Maisy arrived, the waft of fresh blueberry muffins followed her into the dining room. She pulled up a bar stool from the kitchen bench. 'So what now?' she asked, placing the overflowing basket in the middle.

Joe reached for the warm treat but first looked at Keegan. 'Yes, you can have one, son. I think all of us deserve Maisy's baking tonight.'

Ross helped Joe break the muffin into bite-size pieces and was as mute as Joe.

Trevor placed a hand on Ross' shoulder. 'Maisy and I want to ask you something, young man.'

Ross barely lifted his eyes, but Liv paid attention, tilting her head Trev's way. Pepper knew her daughter was angry with Judith about what happened and probably had a million questions for her boyfriend but now wasn't the time. Ross was grieving, and rightly so.

'Yes, luvy, we know you'll need somewhere to stay.' Maisy

passed Keegan a fat muffin. He ate it with gusto. Pepper pondered how men ate under such circumstances while her stomach remained queasy. Food was the furthest thing from her mind.

Trevor continued, 'I suppose it's got around town how many kids we've fostered over the years, so we're not new to having a few teenagers fill our rooms.'

Ross nodded. Liv reached for his hand, and he shot her a weak smile.

'Since you're not eighteen, you'll have to stay somewhere other than your house. I'm sorry, mate, it might feel disrupting, but you'll get good meals, help with your homework, lifts to school and anything you need to get you through.' Trev glanced at Pepper.

'You couldn't find a lovelier family to take you in,' Pepper said.

'Why can't he stay here?' Liv asked.

'You know why, Liv,' said Keegan. He shot Pepper an eye roll, and she stifled a laugh with her hand.

Liv bit her lip but nodded.

'What happens to Mum?' Ross asked. Joe offered him some of his crumbly muffin, but Ross shook his head. 'No thanks, Joe.'

A cough came from the open door. Dane strode in with a female officer by his side. 'Ross Ronson?'

Ross glanced up. 'Yes, sir.'

'They've taken your mother to the Sunshine Coast University hospital for tests and assessments. Her wound was stabilised and is non-life-threatening but will take a while to heal because of the depth. She's going to be okay. Instead of jail, she'll probably need mental care instead. We'll know more after testing.'

Tears slipped down Ross' face. Little Joe adorably wiped them off and cuddled Ross. Pepper glanced around to find everyone around the table with moist eyes.

'And me?' Ross asked.

'I've checked with social services, and the closest foster home is right here.' Dane pointed to Maisy and Trevor. 'The Stuarts.'

Maisy offered the police officers muffins. Both declined with thanks. Sirens no longer sounded in the air. A kookaburra cackled in the trees.

'We've been talking to Ross about if he'd like to stay with us.' Trevor stood.

'Ross, it's the best choice, at least for now.' Dane tilted his head.

'I guess. It's kind of you both.' Ross stood too. 'I'll need to get some stuff from home. Clean out the fridge. Turn things off, and—.'

'It's okay, luvy,' said Maisy. 'We'll all help you. Blueshell Beach will rally as always.'

'But why are you being so nice? You should be all mad about what Mum did.' Ross rubbed his temple before running a finger under his eye.

'No. We're not at all. Poor Judith had a terrible time and acted out through stress and mental fatigue. It's not her fault or yours.' Pepper stood and stretched her arms. 'We can all talk more in the morning, but I promise we will all support you both.' She smiled. 'I'm sure the detectives want to call it a night too.'

Everyone made for their homes and cars. Liv and Pepper waved them off, standing arm in arm. Joe straddled Keegan's shoulders with his little head lolling as he fought the need to sleep.

Maisy and Trevor were in their car, waiting for Ross. He'd noticed blood on the driveway and stood gazing down at it. His shoulders began to shake.

'Mum, I need to go to him,' said Liv.

'Let Trev, sweetie.'

Trevor stepped out of the driver's side, leaving the door open. The tall man put his arm over the boy's back, letting him cry on his shoulder. When Ross was spent, they silently walked to the car.

From the back seat, Ross waved to Liv, who blew him a kiss. Pepper's heart broke for the young man. In the beginning, she didn't give him a chance, not realising the calm, kind influence he could be for Liv. Ross was a son who watched over his sick mother and kept it from the town. He had the world on his shoulders, but he never once complained.

Pepper vowed she would never again assume anything about anyone. It included helping Judith and finding out why she had broken apart.

Chapter Thirty-Seven

Few of the Blueshell Beach town's people were shocked when authorities placed Judith in rehab care. Most witnessed the decline of one of its most well-known residents, from likeable to odd. Some tried to help, but Judith stubbornly coped alone. Her kindness during earlier years made it easier to forgive the fall from grace. All hoped she would make a full recovery. Again, the town rallied around one of their own, aiding young Ross whenever they could until his mother's return.

Pepper observed him with a smile. Ross played in the shallows with Joe. Maisy and Trev stood nearby, watching like proud parents. They'd taken the foster parent role seriously, and as a result, Ross was thriving.

Pepper wrapped her arms around bare shoulders, warding off the sudden chill. Winter arrived late, but it was making itself known. Clouds blocked the sun and billowed above, turning a threatening grey. Wind whipped the ocean to angry white peaks. Inclement weather neared. Keegan and Dane rode waves close to shore, and she hoped they'd paddle in soon.

It was strange that the day she almost drowned when she was ten had been during a random winter heatwave. It had felt like summer.

Maisy's straw hat flew off her head. She chased it along the sand. Trev got to it first, bent to pick it up for her, and placed it on her curly red hair with a grin. 'Looks like we'd better pack up before we get drenched. Come on, Ross.' Trev called.

Ross grabbed Joe's hand and ran towards them. Joe turned back to the surf, scanning the water for his father. 'Don't worry, Joe. He'll be paddling back in before the swell gets messier.' Ross ruffled Joe's dark hair.

Pepper said, 'Liv and I will pack up, Joe. I'll put your jumper on you. It's getting chilly?'

Joe shook his head, taking the blue sloppy-joe and slipped it over his head. He took a while to get his arm in one of the sleeves but grinned when he succeeded.

Liv rolled over on her towel to face them. She didn't like the cold and dressed in jeans and a cotton knit top. 'My towel's wearing more sand than the beach. I've wanted to go for ages. Seriously, I can't understand Keegan surfing in winter.'

'He's got a steamer on. He's probably hot in there,' said Ross. He helped Livia pack up and snuck a kiss on her cheek.

'I thought you'd be surfing too, Ross,' said Pepper, picking up Joe's beach toys and stuffing them in the beach bag.

'Nah. I knew it would get sloppy early. I'll wait until the tides get higher in the next couple of days. We'll take Joe and head up if you want to wait for Keegan.'

'No. It's all good. You go home. Keegan will make his way in.' Pepper turned to the surf, watching the rising swell nearing the rocks. The blowhole would be back any day with the full moon due tomorrow night, and king tides predicted. *Two days to prepare to swim around the rocks.*

***

Keegan knocked on Pepper's closed-door, admiring the intricate carving, not for the first time, but most of the summer it had stood open to allow a breeze through the screen door. Joe stood beside him with the gift in his hands. The door opened. Pepper stood on the other side of the screen, unlocking it and letting them inside.

'I've been shutting the door because of the wind,' she said.

'I guess your mum would be happy people will see it more. It's a special carving.' He kissed her cheek. Joe latched around one leg, passing her the drawing.

'I know. She loved tracing her fingers along the timber. Do you think she'd like the grey paint?'

'Definitely. She'd adore the whole house.' Keegan grinned. 'Why the worries about the house? You were proud as punch weeks ago.'

248

She glanced at the pencil-drawn picture with a smile, holding it close to her face to study it.

He, Pepper, Joe, Liv, Gus and two kittens—family.

'Oh, Joe, this is beautiful. I'll put it on my fridge so everyone can see it.' She showed it to Keegan.

He nodded. 'I know. Adorable, isn't it?' He grinned.

Joe ran to Livia's room, pausing to knock at the door as instructed. Liv did not like unannounced visitors coming into her teen bedroom.

Pepper continued. 'It's just, Mum's birthday is—soon.'

He hugged her. 'The anniversaries of any event are the hardest. It will bring back memories but make sure they are good ones.'

'Mmmm,' she busied herself with the roast lamb in the oven.

'Smells delicious. My stomach is crying happy tears.' He grinned and raised his eyebrows, trying to get her out of the funk.

'Mmmm.'

'Okay, Pep. Out with it. What else is bothering you?'

'Am I that transparent?' She scrunched her nose, shutting the oven and moving into his open arms.

'To me, you are.' It was like they'd spent a lifetime together, but he'd do another lifetime easily.

'I—um.'

'You sound more like me than you.'

'Let's sit.' She took a dining chair, and he sat next to her placing his hand over hers. 'I read the last of his diaries. I wanted to today— because—.' She blinked back tears.

He squeezed her finger. 'I'm here for you, whatever it is.'

She took a deep breath. 'It's not just Mum's birthday.' She took another breath. 'It's the anniversary of Dad's death.'

'Oh, wow. He did it—.'

'Yep. On her birthday. But it's worse. When Tim, Rob's twin, was eighteen, that's 29 years ago, also on her birthday, or how he put it, Dad's departure day, he also departed. It's like the shittiest day, but it was also supposed to be her celebration day. But how could she ever celebrate that day again? So we didn't. Instead, Rob and I made double the fuss on Mother's Day. We'd trick ourselves thinking we could forget it on the actual day.'

'But you never get it out of your head. Oh, Pep, I can only imagine what you all went through. I'm so sorry that happened to you.' He put his arm over her shoulder and hugged her close.

Tears streaked her cheeks. 'See what a mess I am, even all these years later. It's not normal to get so emotional.'

'Sure it is. And it's good for you. Crying releases oxytocin and endorphins.'

She giggled through her tears. 'Of course, you'd know that fact, Dr Dallas.'

'It wasn't my job that made me realise that. It was learning to cope with my anxiety and emotions. Guys aren't supposed to cry. For a long time, I didn't because I thought it was a sign of weakness. When I finally realised there was strength in it, I let myself cry. A bloody lot of crying, actually.'

'I'm glad it worked for you. I can't imagine you ever not being able to cry. Though you're a rock, you're also the most caring, emotional guy I've ever met. I may have already been in love with you before Joe was hurt, but seeing you so broken but strong at the same time at Joe's bedside. It cemented how I felt about you. You touched a nerve.'

'Thank you. I wouldn't have gotten through those first few weeks without your support.'

'That's how I felt when Mum died. I needed Rob—and he came home for the funeral but left soon after. It's days like today I miss my brother so much.'

'I've been through stuff with Danny too. I know what it's like to need your sibling. Maybe you should invite him to stay and see what you've done to the cottage.' But Keegan didn't let on that he'd already thought of it and spoken to her brother. It was bizarre how he clicked with Rob in one conversation about Pepper.

'Yeah, maybe. Anyhow, first things first. The blowhole.'

'You're still doing it?'

She stood to check the potatoes boiling on the stove, opened the oven and shut it again. The roast smell was almost as intoxicating as the woman cooking it. It was the one kind of cooking she excelled at.

'Yep. It's perfect conditions. I need to swim around the headland, wade into Moon Beach and say goodbye to Dad's ghost. I want to say sorry that I didn't understand what he went through in the war, but I do now. And, I'll thank him for explaining himself in his beautiful, poignant, sad diaries.'

'On one condition.' He raised one finger. There was no way she was doing it alone.

***

'What condition?' She sat again, wiping her hands on the apron around her slender waist.

'I'll be on my board following you around. I know you'll make it. I've seen how strong a swimmer you are, but I love you, Pep. If anything happened—.' His jaw twitched though he no longer had the urge to run a finger along the scar on his neck.

'I'd like you to follow me. Thank you.' She brushed the tears under her eyes.

'Great. That's a relief. I didn't think I'd convince you that easily.'

'Why?'

'Well, you can be stubborn.'

She playfully punched his arm. 'Says who?'

'You, actually.' Keegan kissed her lips. He talked more than he had in the beginning. She liked the fact he often punctuated his words with kisses. Pausing for a kiss did not deter the conversation. It merely enhanced it. Every moment with Keegan was easy.

'Let's go about 9 am.'

'It will still be a bit cold. Why not 10 am instead?' Keegan glanced out the window towards the beach.

Why he cared about the cold, she wasn't sure. He surfed in a steamer and hardly missed a day on the waves unless he had to work. Maybe he was worried about how the cold would affect her swim.

'Okay. But I bought a steamer to swim it, remember. I should be warm enough.' She took his hand and squeezed.

'Yes, and it will also protect you from the rocks.'

'Don't plan on going near the rocks because I'm not planning to be in the rip again.' *Just the thought of it gave her the chills.*

He linked his fingers in her's. 'It's a plan. Now my stomach is backflipping for a feed. Is that delicious roast almost ready?'

Typical guy letting his stomach speak.

Her stomach lurched, not because of food but due to the thought of tomorrow's swim. *Is it a stupid mistake? What will it prove?*

251

Chapter Thirty-Eight

The next morning, the surf was like an angry sea god rising to growl at any who dared trespass the shore. Pepper zipped the wetsuit to her neck, flicked the Velcro over and shook her limbs free of bubbling nerves.

Keegan pointed to the rocks, his surfboard under the other arm. 'I'll stay a couple of metres wide of you. If I notice rocks, I'll call out. It's difficult to see a rip in this chop. Are you sure you know what you're doing?'

She gave him a weak smile. 'Yes. I did it when I was only ten. I can manage it at forty-nine. Stop being a worrywart.' Biting her lip, she watched the swell, trying to count the sets, though it was too choppy to do it accurately.

The shore water sucked back quicker than before, whipping their calves. Moments later, the blowhole whooshed spray five metres into grey sky.

'There she blows,' said Keegan. 'Counting twenty seconds.' He lifted his diving watch to show her the face. They waded out to deeper water. 'Ready, set, go.'

She dived under a wave. Icy cold water seeped through her hands and feet, numbing them. The wetsuit provided some warmth to the rest of her body and would protect her from any jagged rocks she encountered. The chill in her bones was fear and respect for the ocean. *For Dad*, she reminded herself—*and Mum too.*

The waves loomed larger the further she got out, but she tried to angle seawards first to avoid the rocks and blowhole. It was a long swim, but it would avoid the sweep that could pulverize her on the sharp stones.

Keegan paddled further out on his board, gazing ahead and shooting her worried glances. He called, 'Keep going. You're clear.' It was difficult to hear through the booming surf and rush of water in her ears.

She felt the water tugging her back to the headland. The pull made it difficult to swim forward. She needed to find an easier path, which meant reaching the rip and letting it drag her to Moon Beach.

Keegan called something but the words caught on the wind. She turned an ear, but couldn't hear him, so she stroked towards the rocks near the blowhole. There was too much swell to see him, but now and then, she caught a glimpse of his dark hair bobbing between waves. His proximity calmed Pepper, making her feel protected. Despite it, she needed to do it alone.

After each stroke, breathing to the right forced her to swallow water if she didn't time her breaths. Pepper sputtered for air. Salt and small seaweed particles dried her lips. She tried breathing to the other side, which worked a little better but wasn't her natural swimming style.

Her foot scraped rock, and it stung. Under the wetsuit, goosebumps spiked her skin. A moment of panic. *The blowhole. Rocks.* Jamming her hands against the stone didn't stop her head from smacking against hard rock. *Pain.* Her vision clouded. She blinked but only saw darkness.

Pep let the rip take her, trying not to panic in the darkening water. It's only those who panic in a rip that drown, Daddy always said. Thoughts of being dragged out to sea lingered, but she pushed them aside along with the dread in her gut. A shadow loomed under her feet. Goosebumps skittle down her back. She tucked her feet under her bum; petrified that sharks lurked below. Though she tread water, keeping her head high to avoid swallowing any, the surge forced her under more times than she could count. She sputtered for breath, eyeing the looming rocks.

The rip sucked her around the rocky headland, her arms scraping rocks. Her knees were bleeding and sore. Her head smacked the north side near the blowhole. She pushed her fingers away from the rock, stunned by the hit. The blowhole rumbled then the water spout showered her like rain. Goosebumps spiked. A close call. Almost sucked into the blowhole. Instead, the rip continued to take her around the rocks to Moon Beach. Coughing, she spat saltwater from her mouth, trying to keep steady breaths.

The water slowed to rolling waves. It happened so quickly Pep barely realised she was out of the rip's grasp. Scratches and bruises hurt her arms. Her knees stung and head ached, but she found enough energy to wade to shore on wobbly legs.

'I made it!' she yelled, spitting seaweed from her parched mouth. Of course, no one heard her boast. She coughed, spitting more salty sludge. Her fingers shook when she pulled seaweed from her hair. With the last of her strength, she punched the air in triumph. Able to negotiate a rip at only ten-years-old. Tugging tangled hair away from her eyes, she glanced up the goat-track path. Wait until I tell Dad.

After regaining her breath, she ran through sand and bush, her bare feet stinging from bindies and stones. Her heart thumped louder than the chorus of cicadas humming in the bush. Would this be the moment he would finally be proud? Might he take her in his big arms and hug her tight? Would he call her Princess Pep, like he did before the war?

Wrapping her hands around wet shoulders to still the shivers, she stepped off the sandy track catching her breath. Her dad strode towards her smiling his encouragement. The cast from his leg was gone, and so was his meanness.

'You made it my Princess Pep.'

'I love you, Daddy.'

'Love you too, my princess.'

****

With panic and dread, Keegan paddled as fast as he could. Pepper floated, lifeless on the top of the water, arms over a jutting rock. He should never have agreed to her swimming in such dire conditions. 'Pepper! Pepper!' he screamed. 'Wake up, Pep.'

Her head shook, eyes wide, blinking. Her body sunk into the water. She resurfaced, spitting and coughing, treading water— *Alive. Thank fuck!*

Keegan glanced to the heavens, his heart pounding like the waves against the rocks. 'Pepper, grab my hand. Quick, before the next set pummels us both.' He watched the rocks. She would have little energy left, and he didn't want to ditch the surfboard yet because it remained the best way to get her to shore.

She spat water. 'No. I feel the rip's current. I can make it now.'She wiped the hair from her face. 'Please, just follow. I'm okay.'

'Your head's bleeding.' *God, you frustrate me.* 'Come on, Pep. Let me get you to shore on the board. You're still doing it, just not swimming all the way.'

Ignoring him, she stroked towards Moon Beach.

Seriously? Paddling after Pepper, splashing her way to Moon Beach, he admired her determination. *But damn it!* If anything happened to her, he'd wring her neck. Didn't she realise how much he loved her? And Joe, Joe loved her too. But it was Pepper's resilience and resolve drawing him to her in the first place—that and her sunny disposition. *And everything about her.*

Keegan noticed the five people on the beach waving and yelling to Pepper to keep swimming. She probably couldn't see or hear them yet. When she did, it could overwhelm her. As it was, he wiped seawater from his eyes. *Saltwater, really not tears.*

When she waded in and spotted them, he wanted to be by her side. He took the next wave, lying on his board, clutching the rim. Shooting past her, he waved with a grin, trying to encourage her on. 'Nearly there, babe.'

She shot a half-smile but looked spent.

On wet sand, Keegan almost tripped, ripping the legrope off his ankle. Dropping the surfboard in the sand, he turned and waded back out to her. She staggered towards him, falling forwards, but pushed herself up. Then she smiled, fist-pumped the air and screamed something to the sky.

***

'You see me, Dad and Mum. I forgive you. Please forgive me.'

My Princess Pep— she heard on the wind. *Dad?*

Spitting pungent seaweed from her mouth, Pepper took in air, filling her lungs and hoping she wouldn't throw up the bile and salt filling her stomach. Her throat was raw. She touched a finger to split dry lips and the wound on her head. Checking her fingers for blood, she was relieved to find only a tiny amount.

Trying to smile at Keegan through chapped lips, she noted the pride in his dark eyes. *My love.*

He reached her, taking her in his arms. 'Lean on me, babe. You made it. There's nothing else to prove.' He always said the right things.

'Why are there people on the beach on such a cold, shitty day?' She squinted at the group of five. A child. *Joe.* Her focus turned to the others. *Liv. Ross.*

And—

Despite being exhausted, she let go of Keegan and ran towards them. She'd almost reached them when her emotions tumbled out with the tears of yesteryears. She faltered, and her body shook.

A kookaburra swooped over them before landing on the sand, staring at Rob with intent black eyes.

Rob ran to meet Pepper. He wrapped his arms around her, holding her and hooting. 'You did it again, Sis. They'd be so proud.'

'You're here,' was all she could manage to say. Instead, she sobbed on her brother's chest. He hugged her close. She sniffed his aftershave, the one he always wore and felt home. After a few minutes, she stepped back, wiping tears from her cheeks and wet hair from her face. 'I can't believe you're here.' She glanced behind him to where the others stood.

Etti held a cat to her breasts, grinning. *Why is she holding a cat?* Livia, Ross and Joe clapped. Keegan joined them.

'It's about time I read Dad's diaries,' said Rob. 'Maybe I can learn something from them, after all. It looks like you have, Pep.'

'You being here is like Dad greeting me on the beach. You know that, don't you?'

Rob nodded, brushing a finger under his eyes.

Pepper, for once lost for words, smiled. Liv wrapped a towel over her shoulders. She drew it close, trying not to shiver. 'Thank you, sweetie.'

'Mum, you're bleeding,' said Liv, gently touching Pepper's head.

'I'll fix it,' said Keegan. Ross gave a towel to Keegan. Joe ran to him, standing between Keegan and Pepper.

'Is that Mum's cat?' Pepper asked Etti. She stepped to her, hugging her beautiful sister-in-law. 'Thank you for getting Rob here, Etti. I needed to see him so much. Especially, yesterday is—.'

'We know, Pepper. Family must be together in times like this. We're only sorry we couldn't have made the trip sooner.' Etti passed Chloe to Pepper.

'Where has Mum's cat been?'

Keegan placed his arm around her shoulders. 'It's a long story, but at least you know she's okay. Your Mum's friend Mrs Charlotte Walters had Chloe all along.'

Liv twirled a finger through her long hair. 'Yeah, Mum, when I'd gone there with the flyers trying to find the cat, she was a bit suss. I told Keegan I thought she might have her. It is okay if Mrs Walters keeps Chloe? She got so attached she couldn't bring her back when we moved here. She's really lonely.'

'Oh, the poor dear. Of course, she can. One cat's enough for us, now we have Rushy.' Pepper petted the marmalade cat, rubbing her nose in the soft fur.'

'And, she said Chloe was pregnant. The kittens were Nana's cats.' Liv rolled her eyes. Mrs Walters said, "I'm so sorry. I just thought I was overfeeding her. I had no idea she'd not been desexed. I couldn't keep so many kittens, and Chloe was exhausted. The kittens seemed chubby enough to survive." Joe wouldn't have Oddball, and I wouldn't have Rushy if she hadn't abandoned the kittens.'

Keegan rubbed Pepper's shoulders. 'Mrs Walters went in the side door of the garage and left the kittens near the old desk. It explains the bloodstains we found.'

'That's a relief,' said Pepper. 'And now I see the resemblance to Oddball.' The cat purred and preened, enjoying Pepper's stroking fingers.

Joe giggled, reaching to touch the cat. They glanced down, smiling at him.

'Did we just hear you giggle, buddy?' Keegan hoped he'd speak next.

Joe nodded. No words followed, but the sound of his laughter was priceless.

Pepper stroked the cat's fur, smiling at Rob. 'Mum would be relieved. Here. I'm sure Chloe will bring back good memories of

Mum.'

Rob nodded with a sad smile reaching for the purring cat.

'Let's head up to the house. You two need to warm up,' said Etti, turning to the track.

'I'll get your board,' Ross said to Keegan, running towards the shore.

Keegan kissed Pepper's cheek, squashing Joe between them. They glanced down at him with a grin.

Joe smiled back. He opened his mouth. Shut it.

Keegan and Pepper shot a glance at each other, shrugging their shoulders. The day turned out perfect. *Can't expect miracles.*

'Daddy? You two are cold and wet.' He wriggled out from in between them wiping his arms.

'We sure are.' They glanced at each other, mouths agape.

'Is this our family now?' asked Joe, wide black eyes looking so hopeful it filled Pepper's heart.

He spoke. Joe finally spoke.

Keegan crouched to Joe's height.

Pepper bent lower, holding the joy close to her chest, feeling like she might explode with the delight of it. She watched Keegan's eyes dance before brimming with tears.

'Yes, buddy. This is our family. We'll always have Mummy in our hearts, but she'd be happy you have a big family.'

Chapter Thirty-Nine

Darius's ghost

Darius smiled. It was time for him to leave the cottage—*finally*. His lovely daughter Pepper was happy, and Rob was too. Plus, Meg was waiting for him. Dear beautiful Meg and their youngest son, Tim.

It was a fortnight later, and his family gathered around Pepper's dining table. Maisy and Trev joined them. It seemed only fitting. They were part of the family, especially since Ross moved in with them, and he saw almost as much of Livia as he did them. The kid was okay so long as he always did right by young Livia.

Aromas of Christmas wafted in the air along with the smoky, woody fire from the newly installed open fireplace. An afterthought because when Pepper did the renovations, she'd been in pure summertime mode and forgotten the chill of winter. He could have warned her about that if he were still alive. He nudged her a few times, but the difficulty of being a ghost is being unseen. There were only so many times he could make her trip to get her attention. Could have told her he'd planned to build a top floor too. He was glad she thought of it—it made him proud.

Christmas decorations and Australian traditional festive foods, ham, turkey, fresh prawns, lollies, fruit cake, salads, candy canes and trifles, filled the dining table leaving little room for the elbows of the occupants.

Joe reached for a candy cane but dropped it when Keegan shot him a look. *One treat after the real food.* Darius would've let the little tyke have his way. It was Christmas, after all—even if they were holding it in July for Rob and Etti before they returned to the States.

Rob raised a can of beer. 'Cheers, everyone. I'm glad we could be here for a true family celebration. And in winter as we usually have it, but at least there's no snow.' Everyone laughed. 'No more living in the past, eh?'

Wow, Rob looked exactly like his old man. Well, if Darius lived to be Rob's age, that is. An age he never reached because of what he'd done. But you can't take those things back—*ever*. However, death isn't always death. Not that any of them could see him. Weirdly, Pepper glanced his way a few times as if she sensed he was there. She studied the kookaburra as if she knew its face. Not that he was always a kookaburra, but he loved the damn funny chuckle they let out. He could have taken on an owl, but he'd never been smart enough.

Pepper would sometimes turn when his ghost stood behind her as she read his diaries too. Even as a young girl, he sensed how deeply she felt things. That made him proud too.

Maisy and Trev grinned at the other end of the table, raising their wine glasses. Maisy was already wobbly and giggly with booze. She shooshed Trev with a finger when he tried to suggest she should slow down.

Keegan clinked drinks with Rob. 'Cheers, mate.' They'd become firm friends, both men gentle and kind. A different breed to the men of the seventies, but that was okay.

Liv giggled, raising a glass of lemonade to Ross next to Joe, who was still trying to encourage someone to sneak him a candy cane. 'Cheers.'

Etti smiled at Pepper. 'The painting is in the perfect spot.'

Pepper and Rob glanced at the wall facing the dining table then at each other. 'Yeah. It was a hidden treasure. Mum perfectly caught us all. It almost looks like a photo.' Pepper sighed. 'Dad looks so happy. It's almost as if his eyes move.'

Darius liked the photo too, though now Meg had faded as well.

Rob said, 'The other treasures were Dad's diaries. I'm glad you opened the garage, plus it's a great place for you to work. I can't believe what you've done with the house and garage's second levels. If only Dad could see it now,' said Rob with a smile and a shake of the head.

Oh, but he can, my son.

Darius was pleased Rob read each diary, and they'd made a difference. At last, he understood some of what happened in Vietnam and why it changed him. He wasn't forgiven, but Rob would get there.

As if reading his thoughts, Pepper said, 'I'm glad you read Dad's journals. I'll keep them in the library upstairs near his desk unless you want to them.'

'No. They belong here.' Rob mumbled with food in his mouth.

Etti raised her glass to Pepper. She whispered, 'You look so happy.'

Maisy butted in, spilling drops of wine on the festive tablecloth. 'She is. It's so wonderful to see. Don't you think so, Trev?'

'Sure, luv. Can we tuck in?' Trev asked, drooling over the feed.

'Go ahead. There are no rules for Christmas in July,' said Pepper. She nudged Keegan. 'I am so happy. It's because of you and Joe coming into our lives.'

'Joe and I are the lucky ones.' Keegan reached for the ham and placed some on Joe's plate with tongs.

'Lucky,' Joe repeated. He sat near his best buddy Ross.

There had been good news about Judith's progress in rehab, but she needed to spend another year recovering. Maisy and Trev weren't about to complain. They'd never had a more helpful, polite foster child and loved Ross like their own.

'Hey, Joe. How's school going?' Rob asked, clearly enchanted by Joe as much as anyone who met him—including Darius, who smiled indulgently. He wished he'd smiled at Pepper more when he was alive. Pepper deserved his smiles even if the war stole them from him.

'Better now I can talk again,' Joe said, glancing at Keegan. 'I love talking.'

'Underwater,' said Ross with an eye-roll.

Everyone laughed. Darius did too.

'And we're all grateful for that.' Keegan smiled at Joe. And the bloke was more than thankful because he knew the child could have died in the accident that took his mother. Since Joe got his voice back, he never seemed to shut up. Not that Keegan would complain about that. Nor would Darius. The kid was cute.

Two days after Joe's voice returned, he confessed he saw the fear in his poor mum's eyes when she was dying. She whispered to him to stay strong. The thing she said before taking her last breath was, *I love you, Joey*. Keegan asked why Joe thought his mum was going to hell instead of heaven. *For being mean to you, Dad.*

Well, if that were the case, Darius wouldn't be joining Meg in heaven any time soon. Though he could hear her calling him now, perhaps he had redeemed himself.

Like the diplomatic bloke he was, Keegan explained that people make mistakes, and Sherry was only looking out for Joe. He'd told Joe his mum was definitely in heaven and to hold her close to his heart. Keegan gave Joe a framed photo of Sherry smiling her beautiful smile right out from the back of the glass. Joe kept it by his bedside and kissed it every night before he went to sleep. Mostly he was a happy child.

Darius could see Pepper adored him like her own. The kid needed her too.

Pepper gripped Keegan's hand under the table while glancing at her loved ones around the table. There was a glow about her.

Everything came full circle, and she could edge forward, no longer feeling anxious about her past. Meg used to urge Darius to stop looking back because it's not the way he's going. He knew it was his fault Pepper hadn't moved on before this. It was the reason he stuck around, hoping she'd read the diaries and understand him.

The portrait Meg painted was a reminder of what could have been. His smile would never fade on the canvas. Poor young Tim wouldn't have faded either. It was the way he wanted to be remembered—smiling at his Princess Pepper.

Pepper always believed in—*love*. Love could make you capable of anything.

The statement wasn't lost on him. Love could make you *incapable*, too—*unable to love in case you lost it*.

***

Pepper turned to kiss Keegan's cheek, feeling the butterflies as always. She glanced at the painting and smiled at her father. *But Dad, love is worth the risk.*

~ ☺ ~

Dedication

I dedicated this book to my siblings, Brad and Karen.

We shared the summers of our youth in freedom and fun. Mossie bites covered in calamine lotion, jellyfish stings, speedboat fumes in Budgewoi, and posing for photos holding fish. Dad's belly-flops from the garage to the above-ground pool, puppies hanging in socks on the Hills Hoist, pet penny turtles, tadpoles from Warragamba Dam, fireworks nights and street parties in front yards. Learning water that goes out must come in (think Little Bay), choreographed dances in front of the parents (Kaz), cubby trees in Kooloonbung Creek, nippers and mermaids at Flynn's Beach, surfboard fin chops at Hat Head (Brad the clubby saved me), waterski weekends camping on the river, and bushwalks with Mum and Dad. Shelly Beach barbecues climbing the Norfolk Pines, riding waves and tanning with baby oil/Hawaiian Tropic (oops), boys (Kaz and I), girls (Brad), tea-tree coke-coloured water at Lake Cathie and the best prawns in the world, Greg's Groovy Disco, and the breakwall sneaky beverages (Summer Wine ha, ha!). My childhood was priceless because I shared it with you both. And we still love each other now we're all grown up.

Acknowledgements

Though my father was nothing like Darius (he showed affection and was a fantastic dad), but he too committed suicide. How did I approach this subject when it touched my so family deeply? Strangely, the second chapter was not as challenging to write as I imagined. The first draft came quickly. I combined a returned Vietnam veteran with PTSD (my Uncle Ivars, also a lovely man) and Dad but twisted and turned them until Darius was neither. He was a family man injured by war, not only in body but heart and mind. Some of the writing brought things to the surface, especially with a son who is an army veteran and dad.

Thank you to my beta readers Debbie, Janet, Bec. My early critique group, Sue, Anna, Sharyn, Deb, Marg, Stephanie. My later critiques Michelle, Lee, Jo and Sally.

Mel and the Sunshine Coast Creative Alliance allowed me to develop the manuscript during the final drafts. A fantastic program.

Beta readers Leanne, Darla and Ivy, thank you for choosing my story.

Thank you, Karla, from Savvy Author, for encouraging my writing and updating me on life in the USA.

Michelle, thanks again for your expert blurb, synopsis and chapter advice—always invaluable.

Sara, you're a sweetheart for driving to my place to help me pitch this story and ask the real questions. Your writing is beautiful.

Thanks to Pamela and others at Authors Unleashed, who helped me design the cover and fix the final blurb.

Angie, thanks for being a sounding board to my woeful author angst.

I want to recognise the agents and publishers I pitched this manuscript to and the near hits and misses. It all makes me grow.

Ultimately, my readers made me realise the book was worthy of its audience and couldn't wait for the long trad route. I'm proud of *Beach Cottage Haven* (it had many name changes). I always had faith in this being a book readers would love.

Thanks (as always) to my people at Romance Writers of Australia. Every connection I've made has helped this author achieve her dreams. If you want to write romance of any kind or romantic element (like mine), RWA is the place to go - www.romanceaustralia.com.

Most of all, thank you, my dear reading fans (you know who you are), the people who have purchased every book I wrote. One day I'll pay you back for the tremendous support you have shown me. In the meanwhile, I'll keep writing books you love reading.

Hugs all around. ☺ xo

Author Bio

Donna Munro is an Australian author of women's contemporary fiction and non-fiction. Born in Sydney, Australia, she grew up in the beach-side town of Port Macquarie, the Gold Coast, Queensland, and now lives on the idyllic Sunshine Coast.

Donna never reached five-foot-tall but don't underestimate her for the shortness. She confesses to an addiction to Peanut Butter, Sydney Roosters, sunflowers and exercise. When not at her work desk with a dog snoring beneath it, you'll often find Donna on a beach. She'll have a book in her hands and her toes in the sand.

She writes beachside women's contemporary fiction and romantic suspense with unique twists—because life gets complicated.

Find Donna at:

Website	www.donnamunroauthor.com
Blog	www.warmwittywords.com.au
Facebook	https://www.facebook.com/donnamunrowarmwittywords
Instagram	https://www.instagram.com/donnadmunro
Twitter	https://twitter.com/warmwittywords
Pinterest	https://www.pinterest.com.au/donnawritings

Croc Brothers Romance Series

A Summer in Paradise: Book One

This book was previously published as *The Zanzibar Moon*.

A magical adventure romance to have you wishing you were on a Zanzibar beach.

A Summer Before: Book Two

Kendwa's earlier life is the prequel to *A Summer in Paradise*.
It was previously published as *Kendwa's Secret*.

A thrilling adventure romance to have you wishing you were on a Borneo beach.

A Summer of Hope: Book Three

The sequel to *A Summer in Paradise*.
It was previously published as *Elephant Creek*.

A family adventure romance to have you wishing you were on a Gold Coast beach.

Excerpt

A Summer Before - Chapter One

The sun hung high in an azure sky, blazing down on the scene below. Sweat poured from the men, dripping down grimy faces and creating wet patches on their armpits. It was chaotic; long grass, mud, tough men and one angry crocodile.

The documentary crew filmed from a safe distance. A cameraman's eyes shifted to the leech attached to his leg. Jumping at shadows, the well-dressed producer took his frustration out on the unfocused camera and the man holding it, yelling a tirade of swear words. Adrenaline surged through the female anchor. Fear gripped her but so did respect.

'It's a well-practised drill,' yelled the head crocodile wrangler, looking up at the camera momentarily before rallying the five men surrounding the croc.

The ancient leather body spun with claws and tail thrashing, splattering muddy water over the men holding the rope tethers. On each side of the beast, a lassoed rope held the ugly jaws tight. Muscles tensed, swear words flung through the air like mud. The beast slowly stopped fighting.

Head wrangler nodded at the boy. 'Mate, you get on her now and strap that gaffer tape on.'

The tall boy with the body of a man, all sinewy muscle, but the face of an angel, didn't hesitate. He straddled the nobbled back of the beast, effortlessly wrapping the mighty jaws in silver tape. His bicep flexed, showing sinewy veins as he snapped the end of the roll with a tight pull.

The reporter couldn't take her eyes off him. She motioned with her hand for her cameraman to zoom into his face. He was an extraordinary-looking male.

The wrangler slapped his thigh, nodding his approval. The young man grinned widely, revealing bright white teeth in a muddy tanned face.

The wrangler said, 'Geeze, Kendwa. Mate, you're a natural. Okay, boys, let's get this croc on the truck and move her up to Thompsons Landing.'

Six Territorians lifted the docile croc onto the flatbed truck. The wrangler patted Kendwa's shoulder as he got into the passenger side of the truck. 'Top work, Mate.' Tapping the tin sides, he sent them on their way.

The reporter straightened her black bob before running a finger over her lip gloss. With the croc gone, the goose bumps that had popped along her arms disappeared. Reptiles terrified her, though watching the wild men catch it also made her horny. Particularly the young man. His gorgeous image remained in her head. First, she would interview the head wrangler. Second get the segment in the can, third – seduction.

'Wow. That was quite impressive. How big was that crocodile?' she asked the wrangler.

Shrugging, he rubbed his dirty hands down his brown trousers. 'That mumma 'd be 'round 600kg and 'bout three metres. She's been scaring stock and the farmers around these parts, so we'll move her on.'

'Why did you let the young man wrangle her? It's such a dangerous job. He looks like a schoolboy.'

'Why not? Did you see how good he was? He's old enough.'

'Yes, he did seem to know what to do. Must have been with the team for a while, then? Is he an apprentice or something?'

'Na. Two weeks. Fastest fella to eva' catch on. Most are shit scared. Oops, sorry, lady. Peeing their pants on their first wrangles. He's fearless and skilled. It's uncanny.'

'So, how did he come to you with so much skill?'

A fly sat on his crooked nose. 'Damned if I know. He and his dad got in touch, asking if he could do some work experience. Most kids will head to the beach and bludge this time of year.' Taking his hat off, he shooed the flies away. 'Just wanted the outback experience and tough work. Kid doesn't talk much, but he's lived all over the world. He's a Yank but originally from Africa. Maybe he was brought up with wildlife or somethin' A bit of a Tarzan if ya ask me.' He scratched his thinning head and then his groin.

They ended the interview by agreeing to meet at the local pub in the small outback town for a post-production beer. Going by the wrangler's lurid looks, she could tell that he wanted her for more than a shared beer. She had other ideas. Seducing young Kendwa.

People spilled out of the hotel onto the dusty red dirt street. A couple of kangaroos bounced past, probably searching for water. They stopped metres from the patio, alert ears twitching for a few moments, then bounded off into the distance.

There were wolf whistles as the reporter sashayed across the timber floorboards, short heels tapping a beat in time with her swinging hips. Ignoring them, she entered through the open doors and let her eyes adjust to the darker inside, scanning the shiny timber bar.

He had his back to her. Broad tanned shoulders, in a navy Bonds singlet, tapered down to a trim waist. Denim jeans sat snuggly across his firm bottom, unlike the saggy bums of some of the other men. Restraining her hands from patting his jeans, she shoved them in her own pockets.

The camera crew tried getting her attention at their corner table, but she only had eyes for Kendwa. As if he sensed her, he turned smiling, raising his glass of beer. A dimple dug into each cheek, one deeper than the other, in dark copper, flawless skin. A perfect smile. As she neared, she realised his eyes were bright aqua, not the blue-green they'd looked with mud around them. Amazing eyes. She caught her breath at his beauty, leaning against the bar so she wouldn't swoon.

'I'll shout you a beer,' he said in an almost-man voice. It wasn't Australian – a mix between English and American.

'Thank you, Kendwa. I'm Abi.' He passed her a cold glass of beer. Their fingers brushed. Electricity shot to her womb.

During her career, she'd met plenty of sexy, powerful, interesting men. None so hot as Kendwa. He had more charisma than a movie

270

star. Something undefinable, putting her a little on edge in an excellent way.

'You're welcome, lovely lady. Abi for Abigail?' He angled his head towards the crew's table. 'Your mates want you over there.'

She didn't look towards them. Instead, she held Kendwa's mesmerising gaze. 'Uh huh. I prefer Abi, and I'd rather drink with you.'

'I'm glad.' He clinked his beer glass against hers, taking a sip.

Abi watched his luscious thick lips and the beer foam on his thin moustache. His beautiful eyes drank her in, even glancing at her exposed cleavage.

Catching her tongue in her throat, she managed to ask, 'How old are you, Kendwa?'

'Eighteen, but people tell me I have an old soul.'

To hide her smile, she placed her hand over her mouth. OMG, old enough for sex. Fidgeting with her hair, she squirmed on the bar stool. 'I'm sure you are. So where do you stay here?'

'Out the back of the pub. There are some dongas. They're small but fit a single bed, a desk and a wardrobe. We share amenities.'

A single bed. Abi grinned, imagining how close their bodies would be. Him naked. There was no turning back after that thought.

'I've never seen inside a donga before. I probably should—while I'm here.' She lied easily with raised eyebrows.

He gulped, his Adam's apple bobbing. 'Research?'

'Of course.' Abi rose from the bar stool. Kendwa knocked his half-full beer over. The beer drenched the front of his singlet. He dabbed at it. Through the fabric plastered to him, she eagerly noticed his chest, nipples and muscles. Yum, yum!

'You mean right now?' His voice broke a little.

Abi nodded, smiling seductively, tilting her head towards the door.

He cleared his throat. 'Okay.'

Ignoring the wide eyes and leers of mostly male pub patrons, she followed Kendwa. At the middle donga, he pulled a key from his pocket, quickly opening the door. She stepped inside, glancing at the bed and back at him with seductive eyes. Their bodies nearly touched, with barely enough room to swing a cat in the tiny room.

Heat radiated off him. Reaching for the door handle, Abi pulled the door closed with a soft click. An air conditioner hummed above the bed, sending cool air washing over them, making her nipples erect.

Kendwa stood like a rock. He didn't look ill at ease; he just didn't seem to know what to do next. Was he letting her decide?

Almost clutching the pheromones in the air, she inhaled the intoxicating male sweat. Inching closer, she placed her hand on his cheek, feeling the soft bristles. Slowly she drew his face to hers. Their lips touched. He proved he wasn't a boy, returning her kiss with experienced lips and a tongue that explored where she wanted it to. His arms went around her, trailing down her back, over her hips pulling her close.

'You have done this before?' she asked, as his erection pressed against her leg.

'Mmmm,' he mumbled, kissing her neck. 'Only with girls, though. You're all woman.' His hands told her so as they cupped her breasts.

'Oh, don't worry, honey. You're all man. You just don't realise it yet. Besides, I'm only twenty-six.'

Turning her around, he quickly unzipped her dress, letting it fall to the floor.

'Show me what a woman likes,' he said, grinning, as he pulled his singlet over his head, revealing a trim six-pack. He unzipped his fly. His package bulged for release in his underwear. Slipping the denim jeans down his hips while his eyes raked her almost made her combust.

Flicking her panties and bra, she edged onto the bed facing him. Her eyes devoured every inch of his sculpted naked body as he stepped closer. Wow! If he still had some growing to do, he would be extraordinary in a few years.

'You are so beautiful,' Kendwa said, his astonishing eyes raking across her body in appreciation. Bracing himself above her, he kissed her deeply. It didn't last long before he crushed his body against hers. There was no denying he was a man when he entered her. A scream of ecstasy escaped her lips. The pub patrons heard it. Some raised a glass, mostly enviously, to Kendwa.

Abi and Kendwa didn't leave the donga until the following afternoon when they both had to return to work. Abi's next assignment was waiting in the city. Kendwa had more crocodiles to relocate away from people and stock. Their paths would probably never cross again.

Kendwa discovered that he enjoyed the long conversations they'd had between the bouts of sex. Perhaps he had some sort of gift when it came to women, just like the talent he had with wild animals.

The lessons Abi taught him in the tiny donga, in the heart of the Australian outback, would remain with him. He liked to think that he had imparted something too. By the look of her satisfied smile and smudged lipstick he had.

After Abi left, the wrangler jibed Kendwa. 'You surprised me, mate. Didn't think you had it in ya.' He lifted his hand for a high-five.

Kendwa left him hanging. 'My business and hers. None of yours,' he said, his jaw tight, facing the wrangler with a steely gaze. 'You need to treat women with dignity and respect.'

The wrangler took a step back, raising his hands. I'll be. The young guy had more integrity than most grown men. The wrangler wasn't scared of crocs, snakes, cattle or most blokes, for that matter. He decided young Kendwa was someone he didn't want to cross.

Reviews:

A Summer in Paradise

"LOVED IT!!! The Zanzibar Moon takes you on a journey from the familiarity of the Gold Coast to an exotic world far away. You never know what lies ahead or what's right in front of you! Congratulations, Donna, on a fabulous novel. Today I thought- today is the day I'm going to sit down and read a couple of chapters in the sun. I was up to chapter 13 and was beginning to think I'd never finish the book (too many interruptions). 21 chapters later and I've gone through a roller coaster of emotions today. I've laughed, cried, empathised, cried again – seriously, Donna, I normally don't cry that much!!! I was so invested in these characters. Congratulations on a fabulous book. I can't wait to tell all my friends and family about the journey it took me on. Now I have to get back to reality and cook dinner. Again well done – I thoroughly enjoyed it!!!" - Paige Burrage

"You actually have a lot of content in the book and the storyline is an interesting "Chick Lit" and reminded me of Janet Evanovich series a lot. The mix of dialogue and locations made the book move and the way that the character travelled allowed you to explore lots of options for material. I could tell you had written it - it really came from your soul and your experiences/loves. There is a real mix of chick lit, travel, suspense and tear-jerking." - Angela Spzjoda, Avid Reader

"I loved it. I really felt like I was walking the narrow lanes of Zanzibar and that I was taken on an African safari. It was a unique and beautifully written story. I haven't read anything like it." - Valerie Ibbotson, avid reader.

"I finished reading The Zanzibar Moon and absolutely loved it, Donna. I didn't predict the ending either. It's exotic, funny and full of adventure. It's also inspired me to go to Zanzibar one day." - Leesa Bennett, volunteer teacher abroad.

"I thoroughly enjoyed being in Africa. I think women will love reading this, as it is most women's fantasy at some point." - Tracy Wilkinson, avid reader.

"I am really impressed by the book, you have really done your homework and if I did not l know any better I would have sworn that you have lived in Africa for a period of time. You have captured life here so well with the chaos, the beauty, the nature, even down to the sometimes not so pleasant aromas (haha). The story line is great and the characters are interesting. I also like how you have put the relevant chapters in the first tense for Alkina and Dr Don. It lets you get closer to the character I think. I showed some of the Swahili to my colleague and as far as she could tell you were spot on." - Kerry Zillner, UN worker in Africa.

"Absolutely loved the Trilogy. Easy read, and highly romantic." - Teebee, verified Amazon purchaser.

A Summer Before

"Glad you had a great launch of Kendwa's Secret!!! Absolutely loved the book, Donna. Looking forward to the next one!!!f Books." - Corine Martin, Avid Reader and bibliophile.

"This was a most unexpected story. Around chapter three, the story kicked off and what a story it was. The author had a distinctly Australian voice which I loved. The story had so many elements, so many complications. I found myself unable to stop reading. The pacing was terrific and the plot was multifaceted and every storyline was intriguing. Yes, this is a romance but it's also a story about families and their loving complicated relationships. I loved that it was set on the Gold Coast. I could see every scene clearly, almost had me tempted to return to live on the coast (nope never going to happen). I enjoyed the back story of the elephant. Noah and Emma were a great couple."- Kirribilligirl 4-Star Goodreads

"Loved the book Kendwa's Secret, Donna. It was a great read I was done n dusted in 2 days. Looking forward to the next one." - Jenny Stedman, Travel Agent.

A Summer of Hope

"I recommend Elephant Creek for an exciting romance and entertaining holiday read.
The story is set around paddle-boarding an inshore creek at an idyllic Australian beachside. The plot has complications with three generations of family members, an electric romance that overcomes dramatic obstacles, climaxing in a helicopter search and rescue.
Emma had started making out with a Tinder date when she met the man of her dreams. Her difficulty in getting rid of the first man and taking up with the second is told by author Donna Munro in this

276

charming novel. Emma is beautiful, smart and loving with a strong interest in pecs, abs and quads.

The story sequels Munro's book 'The Zanzibar Moon'. Emma's mother Ali and her sister continue. Elephant Creek again reveals Donna Munro's affection for and understanding of Africa and pet animals.

The triumph of this book is her portrayal of Hope, who has Downs Syndrome, who is her hot man's daughter. Although Hope is disabled, Munro's story embraces her and she is respected by the other characters for what she is: a lovely young girl.

Because this reviewer is male and enjoyed reading Elephant Creek, it seems more than chic lit. There are critical feminine perspectives on relationships and just the right amount of sizzling love-making. The book chronicles happiness and heartaches in a close family, like Home and Away, with endearing characters whose interactions are closely observed and authentic.

I recommend Elephant Creek for an exciting romance and entertaining holiday read."- Reviewed by: Martin Knox, Author

"*What an adventurest tale this book was, from a heartbreaking New Year's Eve to all the wonders of Africa. This has been the first paperback I have read in a while and I must say I really missed this form of reading. Donna Munro is a new author to me, an this is the very first book she has published. As an Australian, I really enjoyed the Australian lingo and quirks along the way.*

This book is full of wonder, magic, sadness, hope, regret, strength, sorrow, joy, love, chemistry, family, heartache, wildlife and most of all adventure that will fill you as you read."- Ann-Maree is a reviewer. Reading for the Love of Books.

"*I just finished reading yet another amazing book by local author @donnadmunro. Congratulations on yet another great read. I found myself thinking about the characters as if I knew them personally. I didn't want the story to end. Can't wait for your next book. If you love a romantic story mixed with adventures, I highly recommend all 3 of Donna's books. The Zanzibar Moon, then Kendwas's secret and finish off with Elephant Creek. You won't be sorry.*" - Helen James-Doyle

I loved her latest book Elephant Creek. It is set in Currumbin, so that makes it extra special for me, but as usual, Donna has romance, intrigue and a bit of sizzle too with lots of twists and turns. If you haven't read The Zanzibar Moon and Kendwa's Secret, read them first and then grab this one. Guys a great idea for a birthday pressie too!!! Every girl should do themselves a favour and read the three books. They are definitely a nice way to spoil yourself and take some time out to let your mind wander... - Teresa Gartner, Avid Reader

'Absolutely loved the series. Easy read, and highly romantic.'

Beach Cottage Haven reviews

Public Review - 5 Star

Pepper Cassidy inherits the family beach house and decides to renovate it, but must face the memories as she deals with the loss of her mother. Keegan Dallas left the city for the quiet, coastal town as he developed PTSD after a particularly bad case as a paramedic. His neighbor's renovations are causing a few issues for him, but he can't stay away.

I was able to read an ARC of this book and this is my honest, unbiased review. The book's well-written with wonderful characters and it drew me in from the beginning keeping me hooked throughout. While the book is a romance, it also brings psychological issues to focus and does it very well. I seriously loved this book and didn't want to put it down. I highly recommend it.

By Darla J Taylor

Public Review - 4 Star

Another great book by the author, good strong characters. You are transported to Blueshell Beach and the story of Pepper and Keegan and the local community. An enthralling read. Hard to put down.

By Leanne Gordon

Public Review - 4 star

Pepper and Keegan are intriguing characters that drew me in to this story. She inherits the family cottage after the death of her mother and decides to renovate it. Keegan is the neighbor who is captivated by her, but the noise is a bit of an issue because of his PTSD. They both come with baggage that they are trying to weigh through. Will these two be able to heal each other and make it to a happily ever after? This is a well written story that has several layers that bring out several social issues that plagues today' society.
By Merry Jelks-Emmanuel

Public Review - 4 star

This is the 1st book I've read written by Donna Munro; I can't wait to read more of her books.
The story is about Pepper & Keegan; she comes back to Blueshell Beach to fix up her family cottage; he's moved back to get his life back in order to regain custody of his son Joe. After Joe is in an accident, she works with Keegan to help him.

By Jeanne Richardson

www.donnamunroauthor.com

COMING IN LATE 2025

with UK publisher Scorpius Books

Hidden Book of Scars

***Sometimes the past can only remain hidden until the next
heatwave.***

Crime reporter and surfer girl MAKENA KING is engaged and her
career is on track.
Except for her father's ill health and a fire phobia, life is perfect in
Whalebone Beach.
Then ex-Rugby star amputee FINLAY TAHETA comes back to
town as the new Park Range.
Twenty years ago, a bushfire hid their secrets and scarred Makena.
But it was what happened to a homeless man that haunts them most.
When a new fire reveals his remains, Makena and Finlay work
together to find the man's family to ease the Black Beach Fire guilt
and perhaps save themselves.
Her ridiculous attraction to Finlay is an unnecessary distraction.
Plus, how can she crush on him when she's committed to marrying
someone else?
Makena's sister holds dark secrets that could shatter the family.
But she's not the only one keeping secrets.

Who will pay for the scars of the past?